Image of a Man

Image of a Man

A NOVEL OF
THE SHROUD OF TURIN

V. G. Bortin

DELACORTE PRESS/NEW YORK

For
Helen Hayes
and
Margaret Tallichet Wyler

And to the memory of
Victor Chapin

Published by
Delacorte Press
1 Dag Hammarskjold Plaza
New York, N.Y. 10017

Manufactured in the United States of America

First printing

Library of Congress Cataloging in Publication Data

Bortin, V. G.
  Image of a man.

  1. Holy Shroud—Fiction. I. Title.
PS3562.U544I4 1983   813'.54
ISBN 0-385-29264-3
Library of Congress Catalog Card Number: 83-1989

Acknowledgments

The authors' thanks extend to many, but prime in our gratitude are: Donald J. Lynn, image processing expert on interplanetary research projects at the Jet Propulsion Laboratory and participant in the Shroud of Turin Research Project, for his knowledgeable advice; Robert Bucklin, M.D., forensic pathologist, Deputy Medical Examiner, Los Angeles County, and investigator on the Shroud of Turin Research Project, for his impressions of bodily trauma to the man of the shroud; Robert I. Burns, S.J., Ph.D., director, Institute of Medieval Mediterranean Spain, for his learned review of the historical manuscript; Oreste F. Pucciani, Professor Emeritus of French, UCLA, for his counsel on Middle French; John J. O'Neill, S.J., chairman, Classics Department, Loyola Marymount University, for his scholarly thoughts on Roman times; Diana Kathleen Wolf for her illumination of "*la bella lingua*," Piera Velona Koulermos and Giorgio Koulermos for their insights on Turin; Cynthia Vartan, a remarkably perceptive editor; and her assistant, Linda Jordan; John Francis Marion for his special interest; and Janet Hirschfeld and Carla Chandler for tireless assistance in the typing of the manuscript.

Scriptural quotations used throughout the book are from *The Jerusalem Bible* (Garden City, New York: Doubleday and Company, 1966).

Contents

Contents

"Between the idea
And the reality
Between the motion
And the act
Falls the Shadow"

—T. S. ELIOT
"The Hollow Men"

Prologue

At first the assignment did not sound like much. A routine religious feature. It even seemed a kind of hand-me-down story, having originally been given to long-timer Toby Dwyer, recently on sick leave. He covered the Vatican news. But now, after a couple of hours poring over the Rome Bureau's file on the Shroud of Turin, Molly Madrigal sensed her growing fascination.

This just might turn out to be a subject for the far more esteemed business of investigative reporting. There were questions and more questions. And with the American scientists soon to arrive in Turin, she could certainly look forward to some newsworthy answers.

The mail boy placed two letters on her desk. She opened the one on office stationery. It read: "Dear Mollycoddle"—she made a sound of faint disgust—"Sorry the ticker is acting up and this job must be thrust into the delicate hands of my gorgeous associate." Did sweet old Toby actually question her ability? "Do your homework and remember the undisclosed issues are often the really big ones. In Turin be sure to look up my good friend Monsignore Vittorio Monti, Keeper of the Shroud, its historian and prime partisan. He will be a big help. Good hunting. Toby." He P.S.'d Monti's phone number.

The second was in familiar handwriting. "M—Heard you're now at *View* mag's Rome office. If you can get up to Turin, listen in on your old prof." Old prof, hell! Molly's heart executed a tiny flip-flop. Her first love, her first lover. The note was signed, "R."

Enclosed was a notice clipped from the *International Herald Tribune*. "IS THE SHROUD A FAKE? Learn the truth from art expert Richard R. Coolidge, Ph.D. Main Conference Room, Hotel Ambasciatori, Turin. 10 A.M., September 11, 1978. Admission free."

Well, she thought, that surely joins the issue—the pro and the con of it. And one of these two guys, the professor or the confessor, is right.

Toby should be pleased with her homework; she was already well into it. Molly leafed back through her notes. Shadows. Much of the shroud's history, as well as its explanation, was enveloped in enigmatic shadows. She had learned that both Luke and John told of Jesus' empty burial cloth. And some so-called experts questioned in the past by *View* cited uncertain references to the apostle Peter's taking the shroud after Jesus' death. There were even hints of its appearance in Constantinople.

The first documented proof of its existence was in the mid-1350's; its owner, the seigneur of Lirey, France, Geoffroy de Charny. Even then the bishop of nearby Troyes disputed the relic's authenticity and had to be silenced by Pope Clément VII, a relative, through marriage, to Geoffroy's son. Geoffroy's granddaughter, Marguerite de Charny, later presented the shroud to Duke Louis of Savoy, ancestor of its present owner, the now-deposed King Umberto II of Italy. Marguerite had vaguely referred to the cloth as a "booty of war."

What had been its true history if this allegedly ancient cloth had amazingly survived since the first century? And even more astonishing, had survived these years bearing the supposed image of the body it once covered, the crucified Jesus Christ?

If the shroud had enwrapped an even more ancient body, for instance a pharaoh, that would have provoked little contention. But then, this might be the physical evidence of one of the world's most significant figures. The first chapter in the record of a major world religion whose story is still ongoing.

Molly, who considered herself an agnostic, had lent little thought to the subject of early Christianity or any other religious business, for that matter. The world of here and now held more substantial things to merit her attention. Surprisingly, it was not the historians, with their usually conscientious reporting of observed mysteries and man's beliefs, but rather the objective and reality-measuring men of science who had begun to build supportive evidence for the shroud's authenticity.

Virtually all acquisition of nonreligious detail—the hard, physical data—had come in bursts of astonished discovery. Eighty years before Molly pulled the file on the shroud, a photographer, Secondo Pia, was examining his glass-plate negatives, the first photographs of the relic, when he almost dropped them in surprise. The image on the shroud unexpectedly shone forth as a comprehensible positive image. The dark shadows and highlights were reversed and the actuality of the figure became clear. The image had been transposed to the cloth in the form of a photographic negative. But what medieval forger of religious relics—there were many in earlier centuries—would have known about negative images? Or why would he have created such an unimagined thing?

Pia's contemporary, the esteemed French cleric and historian Ulysse Chevalier, thought by some to be the most learned man in the world, studied Secondo's results and pronounced the relic to be a hoax.

A renowned zoologist, Yves Delage, with his assistant, Paul Vignon, attempted to reproduce the figure on equivalent linen cloth with oils and then watercolors. It could not be done. They postulated a vaporograph theory: the tormented body's sweat, which ultimately gave off ammonia vapor, had mixed with atoms of the aloes and myrrh traditionally placed with the corpse, to create fumes which infiltrated the cloth and turned it brown. A majority of the French Academy of Science, when presented with this proposition, was outraged and a continuing, hot controversy was born.

In 1932 the respected French surgeon Dr. Pierre Barbet became interested in the shroud image after studying photographs taken the previous year. He noted the curious fact that the nail wounds in the crucified image were located in the wrists and the heels—not, as invariable artistic tradition placed them, in the palms and center of the feet. Experimenting with cadavers, he discovered that palm spikes could not support the body weight and would quickly tear away. However, the body could easily be supported by nails in the wristbones or in the lower forearms between the radius and the ulna. Again the question was raised: what fourteenth-century counterfeiter would have been aware of this anatomical fact?

It was observed by linguistic scholars that the original Greek Biblical word for *palm* was also used to designate the wrist and forearm. The possibility of some medieval forger/language expert going against the accepted tradition of the time was not believable.

Archaeologists came upon the next surprising revelation. Until 1968 no skeletal remains of anyone who suffered death by crucifixion had been unearthed. That year the bones of a young man named Jehohanan were discovered in the ossuary of a Jerusalem cemetery. Clearly visible was a grooved abrasion made by a spikelike object between Jehohanan's forearm bones. And another spike, still fixed to a piece of olive wood, had been driven into the victim's heels. Dr. Barbet's findings had been remarkably confirmed.

A scientific commission composed mostly of Italian investigators and priests was given permission the next year to remove a small portion of the backing cloth in order to examine the shroud's underside. They observed that whatever had created the image had not penetrated the linen.

In 1973 experts removed seventeen threads and two snippets of the shroud fabric for future study. At the time, Max Frei, a criminologist, collected dust adhering to the cloth in order to examine any pollens which might be found in the surface particles. Frei had been analyzing pollen samples over many years for the Zurich police. He traveled to many places, including Palestine and Istanbul, the former Constantinople, to collect pollens for comparison. He verified that certain species he had lifted from the cloth had existed two thousand years before in the Jordan Valley. Frei compared them with pollen microfossils in the sediment of the Sea of Galilee. Other ancient and identical fossils were found in alluvial deposits near Istanbul. He concluded that the shroud had been exposed to the open air in both Turkey and Israel.

Meanwhile, the director of the Ghent Institute of Textile Technology examined the removed pieces of linen and found their fibers were consistent with species known to have existed in the ancient Middle East. The weave was similar to samples from the first-century Holy Land. Their threads were spun by hand, a method not long employed thereafter. These filaments contained traces of cotton fiber indigenous to the same time and place. Ancient Jews were permitted to mix cotton and flax, but not wool.

Early in 1976 an event occurred which led to the current organization of scientists known as the Shroud of Turin Research Project (STURP). Air Force captain and physicist John P. Jackson and colleague Eric J. Jumper, joined by Bill Mottern of Sandia Laboratories, were making tests on their own using shroud photos and a new space-age machine, the VP-8 Image Analyzer. The VP-8, originally intended for classified purposes, was programed to deliver an exceptional function. Used on two-dimensional photographs of such subjects as terrain and buildings, it created a third dimension based on the intensity of blacks and whites in the image.

Photographs of the most realistic paintings of the human face and figure showed distortion when analyzed by the VP-8. Noses were squashed into faces, and faces bizarrely deformed. Works of the world's greatest artists invariably came out with aberrated shapes. During their experiments, however, Jackson, Jumper, and Mottern discovered that the shroud image on the VP-8 screen became the realistic figure of a man in true form and depth gradations, as if one were to view the body from a few feet away.

The meetings with fellow scientists, the discussions of possible test programs, the raising of funds—much from the Holy Shroud Guild, founded by a dedicated and dynamic priest, Father Peter M. Rinaldi, S.D.B.—took place over the next two years.

The first conference of forty scientists from the Jet Propulsion Laboratory, Air Force Weapons Center, Los Alamos, and Sandia Scientific Laboratories, Air Force Academy, and other prestigious American institutions was held at Albuquerque in 1977.

Out of this meeting came the proposal for a test series to be performed on the shroud. The scientists' hope was to examine the relic following a rare, six-week public exposition, which would honor the four hundredth anniversary of the shroud's arrival in Turin.

In September of the following year, one month before the exposition's close, the STURP team met in Connecticut to prepare a final test program. Actually they set forth both a twenty-four-hour and ninety-six-hour test plan. Although the research group, which included European experts, had not yet received a final commitment from shroud authorities, they planned to transport eight thousand pounds of equipment to Turin regardless. It had become purely a matter of hope and faith. STURP was really rolling the dice.

Rereading her notes, Molly recalled Winston Churchill's comment on Russian intentions, "A riddle wrapped in a mystery inside an enigma." There was that quality about the object of her assignment.

Molly picked up the phone and called Monsignore Vittorio Monti. She hoped she was not disturbing his afternoon siesta. He came on immediately, speaking in jovial and strongly accented English. Monti already knew about Molly. Before he entered the Rome clinic, Toby Dwyer had explained details of the assignment shift. Molly said that she trusted the monsignore could spare some time for her. His help would be welcome. Monti agreed, adding that it was unfortunate she had missed the special press viewing before the shroud exposition. It now took no less than five hours for an individual in the crowd to reach the shroud. Then, in a sizable group, he would be allowed a single minute. Molly was silent. The monsignore laughed, saying not to let all that intimidate her. He would personally get her past the crowds.

"What's the daily attendance?" she asked.

"About eighty thousand, sometimes more."

"Amazing!" she exclaimed. "In the six weeks of the exposition there should be more than three million visitors."

"But of course, Signora Madrigal. What else would you expect?"

Upon her arrival the next day before the clean geometry of Turin's Duomo San Giovanni Battista, Molly's first view was of dense throngs constrained by barricades set up along a side street and far beyond the cathedral. From a local trattoria across the way white-jacketed waiters were rushing espresso to the people in line. They had been standing all morning on this brisk, clear September day. From time to time someone would glance longingly at the chairs under their red and blue Cinzano umbrellas. Yet no one gave up a place in line for the chance to rest tired legs.

Molly rode in a taxi past the crowds and into the piazza of the Duomo. With her was Vittorio Monti. The taxi stopped near the cathedral entrance.

The two stood a moment, watching the pilgrims as they approached the steps of the Duomo.

"Please, would you mind waiting a few minutes," asked Monti, "while I get a press pass for you?"

"That will be just fine. It gives me a chance to interview some of these people."

"Shall I translate for you?"

"I think I can manage," she responded in her fairly respectable Italian.

Molly approached the line of visitors, who were imperceptibly moving, twenty abreast, toward San Giovanni's right front door. With notebook poised, choosing individuals at random, she introduced herself and began her questioning.

There was a short, white-haired man from Palermo, come to pray in front of the image for his wife, victim of a stroke. He had pawned his wedding ring to buy the bus fare.

A well-dressed woman, accompanied by a child, said that she believed this was a unique opportunity to be very near the Savior.

Looking surprised, a nun questioned how Molly should even need to ask why someone chose to see the burial cloth bearing the Lord's image. "The holy shroud," she declared, "reveals the single greatest truth in these times of deception and lies."

An American buyer, in Turin to visit the high-fashion designers, explained, "I finished my job here and I heard this is really quite a thing. Thought I'd try and catch it before I leave. But I may not last out the wait."

Moving to the crowd departing from the left portal, Molly

addressed a middle-aged man, who responded in a choked voice, "When I saw his suffering, I was ashamed for mankind. We are so brutish."

A teen-age girl announced, "Now I feel terribly sinful."

A young man with angry eyes commented, "It is just another of the Church's tricks to fool us into believing all they want us to believe. This will gain them even greater power."

Returning, Monsignore Monti told her that he had visited the Duomo often during this exposition, which had opened August twenty-sixth and would continue four more weeks. It was the relic's first public showing since 1933, one year before he succeeded to the hereditary post as Keeper of the Shroud.

The monsignore led his American guest into the cathedral's dim interior. There it was, suspended like an illuminated billboard above the main altar. This long rectangle of glowing linen in its black-bordered frame commanded the eyes and minds of everyone. Molly could hear whispered exclamations from persons moving down the side aisle.

The two were standing in the nave, directly below a broad platform. Visitors could ascend its walkway for their brief closeup of the shroud.

Staring up at the shining oblong, Molly remembered her research: the linen was fourteen feet three inches long. But at this distance no image was visible. All she could make out were some large, Rorschach-like, mirror-image blotches, burn marks from a 1532 fire in Chambéry, France, when the relic was nearly destroyed.

Monti took her arm and together they moved into the line on the ramp. Now Molly could discern flickering pressure gauges and pipes that hissed faintly inside the shroud's container. This specially built box offered a controlled atmosphere to protect the relic. Its glass covering was bulletproof.

They moved closer. At first she could make out nothing but creases in the fabric and the highly visible array of burn marks. Then something else began to appear. A very pale, brownish-red form. The figure of a naked man, back and front views, lined up horizontally, head to head, feet facing outward. It reflected the course of the original shroud wrapping: starting under the heels, proceeding up along the back, then over the head to return down past the top of the feet.

She began jotting the figure's description. "Mustache and short beard. Tall, nearly six feet. Muscular, genitals concealed beneath clasped hands. Older than expected, handsome." There were more details: reddish stains, darker than the image, which appeared to be marks of many injuries. Some were located around the head—they seemed to be rivulets of blood, as if from thorn punctures. Other wounds were sharply apparent. One on the figure's right side, others on the wrists and heels. The back and legs were streaked with many long markings.

Molly studied the face. It conveyed a sense of tranquil strength and humanity, transcending unmistakable evidence of torture.

"It's quite remarkable," she said, when they had returned to the nave and were again gazing at the distant rectangle.

"So, you are impressed by our shroud."

"Yes. I admit it's truly impressive. But I'm also conscious of the feeling which radiates from all these believers. If you don't mind, Father, I'd like to stay here a little while and let my first impressions soak in."

They sat in a pew near the altar. Monti lowered his head and appeared to be meditating. Molly had thoughts of her own. She pondered for a long time the issues at risk here. Could the Church afford to give these scientists free rein if their findings turned out to be negative and damaging? On the other hand, if these investigators proved the relic authentic in time and place, would it not buttress religious tenets? Would the circumstances of Jesus' death, as possibly recorded on this cloth, coincide with Gospel descriptions? Molly reminded herself to consult a Bible when she returned to her hotel. Had he died on the Cross, or later? Had there been a Resurrection? And if Jesus' burial cloth had survived, was this it? If the shroud was what the scholars seemed to imply, then it was not just another icon or some typical church relic. Rather, it could be a most important historical document, with significance far beyond its religious value.

Both she and the priest rose simultaneously. "I trust I may be of further help, signora. Where the shroud is concerned, I am always available." He smiled. "Besides, I hope we may be friends."

She took a final look at the baffling linen. Beyond it was a tall window which looked into the Royal Chapel. Through its glass could be seen a carved golden sunburst. Like some heavenly asterisk it denoted the relic's usual resting place, a vault enclosed by iron bars above the chapel's baroque altar.

They returned into the bright sunlight. Meanwhile the believers and doubters, the scoffers and the merely curious, stood patiently waiting for their moment with the Shroud of Turin and its image of a man who might be Jesus.

Chapter 1

Jerusalem, 30 A.D.

Mornings in Jerusalem began with the call of Roman bugles stationed atop Phasael, tallest of the three royal towers near Herod's old palace. A moment after, from Antonia Fortress, where the Jerusalem cohort was billeted, came an answering cadence: clear, militant notes, foreign sounds which burned into the soul of every patriot.

Awakening early, Mariamne, young widow of Azariah Bar-Jacob, lay waiting for the brassy challenge. But before it could begin, she heard something else: an insistent, angry hammering at her own door. Quickly she arose from the straw mattress on her brick bunk. Who? And at this early hour? She slipped into a gown. Not waiting to draw up her hair, she climbed barefoot to the roof and peered over its edge. Two Roman soldiers were below. One rider held the dismounted man's horse.

Fearfully Mariamne called down, "What do you want?"

The aide, a *beneficiarius*, shouted back, "Orders from Tenth Legion command. Open up and be quick about it." He renewed his pounding.

Mariamne's door now unbarred, the man stepped inside the shop. He said nothing while studying with interest her figure and her long black hair.

Despite her fright Mariamne snapped, "If you are here to gaze at my body, get out!"

Grinning, the soldier said, "You are directed by our senior tribune, Lucius Flavius Silva, to be prepared for his visit precisely one hour before midday. He orders that no other persons be present." The legionary turned to leave.

"Why does he choose me?"

Not troubling to look back, the *beneficiarius* grunted. "You will find out soon enough." The bugles were sounding.

Gripped with anxiety, Mariamne headed once more for the rooftop. It was there on clear days that she said her prayers. She could see for great distances to the Kidron Valley and Olivet. And down into the shadowed, narrow streets twisting past densely packed houses of the Lower City. Except for times of rain or gritty desert winds, life was best lived up here.

The flame-colored light had softened to salmon. Then, as the sun broke across Olivet, Jerusalem's sky paled to saffron. Dark-feathered swifts laced toward the housetops in endless, curved flight.

To the south, swaying ponderously, a pair of camels entered through the Water Gate, bearing bales of Arabian spices and incense for the Temple altars. A plodding line of wood-laden donkeys followed. The city was coming awake. Below Mariamne street sweepers and water carriers hurried to their tasks. Northward, along the Street of the Sheaves, a bleating flock of sheep was herded along by a small boy wielding a stick. In various quarters of the Lower City merchants set out their goods, preparing for business. "As the Lord liveth" was their oath when hawking dubious merchandise. The more crooked the merchant, the more he cherished that phrase.

It had been this way since the time of King David and before. The promise of the mornings reassured Mariamne. Perhaps things were not as bad as they seemed. Yet, remembering the pounding on her door, she wondered.

After prayers Mariamne descended to awaken her son. Melchi was not there. She sighed with frustration. He had sneaked out again. Probably to meet with that friend, Ezra, whom she suspected of being a Zealot. Melchi was much younger than Ezra, just thirteen—not of an age to be involved with any militant group. What was she to do? Melchi had become unmanageable, thinking himself a man.

Climbing down the wooden stairs into her courtyard, Mariamne stopped to feed the donkey and the she-goat. After household chores she planned to work all day at the loom. The new length of linen was nearing completion. For this she had decided on something special, something more intricate than the typical plain weave: a herringbone twill woven like the silks of Kos. Rich men would prize such an elegant fabric to fashion into a *ketonet* or, perhaps, to store away for a burial sheet. The linen, with its fine even weave, should bring a handsome price.

But first she would prepare a stew her son particularly liked. At sundown the Festival of Lots began. One always had a special meal to end the fast that preceded Lots. Choosing her largest cookpot, she recalled how much Azariah, too, had loved this dish. Melchi emulated his dead father in everything. That was the reason for the boy's fascination with the Zealots. Azariah Bar-Jacob, two years before, had died with other Zealots in an ambush set by Roman legionaries near the Huldah Gates. Much older than Mariamne, Azariah had been a devoted father to Melchi, a gentle and considerate husband to her. But he seldom spoke of his activities outside the shop and their life together. His violent death had been a terrible shock, something totally unexpected.

She took the mina's worth of spring lamb, purchased yesterday, and cut it into cubes. Placing the meat in the cookpot, Mariamne added water, onions, olives, and barley, finishing up with a toss of salt, thyme, and some garlic cloves. Her stew would hang above the courtyard oven, simmering until the meat grew tender.

At the loom Mariamne put aside her apprehensions and fell into the quick rhythms of hand and foot. She had learned the art of linen weaving as a young girl in Jericho, before Azariah asked for her in marriage. Mariamne turned to gaze at her husband's empty loom. Following the Jerusalem specialty he had been a weaver of wool, known throughout the city for his craftsmanship. Now she had to do all the work herself. But Melchi was a clever boy; soon he would be able to take over more of the weaving. That is, if he stayed around long enough.

Concentrating on her work, Mariamne failed to hear the approaching hoofbeats outside, or the street door opening. A man's voice called out, "Anyone here?" It was the hour before noon.

Then she saw the Roman. He was of medium build, strong, and very young, perhaps no more than twenty. His white toga bore a wide purple stripe, designating his high rank. Amazed, she realized he had addressed her in Aramaic.

"I wish to buy a length of woolen fabric—about ten cubits," he began, matter-of-factly. She tightly gripped the edges of the long scarf she wore to conceal her hair.

"There is none." Regardless of her fear Mariamne would not sell to any Roman.

"It's for my mother in Rome," he continued. "They tell us you are the best weaver in Jerusalem."

Though she began trembling, she repeated, "I have no wool to sell."

The Roman walked to the wall niches where finished fabrics were stacked. "Here is something," he called over his shoulder, reaching up to a soft white bolt. Rushing over, she almost forgot herself and was about to tear the cloth away from him, when she saw the warning in his eyes.

He appraised the cloth, running its creamy surface through his fingers; pulling it taut to test its strength. "I like this. What is your price?"

Mariamne sizzled with rage. These Romans, assuming they could go anywhere and take what they wanted. She looked at the sheathed sword by his left hip, at the dagger secured by his wide leather belt. He wore a golden torque around his neck. Its hooked clasp bore a medallion with lion's head and the Latin letters SPQR, "The Senate and the Roman people." She had seen such a thing before around Roman necks. It was a decoration for valor in battle. Probably killing Jews!

"That's not for sale," she responded firmly. "I can sell nothing to you. The few fabrics I weave are reserved for the people of this district who need them."

His jaw set. "I will pay well. My mother requires some wool cloth, and yours is the best. It must come from your shop."

Mariamne determined to stand her ground. She declared, "There are other shops."

"Not so excellent as this. What's your price? You have no choice but to sell to me. I'll make it worth your while. You have my word as a citizen of Rome."

Her hatred spilled out. That this Roman should defile her house by his presence was bad enough. But forcing her to accept his filthy denarii. "Very well!" she cried. "Take it, take the cloth! I don't want your money. Take it, like you have taken everything else."

The Roman looked pained. "You Jews make a political issue out of even a simple purchase. Listen to me, if you're not too stubborn. I know your country well—esteem it. I lived in Galilee as a child. Some of my dearest friends have been your Jewish leaders."

"Then you must know," she bit out, "how much we hate Romans."

"Your troubles are long lived and not created by Rome alone. I believe I know as much of your history as you do. Before us were Greeks and Babylonians, Assyrians . . ."

Bitterly, she cried, "What chance had we against the armies of Alexander, the wealth of Caesar?"

"Yes, that is true." Pausing, he added, "You may not have political strength but you have something else, something very powerful. Ideas."

This was a new one. A Roman soldier speaking well of Jews. But then, he wanted the fabric. "Do you think I'll sell you the wool because you like our ideas?"

His lips formed a hard line. "You will sell me the fabric because I am the tribune and your life rests in my hands." Then he laughed as if his threat had been a joke. But it had not been and she knew he could buy whatever he chose.

"You say you were a child here?"

"My father was chiliarch at Galilee."

She could see he was proud of it. Although she hated him, something about the Roman touched her. "Well, since you seem to like our people, why don't you use your power to stop taxing us until we are paupers and torturing us until we are dead?"

Carried away by her feelings, Mariamne let her shawl drop to the floor. He gazed at her dark, rich hair. It was braided and piled in layers atop bangs that framed a superb face with high cheekbones and eyes like dark gems. Suddenly he knew he wanted her.

When the tribune did not answer her question, Mariamne continued. "The people of this quarter would be very angry with me if they heard that I sold to a Roman." But her voice lacked full conviction.

"How about this? I'll hide it under here." Smiling, he pointed to the hard leather cuirass that served as armor over his tunic. "No one will know. Now, if you please, how much for the cloth?"

She told him and he held out some money, more than she had asked. "I can't take this. It's too much."

"You must," he insisted, "for your trouble in having to deal with me."

Shaking her head firmly, she refused.

Walking to the doorway, he looked into her courtyard. The sun lit his hair and she noticed its warm chestnut color. "I insist." Still she shook her head. "Very well, then," he said. "A compromise. I can smell a delicious odor of something cooking. What is it?"

Despite herself she wanted to laugh. He was so boyish in his enthusiasm. "It is lamb, boiled with herbs. My son likes it."

"Oh, you are married?"

"I'm a widow, with one son. A boy, thirteen."

"You are young to have a son almost grown."

She tossed her head. "Young enough."

He thought her one of the most exciting women in Jerusalem. That elegant hair, those defiant eyes. "Might I share some of your stew—to settle our differences? About the money, I mean."

She glanced around anxiously. What would Melchi think, if he returned to find a Roman dining in their kitchen? But he was probably gone for the day.

"Why not? Of course you may have some."

They moved to the kitchen, and he sat on the clay bench which extended from the wall. Into her best bowl Mariamne ladled a generous portion of the hot, fragrant stew. Then, dropping her eyes, she held it out to the tribune.

He ate with obvious pleasure. "I've had so much to do this morning," he said between bites, "that I am again hungry. This is good."

She studied the torque around his neck. Noticing her glance, he touched the gold band. "This was not, as you are no doubt thinking, obtained for killing your people. It belonged to my father, awarded for valor on the Rhine with Tiberius. He gave it to me when I became tribune."

He put down the empty bowl. "You should know my name and I yours. I am Lucius Flavius Silva."

"Your name is well known," she said, adding in a low voice, "I am Mariamne."

"Mariamne, you are beautiful as the morning sky I saw today from atop Antonia."

She turned away, annoyed by the compliment. Guessing her thought, he said, "I will go, but I shall want more fabric. For my mother, you know. Next time, a length of linen."

"Please, do not come here anymore. My son . . ."

The Roman knew he must see her again. "You will bring me the linen at Antonia."

Jews were tortured there. She shivered.

Briskly he said, "I'll send word of what I need and when you should come. Good-bye, Mariamne." And he was out the door and riding away with his escort before she could say anything.

During the week following the tribune's visit Mariamne worked diligently on the piece of linen. As soon as it was completed, she wanted to begin another length. Flax from the Jordan Valley was now abundant. Her work must go quickly, for Passover would soon come. There could be no work during the holidays. This next project would have to be more simple, something in plain weave.

One morning she was at the loom as usual, when Melchi appeared from upstairs, yawning sleepily. He was tall for his age, with his father's curly hair and the large, thoughtful eyes of his mother. "I'm sorry; I have overslept."

Mariamne studied her unsmiling son. "You don't look very pleased after that long sleep. Bad dreams?"

"They aren't good dreams. How could they be?" He scowled. "Each day I hear of our people being seized by the Roman pigs and never seen again. No one can feel free. Misery is everywhere."

"The times are difficult, but life must go on."

"I'm not doing enough!" he cried.

So like Azariah, she thought. "I'd appreciate a little more help in the shop."

"I don't mean here. I mean outside in the streets. That's what troubles me. The damned Romans. They're polluting our nation."

"And what can a boy like you do?"

"A lot," he responded fiercely. "Father did something about it. And these days my friends are not exactly idle."

Such talk deeply troubled Mariamne. Would she have to sacrifice a son, as well as a husband? "Are you planning to take on the whole Fretensis Legion?"

"I could kill a few."

She became angry. "A few? You aren't talking like a Zealot; you sound to me like one of those cutthroat Sicarii. They're killing our own people, too. Sometimes merely for doing a little honest business with Romans."

"And what do you think my father was?" he shouted at her.

She had never wanted to admit Azariah belonged to the secret Sicarii brotherhood. A Zealot, yes. They were willing to struggle for political reform. But the Sicarii were extremists, in fact, terrorists. "Melchi, you're not actually thinking—"

"Yes, I am," he cried. "I'm a man now. My friends—"

"A man? That dark fuzz on your chin doesn't make you a man, or even half a man! If you don't spend more time in this shop, I swear I'll—I'll thrash you."

Eyes filled with tears of rage and humiliation, Melchi ran past his mother and into the streets of the Lower City. He raced north to the Street of the Sheaves. Then along the Street of the

Potters. Finally, out of breath, he entered the narrow Street of the Merchants.

Not a man. He'd show her. As he passed the stalls of the leather dealers, his mind still swirled in endless argument with his mother. But then the rich odor of food reached his nostrils. Along the rows of little food stalls were hot skewers of lamb, rolled in cumin, spicy pickled fish from Galilee, fat black olives in vinegar and oil, fresh fruit which shone like succulent jewels, fragrant honey cakes.

"Melchi!" The voice of his friend, Ezra. "Over here." Ezra was stuffing the sticky pastry into his mouth. "Come on and have some," he called, and Melchi, his eyes large, staring at mounds of the delicious confection, moved forward eagerly.

"Melchi," said Ezra, "you look like you need something sweet to rid you of that sour face." Ezra was a big fellow with long, curly hair and a scar on his arm he said had been dealt him by a Roman sword. "In fact, my friend, you look so bad, I'm going to buy you several of them."

The two sat in the sun, eating the cakes.

"Now out with it," demanded Ezra. "What's your problem?"

"It's my mother," said Melchi. "She says I'm too young to fight the Romans."

"Well, maybe she's right," grinned Ezra. "All the men in my group are over seventeen. You're about four years younger."

Melchi's eyes flashed. "I may be thirteen, but I'm as strong as you. Want to see?" He grabbed Ezra around the waist and tried to wrestle him to the ground.

Grunting and sweating, the two soon attracted a crowd of onlookers, who encircled them, munching food and shouting advice.

"Down you go," gasped Ezra, placing a leg behind Melchi's and tripping him to the ground. They rolled over, as Melchi tried to get his hands around Ezra's broad ribs. Ezra let out a scream of laughter. "No fair, Melchi, you're tickling me!"

While Ezra howled till tears ran down his cheeks, Melchi made a frantic effort and forced him down, pinning his shoulders in the dust.

"I win," panted Melchi. The crowd roared with amusement and began to drift away.

Still chuckling, Ezra got to his feet and said, "Well, I'll admit you're a very strong thirteen." The young men dusted each other's clothing.

"I'm serious," said Melchi. "I want to do more than just be a lookout at your meetings."

"There are only eight of us now," Ezra mused. "Maybe it could be possible. You have served us and we trust you."

Melchi's face lit with joy. "Yes," he cried, "yes, I want to kill Romans. I could kill all those foreign bastards with my bare hands."

Ezra smiled. "Not all of them, Melchi. Leave a few for me!"

Since the tribune's visit to her shop, Mariamne had been busy, trying to finish the length of fine linen before Passover. From dawn to dusk she toiled at her loom to complete the intricate twill-patterned fabric. And then, one morning, it was done. Her finest work.

Melchi soaked it in hot water to set the threads more tightly. Then, carefully, he laundered it with soapweed until it looked creamy and spotless.

Some days after, the *beneficiarius* returned to the shop. Fortunately, Mariamne was alone.

"The *tribunus laticlavius*, Lucius Flavius Silva, sends greetings. He wishes to purchase nine cubits of linen and will await you at midday."

Mariamne shuddered at the thought of entering the terrible Antonia and seeing the Roman again. But she knew she could not refuse.

She studied the completed bolts of linen. There were three. She definitely would not take that beautiful fabric, just completed. Not for any Roman; it was too good. Choosing a simple length of plain weave, she rolled it into a neat bundle. Then Mariamne left the shop, heading toward the Roman fortress.

Melchi, his mind on the meeting inside, tried to look casual as he leaned against the doorway of Obed's shop. This was his first job for the Sicarii in more than a month. He wanted to handle it well; his hopes of becoming a member of the group hung in the balance. Ezra had told him to watch carefully. Things were tense these days in Jerusalem. Already the Roman Tenth Legion, based in Judaea, had swelled with *auxilia* from Samaria and elsewhere. Loiterers on the streets could be picked up and taken in for questioning at any time. Everyone knew the Romans got their information on the rack. Ezra had hinted a Sicarii raid was planned to take place soon, before Passover. Melchi burned to go with the others and wear the hidden dagger all Sicarii carried as the badge of membership in their terrorist brotherhood.

So far this job was boring. He had been told to inform anyone asking for Obed that the olive-oil dealer was gone for the day and would return to his shop tomorrow. That did not seem difficult, but Ezra warned he would have to be convincing. The Romans had their spies. Ezra promised at the end of the meeting he would introduce Melchi to the others. Melchi already knew most of them, but not well. He hoped Ezra would be able to convince them to let him join the raiding party.

It was hot standing outside. Melchi watched the passersby with little interest. A funeral party, followed by hired mourners; chattering women coming from the well; some donkey drivers hauling charcoal. Once a group of Roman soldiers passed, and he felt a moment of tension as they halted to talk near Obed's door. After they moved on, he relaxed. The hot noonday sun was making him drowsy. Sinking to the ground, he thought he would close his eyes for a moment or two. Sometime later he was awakened with a start.

"What have we here? A lookout, asleep? That will never do." Melchi, jarred by the boisterous voice, opened his eyes and, rising, snapped to attention. Before him was a large man with a full black beard who looked as though he were perpetually about to break into laughter. He wore a dun-colored tunic of rough fabric and smelled of garlic. His eyes sparkled with good humor.

Warily, Melchi asked, "Are you here to see somebody?"

"No," came the reply, "just to report that you are sleeping on the job." The bearded one winked at Melchi.

"It's no job, sir. I'm waiting for my brother."

"Not here you aren't." The stranger leaned closer and said in a confidential tone, "I've been one of them, lad. Know all their meeting places from Jerusalem to Galilee. Obed's father was with us." Melchi wanted to duck his head; the fellow smelled like a tubful of garlics. "Aren't you a little young for this?"

Melchi was scared. "For what, sir?"

"We both know very well for what," said the man.

Maybe, thought Melchi, this was one of those informants the Romans hired to uncover Sicarii meeting places. Then he looked again at the fellow. No. Too much warmth and knowing in that face. For lack of anything else to say Melchi asked whether he was from Jerusalem.

"No, Galilee. My brother Andrew and I were fishermen at Capernaum. The name's Peter; used to be Simon. And you?"

"Melchi Bar-Azariah. And I'm waiting here for my brother."

"Well, you're lucky your brother hasn't involved you any more than this. It's a bad business, Melchi. Don't get me wrong; I'm not for the Romans. But this is not the way to go about righting things. I used to think it was. Oh, I had a boiling temper. Still do, when provoked enough."

Leaning against the doorway, he lowered his voice. "This is dangerous work, youngster. I should know. The dagger of the Sicarii was once concealed in my robe. Though I never had the chance to use it, thanks be to the Lord. There is a better way to conquer. Through love."

It seemed odd, this strapping hulk of a man, talking like a woman about love.

"How old are you, Melchi?"

"Old enough to put a dagger in a Roman!" he burst out.

Chuckling, the stranger clapped him hard on the shoulder. "You've got spirit. Look, I can't say I like them any better than you. But, lad"—he moved closer—"there are other paths. Believe me, there is a greater kingdom than Judaea. And it offers freedom without ever a dagger thrust. I wager I've lived a few more years than you. So listen to what I'm telling you. Hating and killing solve nothing."

Melchi felt the blood rush to his cheeks. "What do you want us to do? Lie down like lambs and be slaughtered?"

"Yes, better that than living your time here on earth hating and seeking revenge. You may think that God is acting within you, but He is not. We believe it is fitting to offer to the Lord those things which are rightly His, and let the Romans have what is theirs."

"What made you leave the Sicarii?"

"I met a great man. He asked me to go with him. It has changed my life."

"Who is he?"

"Jesus, the rabbi from Nazareth."

Melchi recalled hearing about this Jesus. He was regarded by some as a rabble-rouser. "Isn't he the one proclaiming he's king of the Jews?"

"Some members of our Jewish high court, the Sanhedrin, would have you believe that. They hope to catch him in a trap; get rid of him." Peter smiled. "However, his ideas are as disturbing to the Romans as they are to many Jews. For he tells of the greater Kingdom of God, of the redemption of man and a life ever after. The Sanhedrin find him a threat to their religious authority. The Romans, those foolish pagans, fear he challenges their political power."

Melchi, anxious about the decision of the group inside, was growing restive. "I've got to go in the house, Peter."

"Of course, Melchi Bar-Azariah. But believe me, if your forays against the Romans become too much to stomach, and I think that might happen, you come to see me and hear Jesus speak. We're staying on the Jordan's far side, outside Bethabara, at the house of Eliud Bar-Aaron. Eliud was a leper, healed by Jesus."

A leper, healed? Melchi had never heard of such a thing. He would like to have talked more to this unusual man. But Peter clapped a huge arm about the youth's shoulder. "I think I'll be seeing you again." Then he was off.

As Peter strode down the street, Melchi was assailed with the usual bite of guilt, this time because he had lied to hasten Peter's departure. While he was ruminating, Ezra, with a neutral expression, appeared at the open door and said, "The time has come for you to enter; we have decided."

Eight young men were seated on the floor, their backs against the whitewashed walls. All eyes were fixed on Melchi. Obed, the leader of the group, a powerful man with serious brows, spoke first.

"Melchi Bar-Azariah, we fighters for freedom and defenders of the Law have elected to welcome you to our group. If you aid us, may the Lord bless you. If you fail us, may you taste the bitter bronze of our daggers."

Melchi started to proclaim, "As the Lord liveth, you may rely—" but Obed raised a monitory hand and said, "Listen and learn. We have determined," he intoned, "to strike at the Romans where it will hurt and where it is least expected—the military post near Milestone VIII on the Jerusalem–Jericho road. This post has been carefully chosen. It is isolated so those legionaries cannot quickly get help from the Tenth Legion. It is also a key horse-changing station for the emperor's fast messenger service, the Cursus Publicus. Now, pay close attention. I shall review the details of our plan and tactics."

Mariamne arrived late. She had lingered at the Antonia gates, hesitating to enter. When at last she asked to be taken to the tribune, Lucius Silva, the guard, who had been watching her pace back and forth, looked surprised.

Silva had accomplished little that morning. The Judaean woman was on his mind. She aroused in him an unaccustomed excitement. He could be stimulated by a woman of spirit. Further, this one, arrogant and unique, possessed female qualities remembered from his Galilean boyhood. The girls in the marketplace. His first sexual awareness had been directed toward those dark beauties.

As midday came and went, he grew angry. So, she wasn't coming, the haughty bitch. He should not have wasted his time, alerting the guard to let no one near his quarters while she was there. Though a Jew the woman was obviously a person of honor and dignity. Not an easy conquest. But what matter now? She wasn't here. He kicked the leg of a nearby chair.

At that moment Mariamne was admitted. She noticed the tribune wore neither armor nor sword. She held out the fabric, avoiding his eyes.

"I feared you would not come, Mariamne." Taking the linen, he examined it carefully. "This is wonderful work. It will delight my mother." Again he offered more than the requested price. She felt embarrassed accepting so much.

"I promise, no one will know where I purchased this," he assured her. Quickly she turned to go, but he caught her arm.

"Would you like to have a tour of this place? Not many Judaeans ever see the inside."

Pulling her arm free, she laughed bitterly. "Or return to the world, once they have."

"You exaggerate, I assure you. Since you refuse my invitation, you must at least have some wine with me."

His request was phrased as a command. She wondered whether he could hear her heart. Taking the cup he offered, she did not drink, while he began swallowing the wine in great gulps.

"Mariamne, how old are you?"

"Twenty-eight. I was fourteen when Azariah married me."

"Azariah. So that was his name. I suspect you have missed much of life."

She clutched the wine cup, staring into its depths.

Lucius motioned to her to sit across from him. When she remained standing, he rose, saying, "You must think of all Romans as despoilers of your land, indifferent to its traditions and beauty. But I am not like that. Next to Rome I care most deeply for your country and it hurts me to see it dying from the wounds of your hopeless struggle."

Mariamne cried, "We are not without hope. You Romans will be surprised." Agitated, she let her shawl slip back from her hair.

Lucius reached toward her face—he had to touch her—and found himself pulling free the scarf. Loosening her tightly bound hair, he let it spill through his fingers.

"Woman, I am not the crude Roman beast you would make of me." Still holding her hair, he drew her closer.

Trying to move away, Mariamne said, brokenly, "Tribune, you have your linen. Let me leave."

"No! Stay with me." In a quick gesture he pulled her to him. Taking her face in his hands, he kissed her eyes, cheeks, lips. Her mouth was sweet as fresh cream.

With all her strength Mariamne wrenched herself away, but seeing his fury, she was afraid it would go badly for her—maybe even for Melchi—should she resist. An old story, she thought despairingly: the conqueror and the conquered.

She stood rigidly, eyes tightly closed. Silva's hands were around her shoulders.

"You are so lovely. I must see you." He started to lift from Mariamne's shoulders the short-sleeved robe she wore over her tunic. A fibula which drew it closed made a faint tearing sound. Lucius pulled out the metal pin and the robe fell to the floor.

Mariamne tried not to feel his muscled body as he pressed closer to her. His hands caressed her bare arms, brushed across her shoulders, stroked her breasts. Tears were spilling down her cheeks. His lips followed his caresses.

Then, suddenly, he ripped off the bright woolen belt which gathered her tunic at the waist. She tried to pray but the words seemed frozen. Lucius drew off her tunic, and except for her thonged sandals and necklace of colored beads, Mariamne stood naked before him.

Her eyes were still clamped shut as she felt him pulling her toward the couch.

Lucius's words of passion were muffled as his lips sought out her body. Then he took her. Nothing existed in the world but the violence of his need. Yet she lay passive, numb.

When it was over, he buried his head in the softness between her neck and shoulder.

It had been a hollow act, he thought. Like trying to assuage one's thirst from an empty cup. He had not wanted her like this. He had wanted something else. A feeling of inexpressible loss swept through him.

Mariamne wondered why he continued to hold her. At that moment she wished for death. The hopelessness of Israel's plight had become hers.

She heard a sound. His head was still buried in her shoulder. A sob? Could this Roman be capable of regret? Without thinking, Mariamne reached out a hand to stroke his head; then she caught herself.

Chapter 2

Jerusalem—The City of Salt (*Qumran*), 30 A.D.

Sleep was impossible. Melchi paced back and forth on the roof. The city was dark except for some torches burning near the Temple walls. Somewhere a single oil lamp fluttered at a window. Straining his eyes eastward, he thought the night sky looked lighter. The tension in him was a strange amalgam of excitement and fear. From the dark street below a dog barked and in the distance others answered.

Once again Melchi reviewed Obed's instructions. He was to gain entrance to the post, observe the latest conditions there, and report back. At first he was afraid there would be trouble because he spoke little Latin but Obed had told him the legionaries were not Romans but Samaritans. Like all foreigners in the legion, they would gain Roman citizenship after the completion of their service. Melchi saw himself facing the legionaries: he would be calm and convincing.

At first light he hurried down the steps. On the ground floor he slung a leather water bag over his shoulder and rolled up the woolen scarf. Feeling along surfaces in the dark, he found a knife. His fingers closed on its handle. The stripping knife was used to remove leaves and roots from the flax before it was retted. It would not be missed for a while.

He hastened along the darkened streets, guided more by memory than sight, until he reached the south wall of the Temple. Crossing the sheep market, he turned north. A *vigil,* almost finished his watch, leaned into the shadows and grunted indifferently to Melchi, who jumped and spun around. The watchman yawned and spat pleasantly in Melchi's direction. Melchi kept going. A rooster crowed in an invisible courtyard.

The Corner Gate was being opened as he arrived.

"That's a good boy," called one of the guards, "starting out early."

Melchi descended across the terraced expanse of the Mount of Olives. A light rain was falling and he thrust the scarf under his robes.

As he moved northwest on the paved road, he could see two jackals in the distance drinking by a pool. A dog barked on a nearby terrace and the jackals fled. He could make out the hard outline of the mountains to his left as he moved toward the Roman post—still a long way off.

When his mother had learned that Melchi wished to visit her sister, Aunt Rachel, in Jericho, she had laughed and said, "Just another way to get out of work." But she had asked Melchi to carry a woolen scarf as a gift for Rachel.

From far behind came the wispy sound of Roman bugles on the city towers. His mother would be rising now. A hoopoe flew past, in a burst of black, buff, and white, insistently calling out its name.

As he distanced himself from Jerusalem, walking down the Ascent of Adummim, the air became hot and dry. It was as if the rain were a shadow which ended abruptly beyond the Mount of Olives. The route along which King David had fled from his son Absalom now traversed a long range of chalky limestone hills. Melchi was in the Judaean Desert.

He approached the Roman post at Ma'ale Adummim. The landscape changed color and outcroppings of red sandstone burned in the morning sun. The Ascent of Red Places. And then Melchi was in front of the fort. He waved and hailed the legionaries, crying, "*Ave.*" They answered, "*Ave* yourself, little Judaean," and roared with laughter. Melchi moved on. He was only about one *schoinos* from his destination; he would reach it before midday.

Most of the way was downhill along the sides of high slopes, as the road twisted with the natural contour of the hills. At the spring near the Ascent of Salt he refilled his flask and refreshed his face in the cool water.

Finally, to his left, was the critical *miliarium*. Its square stone face was headed by c AUG, for Caesar Augustus, who had commanded the road building. Below was VIII M P, eight *milia passuum*. Eight Roman miles from Jerusalem, HIEROSOLYMA. The route bent to the west, and he was there.

Melchi halted by the front gate tower. A helmeted soldier peered down at him. Clutching the woolen scarf under his arm, Melchi looked up and composed a smile.

"Beat it, kid," growled the sentry.

"Can I see the horses?" asked Melchi.

"It wouldn't do the horses any good to see you, so get moving."

Another man's head appeared at the opening of the little tower. He had gray hair. The sentry turned and saluted, his fist over his heart.

"What's the problem here, Abisha?" asked the officer.

"This stupid one likes horses," snapped the sentry.

"Well, so do I, for that matter," said the gray-haired man, and his head disappeared as he climbed back down the tower ladder.

The gate swung open and the officer, his hands on his hips, grinned and said, "So you're the fellow who likes horses? What's your name?"

He had intended to say Abiud, but he blurted out, "Melchi, O Centurion."

"Decurio. I'm in charge of ten, not eighty or a hundred. Anyway, thanks. Now, what are you carrying there?"

"A woolen scarf for my aunt in Jericho."

The decurio ran his hand through Melchi's hair. "How old are you, son?"

"Thirteen, sir, Decurio."

The decurio laughed and said, "Same age as my own boy, Simeon. What's more, you look a little like him." He drew Melchi past the gate and into the courtyard. "Son, you want to see a real stable? Some fine horses? Follow me."

They were standing in front of a low water-trough. Hitched to a perforated stone in the wall beside the trough was a ready horse, bridled and saddled. Farther back Melchi could make out a large reservoir, its rectangular surface covered by an arched roof. To the north was the rear wall. Next to its small door stood a sentry leaning on his lance. Beyond, atop a hill which looked down on the post, a third sentry could be seen standing in an open guardhouse.

The post's main building had two wings running north to south, joined in their rear by a long east-west structure. Placing a hand on Melchi's shoulder, the decurio said, "Be quiet in here."

They entered the right wing, passing through what was clearly the decurio's quarters, and then into a long dormitory where three men lay asleep on their pallets. Helmets, weapons, and outer garments hung behind them on wall pegs. The rear door must have led to the back gate. Melchi followed the decurio out a door on the left which opened onto the stable. There were ten horses. Melchi, somewhat gingerly, accepted the officer's invitation to stroke their soft muzzles. Then both walked to the rear of the left wing. It was piled with saddles, cavalry equipment, fodder, and supplies.

The decurio opened a central door and moved into the courtyard. "Stay here a moment," he said. "I have something for you." And he crossed past the stone fireplace, where three of the troops were preparing their early meal.

One of the men looked up at Melchi and waved a large biscuit. "Have some *buccellata,* boy!" And they all laughed. The man who was spooning out cereal mush into their mess kits declared, "By Moses' great rod, things are really fouled up at headquarters; our bread is two days late. These campaign cakes can break a man's teeth."

Said another, "That's nothing. What pains me was that quaestor yesterday, not only deducting from our pay for the feast fund, our funeral club, our compulsory savings, our food"—he belched loudly—"our equipment, but then relieving us of a sesterce for a woolen undergarment. Somebody's crazy back there.

It's almost summer; this is the desert. I think the quaestor's girl friend has a family in the woolen business."

The decurio returned. He held out a silver half-shekel to Melchi. "We've just been paid, son. I want you to buy something nice for yourself in Jericho. You're a good boy. I can't get back to see my Simeon for many months." And he smiled with moist eyes.

"Thank you," said Melchi. "I shall buy some flax for my mother's loom."

"Better something for yourself," cried the decurio, as he clapped Melchi on the back. The knife slipped out and fell to the ground at the officer's feet.

May the Lord of Hosts save me, prayed Melchi silently. They both stared at the little bronze knife, its blade no longer than Melchi's middle finger. The decurio picked it up and returned it to Melchi.

"You dropped your flax-stripping knife," he said genially.

Melchi passed beyond the post and, crouching low, returned along the dry ravine behind the sentry on the hill. He reported all he had seen to Obed, adding that the soldiers had been paid the day before and that the sentry at the front gate was named Abisha.

All the men except Ezra were there. Their donkeys, whose hooves were wrapped in rags, were tethered to rocks where the dry watercourse bent out of sight behind the hills to the west. Isaac carried a bound and muzzled young goat like a scarf across his wide shoulders.

"One day after payday," he whispered. "We have picked the right time."

As they watched the fort, the gates swung open and a mounted legionary cantered out, turning in the direction of Jericho. An authoritative voice called out from behind the gate, "Hear me well, Annas. After you deliver that message to the Command, I'll expect you back here by dusk."

Zadok grinned. "Well, that makes our work a little easier."

And then Obed said softly, "Let it begin."

As Obed and Zadok crawled on their bellies behind the sentry post, Isaac crept to the side of the hill in front of the sentry. Untying the young goat's bonds, he slapped it on the hindquarters and pushed it over the low wall of the rain catchment that led from the top of the hill down to the cistern. The animal ran up the hill, passing in front of the sentry.

"Meat," he yelled and, raising his lance, followed the animal out of sight behind the hillcrest.

His death followed the impaled goat's by an instant, as Obed leaped on the sentry's back, cutting his throat.

"Quick, put on his helmet and clothes," he said to Zadok. "Abisha must hear the good news!"

Zadok, already naked, rushed toward the body of the sentry. Standing at the top of the hill in Roman uniform, holding the dead kid high in front of his face, he shouted, "Look, Abisha, a wild goat. Send someone so we may start roasting our dinner."

The sentry on the front tower called down to the decurio, who looked up and shouted to a man at the campfire, "Hiskiah, rise from your buttocks and fetch that goat." And to the camp in general, he added, "The liver is mine; privilege of rank."

Breathing heavily from the fast climb, Hiskiah bent forward to pick up the goat which lay on the ground behind the hill. Zadok was also leaning over the carcass. Hiskiah's last vision was of a small goat turning red with blood—Hiskiah's.

As Zadok carried the goat down to the rear gate, Abisha called from the front tower, "Single cart approaching from the north!" Azor appeared at the hill post, adjusting his Roman helmet.

Then two things happened, almost at once. Ezra, his donkey cart loaded with barley, hammered the front gate, crying, "Provisions from Jericho."

Abisha climbed down to unbar the gate, while Zadok, at the rear door, his voice muffled by the dead goat which he carried in front of his mouth, yelled, "It's a tender young one. Open up." The rear sentry never saw the dagger that flashed from under the goat's carcass to enter his heart.

Ezra led the cart around the tower, out of sight of the men in the courtyard.

"Holy Gerizim!" growled the sentry. "Who cares about horse food? We need fresh bread."

Ezra's dagger struck into Abisha's chest. Ezra pulled the body into the base of the guard tower.

The rest of the raiders silently poured through the back gate. Melchi pointed to the back door of the dormitory.

The off-duty soldiers were still sleeping soundly. Two men positioned themselves alongside each body.

"Blessed is the Lord's name," murmured Obed. As Melchi watched with a sickening feeling, simultaneously each pair cut a throat or pierced a heart of one sleeping Samaritan. There was almost no sound from the victims. Melchi pointed to the door leading to the stable; he was afraid he would vomit. He held the little stripping knife in his hand.

"What is that?" muttered Azor. "Get a sword." And he disappeared after the others into the stable.

By the guard tower Ezra turned from the fallen sentry to face the decurio. A duel between an experienced swordsman and a dagger-wielder is not usually an equal contest. Ezra fell; a horrible thrust had opened his belly and his entrails poured out. Deliberately the Samaritan delivered a slow coup de grace as he pressed his bone-handled *gladius* between Ezra's ribs.

Then the decurio looked back and saw the body of the guard at the rear wall.

"Up, up! We are under attack. The stable—quick." And he raced back toward the dormitory. The two soldiers, swords in hand, ran toward the central door of the stable which opened to the rear of the post.

As the first man entered the shadowed stable, straining his eyes to see, three Sicarii leaped, bringing him to the ground under a flurry of dagger thrusts. The second auxiliary, a giant of a man, dashed in, slashing to the right and left. Matthau screamed as three fingers flew off his right hand and his dagger fell onto the hay-covered ground. Then the auxiliary backed Isaac into a stall and thrust his sword at Isaac's arm, drawing blood. The horses were neighing and rearing. His face white, Isaac pressed against the front of the stall. A horse kicked out, delivering a terrible blow to the auxiliary's chest. He fell back, and Obed stabbed him.

"Kill the horses," yelled Obed to Melchi, who now clutched a Roman sword.

"The horses?" cried Melchi, unbelieving. The decurio entered the stable from the dormitory side. Sword in hand he stared with disbelief at Melchi, who backed away. A look of anguish on his face, the decurio raised his blade. But he hesitated, and at that instant Josiah jumped on his back, toppling him forward over Melchi, who fell backward, his sword driving through the decurio's chest.

The decurio's face lay above Melchi's. His eyes grew dull and he uttered a single, gentle word, "Simeon."

The others were slashing the horses' neck arteries. Isaac, after bandaging his wound, went from body to body, collecting the coins from their leather purses.

"Take heed," called Jonah. "Some of the coins may have graven images."

Isaac cried, "Then they shall be melted into bright shekels."

Quitting the stable, Melchi stood quietly beside the body of Ezra. "You cannot take his corpse through the gates of Jericho or Jerusalem," Obed said. "There will be questions. Head for the City of Salt, the great community of the Essenes. They will bury him." Then he reminded the others who should proceed to Jericho and who should turn back to Jerusalem.

Outside the front walls a man stopped his cart, which was loaded with fresh loaves of bread.

"What's happening here?" he screamed.

"What's in the cart, uncle?" asked Azor.

"Fresh bread from Jericho, for the troops."

"They won't be needing that now," said Azor. "But we have something for those who aid Romans."

The bread dealer was struck down where he stood.

The valley of the Ascent of Salt, down which Melchi was traveling, was an important trade route for the transport of salt, as well as date sugar from the oases of the Salt Sea. The way was slow and Melchi felt a bone-deep exhaustion. He feared that the cart which bore Ezra's body might overturn on this rutted road.

Holding the donkey's halter in one hand, he turned to examine his load. Short of a complete search the body was not visible.

His fellow raiders had sadly bound up Ezra's head, chest, and abdomen in linen which they had cut from the clothing of the fallen auxiliaries. The body lay in the cart, covered with barley. A leather hide, used to protect the grain from rain, was stretched over the load.

He passed a crew of Roman road engineers who were repairing the paving. Sullenly they stood aside. It was hot work for those unaccustomed to the Judaean wilderness. Adar was the most appropriate month for road repair. Soon, Nisan would bring a flood of pilgrims to Jerusalem for the holidays.

An old man, with two salt-bearing donkeys, passed him on the road. They nodded gravely to each other. The sun was beginning to set behind the hills as Melchi came abreast of a small Roman fort.

"What do you carry?" shouted the guard, and Melchi halted. His feelings were curiously numb. He shrugged and concealed the bloodstains on his outer robe by pressing against the donkey's left side. The legionary moved to the cart and reached under the hide. Then he looked at his handful of barley and, with a sound of disgust, threw it on the ground. For barley was the enforced diet of army units who were in disgrace.

"Good enough for those holy idiots in the City of Salt," he muttered and waved Melchi on.

Another six hundred paces and darkness began to shade the sky. Melchi unhitched the donkey and hobbled it near a small mound of barley. At least the animal would dine well. Then Melchi placed rocks ahead of the cartwheels and dropped to the ground. For a while, as he stared up into the night, he was too tired to sleep. Nothing seemed blacker than the desert sky. The stars were achingly bright. Finally he slept.

In his dream Melchi went to his father with sadness in his throat and declared his love. But his father became Ezra, who extended a hand toward Melchi and mouthed many words—soundlessly. "I cannot hear you," he sobbed.

The desert night had been cold and Melchi was stiff when he awakened. At first he welcomed the rising sun but as he approached the City of Salt, the air became hot. Perspiring, Melchi looped the woolen scarf around his middle. In the distance he could see square, earthen pans where dense saltwater was evaporating. Their contents seemed beguilingly like snow. Behind him the dark cliffs looked as though they had been gnawed by a careless giant who had allowed great fans of rock particles to spill out below. Soon he saw white-plastered huts on the edge of land which bordered the Salt Sea. Though the sea was sparkling blue, no birds flew over its dead waters. Here was the principal settlement of the Essenes, a strict Jewish religious order, living a devout communal life, dedicated to the ideal of purity, but above all else, to the study of the Law. The order perpetuated their womanless communities by the adoption of young male children.

Melchi was still some distance from the center of the city when three figures came out of two tiny houses near the road. One, an old man, kept a hand on the shoulder of his slender companion. All were wearing the white robes and headcloths of Essenes. A youth about Melchi's age smiled broadly and said, "Welcome to our city." The others nodded and also smiled.

The old man, his hand still on the other's shoulder, directed his face a little to the left and above where Melchi stood. Melchi realized he must be blind.

"May we aid you?" asked the youth. Melchi stepped out from the far side of the donkey. He pulled away the hide and swept back some grain from his cargo.

"I need help. My friend has been killed by the Romans."

Seeing Ezra's body and Melchi's bloody robe, the younger Essenes reeled backward in horror, dragging the blind man with them.

"All this is unclean," declared the slender man with a sour expression. "You cannot go farther into the city. It is a pure place and may not be defiled by blood nor a dead body."

Then he whispered to the blind man, who announced, "An Essene may take the initiative in only two things: helpfulness and mercy."

"He is the priest Jorem; he is learned in our laws," said the youth, adding that his own name was Sira.

"I am Melchi Bar-Azariah. Would one of you be so kind as to go to the city and bring back some others to help me? My friend must be buried before sundown."

"I regret we cannot enter the city," said Sira. "We must remain two thousand cubits away. We are impure." Then Sira explained that, being blind, Jorem was considered blemished; he must live away from the purity that was the city proper. Josea, the third man, was, alas, also impure. He suffered the curse of Venus and was a gonorrheic.

"And I, too," stated Sira, "am impure. My affliction is a grave one. It seems that while I sleep, I spill my seed on the bedclothes. Purification baths didn't help a bit. My affliction persisted and I am now here. There is no other way."

"Sufficient prayer and it will pass in time," intoned Jorem. "We shall bury your friend. But we may not touch him."

As Josea went to fetch some rope, Melchi tenderly laid Ezra's body on the ground. Then he took the white scarf and placed half of it beneath the body, folding the rest over his friend's face. It reached beyond Ezra's knees.

"This must serve as a shroud," he said.

After digging a grave shaft, each pair of men stood with a rope leading under the corpse. Jorem spoke softly, while they lowered Ezra's body. "The flesh is mortal and its substance transitory. The soul is immortal and now it is released from its prison house. It joyously soars aloft. For the souls of the good, there is reserved a life beyond the ocean—a country oppressed by neither rain nor snow nor heat, but refreshed by a gentle west wind constantly blowing from the sea."

Something inside of Melchi seemed frozen. He closed his eyes tightly, and could feel nothing. The others lowered the impure barley and the defiled cart into the grave shaft.

It was then that Melchi thought of Peter and the invitation to join him and meet his master, Jesus. At this moment he wanted to see the master above all else. "I will go northward now to Bethabara."

Sira said, "First you must bathe and reject those impure robes so that you may pass safely through our city." He pointed to a small structure where the water flowed from a pool out into the ground. It was very cold. When Melchi emerged from the bath, the three Essenes had managed to find sufficient pieces of old white fabric to wrap around his body and head.

"Now you look like one of us," said Sira. "You may go on."

Josea pointed to another small structure and added, "It would be wise to use our privy. There are none closer on this side of the City of Salt. This is the law of our Order. The Sabbath begins tomorrow, and then, until the following sunset, no one may relieve his natural functions. For they are impure and would defile the Sabbath."

Melchi reached out to offer his half-shekel to Sira. How else could he thank them? Sira said, "Leave it on that rock near the road. We will see that it goes to our community. No one may own things of value."

Wanting to be kind, Melchi then turned to Jorem and said, "It is good that you bring the Light to this far-off place."

The blind priest responded, "It is written that those of our community will separate themselves from the midst of perverse men and go to the wilderness to prepare the way. Isaiah has said, 'In the wilderness prepare the way of the Lord. Make straight in the desert a highway for our God.'"

Within an hour, Melchi, riding Ezra's donkey, had passed through the Essene city and was heading toward Bethabara.

He had little trouble finding Eliud Bar-Aaron's house, located in the center of the tiny settlement.

The door was opened by a kindly looking man. "I've come to see Peter," said Melchi. "He said he would be here."

"Just a moment," said the man. And soon there was Peter, his black beard towering above Melchi. "Ah, yes, Melchi the lookout, from Jerusalem. Well, I can see you have traveled a long distance. And you are dressed like an Essene." He winked knowingly. "I understand, a disguise."

Without a word, Melchi pulled off the white turban.

Peter continued, "Have you done battle yet? But of course. You wouldn't be here otherwise. Come in."

Melchi found himself in the center of a small room, surrounded by Peter and several men he had never seen before.

One man sat apart, in the corner. Instantly Melchi realized this was Jesus. He had not expected the rabbi to be so rugged. Very tall, maybe even taller than Peter, though it was hard to judge. He had broad, muscular shoulders, a powerful physique, and great, tender eyes that dominated his face. Jesus appeared older than the others. He wore his dark, silky hair long, pulled back into the single braid of Jewish men. Mustache and beard went untrimmed, according to custom. Dressed in a white robe, he was seated on some cushions, watching the others. Melchi felt so drawn by him he could not focus anywhere else. Rising, the rabbi came forward to greet him.

"Feeling better, lad?" asked Jesus.

Melchi was startled. What did Jesus know? "Yes, Master," he answered.

"Then come over here beside me. I should like to talk with you." He led Melchi back to the corner.

As Jesus directed his gaze upon him, Melchi found it difficult to look into the master's eyes.

"Why do you turn from me?"

Melchi had no answer.

"There are no secrets here. The Father sees into every heart."

The idea that God could know what he was thinking made Melchi wince.

Jesus continued, in a gentle tone. "Melchi, you are dressed in the clothing of the Essenes. I knew one of them, a very great prophet. His name was John and he baptized with water for the forgiveness of sins."

Melchi drew a breath. "I went to the City of Salt. I didn't like it very much."

Jesus smiled. "Not everyone fixes his attention so strenuously on the physical body and its impurities. The Essenes are pious, but no dearer to the Father than other good men." Looking intently at Melchi, he was silent awhile. But the young man saw the compassion in Jesus' eyes. "You had a bad experience with some Sicarii."

Melchi was astounded. Jesus had phrased it not as a question but as fact.

"Some of my followers, in this very room, were once Sicarii.

Peter and Simon over there, also Judas. They well understand what you feel about the deaths you helped bring about."

Melchi stammered, "How can you know this?"

Jesus looked sad. "I know. And my Father."

What kind of magician was this, who could see inside a person, read buried thoughts?

"Do not fear," said Jesus. "I am here to help you."

This troubled Melchi. He did not need any help. Besides, what had happened was his private concern.

"Do you think there can be no forgiveness for the guilt you feel?"

Melchi stared at the ground. Jesus went on. "God will forgive His children."

Melchi wanted to throw himself into Jesus' arms and sob out all his anguish. Instead he responded the way he did to his mother. "The matter is my business and I don't want to talk about it." The Lord would not forgive all those deaths for which he felt responsible: the warm-hearted decurio, the others. Better to let it alone.

"My son, instead of doing violence to others, love your enemies and do good. You must learn the lesson of love, for in the end, that brings the only true victory." And then Jesus asked, "Do you have repentance for your deeds?"

Melchi cried, "Yes, I am sorry. A Samaritan gave me friendship, even a gift, and I—I held the sword that killed him. His face was next to mine as he died." He began pounding his fists against the wall.

Andrew, one of the disciples, came over. "Is he inhabited by a devil, Master?"

"No," said Jesus. "This will pass." He paused, while Melchi grew calmer. "Melchi, do you truly repent?" he asked again.

"Oh, yes, Master, and I regret every moment I talked or thought about killing. I did not understand then." He shuddered.

"Come nearer, my son." Jesus held out his arms. Unhesitatingly Melchi moved into their sheltering arc. He had never known such reassuring love. It was something for which he had yearned since his father's death.

"Begin with this moment, Melchi. Think not of the past. What is done is done, and you are cleansed of it. I promise you that. And I promise the Father's forgiveness."

Jesus affectionately rubbed the youth's head. "And, my son, if our Father in heaven can offer you the gift of His forgiveness, then might you not forgive yourself?"

With those words the dark tensions that oppressed Melchi began to ease. And he could weep.

Mariamne's sleep was filled with dreams. They were all alike: she was undressing before husky Romans in armor. Awakening, she lay in her bunk reviewing the dreams, and it struck her with surprise that they did not seem to be nightmares. She tried to suppress the thought she had actually enjoyed them.

She resolved to banish all thoughts of Romans from her mind as she dressed and ascended to the rooftop to await the bugles.

Looking across the city, she could see a small detachment of the foreigners crossing near the Huldah Gates in front of the Temple Mount. They walked with measured steps, their pleated tunics as dark a red as the blood-spattered Temple level where sacrifices were daily offered. Even this early, smoke curled from the great altar, carrying toward heaven the odors of roasting flesh and frankincense. The altar fires now roared continuously, as priests offered constant sacrifices for Israel's well-being. Its heavy burden of taxes each day grew more impossible. Those who couldn't pay were beaten or worse. Only last month a man in Mariamne's district had been unable to meet the required imposts. While he was absent from the city, his house was entered by agents of the *publicani*, who beat his mother-in-law until her back was broken.

Mariamne thought about yesterday. Lucius Silva. She should hate him. Instead, regardless of that degrading experience, she felt sorry for him. She sensed that he had sought something more from her than just a physical encounter. Her passivity hurt him. She had known it would.

More small detachments of the Roman guard began moving about the open area in front of Antonia. Mariamne found herself watching the soldiers. She admired their strong, manly bodies.

He was a surprising mix of qualities, the tribune. Autocratic, powerful, yet also sensitive and warm.

Maybe he would try to see her again. But did she really want that? It seemed unthinkable, yet . . . Dismissing the revery, Mariamne set about her prayers. Melchi, she noticed, had already gone out. He would be no help today and she had much work ahead.

Lucius Silva scarcely noticed the morning. That woman, Mariamne. She had troubled his rest last night. It was not her beauty alone; there were many her equal in Rome. No, it was something rare, something he had observed in others of her people. A pride that manifested itself as stubborn independence. He admired the quality. It seemed, somehow, Roman. Could he ever possess the heart of such a woman? By all the gods, he shouldn't get involved with her. There was his position to be considered. Here in Jerusalem, at least, he enjoyed considerable prestige.

A *tesserarius* interrupted. Late yesterday, explained the officer, several prisoners had been taken, Jews whom informers had fingered for being involved in an attack on Roman soldiers near the Siloam Pool. Two Romans had been killed and all of the Zealots escaped.

Lucius hurried below to the interrogation rooms. Regardless of the problems he faced in this terrorist-ridden city, the tribune took a dim view of informers. Too often they proved merely to be neighbors settling a grudge. However, in a case of such gravity as this, all leads must be followed up with questioning. As Lucius came near, he could hear the screams of prisoners. The *tortores* were already at their work. Usually they and the *quaesitor*, who undertook the actual interrogation, got what they wanted before many of the Jews died.

All the interrogation rooms were about the same: large, cold, stone places smelling of stale urine. On the walls were pegs from which hung various instruments of torture. The barbed hooks, *ungulae,* that could gouge out chunks of a man's flesh; the lead balls, *plumbatae,* attached to leather thongs, which could easily tear out eyes and break bones; and the *laminae,* metal plates used, when heated, to sear flesh. In one corner there was always the *equuleus,* the terrifying rack—a minor refinement of Roman siege weapons. Sometimes even the sight of these instruments would loosen a prisoner's tongue. For that reason they were always displayed in the interrogation rooms.

Generally the *quaesitor* and the *tortor* worked together, dealing with one suspect at a time. By isolating the prisoners it was often possible to get more information. The Jews were a stubborn lot, and proud. Putting them together might give them mutual courage. But alone . . .

Lucius glanced into one of the rooms. At first, it seemed deserted, wall torches barely flickering. But then he noticed a naked body, sprawled face-down in a far corner. The poor fool must have died during questioning. Long shadows played over the purple welts on his back. Lucius could see blood pooled around his chest. The *plumbatae* had been at work here. Lucius particularly disliked them. They were killing instruments, often defeating the purpose of their application: the extraction of information.

Several chambers were now in use. Lucius heard the thud of metal hitting flesh, the cries of agony. If they could uncover every one of the Sicarii involved in yesterday's raid, it would be possible to move swiftly. But he had never been convinced torture was the best way to deal with these Jews.

Peering into another room, he noticed Marcus, a *quaesitor*—one of the best of them—and his *tortor,* at work on a young prisoner. They had already applied the *fidicula* to the man's right arm. Lucius approved of this method more than many of the others, since it rendered great pain without leaving the prisoner useless for further questioning. Judging from a number of blood-engorged rings, the *tortor* had already used the cord many times on that arm. Now, having reached from the wrist nearly to the shoulder, he was once again turning the metal screw to draw up cord, crushing nerves and muscles.

The prisoner looked dazed, his pale face wet with the cold sweat of shock. Now and then a deep, slow groan escaped his lips. But he did not scream as most would have. They had tied him to the stone bench. His arm, useless by now, dangled limply to the floor. The *tortor,* on his knees, was swearing under his breath as he twisted the cord. "Damned swine, soon we'll begin on the other arm," he grunted, "then each of your leprous Judaean legs."

Marcus, seeing the tribune in the doorway, motioned his *tortor* to halt and stepped outside.

"Tribune, I can see this one's going to be stubborn. We have squeezed the life out of him. He doesn't even yell. But I'll swear he's guilty. We found a dagger hidden under his skirt."

"Was he picked up near the scene of the attack?"

"No, Tribune, at his house, in Bezetha. Name's Achim, though he refuses to admit even that."

The prisoner looked about Lucius's own age. Breathing spasmodically, hair matted with sweat, he lay motionless, with half-closed eyes. Lucius could see he was not the sort of rubbish that Sicarii usually turned out to be. His pale face seemed highly intelligent. "Did the informer tell you anything else?" asked the tribune, his curiosity aroused.

"Just that he's one of the *tannaim*."

So, that explained his intelligence. *Tannaim* were teachers. Probably he instructed at the academy near Bezetha. What in the name of the gods was he doing here? "Do you trust the informer who turned him in?"

"Tribune, like all the rest, he probably had a grudge to settle. These Jews—they're so loyal to that brotherhood of theirs, only the worst of them will give us anything. And then, only for silver."

In fact, Roman law did not allow torture to be carried out on the word of a single informant, except in matters of treason. But in Palestine, where the situation was considered a serious threat to the state, the law was routinely bent.

"I'll question him," ordered Lucius sharply.

"Should I leave the *tortor* here with you?" asked Marcus.

Looking in at the dazed man, Lucius shook his head. "I think not. He's had enough. I want him in condition to furnish answers. Perhaps later, if I get nothing."

Marcus and the *tortor,* glad to be relieved of the problem, withdrew.

Wondering why he had chosen to give himself such an unnecessary assignment, Lucius began pacing the stone floor. He could feel the prisoner's eyes following him.

"So," he began briskly, "you are called Achim." The man was silent. "Can you tell me, Achim, why you have been brought here?" Silence. "Certainly you must know an informer pointed you out. You are accused of being one of the party who attacked our soldiers yesterday near the Siloam Pool."

Thickly the man tried to articulate an answer. Lucius went to the door and called for a cup. Filling it from a pitcher in the corner, he held it out to Achim. At first the Jew ignored it, but when Lucius refused to withdraw his arm, he took the cup in his quivering left hand and tried to drink, spilling more than he gulped. But after he had finished, with a surprising burst of strength he hurled the empty cup against a far wall.

Angrily Lucius stared at him. "Is that how you repay a kindness?" he snapped.

"What kindness is it to ruin a man's arm?" mumbled Achim.

"If you are guilty, it is just," the tribune answered.

"You will never find that out," Achim said under his breath, eyes fixed on Lucius. "I won't give the tribune the satisfaction of being certain. So live with me on your conscience."

Lucius thought of all the men he had ordered to be tortured over the past months. The remark was ludicrous. But somehow he liked the Jew's spirit. It personified this whole nation, sparrows standing before an eagle, yet often displaying courage worthy of Romans. "How do you explain the dagger we found hidden under your clothes? Are you one of the Sicarii?"

Achim made no response. His silence was becoming infuriating. "Answer the tribune!" Lucius shouted. "Are you one of the Sicarii?"

Achim's pain-filled eyes smoldered with hatred. "I don't deal in assassination. Jerusalem is dangerous these days. I protect myself."

Lucius wondered whether to believe him. He wanted to. As a boy in Galilee he had known a *tanna*. The man had profoundly affected his thinking.

Achim struggled upright, leaning on his good arm. "You wouldn't understand, Tribune, but one of our scholars has written, 'Do not unto others that which is hateful unto thee.' I hold with such words."

Lucius stopped pacing. The man he had admired, the *tanna*, had often repeated this phrase. "Yes," he answered quickly, switching to Aramaic. "It was written by the great Hillel. I remember hearing it often during my childhood in Galilee."

Achim's face registered surprise. "You—lived in Galilee?"

"Once it was my home."

Achim had been trembling violently. Recognizing the response, Lucius drew his cloak over the Jew and called for some wine.

After a few sips Achim began to recover. "I, too, was raised in Galilee."

"Perhaps as children we knew each other," said Lucius. Nodding toward the Jew's outer garment, which had been thrown in a corner, he said, "Let me roll up your clothing and place it under your head. You will be more comfortable."

Achim smiled bitterly. "Oh, now you care about my comfort. After crushing my arm."

"I'm sorry for that. Had I known—"

"Known what? I'm the enemy, remember? Your informer told you that. A carpenter, angry about a woman who chose me over him."

Lucius asked again, "Were you involved in the attack on that outpost?"

Anger leaped back into Achim's eyes. "What difference does it make now? You've ruined my livelihood by ruining my arm. I may as well say yes and be crucified."

"Your arm will recover," said Lucius. He moved to help Achim from the stone bench to a chair where he could be more comfortable. But Achim raised his left hand warningly. "Don't come near me, Tribune. I know how to fight, and will do so gladly. I did not attack your men. I'll give you that, because of some memories we share. But let me tell you something else, and you can kill me for it. I sympathize with the Zealot cause. You could call me one of them. I'm no Sicarii, however, leaping on people from the shadows. In a fair fight, pit me against any soldier of yours, and I shall kill him gladly." Struggling to his feet, he tried to hold himself erect. "And never let it be said a Jew could not stand proudly before a Roman."

Watching Achim's attempts to remain upright despite the weakening ordeal he had just undergone, Lucius remembered words of Euripides: "Danger gleams like sunshine to a brave man's eyes."

"You are free to go."

Achim looked unbelieving. "Come now, Tribune, once I walk to freedom out there, you'll order your legion to spear me from the battlements."

"You may trust my promise," said Lucius. "I will order the officers to set you free. I have no proof save your word, which I accept."

Achim stared hard at Lucius, who returned the look. Then tears began to well up in the Jew's eyes. He tried to turn away but, still unsteady, almost fell backward.

Averting his eyes, Lucius moved toward the door. He was thinking of Galilee, the teacher he knew there, and a woman he had just met. "I wish you long life," he called over his shoulder to the Jew, and hurried out without waiting for a response he knew would never come.

Chapter 3

Jerusalem, 30 A.D.

Mariamne was not surprised when one day Lucius Silva appeared at her shop.

"Can you forgive me?" he asked hesitantly.

She wanted to be hard, but could not. Nodding, she turned away from the relief in his face.

"I would like to be with you awhile. May I—just sit here as you work?"

"No, no, that would be impossible," she gasped, alarmed. "I have customers. And my son . . ."

"Then meet me somewhere. I know. Gethsemane. It is a lovely place. I go there often to be alone. We could—take a walk."

She remembered him driving his body into hers. And then his sobs, like a tender woman's. "Very well. Tomorrow, at midday."

After he left, she sat the rest of the day pondering her decision. It was foolish, even dangerous. Yet these two years of widowhood had been lonely. Sometimes she yearned for a man's strong arms. But not a Roman's. And, above all else, there was the Law. God could forgive her yielding to rape but not fornication. No. She would not go tomorrow. Or, if she did, it would be to tell him to leave her alone.

Flavius Silva arrived early at Gethsemane. He had done what

he could to minimize any problems for Mariamne. His escort, waiting nearby, had orders to allow no one into the garden. It would be entirely discreet. He wore a brown cloak to conceal his uniform.

Brooding, the tribune tried to dismiss her importance to him. He hoped not to be disappointed again. Pacing beside a grove of olive trees, Lucius prepared himself for rejection.

Then she appeared, approaching him up a shallow embankment. "Mariamne, how good that you have come."

"I am here, Tribune, simply to tell you something."

"Tell me what?"

"That I—I—" She blushed, not knowing how to say it.

"Please, share my walk." He took her arm. She fell into step beside him, her resolve fading.

Gethsemane was a rocky, moss-strewn garden with clusters of wildflowers, ancient olive and oak trees. It lay on the western slope of Olivet beside a small stream bordered by willows. In the distance loomed Jerusalem's great Temple Mount. The little garden offered an atmosphere of privacy and peace.

"This is my favorite place in all of Jerusalem," he said with pleasure. "The life of a soldier doesn't allow much time alone. This is my sole escape. Sometimes I come here just to think."

She confessed she had never been to Gethsemane. "I work so hard, there is little opportunity for any diversion."

Both had become intensely aware of their feelings. She clutched the dark shawl tightly about her head. Nearby some birds were trilling.

Lucius said, "A *tanna* was brought to me the other day. He had grown up in Galilee." He did not wish to reveal the circumstances of their meeting. "When we talked, it brought back many memories."

"I have been to Galilee several times to visit relatives."

"I decided, after speaking with the man, that when there is time, I shall return for a visit. I would like to find the teacher, Eliakim Bar-Jonah, with whom I studied."

Mariamne was astonished. A Roman tribune, studying with a Jewish *tanna*? "Did you attend the Academy there?"

"It was not formal study. The Academy would not have accepted a Roman boy."

"And," added Mariamne, knowingly, "your parents would not have wished you to be contaminated by Jewish ideas."

Lucius nodded slowly. "Perhaps so. But I recall my early love of the Greek writers began because of Eliakim. I spent much time with him. My father was posted to Galilee when I was a small child. We lived there nine years." He stopped and sat on a large, flat boulder, motioning Mariamne to join him. "Eliakim and I used to talk by the hour, at a spot beside the sea. It was beautiful. Do you recall, Mariamne? In spring the hillsides of Galilee are yellow with wild mustard." He closed his eyes for an instant, remembering. "Those were happy days. Eliakim was, of course, much older than I. I used to think he knew everything. I still do."

"Did you have other Jewish friends?"

"Oh, yes. We shared many things."

Mariamne realized he had again been speaking Aramaic. She felt the danger of this situation, the sense that they were growing closer. "I cannot see you again, Tribune," she said in a small voice. "It is against every law, written or unwritten, to which I am bound."

"I can understand, Mariamne," he responded gently. "I could not behave like the madman I was before. Certainly you are free to go."

She had not expected it. "I might be in grave danger, were it known I had seen you. The Sicarii . . ."

"I would never permit you to be harmed!" he exclaimed. Then his tone changed. "It is a sad affair, Mariamne, when one wishes to love and the other will not accept it."

She heard herself saying, "I know."

And then Mariamne wanted to run as fast as she could, back to the safety of her house. No matter what she might be feeling now, this man was still Israel's enemy. "I must leave, Lucius."

She had never spoken his name before. "Mariamne, dearest—" As he moved toward her, the shawl dropped to the ground. Her long hair was unbound. And he knew she would not go. Cautiously he came closer. She did not back away. Lightly he touched her lips with his. At first she was unresponsive. His arms went around her. Hesitatingly, uncertainly, she returned the kiss. They embraced with increasing passion, holding each other tightly, murmuring little love words. He could feel the yielding firmness of her body, as it urgently strained against him.

"There is a cave nearby," he whispered.

The place was dry and warm. On the ground he spread his cloak and Mariamne's shawl. They knelt facing each other. There was no more hesitation in her eyes, only a tender need. Israel and Rome were forgotten. Slowly they disrobed, drawing in the sight of each other. And as, lovingly, he reached to hold her, Mariamne knew that for them, nothing would ever be the same.

They tried to meet as often as possible, always at Gethsemane. But many things, Silva's duties, Melchi, the shop, intervened to make for frequent separations. And during those times apart Mariamne knew a sad anguish. She had betrayed her faith, her nation, her own son. God would surely punish her.

Though not understanding why, Melchi noticed the change in his mother. Since his encounter with Jesus, he had stayed close to home and the shop. Too sunk in her own thoughts to question it, Mariamne accepted his presence gratefully. She needed Melchi now. More than ever.

One day he turned to her. "Mother, I want you to come with me and meet some new friends at Bethany. There is a rabbi named Jesus. You must see him and hear him speak. I know you are unhappy. He will comfort you."

How caring of her son, hoping to make her feel better. "Yes," she said. "I have heard about Jesus. I will go with you."

"You will also like my friend, Peter," Melchi told her, as they walked the brief distance to Bethany. Then he went on to tell about Jesus. It was clear that Melchi had been moved deeply by him. She had noticed, lately, how different her son seemed. More quiet and introspective. As if he had grown older overnight. The reason might be these new friends. At least they weren't Sicarii, and for that she was grateful.

They arrived at a simple house which Melchi explained belonged to someone named Simon. Melchi's friend, Peter, greeted them at the door. Beyond she could see a group of men who Melchi said were Jesus' disciples, and some women.

Pleased by their visit, Peter explained, "We shall soon leave to go up to Jerusalem for the Passover. At the moment Jesus isn't here. He went out this morning into the wilderness. Said he wished to be alone, to prepare his words for us. I think it is good that you have come at this time." Something in Peter's expression disturbed Melchi. Some sense of urgency, possibly of despair. The youth couldn't quite understand it, but sensed the older man had important things on his mind.

Peter led Melchi and Mariamne into the small courtyard of the house. "I'm certain the master will soon return," he said. "You will hear him teach. I'm glad you've come now," he repeated. Peter turned to Mariamne with a smile. "You can see that women are welcome followers." He led her to the small group of women, who made her welcome. Then Peter, whom Mariamne instinctively liked, took Melchi to chat with the disciples.

Before long, Jesus arrived. He entered the courtyard quietly, but his presence could be felt the moment he came near. He greeted each one with an affectionate hug. All responded with equal warmth. Mariamne thought she had never seen so much love. And the women were not excluded. When he was introduced to Mariamne, Jesus took her hands in his. "We are happy you are here, Mariamne, to share with us the Good News from the Father."

He moved on, to talk with some of the others. Mariamne, watching him, observed how easily he laughed, his joy radiating to those around him. She could not help appraising the linen gown he was wearing. White and seamless, it resembled that of the high priest.

Later Jesus returned. In a friendly voice he said, "I know Peter is fond of your son. Melchi is a fine and sensitive young man. How good that you wanted to accompany him today."

She sensed the importance of this moment with Jesus but, thinking of Lucius, blurted, "Master, I don't deserve to be here."

"Mariamne, it is not by chance that you have come. I do not condemn you; you know well what is right." Then he broke into a smile of pleasure, so simple that it seemed to belong to a small boy rather than a respected rabbi. "I was walking near here a while ago, and I came across something I would like to share with you. Come."

Mariamne was overwhelmed. This great man, this rabbi, offering her the deference paid a disciple. The others were busy with conversation; Jesus and Mariamne slipped away without explanation.

He led her a short distance from the village, where the wilderness began. When the ground became uneven, he took her arm. His touch was manly and sure.

They walked in silence. Then Jesus pointed. "There it is!" She looked around but could see nothing. Just the rocky, hilly terrain, dotted with scrub brush, under a vast expanse of empty sky. "You see? There!" he said. "When I came here this morning, I saw it. Isn't it beautiful?" Smiling with pleasure, he showed her a tamarisk bush in bloom.

Jesus knelt down to examine a feathery branch. "The flowers are tiny, but so perfect." They hung in dense pink clusters. "Did you ever notice them before?" he asked.

"No, Master," she replied. Though she may well, at some time, have passed the lovely tamarisks, they had been just another part of the featureless ground she trod while her mind, as always, turned to itself, preoccupied with worries, injustices, thwarted plans and dreams of fulfilment.

Jesus spoke carefully. "You know, Mariamne, we all live too much of our time on earth in lonely places like this. Filled with our own misery. But what beautiful gifts our Father offers, could we but see." Standing again, Jesus looked at the bush, his handsome features glowing in sunlight.

She felt drawn to him. "I should never have known the delight of these flowers, had you not directed my eyes to them."

He smiled. "And that is exactly why I have been sent. To tell you of the Father's heavenly bounty, that you may cherish His perfection."

Lovingly he touched one of the graceful clusters. Then his expression changed. "It is so hard to leave what the senses find satisfying. As I must do soon." He turned from the tamarisk, and she saw tears flash into his eyes.

Not understanding what he meant, Mariamne nevertheless knew she must hold Jesus in her arms. It was not the gesture of woman to man, but rather something between souls. They clung to each other, and it seemed the embrace she offered him was healing her. She felt a tenderness like nothing she had known before. Love which came from a place within her she had not been able to reach until this moment.

They walked together, hand in hand, back to the others. "I am happy that you, too, enjoyed the flowers," said Jesus. But she knew he had been telling her far more, singling her out for some special reason.

After Jesus and Mariamne had left, Peter came over to Melchi. "Jesus has honored your mother. She will learn much during their walk together. It is good that you brought her today."

"I wanted her to hear Jesus speak, but"—he looked shyly up at Peter—"I especially wanted her to meet you." Peter put a fatherly arm about the lad's shoulders and drew him to a corner of the courtyard, where they continued to talk.

Returning with Mariamne, Jesus went to the middle of the courtyard and settled himself on a cushion brought by one of the disciples. The small group formed a half-circle before him. Peter led Melchi to the front, where he could look directly at Jesus' face as he taught. The young man remembered his first meeting with the master, at Bethabara. What a great day that had been! He listened while Jesus spoke, and knew the Sicarii were far behind him. Their way was not his. Here, things were right. And here was a teaching that offered hope.

"Our Father Who art in heaven," prayed Jesus,

"may Your Name be held holy,

"Your kingdom come,

"Your will be done . . ."

Watching her son's face, Mariamne felt at peace. Melchi was absorbing the master's words like a root come to water.

Melchi returned to work later that day. He was stirred by Jesus' words and presence. His thoughts also turned to Peter. It was good to have been with him. Melchi felt they were really beginning to know each other.

Peter had confided his distress about the trip Jesus would make to Jerusalem, but would elaborate no further. Over and over the disciple had talked of dedicating the rest of his life to spreading what the master's followers called "the Good News." Melchi planned on seeing Peter often while Jesus and the others were in Jerusalem.

Mariamne, too, was profoundly affected by her encounter with Jesus. He had told her, "You know well what is right."

She determined that no matter how painful, she must end her affair with Lucius. Her mind would not know peace until she did.

She approached with dread their next meeting at Gethsemane. As he came toward her, smiling, she knew she had never loved a man so much. This time, at his touch, she gave up her body to him with an abandon born of despair. Though he did not yet know it, this would be their last time together.

Afterward he lay holding her, and she could not say the words. However, sensitive to her feelings, he asked, "There is something wrong. I know you are troubled."

"Yes." Still, she could not speak of it. Lucius would leave her and go on to the young beauties of Rome; he could be happy. She would have nothing but his memory. Yet, that was much.

"You want to tell me we cannot see each other again." Surprised, she sat up and saw the pain in his eyes.

"Lucius, it must end between us. You know the reasons."

"No, no I don't. I was soon going to ask whether you might come to Rome when I return—with Melchi, of course. I could give you a house there. We would be together the rest of our lives."

"As husband and wife?"

He hesitated, and she knew he was not going to destroy his future for her. He came of a distinguished family. In Roman society, she would never be acceptable. And there was also her side of the matter. A deep hatred of Rome had been bred into the hearts of all Jewish patriots. She could not turn her back on that.

"It is impossible for us, Lucius. We both knew that at the beginning."

He was silent a long while. Then, stroking her face, he said softly, "I shall not forget these moments with you."

Looking into his eyes, she knew he spoke the truth. "Nor shall I forget, Lucius."

He thought of some gift he might offer her, something worthy of their love. Removing his ring, he handed it to her. "Please take this, Mariamne. Keep it and think of me."

The ring was gold and bore, in intaglio, his seal, three graceful trees.

She demurred. It was too important a gift for her. She could not accept such a valuable object. But he would not let her leave until she had taken it. Once more they embraced, knowing the moment must serve for all time.

Returning with his escort, Lucius Flavius Silva saw what was to come: Rome the victor, Jerusalem a ruin, and for him, nights beside other women, remembering this one.

Jerusalem's high priest, Caiaphas, occupied an elegant house in the palace area of the Southwest Hill. At midnight he was awakened by the captain of his guard who announced the taking of a prisoner. Caiaphas knew which prisoner; he had left orders to be awakened the instant the man was taken. False messiahs and self-proclaimed prophets were showing up by the score in troubled Jerusalem. Each presented a potential problem. But the Nazarene was far more compelling than all the others. Calling himself son of the Blessed One, this heretic was actually gaining followers. Reportedly people were flocking to hear his blasphemous teachings. He had become an irritant both to the Roman authorities and to the Sanhedrin, over which Caiaphas presided. These times were particularly threatening to the nation. Nothing must be allowed to give the Romans cause for more repressive measures.

As he was assisted into his garments, the high priest pondered his scheme. With the foreigners in control, the powers of the Sanhedrin had been curbed. No longer did they have the decision over life or death in capital crimes. Yet Caiaphas was determined that the Nazarene be brought down, one way or the other.

He wore full ceremonial regalia. It would underscore the high importance of this hastily called tribunal. Caiaphas was relying on the priestly group, the Sadducees, to support him in this matter. They did not want their good relations with Rome to be undermined by a religious pretender. The Pharisees, the predominant opposition group, had often proved troublesome. He could not count on them for strong support in seeking the death penalty under Roman jurisdiction. Yet the Pharisees were the majority. Caiaphas smiled to himself. He had already arranged that more Sadducees than Pharisees be called to attend at this unexpected hour of the night.

Eliud, one of the elite temple guard, and Joda, lowborn like most of the high priest's contingent of *hyperetai,* court constables, waited outside the bronze doors of Caiaphas's reception hall. Within, about forty of the Sanhedrin's seventy-one members were now assembled. They awaited Caiaphas and the prisoner, who was being held in an anteroom.

Joda grumbled, "We could have taken that fellow anytime. This is the middle of the night." Slouching against a wall, he picked his teeth with a thorn.

Eliud, who made a fine appearance in his spotless linen skirt and ornamented sword attached to a multicolored waistband, turned to Joda. "What are you griping about? You are paid well for the little you do."

Joda bristled. "We do all that we are commanded. Jerusalem is not an easy place to police."

Eliud laughed. "Calm down, Joda. I know it can be a troublesome job."

Both men came to attention as they heard the tinkling sound of tiny bells attached to the high priest's robe. A moment later, without a glance at them, Caiaphas swept through the doors they held open.

The sight of the high priest's formal dress hinted that this was no ordinary inquiry. As usual Caiaphas had on the seamless linen *ketonet,* his purple mantle held by the gold buckle of office. As usual the conical golden helmet crowned his head. But this time he had chosen to wear over his mantle the *ephod*, a sacred linen vestment, to which was attached the gold breastplate of judgment. Only for important occasions did he wear this brilliant device with its twelve different gemstones representing the tribes of Israel.

Closing the doors, Joda whispered, "This is something worth losing sleep for."

Immediately afterward the captain of the temple guard and a few *hyperetai* Joda could recognize brought the prisoner to the door. He looked harmless enough. His eyes were gentle. And he seemed remarkably calm for one about to go before the Sanhedrin.

After the great doors were closed, Joda bent over and tried to hear what was going on inside. Eliud remained at attention, remarking scornfully, "You are supposed to be guarding the Sanhedrin, not acting like some Roman spy." Joda, embarrassed, moved his head away from the door crack.

"Were you in the courtyard just now when they flogged that man Peter?" he asked, changing the subject.

"I heard about it," answered Eliud. "They were going to try him also, but he denied knowing the prisoner."

Joda grinned slyly. "I know better. You remember, I was there on Gethsemane, and I recognized him as one of those with the Nazarene. That one is a scrapper. He grabbed a soldier's sword, and we kicked the stuffing out of him. He won't be walking around much for a while." Joda started to laugh, but was silenced by Eliud's look.

He put his ear to the door again. "Some witness is saying the prisoner boasted he could destroy the Temple and build it up again. They are asking him if those were his words." The guard whistled in surprise. "He says nothing, absolutely nothing!"

Eliud nodded. "Very smart. He would have damned himself by trying to explain. This Nazarene may prove difficult. I figure that he is merely another political activist. And that is a matter for the Romans to handle, not the Sanhedrin."

Joda broke in. "There were more Romans up at Gethsemane than Jews. It was those fellows who finally collared him. They obviously want him more than the priests do. Even that Roman commander, what's-his-name, the chiliarch, was there."

Eliud went out into the hallway and came back with two stools. Putting them on either side of the door, he said, "We may as well sit. This will go on all night. Look alive, Joda! When you hear them adjourning, give a warning. I would not like to be caught sitting down when Caiaphas flounces out."

Joda put his ear back to the door. "They are arguing about some legal point."

Eliud sighed. "I know. Those foxy Sadducees will join with the priests and cook up something so the Romans will have to finish him off."

"So, what makes you think the Pharisees like him any better?"

"That's not the point, stupid. Didn't you see who showed up tonight? Mostly Sadducees. They and the high priest will want to avoid trouble with the authorities. They will give him up to the Romans."

At that, Joda dropped off to sleep, snoring softly, his head lolling against the wall.

When daybreak came, Jesus and his accusers finally left Caiaphas's house, headed for the Praetorium and a meeting with the Roman procurator. Eliud had been right. But neither he nor Joda knew it. As the high priest swept out of his chambers, both guards were leaning against the wall, fast asleep.

Mariamne, at home alone, was trying to put Lucius out of her thoughts as she spun some newly hackled flax into strands of linen thread. Gradually she became aware of her animals bleating and kicking at their enclosure. In the streets people were shouting. Running out to the courtyard, she could see that clouds of red dust had covered the sun, darkening the sky to an eerie deep crimson.

Suddenly the ground began heaving. Earthquake! She screamed. A large water jar fell and crashed to the ground. A crack appeared in an upper-story wall. The terrified animals bleated and kicked.

Frightened, Mariamne hurried into the shop. The sky had

grown dark. Not knowing what to do or where to go for protection, she crouched on the floor, trembling violently.

She did not know how long she had been there when she heard Melchi calling her from the street. "Mother, Mother." He rushed in, out of breath. "It's Jesus. He's been crucified! I saw his trial in front of the Praetorium. It was horrible."

Melchi described what he had witnessed. Jesus was accused of sedition. But Pilate asked the crowd to choose between him and a criminal named Barabbas, also condemned to die for crimes against the state.

"Because it's the Passover," Melchi explained, "the Romans allowed one condemned man to go free." Bitterly he added, "The swine planted their own soldiers in the crowd to shout for Barabbas." Then he told how Jesus looked after his scourging: the cap of thorns, the purple robe and blood-soaked gown.

Mariamne found herself weeping. She did not comprehend how this gentle man could be called a criminal.

"I chose not to follow the procession to Golgotha," said Melchi. "I could not bear to watch his execution." His eyes were wet. "Now I must find Peter."

Mariamne begged her son to remain at home. The streets might be dangerous. Melchi explained that the disciples were hiding from the authorities. Peter would probably be somewhere in the Lower City. He wanted to be sure his friend was all right. "Mother, don't worry," he cried, and dashed off before she could protest.

Some time after Melchi had left, the front door opened and a customer entered. It was an old man, quite rich, judging from his cloak's fine embroidery. In a tired voice he asked Mariamne whether she could sell him a piece of linen. He would need it immediately, for a winding sheet.

"I want only fabric of the highest quality," he stated, nervously. "We must rush to take the body from Golgotha and prepare it before sundown."

Golgotha, the place of crucifixions! "Are you speaking about Jesus?" she asked.

He looked surprised. "Why, yes, the Nazarene."

She could remember every moment of that day at Bethany with the gentle rabbi. "I knew him," she said faintly.

The old man looked exhausted. "So many of us believed in his message of love and redemption. He will be buried in a tomb I prepared for myself near the place where he died."

"Why did they do this to him? He harmed no one."

"It was the Father's will. And generations yet to come will know the meaning of it." He began trembling so much she had to steady him. Apologizing, he said, "It has been a terrible time for those of us who loved him."

This old man in fine clothes did not resemble any of the others she had seen with Jesus.

"I don't know who you are, sir, but I believe you mean to do something good for the master." She reached up to the wall niche and removed the beautiful piece of linen she had recently completed, the cloth she had hoped would bring a handsome price. "Here, take it." She thrust the length of fabric into his hands.

"I am Joseph from Arimathea, a member of the Sanhedrin," he said. "This is of superb quality. What do I owe you?"

"Nothing."

"But you must . . ." he began.

"No, let me do this. It is little enough, for the memory he left me and my son."

The old man, touched by her gesture, said gently, "Do not mourn for him, daughter. He is now with the Father, as he promised. I am sure of it."

Taking the cloth, he hurried out. As Mariamne stood at the door watching this generous follower, she thought how strange that this linen she had woven should be chosen for the master's shroud. She recalled Jesus' comment to her that day at Bethany, something about their meeting not having been by chance. Had he known?

Melchi knew that the numerous Zealot groups in Jerusalem ran a highly efficient intelligence network. He began with his friend Obed. Having no information, Obed sent him on to someone else, who sent him to another. For hours Melchi roamed the city, searching for Peter. He realized how much the older man had come to mean to him. Like the father he had lost too soon. For some days now an idea had been forming, a plan to leave home and follow Peter. Now he feared they might never meet again. Perhaps his friend had chosen to flee the city.

When it became dark, he had to abandon his quest. But he began again the next morning, asking merchants in the marketplace, Sicarii he knew, and even strangers, whether they had heard anything about the disciples of Jesus and where they had gone.

Late in the afternoon, exhausted, he revisited Obed.

"No one knows where Peter might be. I'm afraid he may be back in Galilee, his old home."

Obed thought a minute. "Have you been up to Golgotha? I heard the Nazarene was buried in a tomb near the crucifixion site. Maybe some of the followers are there."

The streets were crowded with people visiting for the holidays. It took Melchi nearly until dusk to reach Golgotha, which was all the way across town beyond the Gennath Gate.

He had no trouble locating Jesus' tomb. No other would be guarded by Roman soldiers. He remembered hearing the disciples talk about Jesus' promise to rise from death. No doubt the Romans had heard this talk and were taking no chances someone would sneak into the garden and remove the body.

This was an area of rich men's tombs, tunneled into the limestone cliffs. Usually such tombs had an entrance chamber, then an arched inner chamber, the *arcosolium,* where the body was placed on a stone shelf. Tombs as elaborate as these also included a smaller recess, the *khokh.* After a body became desiccated, it was removed to the *khokh.* Later, when only bones were left, they would be placed in an ossuary. Tomb entrances were sealed with round boulders, rolled into place along a groove carved in the rock floor.

Melchi knew, with the Roman guards looking on, there was no chance Peter could get near Jesus' tomb. He wondered whether the body had been properly interred, the stone put in place. If not, jackals could steal in and desecrate the remains. Perhaps, when I find Peter, thought the youth, he will be grateful I can report that all is well here. Looking at the tough Roman sentries, he shivered. How would he get past them? Night was coming on. His only hope was later, when it got really dark. He must wait.

The burial garden contained olive and sycamore trees as well as flowering bushes. Its surface was strewn with stones and boulders. Not far off rose the upright posts used in crucifixions, standing out against the sky like pillars of a ruined temple. Moving quietly, Melchi concealed himself behind a large rock.

This place of death bore a strange and silent quality, and it was difficult for Melchi to control his fear. Looking over at the guards, he noticed they, too, seemed uneasy, shifting from one foot to the other as they stood their watch. Every so often one would pass a goatskin of wine to the other. The more they drank, the more unsteady they became.

Melchi was hot from the walk, and thirsty. He envied the guards their wine. Resting his head against the stone, he closed his eyes.

Awakening, he peered into darkness. He had no sense of the time. It might be the middle of the night. Everything was black, except for two flickering lamps near the Roman guards who had fallen asleep. Their goatskin, empty of wine, lay near the tomb entrance.

Silently as possible, his knees trembling, Melchi inched nearer. If discovered, he would never live to find Peter. His foot crunched a dry branch and the sound seemed deafening. He stopped and glanced toward the sleeping guards. They snored on.

Now, more bravely, Melchi moved over to them and quickly picked up a lamp. Its wavering light showed him the way to the tomb's entrance. Once inside the entrance chamber, he looked for the sealing stone. Yes, there it was, the large round boulder securely in place, blocking the *arcosolium*.

Suddenly, outside, one of the guards moved and said something. Melchi extinguished the lamp and ran, scrambling blindly over the rocks until he reached the safety of a large tree. Concealed by its thick trunk, he sank to the ground. Looking back, he could see the guards in the light of the remaining lamp. They were still asleep. One of them must have had a nightmare and cried out. Without a lamp, and unwilling to risk going near the Romans for the other one, Melchi thought it best to stay where he was until sunrise.

As he slept, Melchi dreamed Jesus was coming toward him, surrounded by a great brightness. He reached out to touch the master, but Jesus disappeared.

Melchi was awakened at dawn by singing birds. The dream was still with him. It had seemed so real. The guards were gone and the place deserted. It was safe to return for a last look at Jesus' tomb.

At the tomb's entrance he stopped and gasped, unable to believe what he saw: the sealing stone was rolled back from the *arcosolium* entry.

"Melchi, what are you doing here?" Startled, Melchi wheeled around to find Peter. "Mary, the Magdalene, thought I should inspect Jesus' tomb. She said the stone had been moved."

"It *has*, it has. Oh, Peter, I've been searching everywhere for you." Melchi pointed to the sealing stone. "When I came here last night, it was in place. What man could have moved such a thing?"

With mounting excitement Peter declared, "Don't you remember, Melchi? Jesus told us the truth would be revealed after he had gone from among us. Perhaps the answer we have awaited lies in there." He started into the *arcosolium*, moving with some difficulty as a result of his beating.

He was absent only a short while when Melchi heard him shout from deep inside the tomb.

"The Kingdom be praised. Our Lord has risen!"

Never had Melchi heard such joy in his friend's voice. Moments later Peter came out breathing heavily and visibly shaken. Leaning against the cave entrance, he tried to speak. "Melchi, a miracle! Jesus, his body, it is gone. He has risen to the Father!"

Then Melchi told Peter about his dream of Jesus and the light, and the disciple put his arms around the young man, joyfully embracing him.

"Melchi, you have been blessed. It is no accident you were here last night. Our master wants you with us, as witness to what has happened here." His voice broke. "To tell the world of God's work among us."

Melchi felt an indescribable elation. This was what he had hoped for; Peter asking him to stay and help in the work.

Peter could not contain his exhilaration. "We must go back and tell the others. This is the sign, the sign he talked about. Yes! But first I shall bring out the empty burial cloth. It will be our proof."

Peter disappeared again into the tomb, emerging a moment later with a bloodstained burial sheet and the narrow chin cloth which had been tied around Jesus' head. When he spread out the shroud on the ground, so it might be folded properly, sunlight blazed across the linen.

"Melchi, see!" cried Peter, dropping to his knees. There was no mistaking it. The imprint of a man's body filled the cloth. "Melchi, it's Jesus!"

Both were trembling. Never had such a thing been seen or heard of. It was both frightening and wondrous. Melchi was afraid to touch the fabric, wondering whether it had come directly from heaven.

"Here, lad," whispered Peter, "look closely. In every detail, the signs of our master's suffering."

The face, in death, was calm, beatific. It was beyond Melchi's comprehension.

Peter said, "He told us one day we, too, would enter the Kingdom, in full and perfect body. And when we knew the truth, there would be no more fear in this world. He has left us this, so that we might believe his words."

Gathering his courage, Melchi gingerly touched the cloth. It seemed like any other well-made length of linen, the weave more complex than most. Fleetingly he recalled that his mother had recently completed something very like this.

"Melchi, help me fold it," said Peter. "We must carry it back to show the others."

Almost expecting the image to disappear, Melchi carefully lifted the cloth and they gathered it into a neat rectangle, enclosing the chin cloth in its folds. Peter placed his hands upon Melchi's shoulders.

"Will you come with me now, to travel and teach this Good News of ours?"

Melchi nodded, knowing he would have followed Peter into the sea.

As they approached the place where Jesus' disciples were staying, Peter paused, struck with another thought. "You must go to your mother. Help her to understand. You are her only child. It will be hard for her without you in the shop."

"No harder than it must have been for your wife when you left to go with Jesus."

As soon as he had spoken, Melchi could have cut out his tongue. A look of deep pain crossed Peter's face. In a low voice he responded, "It could not be helped. Jesus called me. I had to go."

"So," replied Melchi, "must I."

Peter nodded. "Yes, it is true. Jesus told us, 'Anyone who prefers father or mother to me is not worthy of me. Anyone who prefers son or daughter to me is not worthy of me.' But, Melchi, you must see your mother immediately. Take respectful leave of her."

It was still very early when Melchi returned. He found Mariamne at her loom, setting up for a new fabric.

"Melchi, son, I was so worried. Where have you been?"

With a rush of words Melchi told her of his experience at the cemetery, of the empty tomb, the linen with Jesus' image upon it.

She exclaimed, "That is the shroud I wove. A man came here saying he was going to bury Jesus and I gave the cloth to him gladly. It was the right thing to do."

"Yes, Mother. The shroud will be proof forever of our gratitude to Jesus. And our hope for the great good to be achieved from the master's words in times to come. No payment could be large enough." Nervously he continued. "Mother, I must go with Peter. He is setting out with Jesus' followers to bring the master's message to other people. I know I have not been a satisfactory son to you. But what I have witnessed during the past weeks has changed everything for me. I pray to be a better person. And I shall learn much goodness from Peter and the others."

Mariamne looked at him, weighing the matter. Then she said, "Son, you *are* a good person. But if you want to go, I know you will be safe with those who do God's work. You have my blessing." There were tears in her eyes. "Now we must collect your belongings."

Together they gathered what few things Melchi would need— his other pair of sandals, a tunic, his cloak, the slingshot his father had made him, a few honey cakes baked the day before— and put them all into a cloth bundle. Melchi, impatient to be off, took up the bundle, kissed his mother, and left the house, never turning back. Mariamne watched from the doorway until he was out of sight.

Peter was waiting patiently for him at the hiding place of the disciples. Under his arm he carried the folded shroud.

The mission was to begin in Caesarea. As the two made their way through the Lower City, headed across town toward the Gennath Gate, Melchi asked, "Peter, might we stop a moment at my mother's shop? I would like her to see the image of Jesus."

When they came in upon her, Mariamne had been crying. She quickly dried her eyes and tried to smile. Seeing her sadness, Melchi felt the pain of his decision to leave Jerusalem.

"Mother, this is the linen you wove, is it not?" He spread out the cloth on the rough stone floor. "And see? There is the master's image, just as I described."

Looking at the length of fabric she had so carefully crafted, Mariamne began to weep again. Those terrible bloodstains. The scourge marks that crossed the figure's back. The cruel thorn marks on his head sadly apparent. What sufferings he must have endured. Yet there was the same wonderful face, the muscular physique. Mariamne knew this was the rabbi's image. She did not understand how it could be there, but for her, a miracle needed no questioning. It was the Lord's work.

Going to Melchi, she held him tenderly.

"Mother, take care," he said.

"Go with all my love, son. You are a fine young man. Let no one ever tell you otherwise."

Mariamne continued to cling to him and, anguished, Melchi was forced to pull himself away.

Standing in the doorway, Peter held up his hand, tracing in the air the mark of a cross. Melchi had never seen this done; he thought it to be some ancient sign of protection.

"Blessings on this place and on all who come in the name of the Lord," said Peter.

As Melchi and his companion made their way along the Street of the Kings, once again Mariamne watched from her doorway. Melchi, what a handsome youngster. No, not a youngster; he had grown up.

The travelers turned right at street's end, toward—where? Melchi had not said. She started to call out, but they had disappeared.

Chapter 4

Turin, 1978

The man from *Pravda* sighed from the depths of his Russian soul and deposited another wad of pink bubble gum in his mouth. "I cannot understand," he said, addressing Molly Madrigal. "We build bigger rockets, have achieved more man-hours in orbit, but are unable to produce your American bahble gum."

"Take heart, Korsakov," responded Molly. "Surely someday your physicists will come up with the solution."

The conference hall of the Ambasciatori resonated with the murmur of many languages. Molly could recognize a number of the forty-odd correspondents within the audience. They sat fiddling with tape recorders, reading the handout which awaited them by the entrance, or chatting with their neighbors.

An air of good-humored expectancy could be sensed throughout the room. Richard Coolidge was drawing a quite respectable turnout. The attraction for many may have been his reputation or the provocative subject, but for the news media there was the promise of lively, controversial copy during this slow period before the test series began.

She faced the Russian. "Boris, it just occurred to me. What are you doing here?"

"We are not disinterested in capitalist illusions. Dr. Coolidge advertises to tell the truth about the shroud. You forget—*Pravda* means Truth." Molly smiled.

Her thoughts returned to Richard and back to her senior year at Columbia. His class on Italian Renaissance art. She could see herself, ten years younger, counting the minutes before he showed up. She had come to know the imperatives of love. Scene One of their affair had begun when she stayed after class to ask a silly question. She could still remember how sweet and good it had been between them.

Richard entered then, striding to the podium above a table which held his demonstration materials. A tall, handsome man, he looked older than she had anticipated—a good deal older than his forty-two years. His sandy hair was touched with gray. He quickly glanced across the audience. Would he recognize her? She guessed she might look older to him. Molly's light-brown hair was still shoulder length, though her blue eyes had gained a subtle sensuality. At thirty-two her face showed more bone structure and had about it a certain firm and resolute quality.

"Ladies and gentlemen, thank you for coming. By this time you must be hungry for news, and I promise you, I shall deliver it. As you know, we are facing here an important moment in history. A moment when the Church of Rome has accepted the challenge of science.

"I am here to stake my reputation as an expert in art forgeries on the fact that whatever is determined and whatever the Church says about it, the famous Shroud of Turin is nothing more than a medieval fake. A very good medieval fake, I'll grant you. Still, a fake. And I have traveled to Italy on my own initiative because I know I can prove that to be the case."

He really is laying himself on the line, thought Molly. It seemed a risky thing to do. Yet, given the subject and the odds, he could be right. Surely, if his theory proved out, it would help his faltering career.

She had heard of his failure to win tenure at Columbia. Coolidge and his department chairman had gotten into a brawl over the chairman's effort to prove that the Colossus of Rhodes could have straddled the island's harbor entrance. The man had constructed a model to demonstrate his theory about the statue, one of the wonders of the ancient world. Richard argued that his boss's concept was ridiculous, that the hundred-foot figure of the sun god, Helios, could spread its legs more than forty feet. No galley, with oars extended, could possibly row under Helios's bronze crotch. More likely the Colossus had stood along the bank. In a derisive gesture Richard had struck the model, inadvertently smashing it and, subsequently, his future at Columbia.

On the other hand his determination that the famed Apollonian Marbles were Renaissance fakes had once brought him world recognition.

"I have spent many years studying the subject of medieval fakery," Coolidge was saying, "especially as practiced in Italy and in France. During the Trecento and later, Roman and Greek statuary were avidly sought after. So, naturally, professional counterfeiters of the fourteenth century had lots of business. Amusingly enough, forgers imitated exactly what they saw; their classical statues were cast with broken limbs.

"Most prized were religious relics from the Holy Land carried back to Europe by Crusaders and pilgrims. Fabrication of relics was not difficult. The original, if it ever existed, was not around for comparison. No authentic crown of thorns rests at Notre Dame, no pieces remain of the true Cross. I submit that if you were to take some particularly popular saint and assemble his bones from various reliquaries throughout Europe, the disjointed holy man might weigh half a ton.

"Forgive me, but I take a dim view of relics. And my research has regretfully led me to conclude—there is no shroud of Jesus."

He paused for effect. Molly knew well Richard's penchant for knocking piety and religion. Aggressively atheistic, he relished arguing with people about their beliefs. He could be blunt.

Coolidge stepped down to the table. Holding up each object in turn, he identified them: a metal container, a large camel-hair brush, a square of linen, and a plaque of a man's face in high relief. It looked like de Gaulle.

"I am going to show you one of the well-known methods that could have been used in fourteenth century France to make a 'holy cloth' for pilgrims. There were many such cloths extant during this period. In the thirteenth and fourteenth centuries pilgrims were eager to obtain tangible souvenirs from holy places they had visited. Nowadays we bring back postcards, although there are still a few gullible souls who will buy an 'original' tile from the Alhambra, or an 'authentic' statue from Tut's tomb. Many of those ancient travelers were rich men, prepared to pay substantial sums for a genuine relic of their favorite saint. They would have offered a fortune for something closely related to Jesus. The business of forgery, when skillfully done, has proved immensely lucrative."

Moving to the side of the table, he delivered his charm-laden smile. "By the way, have any of you ever seen what is billed as the only physical evidence of Jesus Christ on earth? You will find it right here in Italy, at Calcata, north of Rome. In a richly jeweled casket, what else? The Holy Foreskin!"

Laughter. Richard was scoring points.

"But I digress. Obviously a foreskin is a foreskin and need not be faked. Yet the matter of *whose* foreskin remains, at the least, controversial.

"Now, as to the shroud—admittedly, a more complex issue. For here we have an actual image, the image of a crucified man, complete in every detail, and looking like a photographic negative. How did such a mysterious figure appear on this piece of linen cloth?

"Ladies and gentlemen, let me explain. Geoffroy de Charny, seigneur of the small French town of Lirey, is the first recorded owner of the Turin Shroud. He lived in the fourteenth century and was a close friend of France's king, Jean le Bon. Jean and Geoffroy were dedicated to the ideal of founding a religious-military order of knights; in fact, they did so. It is my contention that Geoffroy forged this relic and used it as an object of worship for their Order of the Star.

"He and King Jean hoped to revive a great tradition that had ceased when the Knights Templars were crushed some years earlier. Essential to this revival was an important and sacred symbol. The length of cloth you see today above the altar of Turin's Duomo was that symbol."

Molly observed that the assembled journalists seemed fascinated. Richard's theory sounded convincing.

"Allow me to reveal Geoffroy's magic. I shall employ only implements and materials available to an artist of that place and time except, of course, for the hot-air blower and de Gaulle here." He patted the bronze cheek affectionately.

Explaining as he demonstrated, Richard took a piece of white linen and soaked it in hot water. Then he pressed the saturated cloth closely against the likeness, making sure it clung to every surface of the face. Next he trained the blower over the cloth to dry it quickly.

Opening the container, Richard explained, "This is a mixture of powdered myrrh and aloes. These, you will remember, were burial spices the Gospel of John mentioned as being employed to cover Jesus' body. Use of the identical spices should lend a cachet of authenticity to our demonstration. We know from old records that such botanicals could easily be obtained at numerous annual fairs held during the fourteenth century. So here we have, as a pigment, this powder, which I will lightly daub over the cloth."

As he did so, Molly could see, emerging, the characteristic red-brown color of the shroud image, although a few shades darker. Then he removed the cloth from the cast. Excess powder fell away. What remained was a nearly perfect facial image of the famous French leader, with that same soft, diffuse effect she had observed on the shroud.

Holding up the linen, Richard declared, "You will see the face of de Gaulle reproduced like the face on the purported relic. Further, because the powder has fallen away from hollow areas and adhered only to raised portions of the face, we have also reproduced the characteristics of a photographic negative—another 'mysterious' quality of the shroud figure.

"Now, I ask you, ladies and gentlemen, does this not resemble exactly what you saw displayed above the altar at San Giovanni?"

It did look similar, Molly had to admit. Richard then showed a photographic negative he had taken after a duplicate experiment. It was a recognizable positive image of the face, with realistic white highlights and dark shadows.

Someone asked about bloodstains supposed to be present on

the shroud. Richard explained his method allowed for such stains to be carefully added, spilled on, no doubt using real blood.

He appeared to have done it, to have found an explanation for the shroud's miraculous properties. There was little the journalists could think to refute. He had advanced his cause substantially by getting to the media early.

As the meeting concluded, Molly hung back, waiting for the room to clear. She could feel her nervousness. A heavyset man near her was also waiting, but Richard spotted her first.

"Molly!" He took both her hands in his.

"Hi, Richard. I want to tell you how much I enjoyed the demonstration, and your lecture was first rate."

"I thank you, M. It's splendid that you could get up here to hear me. You received my note, of course."

She nodded.

He had not pursued their relationship after her graduation. Their affair had clearly meant much more to her. It all seemed but another example of the old, sorry scenario: another class, another girl friend. For a while Molly had been devastated. A reporter's job with the Associated Press had helped her to get over him. A year later she was dispatched to Rome as a correspondent for AP. When Molly returned to the States two years later, she was immediately hired by *View*. Her career flourished, and she returned to Rome as one of the weekly news magazine's top writers.

Smiling into her eyes, Richard asked, "I assume by now you're married?"

"Nope, I elected the Fourth Estate over the estate of marriage. If you had troubled to write a little sooner than a decade, you might have known."

He questioned her about her work. What articles had she done that he might have read? Had she written much about the art world? What was she doing now? When he learned about her present assignment, Richard's questing gray eyes narrowed. "Admittedly I'm pleased that a very special friend is in a position to do me some good. God knows, Molly, I hunger for some favorable press."

Molly said that she doubted her New York editor would want a special piece on Richard's demonstration, but she would check it out. Meanwhile the Keeper of the Shroud, Monsignore Vittorio Monti, was holding a reception for journalists the following afternoon. At least she would get him an invitation. It should prove worthwhile.

"Right now the big thing for me is INAR."

"Inner what?"

"I-N-A-R, my Institute for Art Research. I started it eighteen months ago. We do expertizations, provenance research, mail out a bulletin of world auction prices. I go on a lecture tour now and then, and when Lady Luck smiles, there's even some fine-arts buying on commission. But alas, Lady Luck is turning out to be a bitch. To say I'm desperate for funds is to demonstrate the meaning of understatement."

Richard wondered if she knew how badly he had fouled up in the recent past. It hurt to think of his authentication of an early Stravinsky portrait by Modigliani. Everything looked right. Even the elderly widow of Modi's agent claimed to remember it. But the composer's pince-nez spectacles supported a dangling black ribbon. Then a couple of Stravinsky's old musician friends swore that there never had been such a ribbon. The painting turned out to be a very good fake, and Richard was hanged by that ribbon.

On an impulse Molly decided to invite Richard to go along with her the next day. She suggested he pick her up at her hotel. Wondering what she might be setting in motion, Molly left.

The man who had been waiting patiently now approached Richard. Bowing, he said, "I come to congratulate you, Dr. Coolidge. Your demonstration and lecture on the alleged shroud was totally excellent. It illustrates the perceptions of an exceptional intellect. Like yourself, I am a doctor of philosophy and a writer. May I present myself?" He bowed again. "Camillo Acciaro."

"Thanks," said Richard, in Italian. "You are very reassuring. However, I am not a writer."

"You will be," continued Acciaro smoothly. "We also share something else: an interest in religious fakery. At present I am writing a book on counterfeit European church relics. It occurred to me, after realizing the range of your knowledge, that you may be of assistance in my current endeavor. Your great knowledge of the shroud. There would be generous remuneration, of course. A few hours' conversation, perhaps over a good wine and a fine dinner. I prefer the very best restaurants—like yourself, I suppose?"

"Well, yes—of course," replied Richard, studying the array of membership keys suspended from Acciaro's watch chain. He was unable to identify any. A gold lozenge with a green crescent and star seemed vaguely Masonic.

Richard found the walk with Acciaro to the Conte di Savoia restaurant pleasant. There was that agreeable camaraderie that often springs up between noncompeting brothers in learning.

Sitting over the remains of their antipasto and beginning a second bottle of chilled Grignolino d'Asti, Richard was feeling more cheerful than he had in months. Being quoted in the Italian's book was all to the good. Camillo had assured him that a prominent New York publishing house was negotiating the rights for an English edition.

Moreover Camillo proposed to pay him five-hundred dollars per conversation, starting that very day. Richard, rather overwhelmed, began to thank him.

"No," reflected Acciaro, "that seems somewhat ungenerous of me. Let us make that fifteen-hundred dollars." Richard could expect a draft in the full amount at the termination of their talks. The collaboration would continue for as long as he remained in Turin. Acciaro was manifestly delighted, he said, with the American's ideas.

"Have you ever thought of the inference which can be drawn from Nicodemus's visit to Christ's tomb as related in the Bible?" asked Richard. "You will remember the Gospel of John informs us that Nicodemus placed one hundred pounds of aloes and myrrh around Christ's body. Now, Nicodemus was a rich and important man, a member of the Sanhedrin. Surely he didn't carry that load of spices under his arm. He must have had a cart. When leaving the tomb, naturally he took the cart with him. What do you imagine was in it on his return trip?"

Camillo hooted with laughter. "So, there is our Resurrection!"

He confided to Richard why he had early become antagonistic to the Church. His industrialist father, left a widower, had turned in his loneliness to a local priest in their town near Milan. The two were together all the time. The priest had stuffed the elder Acciaro with religious ideas. When Camillo was thirteen, he was informed by his father that he planned to study for the priesthood.

"My wealthy father gave all his considerable fortune to the Church. I never got a lira," declared Camillo in a low voice, scarcely concealing his ancient rage. "All of it—the mysteries, the prayers, the ritual—is only calculated to enslave fools like my father. And to grab their money. I have declared war on the Church. My book will be the first salvo."

Richard nodded sympathetically. This was truly a man like himself, unencumbered by religious superstitions and free. "Of course, like myself, you are an atheist," he said pleasantly.

"Oh, no!" replied Acciaro. "I believe God exists. I simply do not respect Him. One reads in the Bible that 'God created man in the image of himself.' But consider—man is so lost in the pursuit of his own desires, so full of angers, insensitive and cruel in so many ways, so vain, so jealous of others, and such a liar, that who in the world could possibly respect God, the model for man?"

"I trust your description of man excludes the two of us."

"Certainly, yes," Acciaro responded, and then both men turned their attention to the arrival of the waiter bearing their steaming *polenta con uccellini*—bright yellow cornmeal with tiny songbirds drowned in gravy.

It was Richard who brought the subject back to himself; Acciaro, he thought, might be of further value. "Camillo, I have recently founded an organization whose purpose you will readily approve. The Institute of Art Research, based in New York, was established to expertize notable works of art; separate the genuine from the spurious. The deceptions of dealers or glamorous publicity never influence us. We would not hesitate to reject the *Last Supper* if we smelled something fishy. But we urgently need more advanced technical equipment, and we are, uh, momentarily underfinanced. It would be a major loss to the civilized world if we were compelled to discontinue our important work."

Acciaro squeezed Richard's arm. "I expect to come into a great sum of money—very soon. I believe there could be a substantial contribution to your worthy Institute. In fact, *caro* Riccardo, I shall promise you that. Incidentally," continued Acciaro, taking a pinch of snuff from a small silver box, "I have little time now for small details and I noticed today that you are acquainted with an attractive American journalist. You Americans have easy access to things. As I said, I should like very much to have some assistance in my research. Those shroud scientists we are now awaiting. It might be interesting to learn what tests they plan, and their schedule. How many people will assist? Et cetera. It could justify inclusion in the book."

"No problem at all," said Richard. "I'll find out everything."

"Very good," replied Acciaro.

Later, after exchanging phone numbers amid declarations of friendship, the two said farewell. Whistling some nameless melody, Richard strolled back along the boulevard.

Monsignore Vittorio Monti hurried to the small house he occupied on Via Alfieri, not far from Piazza Solferino. His mind churned with all the things he must do. Archbishop Severini had called a sudden meeting of the commission this morning which Monti was obliged to attend. But it had set him back. Tomorrow was his reception for the foreign journalists and he had material to prepare.

Serafina opened the door and announced that Count Nicolò Sforzini had come for a visit. Dear Nico, thought Monti fondly. Then he felt a twinge of conscience. Nico would not be pleased by some things which had been decided at the meeting this morning. After all, he was one of the shroud scientists.

Vittorio Monti was a short, stocky man in his mid-seventies, with white hair that tufted at the temples. His ruddy complexion was dominated by dense gray eyebrows. He had assumed the hereditary post of Keeper of the Shroud upon his uncle's death in 1934. As a child he had listened to the legends of his family's connection over the centuries to the relic. It was then he decided to devote his life to it. Throughout most of his forty-four years as keeper he had attempted to trace the relic's history and establish a factual basis for the many stories that had been passed on. Thus far he had been able to locate written records dating to the fourteenth century. And there were clues which led him even farther back. However, six months before he had stumbled upon information he felt compelled to keep to himself.

In the University of Turin library he had come across a reference that stunned him: a footnote in a book by A. Carpano titled *La Venezia di Dandolo*. The author claimed to have found in Venice's Marciana Library a notation that the shroud had been displayed in Venice during the year 1205, the same year the Knights Templars displayed a shroud in Paris. A duplication? Monti hardly dared think of the consequences. He could not find the courage to go to Venice and search out Carpano's source. Better to let the situation rest where it was. Should there have been a Venetian duplicate, it might easily have found its way to Turin. Maybe the original was destroyed. The inference was horrible, unthinkable.

Now Monti's fears were ballooning. Some enterprising historian or journalist might stumble upon the Carpano reference, much as he had. He must set forth all the positive evidence he could to support the Turin relic's authenticity. Bad enough that these scientists, probably atheists all, were coming here—without this added problem.

The priest entered his study and greeted Count Sforzini. "Nico, it is always a delight to see you. But I am afraid that today I have some news which may not please you. The commission met again this morning. Though the consensus is in favor of a test series, we decided against radiocarbon studies of the shroud. At least right now."

Sforzini looked distressed. "How very shortsighted. I know the Americans will be especially disappointed. A proposal has already been submitted by one of the laboratories in the United States."

Radiocarbon testing of the shroud linen would establish a relatively accurate date for the cloth. A method used by archaeologists for many years, it is based on the principle that all living things, including flax, the raw material of linen, absorb carbon during their lifetime. When life ceases, carbon uptake stops. Among the two forms of carbon atoms—isotopes—in the fibers there is a specific proportion of radioactive carbon, C-14, which decreases year after year at a fixed rate. The age of a given sample is determined by the percentage of radioactive carbon which remains.

As submitted, the proposal required only a very small sample of the shroud fabric. This would be reduced by a complex series of steps until only pure carbon remained and then placed in an atomic accelerator, whose high intensity field is often used for this purpose. The atomic accelerator, in a brief time, could separate the radioactive C-14 from the familiar carbon, C-12. The ratio between those two types of carbon would yield the age of the sample within a range of plus or minus eighty years.

"You know," Monti said, "many persons are uneasy about this scientific testing. It is creating controversy. That is not good."

"Vittorio, are you really afraid of us scientists? Do you imagine we will somehow harm the relic?"

"Certainly not you, my son, but the others—they do not care about faith or Our Lord and His message for mankind. Their unique concern is science."

Nico smiled. "Being a member of their fraternity, which includes us archaeologists, I can say something about that. We have the same human sensibilities as—well—priests. Furthermore, at the highest theoretical levels, science and the concept of a Creator, a First Cause, seem to converge. Anyway, Vittorio, stop worrying. Let the Lord take over here."

"But, my dear Nico, we must give Him a little help. That is why I am planning this reception tomorrow for the journalists. I have much material for them. Articles I have written about my historical studies through the years. I trust my small reports will be sufficiently compelling for the journalists to include in their articles. When my material finds its way into print, one hopes it will also nudge these scientists in the right direction."

Nico shrugged. "I understand, Vittorio. You will reach the press with your message before we scientists can announce our

findings. Nothing wrong there. Yet, do you think that will ultimately change matters?"

Nico looked at the monsignore fondly. Since he was eight, he
had known Monti. The priest, who spent his vacations in Venice,
had been a family friend. When Nico's father died, Vittorio became the youngster's confidant and after Nico gave up his career
as a professional race-car driver to attend the University of
Turin, it was Monti who encouraged him in his new specializa-
tion. The count had since become a well-known Biblical archaeologist, associated with the city's Istituto Archeologico.

Nico had hesitated when invited to join the European team for
the shroud testing. He thought it might put him and his friend
Vittorio on opposite sides of the issue. But he had received
Monti's encouragement, and he had accepted.

Monti looked dour. "It is not only the scientists. Would that
they were my sole problem. There is a certain matter concerning
our blessed relic which worries me much more. But I cannot
speak of it."

At Nico's urging the monsignore declared finally that he had a
confession to make. He then confided about the footnote which
might prove the existence of duplicate shrouds. "Just imagine,
we may now be displaying the counterfeit relic! I feel guilty for
having held back this information from you, Nico. But now that
you know, you will alert me to any evidence of forgery. Though,
of course, it simply cannot be so."

Nico well understood how difficult such a discovery must have
been for his friend, and the coming weeks would be a time of
even greater anxiety. Evidence that the Turin Shroud was false
could demolish Monti's world.

The priest went on, "Actually, I did not see with my own eyes
whatever documents were referred to in this footnote. They may
not even exist. In any event, with all that is taking place in
Torino now, I have no time to search for them."

Wishing for an end to his friend's anguish, Nico decided the
thing to do was to confront the issue head on. "I shall go to
Venezia, Vittorio. I am familiar with the Marciana Library."

Nico was the son of a distinguished family, one of Italy's
oldest and noblest. His mother's and sisters' residence was still

the ancient Palazzo Sforzini on the Grand Canal. In recent years, however, he had spent little time in his native city. The place held a painful association for him since the end of his racing days and the subsequent breakup of his engagement to a beautiful model who still lived there.

"The testing will doubtless start at the exposition's end," he continued. "There is ample time, though I feel my search should begin soon."

Monti brought his hands together as if in prayer and extended them toward Nico. "Thank you, dear friend. But then again, perhaps I should not thank you—yet."

Nico embraced the old priest. "I shall be here tomorrow, in the very remote event one of those journalists asks a question which completely confounds you. I might not know the answer but I am very good at scientific double-talk."

As he was showing the count to the door, Monti observed how the younger man's aristocratic bearing, his lean, intelligent face with its dark hair and poetic eyes, gave him the look of a scholar, a romantic scholar. His former bold and jaunty air was gone, replaced by a thoughtful deliberateness. A deep faith had changed Nico, adding a special gentleness to his nature. Yet there seemed also to be a certain brooding sadness which would shadow his face now and then. He was thirty-five. Time to choose a wife. Yet where in Christendom was there a woman worthy of such a good heart? As the old priest closed his front door, he thought, I shall pray for him.

Camillo Acciaro climbed a dark stairway to the small apartment he rented in a run-down building on Via Santa Giulia. He expected two associates to arrive shortly who would assist him in the supremely important project which would make him one of the world's very rich men.

He glanced around the carpetless living room, subliminally noting its water-stained walls and worn furnishings.

Bruno Strà knocked first. Five minutes later Ugo Rozza was at the door. Strà, a short, swarthy man who nurtured a hair-trigger temper and a perpetual surliness, had been a terrorist-for-hire. He showed no evidence of his recent stay in prison. To Strà it had not mattered. The whole world was his battleground. He sported a purple scar across one cheek, memento of the final act in the life of a man who had engaged him in a knife fight.

Ugo Rozza was a technician, skilled in the artistry of devices, most serviceable in the pursuit of crime. He was lanky and unhandsome. One side of his glasses was held to an ear by a loop of string. Apparently the simple and legitimate repair of his own spectacles had failed to engage Rozza's special aptitude.

"Gentlemen," said Acciaro, "I can announce with confidence that our endeavor is now under way. I have met our *babbeo* and the fool is mine. He will be a direct channel to the shroud scientists. We can adjust our plan of action without uncertainty."

"Who is this guy?" asked Strà.

"The man is an American professor and a fool only because of my clever manipulations."

"I don't trust teachers," said Strà.

"If we ever expect to get our hands on the shroud, you had better trust me. I shall teach you how." Camillo offered himself a pinch of snuff and looked steadily at Strà.

"How many lire are in this for us, Camillo?" asked Rozza.

Acciaro replied, "You figure it out. How many millions of the faithful will scrape up money to pay for the return of the shroud? A hundred million, two hundred million? After my sixty percent, your twenty percent shares from the kidnaping ransom will be sufficient for each of you to buy an island and be its king."

"A stinking kidnaping," griped Strà, "with no hostage."

"No hostage?" said Acciaro. "You're wrong. Our hostage is Jesus Christ."

"Holy Mother of God! It is different when you put it like that," Strà said somewhat grudgingly.

"Now, Ugo, there are a couple of things you must start working on. First, I want a blowtorch that is self-igniting. A button or something one can quickly push."

"Simple," said Rozza.

"Then, not so simple, is a small receiver-transmitter radio. I shall decide at what frequency to set it. We shall require a minimum range of two hundred kilometers. Once turned on, the radio should be unable to be switched off. The receiver will always be operating except when a voice-activated switch puts the radio into a transmitting mode. We must be able to hear every sound in a helicopter cockpit. Do you understand?"

Rozza said, "Understood."

"That is not all. Inside the radio must be an explosive charge large enough to bring down the helicopter. It can be detonated by a radio signal set to a very narrow, unused frequency."

Ugo Rozza rubbed his hands together in gleeful anticipation.

"That sounds crazy," said Strà. "Are we going to be radio artists?"

"In a way. The radio will be smuggled aboard an operational helicopter at the airport. Our pilot will be told to take it up with the money in bundles. He will be ordered by radio to fly along the Po at six meters above the river and not use his own transmitter to broadcast any information. We can hear him if he does, and he will understand that we can blow him up any time he disobeys us or allows any pursuit planes to follow. When he passes near our hiding place, he will be ordered through our transmitter—I'll get to that, Ugo—to drop the money on the bank and keep going."

"Suppose he decides to spill the location to the authorities anyway?" asked Strà.

"Then we would hear him. He will be instructed to keep flying along the Po for another eighty kilometers. Our own radio, Ugo, will require a device to explode the charge. The pilot will go down twenty minutes after the drop. At that altitude he will survive, and we shall be far from the pickup area."

"About this teacher," asked Strà, "will he tell us when to go for the shroud?"

"That is my job. I shall tell you when."

"Christ!" reflected Strà. "We are going to snatch Jesus!"

"And Dr. Coolidge," added Acciaro pleasantly, "will be our Judas."

Chapter 5

Rome—Byzantium, 63–64 A.D.

Peter was dozing in the tiny courtyard of Melchi's house in the Weavers' District near the Forum Boarium. His head, with its great white beard, had dropped to his chest and he was deep into a dream about debating Paul in Antioch. At that moment little Priscilla took a flying leap onto his lap.

"Uncle Peter, Uncle Peter, come and play," urged the eight-year-old, gently tugging his beard. He hugged her tightly, suggesting that she sit on his lap. The sun here was so warm.

Soon Priscilla was joined by seven-year-old Rufus, who added his voice to his sister's. They were finally shooed away by Melchi's wife, Julia, who replaced them at Peter's side. Peter watched with regret as the youngsters ran off. They were his joy, the grandchildren he had missed when, three decades before, he left a family of his own to follow Jesus.

What years these had been! Years of hard travel, carrying the shroud and Jesus' message to believers and nonbelievers alike. Melchi was always alongside him, sharing the not infrequent harassment and imprisonment, but also the triumph and growth of a Christian religion.

That religion had remained centered, at first, in Jerusalem, among those who had known or heard Jesus. But soon it began to spread inexorably toward the West. By the time Peter and

Melchi arrived in Rome, a small community of converts had already been established. It was comprised mostly of foreigners, Greek slaves and those who had learned from traders of Jesus' teachings. They shared their goods and cared for widows and orphans. When it was learned who Peter was, he was acclaimed and immediately given leadership.

He and Melchi found life in Rome to be remarkably peaceful. Imperial authorities were little concerned with a small community representing the poorest classes. However, of late there were ugly rumors. These Christians, it was said, practiced orgiastic and repugnant rituals. Their superstitions were perverse, wicked.

Peter recalled a day at Lydda. The bright sun had been like this. It was a time long past, when he had cured the paralytic. Aeneas, was it? Funny how one's senses can jog the mind about an event. The warmth, the long shadow of a fig tree. The cripple had been lying under such a tree, his stiff body mottled by the shade from its branches. Somewhere, he remembered, a bird had been singing. Yes, a day like this at Lydda.

Julia was speaking. "Peter, you're not listening," she declared loudly.

He smiled apologetically. Julia was a diminutive, plain-looking Roman girl Melchi had married a decade ago when they decided to settle here. Full of kindness and easy laughter, she also loved to talk. Peter was the person to whom she directed most of her discourses. Julia enjoyed his companionship, since Melchi had little time for idle conversation. When not leading the small group who worshiped each week at their house, he was busy making a living at his loom.

"Peter, you haven't heard anything I've said. I'll simply have to begin again."

He pulled his thoughts from the past. Julia's information suddenly drew his sharp attention. Paul had just been released from military custody. He had sent word he would join them at the Lord's Table this week.

The news brought Peter both pleasure and pain. Paul, who had taken much of the leadership from him. A bitter draught to swallow, this Paul. Younger, dynamic, obsessed with his mission;

he was not even one of the original Twelve. Peter wondered whether Paul was planning to stay here in Rome and take over the Community. It made sense. The time had come for someone else to assume the responsibility. Peter was sixty-two. His body had slowed down. How infuriating, this unwillingness of the body to do what the mind commanded. But that was as it was. Yes, it would be good if Paul stayed.

There was great excitement at Melchi's the following Lord's Day, as Christians gathered to await Paul. Since his arrival in Rome two years before, the evangelist had been under house arrest and had never worshiped with them. Peter noticed that Melchi took special care arranging the offering table, and Julia explained to Priscilla and Rufus that a great man would be their guest for the agape, the feast of communion they all shared during worship.

After everyone, about thirty Christians, had assembled, there was a knock at the door. Peter, in the upstairs meeting room, could hear Melchi welcoming Paul. And, at last, there he was, standing in the upper doorway. Small, intense, Paul quickly scanned the room until he recognized Peter. Immediately the old man rose. They had not seen or communicated with each other for ten years, since Paul's outburst toward him at Antioch. Peter had left for Rome because of Paul.

Paul waited while Peter made his way over to the doorway. The older man was annoyed that Paul could always work things around in a gathering to become the commanding figure.

As Peter led him before the congregation, Paul nodded to all with easy assurance.

"Your companions in Christ are here, Paul, awaiting your message."

"Peter, dear friend, it is good to be back with you." Again Paul looked around, pausing at each face. "As you know, I have had a long imprisonment here in Rome. Not so harsh as some places I remember, but harsh enough. Still, most cruel of all was my inability to join you, my spiritual brothers and sisters, in the celebration of Our Lord's feast. I have deeply missed this. Though, of course, my prayers and thoughts were always with you."

He looked upward and Peter noted again the compelling power in his eyes. "But what great benefits we are given when we can suffer in the service of Our Lord and his Word. My friends, what a blessing! I am profoundly grateful to offer this unworthy body, if in so doing I can further Jesus' plan for humankind."

Conviction lighting his face like a lamp, Paul continued to speak, praising God for the blessings of his imprisonment. Peter felt the bite of jealousy. As always Paul was deeply convincing, his rhetoric polished and cultured.

Why couldn't I have such learning, such grace of tongue? thought Peter. What has the Lord given me to use in His service? I speak clumsily. The followers do not drink up my every word, as they do Paul's. My mind is slow; I have traveled the world and know nothing of it.

It was time for prayers and Peter led the worshipers, but thoughts of Paul kept insinuating themselves into his consciousness. His words seemed to come with even more difficulty and he felt a painful resentment.

Before leaving, Paul took Melchi and Peter aside. "I will soon depart for a long visit to Hispania," he said. "Before I go, I must talk with you about certain matters here in Rome. Could you join me tomorrow?" So, he wasn't going to stay! Peter tried to repress a smile though reason told him that, soon enough, he must name a successor to take over his duties. He would approach the subject tomorrow.

Awakening the next morning, Peter prayed at length, asking the Lord to grant him freedom from the bitterness he felt toward Paul. By midmorning he and Melchi were on the Via Sacra, headed toward Paul's lodgings. They passed through the teeming Forum Romanum, where tradesmen and prominent citizens jostled the populace for space and advantage. A few in the crowd recognized Peter by his great height and flowing white beard. Even in Rome, center of the world, he was known as a miracle worker, somewhat feared by the pagans who whispered that he and his followers practiced cannibalism in their secret rites.

Near the Tabernae Argentariae someone roughly clutched

Peter's tunic from behind. It was a woman carrying a tiny infant. She implored Peter to cure the baby, who had refused nourishment and was covered with sores. Peter, perceiving the young woman's anguish, turned to the child. Taking the infant, he closed his eyes in silent prayer. Melchi could see the deep concentration transfigure his face. He had watched this a hundred times but it never failed to move him. Melchi thought he could almost detect a thin film of light emanating from Peter as his energy flowed into the little one. A moment later Peter opened his eyes and handed back the child. He was visibly tired from the effort. A crowd had gathered, demanding that the woman lay back the child's woolens. She did so, and gasped with joy. The skin was clear, the babe crying for food. Gratitude shining from her eyes, she put him to her breast.

Sighing, Peter turned to Melchi. "I'm an old man, Melchi. Could we rest a moment?"

As they sat on a curbstone, someone from the crowd moved close and began cursing Peter. It was obvious from his hairstyle and clothing that he was a Jew. Berating Peter, he heaped curses on the false god, Christus. Melchi was hot with anger but Peter put a hand on his arm. The two said nothing and soon the Jew, anger spent, went away. There were other mutterings from the crowd against foreigners and their magic. Gradually their hostility dissipated; the revilers moved on.

Paul greeted Peter and Melchi happily. "You're in time for the midday meal. Come, join me."

Peter was still fatigued. As they dined, he complained to Paul. "The Community in Rome is growing larger every day. It is your turn to lead us, Paul. You are more qualified than I. That was obvious to me yesterday."

Melchi felt much sympathy for Peter. Through the years he had watched the two men clash, with Peter usually ending up the worse for it. Now his friend was giving up altogether.

Paul regarded Peter intently. "This is the very reason I asked to meet with you today. I sensed at the agape your strong feelings against me. So, nothing has changed since Antioch?"

Peter could not hide his sentiments. With Paul it would have been useless to try. "I suppose I've never stopped resenting your leadership, when it was I—not you—who personally knew the master."

Paul grimaced. "At its roots this has always been our dispute. Even our theological differences have stemmed from the fact that you knew him and I did not." He paused, then gazed piercingly at Peter. "But you forget. I *have* known him. On the road to Damascus. And didn't he say that only after he left us would we fully understand all, through the Spirit?"

Peter remembered Jesus' words; he had sat at table with the master that last night.

"So," continued Paul, "you who knew him as a man, knew him no better than I."

"What you say is true, Paul," remarked Peter wearily. "I do not dispute your leadership. It is you who have the youth, the energy, the ability. No one wants an old fellow like me anymore. They all want you. Yesterday I saw it in their faces."

Standing, Paul banged his fist on the table, so forcefully that both Melchi and Peter were startled.

"It has been too easy for you, this life in Rome!" cried Paul. "No persecutions, no prisons to keep you striving. You've gone soft, old man. And what's more, you've let the master down. You should be ashamed."

Peter, aghast, gaped at the wiry Paul, who continued his diatribe. "I'm telling you the truth, if you have the brains to comprehend it. You must pray for release from your indolence, from the ease of your good life."

Melchi was embarrassed for his friend. But, surprisingly, Peter seemed moved. Suddenly he felt young again; once more the scrappy Galilean. Rising to his feet, he towered over Paul, challenging the younger man with his intense glare.

"Agreed your criticism is fair. But I haven't lost my will. I warrant that this year I shall collect more souls than you. Don't forget, I have before."

"Just try it," countered Paul. "I would like to see the day . . ."

Then they both laughed and embraced each other.

"God's blessing on you if you succeed, dear friend," said Paul.

From that day Melchi observed a new fire in Peter. The kind of fervor he had had upon first leaving Jerusalem to preach the

Good News. Then, people had waited for Peter's shadow to pass near them, believing even it could heal.

One day, after the visit with Paul, Peter asked Melchi's help in composing a letter to the converts in Asia Minor. Peter had had a dream that soon they would suffer terrible persecutions and he wanted this letter to stand as a testament of faith. Melchi wrote down the words as Peter spoke.

"All flesh is grass and its glory like the wildflower's. The grass withers, the flower falls, but the word of the Lord remains for ever. What is this word? It is the Good News that has been brought to you."

Melchi had never known him to be so eloquent.

It was early the following summer that Julia announced she was again pregnant. Peter rejoiced with Melchi, already loving the child-to-be. On the first day of the week, after Julia's announcement, the small Christian community gathered in Melchi's house for the agape. They prayed for the health of Julia in her pregnancy and Peter thanked God for the safety allowed their group by the Roman authorities. Later Melchi presided over the common meal. Peter felt great joy for the love in Melchi's face as he looked at his wife. The apostle seldom regretted his celibacy, but tonight he did so, as his old frame stirred with memories of women he had once known in Galilee—the wife he had left behind.

One sultry day in midsummer Julia quit her weaving and joined Peter under the fig tree. She was already beginning to show the outlines of her pregnancy. She rested her head in Peter's lap; he felt profoundly happy to have her trust and affection. Breathless, Melchi rushed in from the street, startling their tranquility.

"I was delivering fabric in the Palatium district when a shopkeeper stopped me. He had terrible news! This morning Emperor Nero crucified four hundred slaves, all because one of them killed his cupbearer."

Peter felt the blood leave his face.

"Their crosses are standing in rows along the Via Appia just outside the city. The shopkeeper is one of our brethren, Peter.

He urges you to go there. Many of the slaves are Christian; they cry for your blessing."

As they hurried south, Melchi told Peter all he had learned. That the slave who committed the murder had been clearly identified. Regardless, Nero had proceeded with the mass slaughter. People were stirred to fury by such injustice. There had been a few quickly suppressed street riots. Peter lamented the increasing madness of the emperor: his whoring on Mars Field, in brothels staffed by women of his own court; his insane musicals that went on for hours with no one allowed to leave on pain of death; his spies planted everywhere, betraying even their own relatives for personal gain.

The two could hear a wail of groans and cries and smell vomit and excrement long before they came near the crosses lining both sides of the road. Peter, agonized by the ghastly scene, moved among the dying, praying for pagan and Christian alike. Many called out his name, begging for a quick death. He tried to comfort them, urging them to remember Christ's salvation. An old man no longer, Peter scrambled over boulders and ignored brambles to touch the feet of the tortured, to call up to them his blessing.

Finally a guard spotted him, came over to where he was praying with one of the wretches. "Clear out of here, old man. This is none of your affair. Leave the dying to die."

Peter paid no attention. The guard drew back a leg as if to kick him, and shouted, "Do you want to hang up there, too? Get going now!"

Peter turned toward the legionary. His powerful frame towered above the stubby Roman in his crimson and metal. Looking toward the heavens, Peter prayed in a loud voice, "Father, deliver us from tyranny. Give these, Your faithful, a home in the Kingdom. Be with them now, in their misery and pain. Take them unto You and let them know the only true freedom."

Abruptly the guard moved off, without making the arrest. Melchi had seen it before, and always it filled him with wonder.

At twilight the two weary, grimy men stumbled home. Julia had supper waiting but neither could eat. Melchi fell into bed, exhausted. Peter went outside to be alone. He sat down, staring up at the stars as they blinked into view above the small square of courtyard. He remembered that other cross, the day he thought his heart would split.

Jesus' shroud was folded among his belongings. Since that moment outside the tomb he had tried to avoid looking upon its stained image, leaving that part of the teaching to Melchi. He knew it was the dread of reliving so much agony.

But now the four hundred had brought it all back. The years of peace were over. This was a portent of things to come. He felt a chill spread through his body. Could it be fright, as it had been that night, long ago, when he had denied Jesus? Could he, after all the years of trial, be afraid to suffer as did those wretches today? On his knees Peter began to pray.

He was still at prayer when he looked up and saw the reddening sky. Suddenly he was aware of a vast murmur across the city. Slowly it became a low roar. He awakened Julia and the still-exhausted Melchi. They went into the street to learn the full horror of what they were seeing. Rome on fire! The emperor, some said, had set the torch to it himself. Even now Nero was standing in the Maecenas tower, chanting of the destruction of Troy.

They could see the flames, moving in a southerly direction through the Forum Romanum, toward the Regio Palatium and Circus Maximus. Melchi told Julia that none of the *vigiliae* who fought Rome's fires were equipped to handle such a conflagration. The city would be destroyed. At this Julia began to weep hysterically. Peter realized there was nothing they could do now but take the children and flee to the cemetery outside town. There they might be able to find shelter in one of the tombs until the flames subsided.

The small group of Christians led by Melchi and Peter left their homes and shops to the mercy of the flames and, amid the clutter and din of a terrified populace, made their way out of the city. The stench of burning wood and flesh made breathing difficult; black clouds of smoke hid all light; day seemed like night. Screams of those losing property and loved ones ripped through the flames and clamor to shake even the bravest of them. They tried to calm neighbors, while hurrying through the soot-blackened streets, stamping out small fires wherever they could, carrying in their arms what food and clothing they had been able to gather in their haste.

As they moved along with the surge of humanity filling the Via Appia, Melchi and Peter saw the grisly crucifixes still in place. Most bodies had been removed, but some remained, sagging in death.

At the cemetery the group separated, each family seeking an empty mausoleum in which to take refuge. In the distance Imperial Rome burned. Flames colored the skies with a brilliance which would have been magnificent were it not so tragically mad. Finally, near a tiny stream, Melchi located a damp, evil-smelling tomb, large enough for adults and children to huddle inside while they tried to ignore the acrid smoke that penetrated even here. Julia gave the children a small bit of the food she had brought, and tried to make them comfortable on cloaks she spread about the moldy stone floor.

Six days and seven nights they waited and prayed, supposing the flames had already destroyed their home and livelihood. On the seventh day, after a few hours' sleep, Peter awakened. Young Rufus, also awake, walked outside with him for some air. It was surprisingly quiet. Somewhere Peter could hear a bird. He looked toward Rome. The flames had burned out. An exhausted, ruined city was now quiet. When Melchi and Julia awakened, the family prayed, thanking God for their deliverance.

Upon returning to Rome, Melchi and the others discovered that the Forum Boarium had been spared. Although their house and its contents were blackened by soot and ashes, everything was intact.

A few days later Julia and Melchi were still at work clearing away the dirt and debris when Silvanus, one of the Community and a neighbor, stopped by with news.

"People are rioting again, near the Golden Palace. The Praetorian Guard has had to call in reinforcements to protect the emperor. Several cohorts from the Roman garrison have been summoned to duty near the palace."

"What does it mean?" asked Julia, alarmed.

"I cannot say," answered Silvanus. "But citizens are angry.

Those with burned-out properties were not permitted to return to them. There are rumors Nero has looted these places for his private gain."

"That vile pig," growled Melchi. "He is no better than the lowest criminal!"

Julia threw her arms around Melchi. "Where will it end?"

Silvanus gave a bitter laugh. "Where will it not end? That maniac won't stop till he's destroyed everything."

Melchi added, "And all of us."

But Nero was not without a plan to exonerate himself. This became painfully apparent to the Christian community in Melchi's quarter as they held their weekly meeting six days after the fire. As Peter commenced that part of the service in which the faithful are offered fish, bread, and wine, there was heavy knocking at the front door. Everyone instantly sensed it meant trouble. Then came a louder thunder of knocks. As Melchi started for the stairs, Julia began to weep uncontrollably, clutching his arm. Gently he set her aside and continued to descend.

There was silence in the small room as rough voices of soldiers were heard shouting that they were authorized to arrest one Simon Peter and take him for questioning. Melchi tried to protest, but was shoved aside. Two guards burst into the upper room. The Christians, who had been standing to receive the Eucharist, waited silently.

One of the guards demanded to know who was the man called Simon Peter? Peter stepped forward and was arrested. At that moment he knew he would never see the brethren again. He feared for them and for the continuance of this little band Jesus had given him to shepherd. He asked for a word with Melchi.

Taking Melchi's hands in his, Peter looked deeply into the face of this man he loved like a son. "Do not fear. They want only me and will not harm you, if you do not resist."

Melchi remembered his feeling years before, when Ezra had been killed. It came upon him now; a numbing heaviness.

Peter trembled. "The shroud," he whispered to Melchi, "it is now yours. Cherish it, and forever tell of its great miracle."

"Come on, old man," growled a guard.

Hugging Melchi's children to him, Peter faced the brethren.

"The Lord's peace be upon you," he cried. "We shall meet again in the life to come, as Jesus promised."

Kissing the children, he traced in air the sign of the Cross, the sign of blessing and protection.

The *praetoriani* laughed and grabbed Peter, brutally dragging him downstairs and out of the house.

In the street Roman citizens who recognized Peter jeered at the guards and shouted that the emperor had chosen the lowest of the low, a Christian, to bear his own guilt. The helmeted soldiers jabbed at passersby with the butts of their spears to clear the path.

Peter had expected to be taken to prison. He was surprised to find he was headed, instead, for the Golden Palace. He and a guard passed through the main porch where the famed hundred-foot statue of Nero stood. Gold, jewels, mother-of-pearl, gleamed from its surface. The walls of the long chambers through which they walked were lined with ivory panels. Mosaic floors glimmered with gold inlay. Peter was revolted by this show. Although the air in these rooms was heavily perfumed, to him it was the stench of decay and death; the death of Rome. Rome in the clutches of Satan.

"You are to be interrogated by the emperor himself," said the guard importantly, as if offering him a gift.

They arrived at great bronze doors which magically swung open for them to pass through. At first Peter did not notice the emperor, so vast was the circular room into which he had been taken. Periodically ivory wall panels opened, emitting a scatter of colored flower-petals. Here the reek of scented oils was overpowering. Fountains jetted colored water at opposite sides of the monstrous chamber. And—wonder of wonders—its floor, a giant disc, was slowly revolving.

In the middle of the room, on a yellow silk couch, reclined Nero Claudius Caesar Drusus Germanicus, Emperor of the World. This is the center of the material world, thought Peter, and I'm slightly dizzy turning about on it. Despite his sense of vertigo, the old man managed to stand upright until the guard gave him a shove that sent him to his knees.

Nero leaped up disapprovingly, chiding the guard for hitting such an ancient fellow. Then the emperor helped Peter to his feet and walked slowly around him, appraisingly. The two men were of nearly equal height but comparisons ended there. Nero had a heavy, indolent face, pustular and freckled. His carefully dressed curls were a dull blond, his eyes gray and small, buried in fat.

"So, you're the ringleader of those Christians," he began. "A very old man! It seems rather late in life for the incest you are reputed to practice." He laughed, a rusty, high-pitched cackle that echoed against the room's tall ceilings. Coming closer to Peter, in a friendly manner he asked what it was Christians actually believed. Peter, knowing any response would only provoke another sardonic comment, answered noncommittally. No fool, Nero realized the old fellow was clever. Motioning the guard to leave them, he invited Peter to sit on a chair near him. Peter continued to stand. Angry at this rebuff, Nero shrilled, "When the emperor tells you to sit, you shall sit! I will not be disobeyed by garbage like you."

Nero proceeded, earnestly at first, to question Peter about Christian beliefs. Thinking that perhaps the Lord had brought him here to save his flock—the Empire as well—Peter tried, in his halting way, to explain the faith of Jesus. Surprisingly Nero listened carefully, questioned intelligently. Then, at last, with a leer, he said, "It is known you can perform magic. Are you a sorcerer?"

"No, Emperor. It is not I who perform the healings but the Holy Spirit working through me and all others who believe."

At the words "Holy Spirit" Nero's small eyes gleamed. He leaned closer to Peter. Confidingly he whispered, "There is a figurine in my possession. . . ." He told of a doll given him by a common man in the street—"someone as low of station as yourself"—which he'd discovered had magic powers. He prayed to that figure in secret three times each day. Now the emperor was glowing with excitement—"This doll has won me battles; has given me brilliant musical powers; made women in bed cry for more of me."

Peter began to pray silently for deliverance from this maniac.

"Does your—ah, Holy Spirit—do all that?" Nero asked, triumphantly.

"The Holy Spirit is concerned with goodness, Emperor," answered Peter quietly.

"But so am I!" said Nero, leaping to his feet. He ran to one
panel of the cylindrical wall. Pulling aside a silken curtain, he
revealed an altar of gold and precious stones. Seated atop it was
a tiny rag doll, the type small children carried to bed with them
for comfort in the night. He fondled the object, which was grimy
from much handling. "Now, Master Peter, you—you Christian—
join me in worshiping *my* God. A *true* worker of miracles."

Peter could feel his anger rising. No longer did he think of his
own safety, of the safety of his friends, or of Rome. Only that he
wanted to strike out at this poisonous villain who fouled the very
air they breathed.

"You, Emperor of filth," shouted Peter, "are a fool. You will
suffer eternally for your evil and wickedness."

In a blind moment he lunged for Nero, knocking the big man
to the floor. Although he was more than three decades older,
Peter pinned the emperor firmly against the marble. He could
see fear cross Nero's face before the ruler screamed shrilly for
help. Guards rushed in and would have run Peter through that
moment had not Nero stopped them.

"Leave him for now. I have better things in store for this
Christian and his fellows," he whispered in a choked voice. Unsteadily he pulled himself to his feet. "Get out! I must not speak
anymore. This disgusting clod of dung has made me shout. I
may have injured my voice. And the musical games are next
week."

Peter was thrown into the Tullianum, that fearful place few
ever left except to endure worse tortures. He was detained in the
carcer, a small cell at the upper level, rather than the dungeon
below into which criminals were lowered by rope. This was
hardly reassuring. He feared what Nero's fertile brain would devise for him. Even more did he fear for the other Christians, especially Melchi and his family.

The captain of the prison guard was a powerful young man,
with massive arms and shoulders. Lacking an eye, he appeared

otherwise fully capable of crushing a man. Yet his manner was kind, even sympathetic. Peter remained quiet, spending his time praying, trying to disregard the dark cell's filthy conditions, the damp that made his joints ache.

When the guard brought Peter his piece of bread the first night, he said, "Here, eat this, old fellow, before the rats get it. This will be better for you than prayers. And maybe I can find more for you."

Peter rose from the corner where he had been kneeling. "What is your name, my son?" he asked in a gentle voice. "Since we will be sharing this small corner of God's earth, we might as well address each other as men."

Taken aback, the guard said he was called Gallus. When Peter introduced himself, Gallus seemed interested. "You're the leader of those Christians."

Peter felt impelled to explain something about Christians, and the following day Gallus was back with more questions. Peter patiently answered them, then asked the guard what was to become of him. Gallus told him he had heard rumors that Peter and the other Christians were to be condemned for torching Rome. He and others realized it was the emperor's doing, but Nero, to save his skin, required scapegoats. The Christians. Leaving, Gallus said quietly, "You are to hang on a cross, like Christus your master did."

Peter spent an agonized and sleepless night. But by the time Gallus entered the cell with some watery morning gruel, the apostle had quieted himself.

Gallus was surprised to see his prisoner so calm and when he remarked on it, Peter explained that to Christians, life was everlasting. The soldier's good eye widened with fascination. This time he sat on the floor for a long time, asking questions, until Peter's strength was exhausted. Later Gallus, carrying a tattered woolen blanket, returned to the cell where Peter had fallen asleep. Looking over his shoulder to make sure he was not observed, Gallus tossed the blanket over the sleeping prisoner. He stood a moment, studying the old man. Then, in a guarded gesture, he smoothed out a fold of the ragged covering.

During the night Peter had a dream that Jesus came to him,

saying his time was near. Awakening, he stayed up till dawn, praying for courage to face the coming trial. Next day, when Gallus arrived, Peter asked whether he would soon be tried. Gallus looked uncomfortable.

"I shouldn't be talking. But I've heard there's to be no trial. You're a foreigner, a state criminal. As chief magistrate, the emperor himself has already passed sentence."

Now Peter could expect the worst of brutalities.

"For you," continued Gallus, "it's to be crucifixion, tomorrow at sunup, on the Vatican Hill."

Peter stood quietly, staring at the pattern of flooring stones wavering in the light of Gallus's oil lamp. Not raising his head, he asked, "Will you request one thing for me? Have them crucify me head down."

Gallus was shocked. "But why? It's more painful."

Peter replied, "I'm not worthy of suffering the same martyrdom as my master, Jesus."

The guard nodded. "Death comes more swiftly that way. You'll not be able to raise your body on the nail to bring relief."

Peter began to shake. He leaned against the wall for support. Coming over to him, Gallus promised to make the request. "But I can do no more than that. I lack your courage, Master Peter; I am an ordinary man."

That night, however, Gallus gave his own dinner to Peter, saying it was all he could think of to do. Touched, Peter blessed the man.

Looking into Peter's eyes, the Roman said he wanted to become a Christian. Secretly, of course. "How do you become a Christian?" he asked. The apostle explained about baptism by water. Gallus said tomorrow he would bring some pure water from a spring. Could Peter please do it then, before they took him away?

Peter passed the night in prayer. And very early Gallus arrived, carefully carrying a pottery cup of water. He knelt before Peter, who three times sprinkled his forehead, then, tracing the sign of the Cross, pronounced a baptismal blessing. Gallus had tears in his eyes.

"Thank you, Master," he exclaimed. "Already I feel different.

Now, though I have to work here and send good persons like you off to death, I, too, can be forgiven. Isn't that right?"

What Gallus did not reveal to Peter was that Nero had ordered a series of horrible tortures to be inflicted on the old man prior to his crucifixion. The jailer had simply ignored the Imperial command. Though he could not save Peter from death, Gallus was determined that the apostle should walk to his end in dignity.

Soon a detachment of soldiers arrived. As Peter prepared to leave, Gallus whispered he would pray to the great God Christus for his deliverance into the new life. The legionaries shouted from outside for them to hurry. Gallus grabbed Peter's hand and kissed it, then delivered him to the soldiers.

It was not long after Peter's arrest that Melchi heard about the events at the Golden Palace. Knowing Peter was doomed, he wished to see his friend a last time but he was turned away at the Tullianum. In the square outside the prison he learned that the apostle was to be crucified.

Wrenched with misery, Melchi went to Vatican Hill to witness Peter's end. He was not permitted to go near the area where the old man hung, head down, on a cross. Eventually, however, the thought of Peter's suffering became too much for Melchi; he forgot his caution. Breaking through the line of soldiers, he rushed to the foot of the apostle's cross. Peter's beard had been shaved off and his head, hanging down, was a cruel red. As Melchi reached up to touch his friend, he realized gratefully that Peter had lost consciousness. At that moment two soldiers grabbed Melchi. Saying he must be another Christian, they arrested him and took him to the *carcer*.

Meanwhile, to divert attention from his own crimes against the city, Nero began his purge of the Christians. Julia, fearing for Melchi, who had not returned home, remained indoors, trying to work. She had heard terrifying stories of Christian neighbors disappearing in the night. Even so, she did not think of her own danger until the day following Melchi's departure, when she learned that a woman of their Community, a widow with one small child, had been taken—the child, too. She knew she must get away, out into the countryside where she and her children would be safe. Quickly she gathered together some warm clothing and a bundle of food, and, with Rufus and Priscilla, headed once more toward Via Appia and the tombs. She prayed Melchi might go there, too, and they could find each other.

Moving carefully, Julia tried not to attract the suspicions of patrols that were everywhere. In her district they had already rounded up many people. Some she recognized as Christians from their own Community, others she did not. She supposed the legionaries, not knowing whom they were supposed to arrest, had seized all who seemed suspicious, labeling them "Christians." She calculated she was probably safer without Melchi for the moment. Gently she cautioned the children to be quiet, as they made their way slowly toward the city's outskirts. When they were nearing the Porta Capena, Julia's every nerve fought to keep going, but finally she felt she must rest or collapse. Were she not pregnant, she could have forced herself to go on.

As the three stopped to rest, a group of soldiers passed by leading a large group of prisoners toward the north of town. Suddenly Rufus recognized someone in the group.

"Mama, Mama, there's Ananias!"

Indeed, as she looked to where the child was pointing, Julia could see their very close friend, a leader of the Community. Ananias looked away hurriedly, hoping not to draw the guards' attention to Julia and the children. It was too late. One of the soldiers halted the prisoners and came toward Julia.

Mad with panic, she screamed at the children to run. Rufus burst away from the soldiers but Priscilla clung to her, sobbing. As they both tried to escape, the praetoriani easily closed in and took them. Julia held her daughter closely, crying Melchi's name over and over.

Raging at his impotence to protect Peter from such a terrible fate, Melchi put up a struggle at the *carcer*. But he was knocked unconscious and thrust into one of the smallest cells. He awoke several hours later, his head aching terribly. The space was so constricted he could not stretch out his legs and had to sit tightly against the wall. Frantically he wondered about Julia and the children. What would become of them? He was somewhat comforted by the thought that the Community would care for his family should he not return. He ached everywhere and it was difficult to think. But the crucifixion—that dreadful vision of Peter dying—refused to leave him. Peter had been a true father. He loved the old man who had brought reassurance and affection into his life. They had been through much together. Rome—that had been the best time. Until now.

The heavy iron grate was unbolted; a guard entered. Melchi pretended he was still unconscious. Suddenly a huge rat ran across his legs, causing him to flinch. The guard laughed. "I don't know why the rats here are so big. There are no feasts for them to fatten on."

Melchi stared at the man. There was unexpected friendliness in his tone. He leaned down and spoke softly: "What is your name, prisoner?" Melchi found himself responding, though he had promised himself to remain silent. The guard smiled. "I'm Gallus. Let us know each other as men." Then he straightened up and was gone.

Upon his return the next day he said, "The other guards tell me you're a Christian. Did you know the man Peter? He was crucified two days ago."

Again there seemed more to Gallus's manner than mere curiosity. Melchi answered, "Yes, I knew him—well."

"Is that where they arrested you? Up on Vatican Hill?"

"Yes," responded Melchi, adding angrily, "I suppose that I am also to be crucified? What will become of my family?"

"I know nothing about your family. The emperor has his different methods with prisoners. Some are sewn in animal skins, to be torn by wild dogs. Some are smeared with pitch and set ablaze. Since you are a suspected Christian and a foreigner, it will probably be the usual crucifixion."

The jailer lowered his voice to a whisper. "I knew your friend Peter. He was here. Perhaps I can help you." Melchi looked at Gallus suspiciously, wondering if he could be believed. "Not all Romans like what the emperor is doing. I don't. And in fact, I'm quitting this job, walking out tomorrow. I can no longer be one of those who send innocent men like your leader to their death.

Tomorrow I'm taking off. And while I'm about it, maybe I can help you, too."

Melchi lay awake all night, thinking of what Gallus had said. Was there reason to hope? In the morning he had his answer as soon as Gallus opened the iron door.

"Quickly, come with me. Not a word. Let me do the talking. My uniform will protect us—for a while, I hope."

Several times they were stopped in the crowded streets by squads of soldiers. But Gallus simply declared he had orders to take the prisoner to the palace for questioning. "The emperor's business," he would impatiently announce. That stopped further inquiries.

When they had walked a distance from the prison, Gallus told Melchi he had learned of a ship leaving for Byzantium that week and he intended to be aboard. Melchi could do what he liked.

"I must join my family in the Forum Boarium," replied Melchi.

"You should be very careful," warned Gallus. "That's where a lot of arrests are being made." He pondered a moment, then said, "I'd better come with you. You'll be safe with me."

Together they made their way back to Melchi's house and shop and found it empty. Neighbors told Melchi they had heard that Julia and Priscilla had been arrested while trying to flee but that Rufus had gotten away.

"But he is only seven. He will never find his way home!" cried Melchi in despair.

"There is no hope for your wife and daughter," Gallus said, "so let us pray the boy can be found."

Melchi, feeling more anguish than he had known on Vatican Hill, now turned to Gallus and thanked him for saving his life. He must stay in Rome, he said, to search for his son and try to help Julia.

Gallus begged Melchi to come with him to Byzantium where they could be sure of safety. "If I leave you here," he said, "you remain in great danger. And I must depart soon to reach Puteoli before the ship sails." By now their flight had been discovered, he felt sure, and both were fugitives.

"I have to find my family," insisted Melchi.

Gallus replied, thoughtfully. "So be it. I have gone this far with you. I will stay here until tomorrow night. With great luck we just might locate the boy."

While Melchi, remembering Peter's last request, was looking through the apostle's belongings, Gallus went into the Christians' meeting room. So simple, this Christianity, thought the Roman. A wooden table, a font with water in it, and, drawn on the wall, a fish and some loaves of bread. But Peter's few words had already taken hold. Even now Gallus knew that in Byzantium he would seek out a group like this and find more answers.

Melchi easily located the shroud along with its chin cloth, which Julia had long ago sewn onto the larger piece. He carefully rolled the linen in a piece of fabric from the shop. Then, taking a handful of coins from a hidden wall niche, he joined Gallus, who looked at the shroud inquiringly.

"This belonged to Peter," explained Melchi. "It is the master's burial cloth and bears a miraculous image of his body."

Because Gallus was eager to see the figure, Melchi carefully unrolled the cloth. The Roman moved slowly along its length, gazing wonderingly at the image. Then he dropped to his knees and touched it.

"The master Christus—Peter told me he was sent from the great Lord." He spoke softly, almost to himself. "Yes, it is so. Now I know in my heart it is so."

They spent two days in a fruitless search for Rufus. As evening of the second day neared, Gallus reluctantly said they must go. It would be dangerous to remain. But Melchi refused, saying he would not leave without his family. Again Gallus reminded him that an alert had certainly gone out since their disappearance from the Tullianum. If caught, they were dead men. "And then what use will you be to your family?"

"What good will I be to them in Byzantium?" lamented Melchi.

"You are a Christian," Gallus argued. "Pray to the great Lord that He help you. Then leave it to Him. Peter explained to me about faith." It was then Gallus confided to Melchi that he had received baptism. Surprised and touched, Melchi said he didn't want to endanger his new friend. But he must return to the

Forum Boarium once again. Maybe he would hear some word of Julia or the children. Shrugging his shoulders and wondering why he was risking himself for this man he scarcely knew, Gallus announced he would continue to accompany Melchi for a brief while; then he must go. Melchi turned toward home, hoping by now that there would be news.

Later he was to wish he had never returned. It would have been better not to know. Theudas, one of the brethren not yet taken, told Melchi that Julia and Priscilla were dead. The night before, with other Christians—many of them women and children—they were smeared with pitch, tied to poles, and burned in the emperor's palace gardens, which Nero had ordered to be opened for a public spectacle.

"She was expecting our baby," was all Melchi could groan, over and over. Gallus took Melchi by the hand and, as one would a child, led him out of the city. In three nightmare days they made their way to the coast, Melchi unable to speak or reason.

By the time they reached Puteoli, Melchi's clarity of mind had returned. The dazed expression disappeared, replaced by something else, something hard and deeply angry. He thought constantly about his son; what might become of Rufus should the child survive. The possibilities were ugly or unthinkable. And the shroud. Why had he bothered to hold on to it after losing everything else? He and Gallus argued constantly about Christianity. For Gallus it promised a fresh start; for Melchi its very mention brought bitterness.

At the harbor they found space on a Roman merchant vessel headed toward Asia; final destination, Byzantium. The captain, a stocky old salt with squinty eyes, looked inquiringly at them.

"I'm returning to my post at Byzantium," lied Gallus. "This is my friend from Rome. I'm bringing him home for a visit." He hoped his native Greek would be convincing. The captain, also a Byzantine, seemed satisfied. Nevertheless he kept glancing at Melchi's cloth-wrapped packet. Feeling uncomfortable, the two looked about the hold for a safe place to stow the shroud, not realizing the captain was surreptitiously following their every move.

The ship was an old three-masted square rigger, used to transport passengers and trading goods throughout the Mediterranean. Following the coast, it called at frequent small towns
and harbors along the route, and at night would anchor, when
possible, in sheltered coves. It carried a full cargo of Falernian
wine and little space remained for the half-dozen passengers. It
was an uncomfortable and dangerous trip—two fierce gales almost wrecked the old vessel—but Melchi was indifferent to everything. His son, all that remained of life, was somewhere far
behind him. He tried to pray that Rufus was neither taken by
perverse men nor starving, but the words would not come.

Gallus endeavored to revive Melchi's spirits during the three-
month voyage by teaching him Greek, which was spoken in Byzantium, and by telling him some of his own experiences. Gallus
had been born in Corinth to Roman settlers. Later he had served
with Suetonius Paulinus in Britain and it was there, during a
skirmish, that he'd lost an eye. Following his injury he was sent
back to Rome and appointed captain of the guard at the Tullianum. "That was your lucky day," he reminded Melchi, adding,
"and mine, too!"

Whenever the ship lay over in ports such as Malta or Lasea,
Gallus did what he could to interest Melchi in the strange and
exotic scenes each place presented. At one port in Crete he
found a couple of lissome women with painted eyes who were
glad to be accommodating. But they held no interest for the
dispirited Melchi. It was not like Gallus to be long without a
woman, and he disappeared with both for a few hours.

After Crete the ship traveled past Cape Salmone, almost
broaching in the heavy seas, and on to Cnidus, where they lay
over eight days for repairs. Then along the Asian coast to Mity-
lene on Lesbos, and on up to Troas, site of Homer's fabled city,
in actuality little more than a dirty commercial port. Once past
Troas, they headed into the Hellespont. Standing on the ship's
prow one clear day, the fresh wind hitting him full, Gallus felt a
surge of excitement. Just across the Propontis waited a new life.
Byzantium!

As the city moved into view, Gallus yelled down to the hold
for Melchi to come and look. Byzantium's white buildings,

sprawled across distant hills, grew more dense near its harbor. Gallus had never known water so blue. Sun dappled its rippling surface. Even from a distance both men could see that the city was astonishing. It was clear why the town's inhabitants were notorious for their idleness and depravity. One would find it hard to live in such beautiful and exotic surroundings and be concerned with anything but pleasure.

As their ship came alongside the quay, Melchi and Gallus hurried below to gather their few possessions. They had hidden the shroud behind an old sail, but when they looked for it, it was gone. In desperation they searched the entire hold but found nothing.

A crew now moved in to carry off the cargo while the other travelers clambered onto the broad sea wall. Melchi and Gallus stood on deck, watching carefully to see whether someone had mistakenly picked up their property.

They could come to only one conclusion. The shroud had been stolen.

Chapter 6

Byzantium—Melantias, 64–69 A.D.

By 64 A.D. Byzantium, originally founded and settled by Greeks, had become a Roman protectorate. Its wealth was largely the result of a deep-sheltered harbor and control of the straits through which all shipping to and from the north must pass. Spilling across two hills, surrounded on its land side by a great wall, the city overlooked a beautiful curved inlet called by the Greeks "Chrysoceras," the "Golden Horn."

Since the shroud could only have been stolen by someone aboard their ship, Melchi and Gallus immediately suspected the ship's master, who had eyed the shroud bundle with such curiosity when they sailed from Puteoli.

After the ship had tied up at the port, they followed the old captain ashore. He was carrying a packet wrapped in coarse hemp cloth which they suspected contained the shroud. The man headed directly for a marketplace located behind the port where he greeted and conversed with a black-robed magician. Evidently the two had done business before. Eagerly the magician opened the bundle and spread out its contents. Moving closer, Melchi and Gallus saw that it was indeed the shroud. The magician was obviously pleased. He nodded his head vigorously and after rewrapping the shroud, gave some coins to the captain, who disappeared into the crowd. The magician then gave some inaudible instructions to his assistant, a willowy boy, and sent him off.

All the two could do was keep a careful watch on the man from a nearby food stall. Since Melchi had exhausted his small store of coins on expenses of the passage, Gallus insisted upon sharing the ample remainder of four months' pay he had received shortly before deserting. As they waited, the two wolfed down mounds of large, succulent oysters and slices of cool, sweet melon.

Within an hour the magician's assistant returned and spoke some words to his master. The boy was directed across the marketplace with a basket he retrieved from inside the magician's small shop. Returning with food, the assistant followed his master within. The door was slammed shut and they could hear the thrust of a bolt. It was time for midday closing. Most of the merchants were shutting up their stalls.

While Melchi stood watch near the magician's closed door, Gallus sought out a clothing merchant and purchased a toga. He was afraid his military trappings might provoke too many questions. He chose an unadorned, good-quality linen and a blue cloak against the cold winds he had heard would sweep down upon the city in winter. The Roman felt odd divesting himself of his militia's leather and crimson. Until so very recently he had worn it as a proud soldier. It would take getting used to—walking the streets without people stepping aside for him.

A public bath was his next objective, a place to wash off the grime and salt of three months at sea. He was unprepared for anything quite so impressive as the ornate structure he found a short distance away. Within, the facilities were unbelievably luxurious. Bathing was a highly favored diversion of the Byzantines and their Roman-style baths were built with Oriental splendor. Gallus reveled in the almost forgotten pleasures of hot water and steam, followed by the icy *frigidarium*, and in the fragrant oils with which an attendant slowly and sensuously massaged his body. Already he was becoming aware of the languor which hung like a silk coverlet about this city.

Three hours later, after Melchi, too, had visited the bath, the magician reopened his shop. Keeping a watchful eye on him,

Melchi and Gallus explored the lively square, a place of noise and confusion. Food, jewelry, embroideries, apparel, and kumiss, an intoxicating liquor made from fermented mare's milk, were all selling briskly. Astrologers, healers, scribes, and moneylenders sat about awaiting customers. Among the passersby were rich women borne on litters by powerful, large-bellied eunuchs. Gallus found a certain excitement in speculating what charms might lurk beneath their colored veils. He could feel his lust rising. It reminded him of his long deprivation.

A young Greek approached the magician's shop, carrying two squawking braces of ducks. The youth stopped and spoke to the magician. Then he handed the smiling old man a bag of coins, took the packet containing the shroud, and hurried off, pursued by Melchi and Gallus.

The young fellow finally stopped in a public garden, a charming escape from the extreme heat of the summer noon. Dropping the bundle to the ground, but still clutching the ducks, he settled on a semicircular stone bench by a grove of pomegranate trees. Melchi and Gallus sat beside him.

"Are the days always so hot here?" Gallus asked.

"Not for long. The winds from the north will soon enough be here. And I cannot say I'll be sorry. You are strangers?"

"Yes. I am Gallus, my companion, Melchi."

"My name is Ion. Have you traveled from a great distance?"

"We come from Rome."

"Rome. Some say it is a great city. But no place on earth could be so beautiful as our Byzantium."

Gallus was pleased that Ion was talkative. It would not be difficult to get the answers they sought. Melchi, who knew only the little Greek Gallus had taught him on the ship, fidgeted impatiently as he tried to concentrate on the conversation and find out where the shroud was headed.

Gallus quickly discovered that Ion, a steward's errand runner, worked for a rich widow named Olympia.

"Just what do you have in the packet there?" he casually asked.

"Oh, that. An old piece of cloth my mistress wants. It has great magical powers. She says it must be installed in her new house to protect against evil spirits."

At this Gallus exploded, "Look, Greek, that cloth is our property. It was stolen from us."

Ion was frightened by Gallus's threatening manner. "It was not!" he cried. "We bought the cloth honestly, for a great deal of silver. It belongs to my mistress. Take care! She has very powerful friends."

Gallus forced a hearty laugh, saying, "That was just a little joke to lighten the day." He patted Ion's shoulder. "Now tell me all about your fascinating mistress and her new house."

Ion explained that just the month before his mistress had moved into the new villa in the Novae Athenae district.

Gallus inquired whether there was employment at Olympia's residence for him and Melchi.

"If you do not mind working outside, you might find employment as gardeners."

Gallus convinced Ion to take them to the head steward. A small silver coin helped.

The three set off toward Novae Athenae. Along the way Ion chattered incessantly about his mistress, who was childless and had been married to a much older man.

"Some say she helped her husband across the River Styx," he confided with a smirk. "Then, with her enormous inheritance, she purchased this elegant villa and now lives a grand life. Though the woman comes of common stock, her beauty is exceptional." Regretfully he added that he had seen little of her, since only female slaves and eunuchs were permitted to attend women of a Byzantine household.

"But once," he recalled, "when she gave a large dinner party, I had to carry in one of the platters and set it before her." He rolled his eyes at the memory.

As the youth prattled on, and Gallus translated, Melchi tried to picture the woman being described. He imagined her to be a self-indulgent person who took whatever she wanted—someone of little merit. With an aching heart he thought about his dear Julia, her unselfish nature and loving concern for him and their children.

They halted before the magnificent residence and waited for the arrival of Olympia's steward, the eunuch Boas.

Boas was of great size, and handsome, with an expression that seemed strangely malevolent. Melchi took an immediate dislike to him. After telling them at length about the mistress and her endless rules of conduct for servants, Boas announced that they were hired. They would receive board and a small wage. He would escort them, he said, to meet the senior gardener.

Olympia leaned back against a dove silk couch in her sitting room, trying desperately to focus on plans for the first of a series of dinner parties she was giving. Boas had just left after dressing her long copper hair. She loved the way he cared for it, so much better than the women. Fingering a curl, she thought about what Boas did even more expertly than that. Her catlike eyes half-shut in sensual recollection. Yes, older men like Boas were most desirable as lovers. Except for old Theophrastus, her late husband, they generally turned out to be more considerate and effective than the young stallions, always too concerned with their own gratification. She giggled, thinking of the exciting challenge she had devised for herself: discovering which of her eunuchs could perform like a real man. With eunuchs no one was ever the wiser. People thought they had no desire, no virility. And this was almost always the case. However, it depended at what age the castration occurred. Boas told her he had been captured and made a slave when nearly twenty. Before that he had had many sexual experiences. She felt sorry for Boas. He was taken by Greek slavers at Troas, along with many other boys and men. After their testicles had been severed, the bound slaves were buried up to their waists along a stretch of the Aegean shore. For those who survived, the salty sand helped prevent infection while they healed. Olympia knew of the practice. Theophrastus had described sailing past the infamous beach during a sudden fog. The eunuchs' moans were an aid to navigation, helping pilots keep their vessels from running aground.

She had once enjoyed another eunuch, but Boas was better. A great phallus that gave such pleasure, she throbbed each time she thought about it. That detestable dinner party! A lot of stuffy friends, mostly leftovers from her dull marriage. Theophrastus. She smiled cynically. I know they all think I poisoned him. Well, let them. He didn't need any help from me, the old ram. Rutting with me all the time. At his age. I hated it! He smelled bad and besides, he was selfish. Making us live in that hole of a house across town. Such a pinchpenny. Well, that's that. I make the decisions now.

Loudly she called for her women. Time to get dressed and confer with Boas. She sighed, reminding herself she must keep her mind on the party.

When Olympia was dressed, she ordered Boas sent to her. As he waited for her to speak, she could read his desire. She had put on a particularly transparent gown. It was exciting to watch the way he ran his tongue over those heavy lips, his eyes traveling up and down her body. She began discussing a menu for the dozen guests she had invited. For the *gustatio,* a first course to awaken the appetite, pickled vegetables, fried peacock eggs, artichokes with a white garlic sauce. Olympia lazily brushed her sandaled foot against Boas's leg. Then perhaps roast pork and grilled sparrows. She moved her leg against his, feeling the attraction which drew their flesh together. Minced hare, turbot with the *gakos* sauce her kitchen made so well. Olympia hooked her leg around Boas's and pulled him closer; he was almost crazy with bridled lust. She could see it. A delicate mussel soup. Her friend Dorcas had served it at a recent dinner party. Boas had bribed Dorcas's cook for the recipe. And a spiced tripe to finish off the main course. Boas fell to his knees in front of her, but she was not ready to let him touch her yet; she ran one finger up his massive chest, planning the delicious moment of surrender.

"A fine cheese—you be the judge of that. Oh, and perhaps some biscuits. They must be light; not those little millstones the cook baked last week." Bringing her face close to his, she whispered, "You want me, don't you, Boas?"

"Yes, mistress," he breathed in a strangled voice. Sweat was beginning to form on his face and upper torso. She loved its glisten, wanted to run her tongue across the salty wetness.

"Oh, and I expect you to find mushrooms somewhere. I know they're in short supply. I wish them dipped in oil and vinegar like we've done before. Soon, Boas, soon," she whispered, sliding off the couch to face him. She watched the great phallus rise, throbbing beneath his short skirt. Still, he did not touch her; a slave wouldn't dare. So exciting!

"Find some blueberries and apples for the last course. Oh, yes, and the various wines. Use your judgment."

Although still giving orders, her voice had grown lower, husky. Not touching him with hands or arms, she rubbed her silk-sheathed body against his chest so he could feel her hard nipples thrusting forward. He was on his knees, obediently unmoving, as she began touching his face, his neck, his shaved head with her lips and body.

"Now, Boas, now," she breathed, and she felt his huge muscled body urgently reach to engulf her.

As soon as he began to work for Olympia, Melchi ceased worrying about the shroud. It was certainly safe with her. And one day he would get it back. He wasn't even sure he wanted it again. The events of Rome still burned in his memory. He could not bring himself to think of anything associated with the Christians. Only the fact that Peter had entrusted the shroud to him made the regaining of it seem worth his efforts.

He and Gallus enjoyed their work in Olympia's gardens. The senior gardener, Damon, was a good man, completely devoted to his world of flowers, trees, and hedges. Their first job was to dig and line the network of tiny irrigation ditches around the new gardens encircling Olympia's extensive property. The villa had been in poor condition when she purchased it; the gardens quite ruined. Olympia had casually spent a fortune restoring the house. Outside was a dazzling composition of fountains, columns, and marble walkways with bright mosaics. She had commanded Damon to make certain that the grounds would be as sumptuous as the villa. Now he was embarked upon his grand plan for achieving this.

Melchi and Gallus worked hard to help Damon complete the task before summer ended. They shared a small room in one of the villa's outbuildings, an old wreck of a structure Olympia had not bothered to restore. Gallus spent very few nights there; he had met a pleasant young female in town. When Melchi chided him for being a Christian and consorting with an unmarried woman, he looked surprised. He had not known of this idea among Christians; besides, he thought he might marry Blandina, who worked in her father's pottery shop.

Although he, too, sometimes felt the need of a woman, Melchi had no heart for anything beyond his work. He wanted no more deep feelings for another. It was dangerous to love; never would he do so again. Besides, he reminded himself, I'm forty-six—an old man. His dark hair was now touched with gray. Unhappiness had lined his face, and the sun had tanned it. His muscles had hardened. Though no longer young, Melchi was still arrestingly handsome.

Olympia noticed his good looks when she happened to glance from the window of her second-story dressing-room. Below, Melchi was studying a pear tree he had just planted. He was stripped to the waist, for the sun was hot. His body glistened. Olympia asked one of her women who he was. A slave? Told he was a foreigner, newly arrived in Byzantium and hired to help in the gardens, Olympia was intrigued. A real man! Not exactly the kind of challenge she was enjoying with her chief eunuch. Yet, watching the purpose in Melchi's movements, the hard set of his jaw, she recognized that here was another sort of adventure, one she planned to pursue immediately. There was her next dinner party. He was her gardener, wasn't he? Well, she would call him in to tell her whether all the plantings would be completed in time.

Melchi was surprised to receive a summons to Olympia's private apartments. He was mildly curious to see this woman about whom he had formed such a negative opinion. As for Olympia, some feminine instinct told her she must not appear obviously interested in the handsome foreigner.

When he arrived, he found her in a soft, embroidered gown and deep red silk cape, caught at the neck by a pearl and gold fibula. She was far more beautiful than he had supposed, with creamy skin and widely set green eyes. Her carefully dressed curls were tied with a looping golden cord.

Despite himself Melchi could not pull his eyes from Olympia.

She sensed this, and knew what to do. With artful interest she inquired about his work in the gardens. Standing before her, he made a politely neutral response. She had expected more of a reaction.

"I would like to see what you have done with my herbs."

"Whenever you wish, mistress, I shall be honored to show you."

"Tomorrow?" she asked in a buttery voice.

"As you wish," he replied, backing out of the room.

In their hut that night Gallus told Melchi that everyone was talking about the mistress's summoning him to her quarters—evidently a most unusual occurrence. He warned Melchi to remember Boas. The big steward was zealously protective of his relationship with Olympia. Melchi declared that there was no cause for worry. He recognized his employer for what she truly was and had not the slightest interest in a closer association. But somewhere within himself, he sensed an unvoiced warning. That night he dreamed of Olympia taunting him with lewd and inventive postures.

The following morning Melchi awaited Olympia in the herb garden. He had just finished planting thyme and marjoram when she arrived wearing a seafoam-green mantle the color of her eyes. As he answered her questions, she stood close by and he caught the scent of myrrh with which her servants had massaged her body. His heart started to pound and he felt a pull he wanted to resist with all his might. She realized his resistance, and it inflamed her. As she left, she brushed her hand against his thigh. His skin seemed to strain toward her touch. He knew he wanted Olympia as he had never before wanted a woman. Neither saw Boas, watching from the upper story, his dark eyes hard.

Later Melchi said nothing to Gallus, who happily reported he had located a small Christian community west of town, at Melantias, on the Via Egnatia. The Christians earned their living by helping to tend vineyards. The area produced a much esteemed wine.

"Melchi, come with me. You will like it there."

Melchi was not interested. "I've had enough of Christianity for a while, my friend. It has done nothing but ruin my life."

"You are wrong," argued Gallus. "What Master Peter said about prayers being answered is true. I know it now. I prayed to find some Christians in this place, and one day my Blandina just happened to tell me about Melantias. She did not even know I had received baptism." With pride he added, "Blandina will go with me. She also wants to join the Community."

Melchi was pleased for his friend. But he preferred to hear no more about Christians.

However, Gallus was not to be put off. "You must pray to Christus about your son. He will send the boy to you."

Melchi snorted angrily, "Gallus, you are an innocent about some things."

Hurt, Gallus retorted, "That's not so strange an idea. The boy is a foreigner, a child wandering the streets of Rome. Some rich slaver could easily grab him, put him on a ship. Great numbers of slaves are sold in Byzantium every day."

Though he did not admit it to Gallus, when time allowed, Melchi haunted the slave market, searching for Rufus among the weekly cargoes of wretched beings offered for sale. The thought that Rufus might be a slave sickened Melchi. But Gallus, untroubled, said, "Very well, Melchi, if you won't pray for the boy, I shall. And I'll keep looking. Christus won't let you down."

Melchi was touched by the Roman's naive faith. It had never been like that for him. His Christianity had been closely tied to his love for Peter. Now, with the old man gone, Melchi's last tangible connection to the past hung on the wall behind Olympia's sleeping couch: the shroud. Perhaps when Gallus joined the Community at Melantias, Melchi would somehow try to get it back from her. And give it to his friend.

Olympia had a bad night. She lay sleepless, tormented by the memory of Melchi's muscled thigh against her skin where they had momentarily touched. It was hard to sleep when she wanted a man. She considered summoning Boas, but now she could not bear the idea of him. Only Melchi. She feared, however, that if she possessed the well-built gardener, he would not be easy to hold. He was accustomed to freedom and male dominance. Where he came from, what his life had been, she did not know. But with womanly awareness she could tell that his experiences had made him more than a match for her. This was not reassuring, but the desire which coursed insistently through her was unremitting; she must get him, no matter what it took.

Once again she was in the garden watching him at work. He was unaware of her presence. Suddenly she hit on a bold tactic. She would simply tell him of her wish to sleep with him. She had never before done such a thing. But she was certain of her allure. Yesterday she had felt his response. Olympia's excitement rose at the thought of such daring.

He was bending over a low hedge of Grecian laurel as she came near. Her voice startled him. Hurriedly he stood up.

"Come and walk with me, Melchi," she said softly.

She gazed at him, and he thought he had never seen anything so wonderful as her eyes. They moved together toward some apple trees Gallus had planted near the elliptical pond. On a pale onyx bench at the pool's edge Olympia sat and asked Melchi to remove her shoes. He bent down and did so. She dabbled her feet in the water as she looked at him, her clear eyes never leaving his face.

"Please join me here, Melchi," she invited. He could not think of refusing. "It is difficult for a woman like me. I am young, passionate"—she watched him carefully—"and I am mistress of a great house; widowed so early." He seemed anxious to get away, but she noted the tension of his jaw, the tight fists. "I must take my love where I can find it. There are so few opportunities in Byzantium for a marriage of equal rank and status. So—I use my body as it directs me. And you, dear Melchi"—she surprised herself at the word "dear"—"would suit me." There, she had done it! She wished he would not notice her trembling, but knew he did. His face grew gentle. She had not expected that.

"Mistress," said Melchi, "there is much you do not know about me. I was married once; we had children. I loved her deeply, but she died. And, when that happened, all feeling died in me. All *desire*, let me say. You are very beautiful. The most beautiful woman I have ever seen. Many men would want you. . . ."

Olympia straightened quickly. Fury smoldered in her eyes. Never before had she been rejected. And by a hateful, soil-smeared servant. Seizing her sandals, she stood up and flung them in his face, then turned and rushed away.

Melchi wondered that night why he had refused Olympia. Her rage had only further fired his passion. He lay on top of his bed, consumed with thoughts of her. Holding the sandals to his nose, he could detect the odor of myrrh still clinging to them.

He expected to be discharged, but next day, when no such order was given, he knew Olympia was still his for the taking. Why hesitate? He decided to go to the house and return the sandals. Olympia sent a servant at once to show him to her apartments. Despite himself he was filled with anticipation.

But he was unprepared for her reception. Entering the room, he saw Olympia locked in the beefy arms of Boas. She stopped her caresses just long enough to order him to drop the sandals and leave. Confused and embarrassed, he fled the room.

Melchi could not erase the memory of Olympia and Boas. He felt revulsion and, at the same time, jealousy. Still, he said nothing to Gallus, who, having heard rumors, looked at him questioningly. Gallus was making plans to soon quit Byzantium for Melantias. In these last days it seemed to Melchi that his friend did nothing but babble about praying and the Community. He was tired of hearing about it. Possibly it might be a good thing to see the last of Gallus. Melchi found his thoughts lingering on other things. For some perverse reason he wished he had not rejected Olympia. He could protect her from grotesques like Boas. She needed a real man to take care of her, to let her know how splendid she truly was.

Four days after the incident at the pool Gallus departed. When they said good-bye, Melchi felt a rush of affection for the man who had saved his life less than a year before. Gallus promised to pray for him and Rufus. As he left, he took Melchi by the shoulders and looked squarely at him. "You have my word," he said, "by the great spirit of Christus, I will pray that you find your son."

Melchi placed an affectionate hand on his friend's shoulder and wished him happiness in his new life. Gallus and Blandina had decided to marry. She would be baptized at Melantias. Gallus was in good humor as he said his farewells to the gardener, Damon, and the others. But he was concerned for Melchi. He wished they could have talked about Olympia and the unmistakable rancor Boas was exhibiting toward him. Ah, well, Gallus thought as he set off, Melchi can take care of himself. I guess I've watched out for him so long, it's become a habit.

That watchfulness had served as a constraint for Melchi. When it was there no longer, he gradually moved toward a style of life far different from his previous one.

The day of the dinner party Damon told Melchi he was wanted in the kitchen. Upon arriving at the villa, he was given a fresh toga and sandals, told to bathe and prepare to serve the mistress at her table. Boas, in a particularly black mood, ordered Melchi about the banquet hall in surly tones, several times deliberately confusing him in order to scream at him later in the kitchen. Melchi did not care. Never having seen such luxury, he was completely enthralled. Olympia's dining room was divided into two areas. At the upper end, around a huge oval table with ivory legs, reclined the guests on bronze couches, cushioned in gold-embroidered blue silk. The room's lower portion was open for serving and entertainment.

Melchi's eyes were fixed on the hostess as she entertained her guests. Olympia was dressed in a pure white, gold-bordered garment; her lush hair caught the sunlight from the open courtyard beyond her couch. Several times he caught her watching him. And once, just once, he returned a look as arrogant as hers. She flushed and ignored him for the rest of the afternoon.

By twilight the guests, groggy with a surfeit of food and wine, lay on their couches, awaiting more entertainment. Two elderly men snored placidly.

The servants lighted torches in the wall sconces, casting a warmth about the beautiful dining chamber with its fantastic murals. Olympia clapped her hands, and a pair of dancing girls from Pamphylia began their sinuous movements, accompanied by pipes and a cithara. Holding a diaphanous drapery above their heads, they undulated in slow rhythms, as the musicians piped and strummed their exotic runs. Melchi watched from a doorway. The music and the swaying dancers were hypnotic, the rhythms insistent. By now more of the guests had been lulled to sleep by the wine and music. Their heads lolled on the soft cushions. In a faint breeze the torches danced.

Melchi felt himself roused by the fleshly spectacle and by a desire for Olympia he could no longer suppress. He watched her every movement from his position in the doorway. Olympia glanced at the sleeping guests, put a hand to her breast, and slowly caressed it as she looked at him. Hot desire surged through him. Finally she nodded to him and stood up. Motioning to Boas to stay where he was, she beckoned with her eyes to Melchi, who followed her from the room. Boas, watching them, struck an overturned silver platter beside him, imprinting the dent of his huge fist.

In her private quarters Olympia asked Melchi to be seated as she called for a servant woman. Standing boldly before him, she slowly disrobed and mounted an unpolished marble table. Languorously she allowed her body to be massaged with warm, scented oil. The masseuse was dismissed. In a husky voice Olympia invited Melchi to strip and join her. Her lust heightened as he dropped his clothing to the floor.

Then he was in her arms as they stroked and searched each other's slippery body. Her firm young breasts slid across his chest. The perfumed oil added an intense sensuality to the meeting of their flesh. The world narrowed to nothing but the urgency of their need.

"Now," she cried, "now." And he entered her fiercely.

After that night Olympia directed that Melchi be moved from his ramshackle hut to a rich accommodation near her in the main villa. She inundated him with gifts and fine clothes. Sometimes it made him uncomfortable to be the recipient of so much largesse. But it was not difficult to overcome these scruples and give himself over to the pleasures of Olympia's passion.

There was no sexual feat at which she wasn't skilled. Each night her excitement with his body reached new heights. It was an incredible experience to let himself surrender totally to his senses. But sometimes, lying exhausted beside her after lovemaking, feeling her relentless need for his caresses, Melchi would recall the sting of his former bitterness. Olympia would notice the look in his eyes and question it. Yet he never talked to her about the past; he could expect little solace. So Melchi accepted Olympia for what she was, admired her beauty, and gave his body with mindless abandon. She, sensing that he withheld himself, heaped more costly gifts upon him.

When Olympia was alone one day, Boas asked permission to speak with her. On his knees he bowed to the floor, remaining in that position.

Impatiently she cried, "Oh, get up, Boas, and tell me what you want."

"I cannot, mistress. I am heavy with sorrow."

Surprised by Boas's unaccustomed sensitivity, Olympia asked him to explain.

"My mistress no longer welcomes my caresses. Did I not please?"

Olympia wanted none of this, but felt a certain pity for the eunuch. "Yes, of course you pleased me, Boas—once. Now I have discovered I prefer a complete man to a castrate." Her voice softened somewhat. "You have served me well. But there must come an end to all things. Now, please get to your feet. You annoy me down there."

Boas rose and she could see that his face was contorted with pain and rage.

Briskly, she said, "I'm busy now. Leave me."

Bowing, his eyes turned downward, the eunuch backed out.

That night Melchi was alone in his room. Being indisposed, Olympia regretfully passed up her usual pleasures. Melchi was relieved. His thoughts turned to Gallus and the Christians at Melantias, and to the shroud, as he reviewed in his memory every detail of its ghostly image. Suddenly he began to weep, something he had not done when Peter or his family died. It was as if a giant stone within him were crumbling away. Then at last he snuffed out the lamp and fell into a deep sleep.

A short while later he was awakened. A sound—was it a sound? He tried to focus a mind drugged with sleep. Opening his eyes he saw the arm raised above him. Through the window a beam of moonlight caught the glimmer of a blade. Summoning all his strength, Melchi reached up, grabbing the powerful arm. He twisted it downward and somehow managed to shake loose the dagger. The weapon lay on the floor between him and his assailant, Boas. Silently they struggled, the eunuch bigger and more powerful, Melchi more nimble, smarter. For an instant Boas was pinned to the bed. Melchi grabbed for the dagger. Boas began to break loose and Melchi thrust the blade into the soft folds of the eunuch's throat. There came a liquid gurgle from Boas, who fell back, dying. In a moment he sank to the floor.

In horror Melchi looked at the huge body, remembering another time he had been involved with killing. That day on the Jericho road . . . the decurio. He began to retch.

Olympia treated the killing of Boas as a casual incident of the household. Melchi was disgusted that she should show no regret for the death of someone she had once regarded with intimacy. More than that he was sick with conscience about the incident. He could understand why that poor mutilated slave should hate him. The fool knew no better than to try to rid himself of a rival.

Though still enjoying the fleshly pleasures Olympia offered, Melchi began to feel trapped in the shallow world of her gifts and endless parties. Though his senses were sated, his other needs cried out. He thought more and more about Melantias and Gallus. Finally he decided to make a visit to his old friend; see what the life was like. Telling Olympia he must restock her wine stores, he set out.

The day was cool. A fresh breeze from the sea washed across his face. The escape from the city lifted his spirits and he felt renewed as in the good days of Rome. At Melantias he easily found Gallus, who greeted him joyously.

"So, my friend," said the Roman, "you have decided to join us?"

Melchi smiled but was silent. Gallus introduced him to the other Christians and to his wife, Blandina, a simple, pretty girl who was clearly pregnant. Melchi had forgotten how good it was to experience the mutual concern and sense of well-being in these Communities. As they feasted together, he remembered how it used to be in the old days: Peter, Julia, and the children, together, sharing the Life of the Spirit with their friends and neighbors.

After they had finished the late afternoon meal, Gallus asked Blandina and the others to leave them so he could talk alone with Melchi. When they had departed, he sat back.

"What is going on with you, my friend?"

That was all he needed to say before Melchi began pouring out the whole story of his affair with Olympia; the gifts and parties; the nights of passion; finally, the death of Boas. Hearing himself discuss the sordid tale, Melchi was filled with self-recrimination. "I am little better than an animal," he admitted to Gallus. "Fornicating, killing—I deserve to die."

"Melchi, you have closed the door to God. But He will not desert you. Can't you remember the words of Christus? 'Ask and it will be given to you; search, and you will find; knock, and the door will be opened to you.'"

The two talked together long into the night, and when Melchi finally fell asleep, he was comforted. Still, he would not join Gallus and Blandina in the morning prayers. He made a weak excuse about having to hurry back with the wine. Gallus said no more, but urged his friend to come again, soon. As he walked with Melchi toward the door of the simple house, he paused, smiling. "And I have not forgotten my promise. Each evening I pray God to return Rufus to you. One day He will." Gallus was a deeply happy man.

Olympia could sense a change in Melchi after he returned. He would say little about his trip, except that he had met an old friend and found some excellent wine. She knew she could not draw more from him, so she made no further reference to the matter. That night in bed he seemed preoccupied and unresponsive. Was there another woman? No doubt a low wench of Melantias, her feet stained with the juice of the wine press. As she lay caressing this man who had come to be her life, Olympia resolved to seek new means of pleasing him. She thought about a beautiful ring she had seen yesterday in the market. She would buy it for him. And she knew an old sorceress who had a powerful potion to renew lagging passion. She would visit her first off, in the morning.

But as months went by, she knew Melchi was slipping away from her. His absences grew more frequent. He never explained where he was going, and she knew better than to ask. She took to drinking too much wine at dinner. Sometimes she was so drunk he could do little more than put her to bed. Even then she would raise her torpid lids, reach her arms toward him, and beg him not to leave her. Then Melchi would feel a stab of guilt. He realized that Olympia had come to love him with a childish dependence younger women often feel for an older lover. He was sad that he could never truly return her love. More and more his life centered on Blandina and Gallus at Melantias. Still, he could not pray with them; he had not yet found the resolve to rejoin the Christians. If they would even have him.

Certainly he knew his affair with Olympia was ending. She had made him wealthy with her gifts. In return he had offered an impoverished affection. He wished to give back all the gifts; leave the way he had come, with nothing more than the clothes on his back—and the shroud. As the days went on, Melchi grew increasingly restless. Then Gallus arrived for a two-day visit. He had business in the city. Unexpectedly he asked when Melchi was leaving.

"Why should I leave Byzantium?" asked Melchi, surprised.

Gallus looked knowing. "Because you are not content here. I can see the difference in your face when you are with us in Melantias. Come back with me, Melchi."

That evening Melchi was totally distracted. He could do nothing right, even spilling a cup of wine on Olympia's gown at dinner. Later, in her bedchamber, pretending nothing was wrong, Olympia reminded him about his promise to accompany her to the marketplace next day. She hoped to have a famed astrologer cast a chart for her.

"Olympia, I cannot go. I am sorry," said Melchi quietly. He had decided it must now be finished between them.

In a fit of temper Olympia accused him of having an affair with someone else. "I want you to leave. At once!" she screamed. "I loved you as I never loved any other. I said nothing when you were coming and going as you pleased. But I will stand no more of it. Who are you but a common gardener?" She fell back, sobbing.

Melchi rose from Olympia's couch. But he did not leave. He regretted having hurt her and wished to say one last thing. When her sobs grew still, he declared, "There is no other woman. In all this time I have had only you."

Olympia leaped from the couch and threw her arms around him. "Then why do you choose to leave me? I have been so happy to offer you a home here, a good life, gifts that reflect your value." Standing away from him, she lowered her eyes. "I am not unhandsome."

He took her hands in his. "You are the most beautiful woman I have ever known. But this place, this Byzantium—for me, the life here is empty. I must have something more, something I once had, and lost."

"What is it?" she implored. "I will buy it for you. I will give you anything you desire."

But he could not articulate what he sought, not to her. "Olympia, please take back the presents you gave me. I shall not need them where I am going."

She started crying again. "No, never. I will not take back anything. They were my love gifts to you. And I still love you. What can I offer you? Tell me. Please!"

There was something. "That cloth on your wall; the miraculous shroud. May I have it?"

Relieved, she cried, "Yes, yes, that and a hundred more like it. Will you stay, then?"

"No, I cannot."

Running across the bedroom, she pulled down the shroud and, roughly bunching it, flung it at him, screaming, "It has brought me evil luck. Take it. Get it out of my sight. And you, too."

As Melchi left, he looked back and saw Olympia sitting on her couch, tears streaming down her cheeks, gulping from a silver wine pitcher—the pitcher she had of late kept close beside her bed, always reassuringly filled.

Because it was still night, Melchi stayed with Gallus, whom he had lodged in the old shed they had once shared as gardeners.

He packed the shroud, his clothing, and, as he realized when he saw it spread out before him, a fortune in jewelry.

Gallus awakened, surprised to see Melchi. He nodded with relief upon hearing that the affair with Olympia had ended. Before dropping back to sleep, Gallus breathed a prayer of thanks for his friend's deliverance. Melchi, beyond sleep, lay staring into the night, thinking of the pain he had caused Olympia, of his decision to forego the easy living he had known with her, and to settle instead in Melantias.

By daylight he was ready to leave. But before setting out, he asked Gallus to accompany him to the marketplace. "For one last look." The Roman nodded, understanding.

Though the hour was early, the market was crowded with buyers, there to look over a newly arrived shipment of slaves. The sad group of about one hundred men, women, and children was penned in a cagelike enclosure. Melchi had come here often, scanning the naked, shivering humanity for someone who might be Rufus. The search had become second nature to him. Yet each time, the specter of these humans, waiting to be purchased, appalled his sensibilities. This might well have been the fate of his own son.

Carefully he sought out each face in the pitiful gathering. He was about to move on, when his heart stopped. A boy—a tall, handsome lad of about twelve, with red-blond curls, the same color as Julia's. No, it could not be. He turned away. Gallus was staring at Melchi. "What does your boy look like?"

Melchi, his heart pounding with fear and longing, pointed at the youngster. "Like that. But, no, Gallus—it could not be!"

Gallus, excited, told Melchi to call to the lad.

"Rufus!" cried Melchi sharply. For an instant the youngster turned. "Rufus!"

The boy started and looked again, but without comprehension. There was a hardness about his face, a cunning that spelled survival for children of the streets. Melchi could not believe his Rufus would carry such a look. Besides, there was no recognition in the lad's eyes.

"That means nothing," cried Gallus. "It has been five years. You've changed."

But, Melchi realized, if this were Rufus, it was the boy who had changed. Suddenly he thought of Peter and, for the first time after so very long, found himself praying to a God he believed had deserted him back in Rome. If You exist, Lord, he thought, let me know You can enter into this wretched life of mine. Forgive me my sins, and let this be my son. Grabbing Gallus's sleeve, Melchi said in a trembling voice, "I think it's Rufus."

Gallus's face shone with the joy of one whose belief has been justified. "You see," he shouted triumphantly, "I told you Christus would help you."

Quickly the two made their way over to an official-looking man stationed at one side of the pen.

"I want to buy that boy—that one there," called Melchi, his voice breaking as he pointed with wavering hand toward Rufus.

The slave dealer turned crafty when he saw how anxious Melchi was. Another pederast, desiring fresh young flesh, he thought gleefully. And he named an outrageous price. Melchi, who would have agreed to anything, held out half the gold Olympia had given him and asked if that was enough. The man's eyes widened. Hastily he grabbed the money, unbarred the cage door, and roughly grabbed the naked boy by the hair.

Melchi took off his cloak and wrapped it about the boy. He tried to embrace him. But the youngster would have none of it. Eyes smoldering, he spat out, "Can't you wait to paw me until we are home, old man?"

Melchi recoiled as if he had been struck. "Rufus, Rufus, don't you recognize me?"

"Why should I recognize you? You're just another old man wanting a beautiful boy."

"Oh, my son, what have they done to you?" cried Melchi. "I am your father—your father."

The boy pulled away and wrapped the cloak tighter around him. "I have no father. He was killed by Nero long ago. Take me to where you live and tell me what to do. I'll be obedient. I never want to go on another ship and be sick all the way."

Gallus came over to where Melchi stood, trying to think what to do. "Let us be off to Melantias. You two can stay with Blandina and me for a while."

Before leaving, Melchi bought the boy a toga and sandals. That seemed to please him. But during the walk of several hours Rufus was silent whenever Melchi tried to make conversation. However, Gallus, with his easy manner, was able to elicit some information from the expressionless youth about his experiences since he had run from the soldiers that day in Rome. After a couple of weeks of foraging about in the alleys to keep alive, he had been taken in by a man who gave him plenty of food and who he thought was kind and good. The man turned out to be the first of several slavers who took Rufus into the life he had lived up till now. First, he had been shipped to a brothel at Syracuse where he served the women who worked there; later he had been sold as a bodyservant to a rich merchant who took him off to Crete. When that man died, he had been sold to another slave dealer and shipped up to Byzantium. Hearing this terrible recital of events was almost too much for Melchi. What indignities and depravities had this child—his son—been subjected to, at such a tender age! Then he thought of these years in Byzantium, of Olympia and Boas with the knife in his neck. He, too, had been marked. It would take time, it would take time . . .

When they arrived at Gallus's house, Blandina, pregnant again, was overjoyed to hear what had happened. Gallus's small son clutched Melchi with delight at his return.

"We will stay here until I can find a house for us," Melchi told the boy. "This is a Christian community, like one in which you used to live."

At that something seemed to come alive in Rufus's eyes, some recognition attempting to surface out of the dimness. But he was still not ready to believe. "How do you know that?" he asked sharply.

Melchi took the boy outside and the two of them sat, leaning against the plain whitewashed side of the house, in the cool, bright sunshine. Gently Melchi spoke. "Do you remember Peter —you used to call him Uncle Peter?"

The boy, who to survive had learned quickly the habit of not trusting, simply stared at Melchi.

"Have I changed so much?" Melchi asked, miserably. In truth he had. The years of bitterness had aged him.

Gallus was standing beside the doorway. "Would he remember the shroud?" he asked.

In a flash Melchi was up and bringing out the piece of cloth. He spread it on the ground. There was the faint image, the bloodstains. The boy got down on his hands and knees and moved around it, examining. Melchi remembered Rufus used to do that as a child. His heart ached with wanting to hold him. Dear Lord, he prayed, You have given me the miracle of my son, back again after so long. Let him open his heart and take me back, too.

The boy stood up. His face had changed completely and he was gulping, manfully trying to keep back the tears. "Father," he said, "Father . . ." And then Rufus was in Melchi's arms, weeping and holding him as if he would never let go.

Chapter 7

Jerusalem—The Salt Sea (Dead Sea), 70 A.D.

In the weeks and months after Rufus returned Melchi knew greater happiness than he had in many years. Father and son found a house on the outskirts of Melantias, where Gallus's small son was a frequent visitor. Rufus had become his beloved brother, and the older boy relished his new role. Melchi helped Gallus care for his vineyards. In addition he purchased adjoining land and together they planted new vines and shared the profits.

Although he believed with Gallus that God had directly intervened in returning Rufus, Melchi still hesitated to attend the weekly gathering of the Christian community. He felt unworthy because of his life in Byzantium. But there was something else. A certain thought he seemed unable to bring to mind. Whenever Gallus invited him, Melchi would find some excuse to decline.

One spring morning the two, assisted by Rufus, were at work in the vineyards when a traveler approached them. He said he was on his way to Byzantium. Gallus promptly invited him to his house. Too little news found its way to Melantias; they were hungry for it.

That night, dining in Gallus's *triclinium,* the two families eagerly questioned the traveler, whose name was Philo. He had come up by ship from Alexandria after a tour of Egypt and was on his way back to his home. Never having been to Egypt, Gallus and Melchi had many questions.

"It is a place of marvels," related Philo. "I followed the Nile south for many miles and saw some of the wonders of the world still standing on that soil. At Thebes there are two magical statues in the desert—huge, seated gods—and when the sun touches one of them each morning, it sings a hymn of praise."

Hymn of praise? It was hard to believe.

"I swear it. And halfway between Thebes and the Delta I saw three great burial piles with four immense triangular sides. I am told they were once covered with white marble, their pointed tops sheathed in glistening electrum. Their size is so great, when I stood at the base and looked upward, I could not see the sky for stone."

"Alexandria—what did you see there?" asked a fascinated Melchi.

"It is not what I saw there, but *whom*," said Philo, importantly, as he reached for his wine. "Have you heard of the famed healer Apollonius of Tyana?" They had not. "He is reputed to have powers similar to those of your Jesus. I encountered him in Alexandria, where he is staying awhile."

It was obvious that Apollonius had impressed Philo more than all the sights of Egypt. "He is a powerful man, of rare form like a god. But his dress is bizarre. He wears only linen and sandals of papyrus because his Pythagorean philosophy forbids him to use animal substances for his own comfort. He sleeps in the temples and lectures each day on the stoa of the great library. He discusses his philosophy with all who wish to listen."

Philo's audience did not find this unusual. There were many philosophers about.

"What is he doing in Alexandria?" asked Melchi.

"Some say he has come there to meet with the new emperor, Vespasian, who is his disciple. Vespasian's son Titus has laid siege to Jerusalem."

For an instant Melchi stopped breathing. "Were you there?" He was thinking of his mother.

"I did not travel to Judaea," said Philo. "The country is in a tragic condition. Factions within are creating civil war. Those assassins the Zealots appear at festivals and stab innocent Romans and their families—even Jews, if they are rumored to be Roman sympathizers."

Melchi wanted to learn much more about Jerusalem. He asked many questions.

"I am told," said Philo, "that Titus set out with the Tenth Legion—the Fretensis—to take the Jewish capital and destroy this troublesome nation, once and for all. On the eve of their Passover he laid siege to the city. But even before that, famine and civil war had broken out. I do not know what has happened since then."

Gallus shook his head. "That is not like the Romans. They prefer to leave inhabitants of a subject nation alone. Take their taxes, yes, but leave them to their own ways. For years they allowed the Jews to be governed by their own rulers."

Philo snorted. "Those Zealots! They got out of hand, massacred troops, and tried to seize power. Vespasian had little choice."

Melchi recalled the Jerusalem of his childhood; the great walls within walls and beyond them, olive groves cascading down to the Valley of Kidron. The Temple Mount, its sacred enclosure thronged with believers during the Passover season. He could almost smell the frankincense that burned on its altars as the jeweled vestments of the priests blazed in the light of a thousand lamps. What a glorious, unassailable fortress of the Lord. It saddened him to picture the Street of the Kings, the shop where he had helped his mother in her work. Obed, Zadok, Azor, the Zealots who had been his friends. What had become of them? Did they go on to kill more Romans or had they themselves been killed? It was in Jerusalem that he had met Peter. And Peter had led him to Jesus.

"Melchi, more wine?" Gallus was looking at him with a thoughtful expression. "I say, friend—more wine?"

"Ah—oh, yes." Melchi held out his cup. He knew now he must return to Jerusalem. The reason he could not bring himself to worship with the Community was simply that he still, in his heart, believed as a Jew. The travels from Judaea, the years at Rome, then Byzantium, had not taken from him that core of himself, and that core was Jewish. He must rejoin his people, fighting for their lives and their nation. His mother—he wanted to find her; take her to safety if she was still alive.

After Philo and the others had retired, he sat with Gallus and confided his plan. His friend understood. "I know what you are feeling. Each time I hear a bit of gossip about Rome, or see a legionary, something in me says, 'Go back.' One can never completely cut the old bonds. Every once in a while some memory tugs at us, and our thoughts return to former times. Sometimes even the bad things come back as good. But what about Rufus? He loves you."

"And you, too. You and Blandina and the children. You are as much his family as I. It is best he remain. Rufus is a true Christian, the first in my family."

"But you—you're a Christian, too," protested Gallus. "Those years with Peter. The shroud . . ."

Melchi sighed. "There is something in the blood of everyone born in Jerusalem. A need to return. I must see my mother. I have always felt the guilt of abandoning her."

Gallus broke in. "But your son is here. He needs you."

"No. He is like me at that age, independent. He must lead his own life. Once we found each other, the pain was healed."

Gallus put his hand on Melchi's shoulder. "Rufus has a home here with us, always."

"I know, dear friend, and I am deeply grateful. You have given me my life."

In the lamplight Melchi studied Gallus's worn face. It reflected a profound peace. Had Christianity done that for him? For Melchi it was his Judaism and his conscience—were they the same?—which were pulling him back, whatever the price.

Later he told Rufus of his plans. The boy could not truly understand. Why should he? He had never known Jerusalem or his grandmother.

"When will you come back to us, Father?" Melchi could not answer.

The week passed in preparation. Rufus moved his few belongings to Gallus's house, where he was already accustomed to spending much of his time. Melchi gave most of his possessions of value to Gallus and Blandina. The remainder were shared by the Community.

"The shroud—what will you do with the shroud?" asked Gallus the night before Melchi's departure. Melchi had thought long about this. He knew Gallus would like to possess it to pass on to his sons and their sons. But this should rightly be his legacy to Rufus. It had brought them together again. Sometimes he saw the boy, alone, studying it.

He said, "I wish to leave it for Rufus. He is now a Christian. Peter would have wanted him to own it."

At the sound of Peter's name, the anxiety in Gallus's face disappeared. "Of course, you are right."

Melchi called Rufus to him. "Son, I do not know how long I shall be gone. Perhaps a very long time. But you are now a man. One day you will marry and have sons of your own. For yourself and for your sons I wish you to have the shroud. It is our family's sacred possession."

"But, Father, it belongs to you." A troubled thought shadowed his young face. "Are you not coming back?"

Melchi could not lie. "I must go to Jerusalem and find your grandmother. There is a terrible war that rages between Romans and Jews. I cannot promise what will happen, only that I must go."

Rufus fingered the folded relic. "I shall pray to our good Christus every day, that he will protect you."

"Care for the shroud, Rufus. It belonged to a very great man. You remember him."

"Uncle Peter? I remember. The soldiers took him away." Holding the cloth to his breast, Melchi's son ran from the room.

Next morning townspeople, bringing gifts of dates and figs, gathered outside to say good-bye. At the moment of parting Gallus had a heavy look about his face. Rufus did not want to let go of his father. "Come back," he kept repeating.

"God be with you, my son," said Melchi, turning quickly.

As he headed away from Melantias, toward the city of his ancestors, Melchi Bar-Azariah could hear only one thing: the sound of his son's voice calling, "Come back."

For many years Mariamne continued to maintain her weaving shop in the Street of the Kings. Eventually it became necessary to hire her cousin Rebecca's grandson, Zebedee, to help weave wool on the other loom and do chores she could no longer manage. Zebedee was married, with his own family, but he remained a loyal and devoted worker. She came to regard him like a son. Yet she never stopped thinking of Melchi. Where was he? What had become of him?

As she grew old, Zebedee had to take on more of the work. He would inherit the shop one day. He was a moderate, not involved with Zealots as Melchi had been. Yes, thought Mariamne, she was fortunate to have Zebedee.

With growing apprehension Mariamne watched the factions developing in Judaea. No longer were Romans the only threat; equally dangerous were the Zealots. And they grew more numerous each day, turning upon their brothers, those Jews who preached moderation toward Rome.

In Galilee a bloodthirsty Zealot leader, John of Giscala, began a reign of terror and civil war. Vespasian, soon to be ruler of Rome, advanced on the town to put down the disturbance. John, with a large body of fugitive Zealots, fled to Jerusalem. Mariamne watched their entrance into the city with dread. Moderates like Zebedee believed the Zealots could not long hold out against Rome. Yet never could she have guessed what was to follow. John of Giscala and his followers began killing all the city dwellers who appeared to oppose them. John's forces opened Jerusalem to their allies, slaughtered the high priest, and seized the Temple. In a single day the Zealots slew eight thousand Jewish moderates, Zebedee and his entire family among them.

Another rebel leader, Simon Bar-Giora, came with his robber bands to join John in Jerusalem. But soon civil war broke out between the factions. Worst of all, their bloody struggle for supremacy led to the burning of Jerusalem's grain storehouses. Before the Romans ever arrived at Jerusalem's gates, famine had gripped the city.

An old woman now, compelled to care for herself, Mariamne tried to conserve what stores she had. Though her courtyard cistern provided drinking water, her kitchen grain bins were slowly growing empty. She kept the heavy wooden bar in place across her door and never went out. Once Cousin Rebecca came to the house and banged on the door, screaming for her. But Mariamne knew better than to open to anyone. No longer could Jew trust Jew or be united against a common enemy. There were many enemies, not the least of them starvation.

Yet, when Passover came, the people of Judaea, as they had for centuries, flocked to Jerusalem. Conditions became intolerable. It was then, the city swollen with thousands of pilgrims, that Titus chose to lay siege. Marching from Jericho with an army of eighty thousand, he set up camp upon the Mount of Olives.

Standing on her rooftop at night, Mariamne could see the Roman campfires. They seemed numerous as the stars. Above her was a comet which for days had been slowly moving over the city. She regarded it with terror; it was a bad omen.

Little by little her stores were disappearing. Once she was forced to leave her house and go to a neighbor to trade her goat for grain. When the grain was exhausted, there would be nothing.

Sometimes, hearing the cries and groans of death which rose throughout the city, she wondered what difference it made whether she lived or not. No one was left who cared.

Melchi decided to take a ship from Byzantium which sailed down to Alexandria. From there he would travel on foot to Jerusalem. It was the quickest way.

The trip from Alexandria was long and dusty. After he had crossed the border into Nabatea, Melchi was immediately aware of an unsettling development. Streams of Jewish refugees were making their way past him, headed toward Egypt. He addressed one man who had paused with his family.

"Tell me, what is the situation in Jerusalem?"

"Hopeless," the man replied. "Titus has broken through the inner walls. The Romans have set up their standard in the Temple precinct. They prefer us either exiled or dead."

Long before he arrived in Jerusalem, Melchi could see smoke coiling toward the sky. Great gray billows of it. He tried not to think what it meant. A little farther on he could make out a vast Roman encampment stretching from the Mount of Olives down into the Kidron Valley at the base of the Temple Mount. With agonized heart he realized that the smoke was rising from the Temple. They had fired it. The center of the Jewish world, smoking rubble. The very idea was almost impossible to accept. Jerusalem's air, acrid with smoke, was also tinged with something else. Frankincense. The chambers where the precious incense was stored were being consumed by the holocaust.

Refugees surged out of the gates. They appeared dazed, half starved.

Melchi's toga and cloak looked Roman. When stopped, he concealed his anger in cheerful Latin. They thought him to be an official. The legionaries, sturdy and well fed, were methodically working their way through the city, quarter by quarter, breaking down doors, seeking out rebels, ransacking houses for food and valuables, expelling the old and enslaving the young. Males were assigned to labor units. Females were shipped to Rome to be sold as house slaves or delivered to brothels. Although the Romans had not yet descended on his mother's quarter, from snatches of an overheard soldier's conversation Melchi was certain the Romans would not long delay their sweep through this part of the Lower City. He hastened his pace; time was running out.

When he reached his mother's house and tried to open the door, it was barred. Knocking loudly, he called to Mariamne and shouted his own name. At last he heard the bar being removed. And there stood his mother, resembling a wretched beggar with soiled white hair and a frail body, little more than bones.

"Melchi, my Melchi," she cried, sobbing, as he took her into his arms.

It was forcibly clear to Melchi that he and his mother must quit Jerusalem at once. He thought of his Zealot friends. He had learned that some were still holding out against the Romans in a western district of the city. Obviously they would be impossible to approach. If any were hiding elsewhere, they might have some practical plan or advice. Assuring Mariamne he would be gone but a brief while, Melchi returned to the streets. On impulse he went to the nearby house where Obed had lived.

He pounded on Obed's portal, calling out his name. There was no response. The door to the adjoining house opened a crack and from its shadowed interior came an old woman's voice, crying, "He has gone away."

"Where? I must see him."

The woman thrust her face out and stared suspiciously at Melchi. He was not dressed like someone from their city.

"Who are you? What is your business with that old fellow?" He explained that his name was Melchi and Obed was a friend from long ago. Then he added that he sought help and advice for himself and his mother, Mariamne, the weaver.

The door opened wider and Melchi could see a shrunken old man standing behind the woman.

"Then tell me, Melchi—if that is your name—who is your father?"

"He was Azariah Bar-Jacob. He died when I was a child."

"Come in quickly," said the old lady. Her bony fingers clutched at his cloak, drawing him into the house.

"It is Mariamne's son, Melchi Bar-Azariah," muttered the old man. Melchi could barely see the persons moving about the dimly lighted room. He felt many fingers probing at his body and pinching his arms as if he were a fowl being considered for purchase.

"He is too fat," said someone. "He is one of them."

Melchi explained that he came from a distant land where he had lived for a long time. He could count the people in the room now. There were eight of them. They all seemed very old.

Someone challenged Melchi to name Obed's profession. He answered correctly. There was little to lose, so he added, "I once went on a raid with him. Romans were killed."

Suddenly arms were embracing him. A woman bent down and kissed the hem of his cloak.

They told him that Obed had quit the city four years previously to join other Zealots, men and women, on Masada. This was a thirteen-hundred-foot-high rock citadel at the edge of the Dead Sea with formidable walls, defense towers, arsenals, vast cisterns, and storehouses fortified by King Herod a century before. The Roman garrison there had been overcome by Zealots, who now occupied it. They would descend in small bands to successfully attack Roman sentries and garrisons in quick hit-and-run raids.

Melchi told the old people that they dared not lose a moment; the legionaries would surely strike their district within a day. He advised them to take blankets, collect their food, and fill their water bags while he was returning with his mother. They could trust him to lead them to Masada.

But, they complained, there was only a little flour and some dried fruit left between them. Then he said, as the Jews had done during their exodus from Egypt with Moses, they should quickly bake unleavened bread for the journey.

Melchi went back to fetch Mariamne. While his mother was baking bread with the last of her flour, he climbed to the rooftop. In his youth he had come here often to look out over the great city of his ancestors.

He could see smoke rising from the Temple Mount as Roman legionaries swarmed through the broken wall toward the sacred enclosure where, in former times, trespassing Gentiles would have been instantly executed. Such a deliberate policy of desecration and destruction meant the end of the Jewish nation.

The anger Melchi had long contained flared up in his gut. And now it was coupled with profound sadness.

That afternoon Melchi led Mariamne and the others through the Tekoa Gate toward the south. The old people walked slowly, though Melchi constantly urged them to go faster. Light was failing when they halted, exhausted, at Bethlehem. That night a kind villager allowed them to sleep in his stable. The next evening they rested near Tekoa, under a thick grove of trees. There was no available food, but fortunately the old peoples' hunger was limited by long months of privation.

On the second day of their descent to the Salt Sea one old man complained of crushing pain in his chest and could not go on. The group watched helplessly until, within the hour, the man died. Melchi buried the body beneath a pile of rocks. Then he stood with his grieving fellow travelers, who were reciting prayers.

The tired group was a few miles from En-gedi, the Spring of the Kid, when they were halted by a mounted Roman centurion at a fort of the fifth circle. The Romans had strategically located forts in a series of roughly concentric circles at towns and cross-roads which surrounded Jerusalem. As his scowling legionaries blocked the road, the officer raised his palm and snapped out, "It is forbidden to go farther. Turn back."

Melchi stepped forward, and in his excellent Latin, mildly asked the reason for this.

The centurion stared down from his horse at this fellow who dressed and spoke like a citizen of Rome. "If it makes any difference," he said with amusement, "Lucius Flavius Silva, deputy to the emperor's son, Titus, who commands our Fretensis Legion, has issued orders that no one may come closer to the Masada region. We have our troubles there." Melchi translated.

Mariamne gasped, raising a hand to her breast. For an instant she thought she would faint. Lucius had come back! After forty years. The people, terrified and confused, began to wail and lament as they turned away. Mariamne clutched Melchi's arm, pulling him into the group. Reaching below the neck of her robe, she withdrew a tiny sack on a cord and, hidden by the others, extracted a gold ring which she handed to Melchi. She whispered some words in his ear. Melchi gaped at the object, drawing in his breath sharply. Quickly recovering, he put on the ring and returned to the centurion.

"These old people do not understand that I am taking them to Masada at the express order of Flavius Silva, whom I represent."

The soldiers started to guffaw. But the silver-haired officer, wise in the unexpected ways of those in high authority, asked to see Melchi's warrant of passage. Melchi, extending his right hand, said calmly that he had something far better. Flavius Silva had loaned him his personal ring and with it all the authority necessary to pass freely and carry out his orders. The centurion examined it and let out a low whistle of astonishment. One could never be too careful about the eccentricities of these leaders.

"Stand away from the road," he barked at his men. "These people may pass."

As the centurion escorted the old folks toward En-gedi, he leaned down and asked Melchi politely whether he cared to reveal the reason for this curious order. Melchi motioned the officer to move to one side. Drawing closer, he explained in a confidential tone that these persons all had sons who were Zealot leaders on Masada. It was Flavius Silva's idea to lure them down from the citadel by threatening to execute their parents. The centurion nodded sagely—it was a clever tactic. There was a Roman post not far from Masada.

At En-gedi the centurion directed Melchi's people to be fed and watched over. He invited Melchi to join him for dinner in his quarters.

"My surname is Melicus," said Melchi, biting into a rib of roast lamb. "My father, a close friend of the Silva family, named me after his love of lyrical music."

"Ah, the gentle niceties of civilian life," said Servius, the centurion, wistfully. "But what would I know? I am an army man. I have served in the legion for thirty-seven years."

Melchi asked Servius about his plans for the future.

"The future? There is only one future for a man with no wife and no family. The legion. You know that as a centurion, I can serve so long as I choose. Between the two of us, sir—Melicus"— he lowered his voice—"I am tired of this duty in the field, watching my good men being killed. There can never be an end to it. One month from now, the first week of October, I qualify for the rank of *princeps* and shall be transferred to Caesarea. It is pleasant by the shores of the Mediterranean. My responsibility there will be the directing of the headquarters staff and training." Then, sitting erect, Servius asked, "I shall be notified, I suppose, when we are ready to act at Masada?"

Looking the centurion in the eye, Melchi replied, "Servius, you may rely on it."

At first light Melchi led the refugees southward toward Masada. An hour later they came upon three soldiers who were bearing the bloody corpse of a fellow legionary back to En-gedi. Melchi flashed the ring and started to repeat his earlier story. One of the soldiers bellowed, "Get those Judaean bastards.

We've seen enough of them for one day." Dropping the body and drawing their swords, they charged into the group.

"Run!" yelled Melchi.

The old men and women scattered in all directions as the soldiers ran forward, slashing and stabbing. Mariamne received a gash on the shoulder. Melchi swept her into his arms and raced up a dry water course toward the foothills above.

Her body felt very light, but the rapid climb was exhausting. From far below came the faint screams of the fallen. Melchi rested to catch his breath. He comforted his mother and bound her wound. She had lost much blood. Lifting her up again, he searched for a place to conceal her.

It was there, in the foothills of the cliff, that he found a small cave.

He added his water bag to Mariamne's and gave her all his food. He told her that their only hope was with the Essenes in the City of Salt. Somehow he would bring them over the hills to carry her to safety. But he must set out at once. It might take a few days.

Mariamne held out her hand and asked Melchi to place the ring on a finger. "We loved each other once," she said, gazing at the gold band.

Melchi kissed her forehead. "Now I can understand. Love, when it comes, is blind to everything but itself. It is good that you have known such a love." But still, there was the anger, and the ache of sadness within him. "Pray for me, dear Mother, and I shall soon return." He embraced her once more and turned to go.

"My prayers have always been with you, my son," she said.

Mariamne sat by the cave wall and looked again at the ring she had concealed near her breasts for so many years. She closed her eyes and saw the tender face of the young Lucius. His arms reached out for her. She, too, was young and her hair shining black and her heart filled with overwhelming joy. Mariamne leaned back against the rocks. She was very tired.

Melchi made his way laboriously across the upper hills and steep valleys. Below was the easy, dangerous route along the paved road. It was midday when he saw En-gedi in the distance. He was perspiring heavily. His thoughts turned constantly to Mariamne and the water bag he had left with her. He clenched his jaws and began to climb another ridge. His clothing was soaked with sweat. The savage heat of the Judaean wilderness bit at his flesh like a ravening beast. And always, from far off, sparkled the unspeakably blue waters of the Salt Sea. His tongue stuck to his dry mouth. He was forced to rest.

As the sun moved beyond the mountains, deep purple shadows brought him a slight respite from his torment. He lay on his back, staring up at the stars, thinking of the long path of his life which had brought him to this place. Of Jesus telling him to love his enemies. And Peter saying, "There is a better way to conquer."

That better way was love. Though the Romans had succeeded in destroying his nation, Melchi perceived they had won nothing. Such triumphs were short-lived and valueless in the life of the spirit about which the master had spoken. His beloved Peter had once been a Jewish Sicarii; his friend Gallus, a Roman legionary. Yet each had abandoned the sword for a greater power. Now, at last, Melchi could understand the truth they had sought and found. He must finally let go of hate so love could take its place. As time passed, the anger which had smoldered within him for so very long slowly went away. And the sadness. He was free.

In the cool of dawn his body burned with fever. He descended to the sea. At times he felt dizzy. When the sun began its relentless onslaught, his skull pounded from a violent headache.

Reaching the water, he waved his bare arms through its wetness. This sea, five times saltier than the oceans, had a smooth, oily feeling. He plunged his face below the surface and gulped great draughts of the disagreeable liquid. It burned his eyes and face, leaving a rough, salty crust. Melchi vomited and retched for many minutes. His skin was flushed and dry. He had stopped sweating.

It was excruciatingly difficult to keep going. His vertigo had increased. He collapsed for an hour, seized by terrible abdominal cramps. Ahead was still another dry water course.

As he lay staring dully at the parched rocks, with a rushing sound, water—sweet, sweet water—came splashing down the ravine to pour into the Salt Sea. Beyond the mountains there had been rain. Water! Frantically Melchi lurched forward toward the cascading torrent. In his unsteady state he slipped and fell near the edge of the stream, heavily striking his head.

When he regained consciousness, it seemed there was another person with him. He thought it was Peter and he tried to call to him. Somewhere the voice of Jorem, the blind Essene priest, said, "In the wilderness, prepare the way of the Lord; make straight in the desert a highway for our God." Then he saw the figure on the shroud.

He fell back into coma. When his senses returned, the flow of water had ceased, and there were only the dry rocks. Melchi knew he was dying. In a faint voice, he recited his people's ancient prayer: "Hear, O Israel, the Lord our God, the Lord is One . . ."

But then, feeling himself slipping away, he also spoke words he had heard from the lips of Jesus: "'Our Father, Who art in heaven . . .'"

Chapter 8

Turin, 1978

Molly Madrigal stood on the diminutive balcony of her room at the Hotel Regno. A wave of sound rose from the late-afternoon rush-hour traffic. But her attention was on the distant scene. She had ordered a Cutty Sark and soda while awaiting Richard, and now sipped it as she watched the sun descending toward the crescent of mountaintops which surrounded Turin. Light glowed across the snow-topped Alpine peaks: Mont Blanc, Gran Paradiso, Monte Rosa. Beneath, in deep shadow, lay pine forests marking the famous French and Italian ski resorts. Off to the right, through foothills down to a great plain, the Po rushed like a ribbon of cappuccino.

Turin provided an interesting mélange of old and new. The factories of Fiat, the Cinzano distillery, the elegant shops, office buildings of glass and steel. This was modern Turin declaring its prosperity. But there was another city. A city whose memories reached back to Imperial Rome. Old Turin had fallen on hard times. Still, Molly had chosen old over new. From the balcony of the aging hotel she could look down on villas which two hundred years before had been elegant palazzi. Now they were apartment houses fallen into varying stages of decline. Many were inhabited by people up from the south to work at Fiat. The southerners hung their washing out of windows. Sharing no part in the sleek, contemporary pace of modern Turin, such old neighborhoods had been left behind, like the grandfathers who talked of times past and smoked their pipes in barren yards.

Molly struggled with the same tension she had felt at the Ambasciatori the previous day. Perhaps one never did get over a first love. In fact there had been very little love in her life since Richard. The work kept her busy, on the move. There were always new people. Had she contrived it that way? The unceasing activity for the sake of her career kept her from commitment to any of the several men who had wanted something more permanent.

When Richard arrived, he accepted her offer of a drink before they departed for the monsignore's reception, and she called down for another Scotch. Contemplating her, Richard realized that Molly was no longer the pliant, wide-eyed college girl. She had become more positive, more self-assured. He had not remembered her being so lovely. The truth was, he hardly remembered the details of their affair at all. It would not, he decided, be overly difficult to warm things up again. And now she could be helpful in his need for publicity.

They moved onto the balcony. He felt an unaccustomed awkwardness. From the hotel kitchen below came the muted clatter of dishes, the faint smell of garlic. "Tell me," he said, "how have the gods been treating you since last we knew each other? How is your life—outside the work, I mean? Anyone important since . . ."

"Since you ditched me? Oh, there have been some near misses. But as you may perceive, I'm still quite independent. And I very much prefer it that way."

He said, "I'm sorry if I inadvertently hurt you then. If it makes you feel any better, I've gone through some rough times myself. I'm different now, Molly, from that amoral young dog you once knew."

Old feelings were slipping back. She said, "At least we are both doing what we prefer."

They stood together with their drinks, watching the Alps turn a metallic rose in the sunset. Then, putting down his glass, he took her in his arms. She had feared it would happen, but she did not pull back.

"Richard," she murmured. He stilled her with a kiss. And then his hands were caressing her slim, tense body.

She broke away. "This all seems to be happening too fast. You walk back into my life and we're headed for the bedroom, just like that. Damn!"

"You have a point. I am being insensitive. But, Molly, you've become more lovely than ever. I just can't help myself. My only hope is that we shall see much more of each other. What do you say to that?"

She wanted to move back into his arms. But they were late for Monsignore Monti's reception. It was professionally important to them both.

By the time they arrived at Via Alfieri, the monsignore's handsome Italian-Louis XVI drawing-room was packed. Monti hurried over to greet them, then moved on to other guests. After a while Richard wandered away, seeking important journalists with whom he could make contact.

As Molly stood alone, sipping a glass of Monti's Barbaresco, Nicolò Sforzini became aware of her. She was one of the most attractive women he had ever seen. As lovely as Livia, though her look was of a different sort. Bowing slightly, he introduced himself. She smiled, offering her hand. "I'm Molly Madrigal."

Nico kissed her hand. She thought he looked familiar. Where had she seen that face before?

"Tell me, Signora Madrigal, you are a journalist?"

She spoke of her assignment in Turin for *View*.

"I read your magazine frequently," he said admiringly. "In Europe everyone is familiar with *View*."

Molly returned the bow.

"Your name—do you spell it *Madrigale*? How very charming; early romantic music. It is Italian, of course. Your ancestors, are they Italian?"

"Could be. But as far back as I know, it was without the 'e.' There's also a lot of Irish in me." She laughed. "The Irish wins out, at least in an argument."

Looking into her eyes, Nico recalled delphiniums he had seen years before during a summer vacation in England. He told her he was an archaeologist and would be examining the shroud with a group of European scientists. His work was primarily in the Holy Land and he had begun to describe the site near Masada he was currently excavating, when Monti joined them.

Molly said, "Monsignore, might I steal you for just a moment? I've done some homework on the shroud, but not nearly enough. Can you tell me more about earlier testing?"

The priest smiled. "I love to talk about the shroud and, Molly, I would be happy if you called me Vittorio." He told her there had been examinations in 1969 and briefly again in 1973, after the shroud's first appearance on television. "Several things were conjectured following these observations. Which, you know, were not so extensive as those that will take place during the coming month." He spoke of the pollen grains found on the shroud, especially from a variety of tamarisk bush, with clusters of small pink flowers. The plant grew in places with high salt content, like the Dead Sea region and the wilderness areas around Jerusalem.

"I can tell you, signora," Nico said, "that I have seen such plants near the site I am excavating in Israel. Their flowering is subtle and on closer examination, quite beautiful."

Richard Coolidge, talking nearby with a woman writer from the Italian daily *La Stampa*, overheard Monti's remarks, excused himself and came over, just as the priest darted away to greet some new arrivals. Molly introduced Richard to Count Sforzini, explaining that the archaeologist was a member of the scientific team from Europe. Immediately Richard looked interested. "I should very much enjoy hearing details of the testing when everything is decided. By the way, Count Sforzini, you are in a position to explain why it has been announced that radiocarbon dating will not be included as part of this test series."

Richard grinned, knowing he had raised a major issue. He enjoyed homing in on sensitive subjects.

"I cannot speak for the commission," replied Nico. "But as an archaeologist with some experience, I believe the new technology for age dating is still not refined to the point where the Church thinks a result would be unimpeachable."

Richard warmed to the subject. "Come, now, Count, isn't the

Church just a little afraid that the cloth will turn out to have been made in, say, the fourteenth century?"

Nico shrugged.

"You will agree, won't you, that if this relic proves to be false, many persons will have less faith in Christianity than before?"

"I cannot speak for all people, Dr. Coolidge. Only for myself. And it will not change my belief at all."

Richard shifted to a new subject. "You can solve a kind of mystery for me. The Gospels reveal that when Peter entered the tomb, he found a shroud lying on the ground. But Jesus' chin strap, the piece of cloth that was wrapped around his head, was in the corner, rolled up like a dinner napkin some well-mannered schoolgirl would leave neatly by her plate." He chuckled at his simile. "Why should the process of Resurrection be interrupted by such attention to etiquette?"

Anxious to know just exactly what the Gospels did say about a shroud, without Richard's derisive inferences, Molly bowed out of the conversation and went searching the monsignore.

Matthew, recalled Vittorio Monti, noted that Joseph of Arimathea wrapped Jesus' body in a clean shroud; Mark said Joseph bought a shroud and wrapped the body in it; Luke also mentioned the shroud, as did John, who further recounted that a hundred pounds of myrrh and aloes were wrapped in the linen.

Molly remembered Richard had used powdered myrrh and aloes in his demonstration the previous day. "Is there any further mention of a shroud? That is, after Jesus is supposed to have ascended?"

"*Supposed* to have ascended?" The priest pretended shock.

Molly felt embarrassed. "I should admit, Vittorio, that my religious upbringing was, at best, sketchy. And, to be honest, I retain a certain skepticism." She smiled suddenly. "However, after working on this story . . ."

"A miracle, perhaps," he shot back.

The Gospel of John offered the most detail, he said. From memory he recounted it for her: "Peter set out with the other disciple to go to the tomb. They ran together, but the other disciple, running faster than Peter, reached the tomb first; he bent down and saw the linen cloths lying on the ground, but did not go in. Simon Peter, who was following, now came up, went right into the tomb, saw the linen cloths on the ground, and also the cloth that had been over his head. . . ."

"Who took the shroud from Jesus' tomb?" Molly asked.

"Simon Peter. Ancient documents relate he kept the cloth with him throughout his lifetime."

"And after that?"

"Little is known. There are certain doubtful references. But I have been able to find nothing until some possible notations occurring around the time of the Fourth Crusade in Constantinople."

Molly looked at him sympathetically. "It must be a great strain for you, Vittorio, to have these scientists poking at your relic. I truly feel for you. Who knows what they might uncover—rightly or wrongly?" She took his hands in hers and held them tightly.

At that moment, because she seemed to understand so well, the old priest forgot this sincere and caring woman was a reporter and did something he immediately regretted: he confided the possibility that there may have been another shroud. Molly jumped on it. Upon closer questioning, she learned one could not, at this point, be sure whether or not Turin's shroud was the duplicate. However, the facts were not thoroughly researched. Monti hinted more information would soon surface.

Molly felt exhilarated; this could be a great angle. A *View* exclusive—if, of course, the monsignore could refrain from further confidences. She wanted to get to Venice in a hurry, pay some researcher to help her check out the Carpano reference. It must be done before the American scientists arrived; after that she could not leave Turin.

Feeling she had gotten the best story of the day, Molly was soon ready to depart. She glanced toward Richard. He was absorbed in conversation with a woman journalist, a chic Italian.

"Richard," she said quietly, touching his elbow. "I'm leaving. See you soon, I hope."

"Yes, yes, of course. Thanks, Molly," he answered abstractedly.

She felt a flicker of annoyance. That was Richard. For him the object of prime interest was whoever he required to fulfill the moment's purpose. Walking toward the entrance hall, she chided herself. As a journalist she frequently had to adopt the same attitude.

Nicolò Sforzini followed her. "Signora, might you care to join me for dinner?" he asked.

They strolled toward the cathedral, then down a side street to a rustic-looking place with a sign in archaic script, IL DUOMO. The decor, with its small gilded cherubs, was delightful. A waiter, recognizing the count, hastened to seat them in a secluded corner. "Signore Cavaliere," he said importantly, "we welcome you."

When they had settled down to a couple of Americanos, Molly inquired about the nickname. Like Nico himself it seemed familiar. At first Nico was reluctant to discuss the matter. Then he made a face and explained that he used to race cars for Ferrari. The appellation, meaning "knight," identified him with the Ferrari insignia, a black horse, and possibly with his gesture, once, in abandoning the lead to go to the aid of a fellow racer whose car had struck a wall and was on fire.

Suddenly it all fell into place. She remembered a photo after he had won the Targa Floria: Nico in his car, checkered flag in hand, and the requisite beautiful woman alongside the Ferrari.

As the two were served a regional dish of grilled chamois and white truffles, Molly wondered aloud why he had quit racing to become an archaeologist. It struck her as a quite divergent vocation.

Nico shrugged and said that archaeology offered the quiet, introspective life he really preferred. Something about his explanation did not ring completely true to Molly. She thought it best to drop the subject.

Then he continued, "Vittorio helped me so much. He steered me to the university and Biblical archaeology, an enthusiasm we had always shared. Those first years of the changeover were what one might call my 'dark night of the soul.' I finally emerged with a new perception of Our Lord and His goodness." Nico dropped his eyes momentarily, embarrassed by this revelation of himself to someone he scarcely knew. Molly, who had never even imagined such a spiritual struggle, remained silent.

"It is time I stopped talking about myself and learned more about you. May I call you Molly?" She nodded.

"My life has been centered on one area alone, journalism," she said. "I always wanted to be exactly where I am now. As for my religious convictions, I suppose a God is out there somewhere. I just haven't met Him yet." She laughed self-consciously. Nicolò Sforzini had a warm, sympathetic manner which invited one to open up. This was the sort of man she came across all too rarely. The kind Richard had seemed to be in the beginning, although the count lacked Richard's cynicism.

She turned to another field. "Since you're on the scientific team, could you give me some information about the tests to be performed? And is there any way you can explain in uncomplicated terms? I'm a scientific idiot."

Nico smiled and said he had yet to meet with the American scientists. But of course he had a general idea of the program which was planned. All of the tests would be nondestructive, excluding radiocarbon testing. They would certainly include wide-spectrum photographic studies, particulate sampling of the shroud's surface, and X-radiography to detect any painting beneath the image. This would be followed by X-ray fluorescence studies. Fluorescence, he explained, would provide clues to the chemical makeup of substances on the shroud. While the cloth was being bombarded by primary wavelengths of the spectrum —X ray, ultraviolet, and infrared—secondary light radiations, or fluorescence, would be emitted, identifying certain chemicals or revealing contrasting substances. The results would be photographed and each test would provide exact information about the shroud image. For instance, the scientists would be highly interested in checking whether the so-called bloodstains on the shroud would glow, it being known that blood does not respond by fluorescing.

"Macrophotography will also be done," explained the count. "We hope to magnify portions of the cloth up to forty times original size. Some of the American scientists are experts in computer analysis. In fact, I know two men on the team who work at California's Jet Propulsion Laboratory. They have analyzed computer information sent back from the American space explorations. We hope by applying the same computer enhancement techniques, which were used on material like the Mars pictures, to achieve much clearer detail than has ever been obtained before. Perhaps we shall see things not possible without this special equipment." Previous photographs of the image seemed to show round objects over the eye areas. "These may be coins," said Nico, "though I doubt it. They are most probably pottery shards. If not, image enhancement might be able to distinguish details of the supposed coins and provide a unique means of dating."

Nico also explained that a special, chemically inert tape would be pressed into various portions of the cloth to collect surface particles, and a few tiny fibrils would be drawn from the fabric. Later, in other laboratories, chemists would analyze the tapes for hemoglobin in the suspected dried blood; pigments, if any; and foreign matter.

Molly broke in. "Do you think radiocarbon testing will ever be done?"

"In the future, I suppose. Dr. Coolidge was baiting me, claiming that the Church would obviously avoid cutting away pieces of the shroud for the destructive C-14 tests. Coolidge is quite knowledgeable about the process. He told me a friend of his works with the Van de Graaff accelerator. He seemed surprised when I informed him that there are already shroud samples available and that Vittorio keeps these specimens in a drawer of his desk between the pages of an old stamp album."

"I'm rather surprised at the casual attitude of the Church regarding the testing," Molly said. "I was told in a phone interview with one of the scientists that the American STURP group would probably take off for Turin without knowing for certain whether the tests are 'go.'"

"I am certain that we will get official permission," explained Nico. "However, the Church is not precisely concerned with the shroud as a historical object. No pope has ever formally declared the relic to be genuine. Though the Vatican acknowledges it as an object of veneration. It is what it is. They are not worried, one way or the other."

"Do you believe it is the shroud of Jesus?"

He looked amused. "Off the record, please. I do not presume to know, what with two thousand years gone by. Yet our great museum of Egyptology here in Torino has several fine examples of ancient linen far older than the shroud."

"But it's the enigmatic image, more than the fabric itself, which seems to defy explanation, isn't it? Some call it miraculous. How do you, a scientist, feel about that?"

"I can only speak as a Christian, Molly. I believe in the life and Resurrection of Our Lord. I know he is divine and can work miracles. Might this not be another of them?"

She continued to pursue the issue, more to answer something for herself than to challenge him. "But what absolutes are there to verify all this? It seems to me that all we have are some scant writings after the fact. I find it implausible that a major religion could flourish on something so remote and unprovable. Surely, in this age of science, we will have to do better than that."

"Oh? It appears we find ourselves too sophisticated to accept the miracles of the Biblical era. So here in 1978, perhaps the Lord is providing us with a twentieth-century miracle: the validation of his image on that cloth through state-of-the-art technology. The verification that he lived and died and exists for us today. Do you not see?"

There seemed some reason to his argument. In a wistful tone Molly said, "I wish I had your faith. It appears to provide all the convenient answers."

"Oh, no, Molly. I think Jesus did not intend us to look for miracle cures that would solve, magically and instantly, all problems. Maybe the true miracle lies in our becoming: our approach to something higher; our awareness and identification with it."

As they walked back to the hotel, Molly mentioned the monsignore's accidental disclosure of duplicate shrouds and her decision to go to Venice and try to uncover the truth of the matter. Nico instantly invited her to be his guest at the Palazzo Sforzini. "You must meet my family. I have promised Vittorio that I, too, would search for that reference. And though our aims are not exactly identical, perhaps, together, we may learn the truth."

She was surprised to hear herself accept his invitation without any hesitation. But then, she quickly reminded herself, this was business. Certainly nothing more than that.

Richard Coolidge continued to linger at the monsignore's reception. He had made some excellent contacts. The good-looking journalist from *La Stampa* was still smiling in his direction. At the least she would interview him for an article. Tomorrow he planned on inviting her to dinner.

He kept brooding about what the archaeologist Sforzini had said. It seemed preposterous that his host actually held pieces of the shroud in his desk drawer. Certainly the Catholic Church would not go so far as actually to mutilate their precious cloth, even to the extent of a few threads. He determined to have a look. It was altogether too tempting. Peering toward the far corner of the salon, he saw Monti lost in conversation with a couple of the remaining journalists. Quickly Richard made for the door. Just as he was about to leave the room, Monti called, "Oh, Dr. Coolidge!" Richard grimaced.

Beaming, Monti came over. Count Sforzini had told him, he said, of Richard's comment about the rolled-up chin cloth.

"It strikes me," said the priest, "that there is a perfectly logical explanation for its presence in a corner of the tomb. Mark writes that Christ died in the 'ninth hour.' For modern scholars that translates to three o'clock in the afternoon. After his crucifixion there were a number of things certain disciples were obliged to attend to. A proper shroud had to be obtained, and the spices which Nicodemus placed around the body must be sought out and purchased. There was the laying out of the corpse, the prayers and, doubtless, other duties. These took time and the Sabbath was rapidly approaching. For Jews all labor ceased at dusk. It would have been a sacrilege to flout the Law and remain to complete their final tasks. The men suddenly realized they had lingered too long. Perhaps they had failed to observe the setting sun in the darkness of the *arcosolium*. One surely cried out a warning and they fled the tomb, letting the chin strap fall in their haste."

Richard shook his head doubtfully. "That," he commented, "is your interpretation of it."

"It is indeed, and I suggest it makes better sense than—as you put it—that the Resurrection included a deference to etiquette. But before all this occurred, there was an important task for Joseph of Arimathea to perform: the removal of a strip of linen from the shroud to serve as chin binding. It was to be wrapped around the head in order to keep the mouth closed."

"And what's your evidence for that?" Coolidge mentally kicked himself for his question. This old pedant would now bore him with another long-winded theory. Richard wanted to get out of the reception room while others were still there to occupy Monti's attention.

"This is really just my own opinion. As these journalists might say, 'off the record.' We have found a narrow strip of the same sort of linen sewn along the relic's edge. I have an intuition that this could be the chin binding, attached at a later time so it would not be lost."

Monti caught his listener yawning. He moved away. Richard took another drink and tried to look casual until he could be certain his exit would be unnoticed. Then he slipped out of the reception room and into the hall. The study was close by, its door open.

The room was a monument to disorder: books piled everywhere, even on the carpet; papers strewn on all the horizontal surfaces. A purple sock was lying on the big oak desk.

With a glance toward the study door, which he had closed, Richard commenced his search, beginning with the upper left-hand drawer. How easy—there it was! An old stamp album. Lifting it from the drawer, he set it on the desktop, then quickly leafed through its pages. Inserted in the album's center was what he sought. What he had believed could not possibly be there. Enclosed in separate glassine envelopes were the shroud samples. Most just single threads of varying lengths. But among them were two pieces of larger size, one about a square inch. Big enough to be tested by an atomic accelerator. Occasionally, in dating an artifact of organic material or authenticating an old piece of artist's canvas, he had made use of the Van de Graaff machine. He had gotten to know Scott Nordlinger, one of the scientists at the New England nuclear research laboratory, rather well.

Coolidge was convinced that age dating would be the decisive factor in proving his theory. Everything for him, a top university post, the future of his Institute, the recovery of a fading reputation, rested on what the carbon atoms in that little sample had to say.

Fingering the envelope which held the larger sample, he thought, why not? They will never miss it. The Roman Catholic Church would avoid putting their prime relic at risk, he rationalized. The samples would rot away forever in this desk.

He pocketed the envelope and put the stamp book back in its drawer. Inspecting the empty hallway, he stepped out into the street. Scotty was a friend. He would do it. Whistling his unrecognizable melody, Richard walked briskly toward Corso Vittorio Emanuele and his hotel.

Chapter 9

Melantias—Byzantium—Rome, 324–326 A.D.

Licinius hated Christians—a matter made savagely clear at Melantias, where a group of worshipers quavered before the ruler of Rome's Eastern Empire. At their feet lay three bodies, a woman and two men, casually slain by the emperor's notably handsome bodyguards. In shackles, beside the villagers, stood the renowned Christian bishop of Egypt, Paphnutius. This revered ascetic was the means by which Licinius now hoped to uncover and destroy the shroud of their god.

The emperor considered himself a reasonable man, but his feelings about Christians fell beyond the limits of tolerance. Why should these people seek some sort of heavenly redemption for their sins when Romans—far better persons than they—had no such need? And then there was that sacrament called the Lord's Supper which he had learned about from interrogation of a captive Christian. The Christians' barbaric practice of devouring the flesh and blood of their god utterly disgusted him. They were beneath contempt.

This former Illyrian peasant found their Christus to be singularly absurd. He could no more fit into the Roman pantheon of understandable, intemperate, and libidinous gods than could these repulsive Christians, most of them lower-class Greeks and Jews, become part of the Roman scheme of things.

Today was typical of their idiocy: they virtually threw themselves at martyrdom to gain some ambiguous end, far from the refined delights of Elysium. They were dangerous, he reasoned. Their intransigence was a threat to the foundations of empire. Even more distressing, they evoked certain personally galling memories. Always, in these recollections, hovered the classical features of the ruler of Rome's Western Empire, Constantine.

O Iuppiter! Once he had loved that tall young Apollo, with his golden curls, like a brother. At Milan he had become Constantine's actual brother-in-law. That was the beginning of the humiliations. The string of disasters which had brought him to this place, astride a white horse, looking down at the Christians.

A past emperor, Diocletian, had established the principle of two senior emperors, augusti, commanding the defenses and government of an empire grown too vast for a single *imperator*. According to Diocletian's constitution, the Western Emperor, Constantine, outranked Licinius and, embarrassingly enough, Constantine was younger than he by twenty-five—call it twenty— years.

Before his marriage to Constantine's half-sister, Licinius had been compelled to agree to an edict decreeing that Christianity was to be tolerated as a legal religion throughout the empire. It was humiliating. After all, he had only been doing what other emperors did, following Diocletian's official policy of suppressing the Christians. Licinius felt that he was being slapped in the face for his extra zeal in this State matter.

This led to their first armed conflict. Constantine had suspected the existence of a grave conspiracy against him. The plot was to be instrumented by Bassianus, a young man from a rich Roman family Constantine had appointed junior emperor, or caesar. Licinius was proved to have instigated and backed Bassianus in his sedition.

After Constantine won a victory over Licinius's larger forces, the emperor of the West allowed Licinius to live, but confiscated five of his provinces, including his native Illyricum. Calling him "friend and brother," Constantine had left him only Thrace, Asia Minor, Syria, and Egypt.

The final affront was Constantine's stipulation that two of his sons, Crispus and young Constantine, be named caesars, with the hope for succession in the West, while only a single son of Licinius, his bastard, received the same honor in the now-diminished East. What reasonable man could fail to understand Licinius's present resentment?

He turned in his saddle. One of his bodyguards, Ansatus, meaning "man with handles"—he renamed them all according to his whim—was staring at a boy beside an old, gray-bearded Christian.

"Ansatus," called Licinius, placing one hand behind his back, "we shall throw fingers. If you win, that boy is yours. If you lose, you will nail him to an olive tree over there." Constantine had passed a law forbidding crucifixion; Licinius's response had been one of utter contempt.

Ansatus threw out five fingers, calling, "*Par*"—an even sum. Simultaneously, Licinius showed his hand, with the index finger extended. Six. The guards cheered their emperor's fairness.

Matthias's cheeks paled as he held his grandson, a visitor from Byzantium, tightly against his side. He watched Licinius, seeing a man who looked like an aging gladiator. The emperor's face, with its broken nose and outthrust jaw, was molded from deeply tanned skin which resembled ancient leather. It appeared in strange contrast to the royal diadem, with its delicate ribbon of pearls, tied in a neat bow behind the thin white fringe of his hair. Licinius's body was squat, barrel-like. Matthias could see the heavy tufts of white hair on the emperor's shoulders and chest, which showed through his diaphanous, purple silk gown. His gnarled legs looked like limbs of an oak.

Licinius addressed Paphnutius. "Illustrious bishop, it is my intention to bury Constantine, that great lover of Christianity, in the shroud of your Christus. You will direct your people to deliver the shroud to me at once. I know it is here. Yesterday a Christian in Byzantium confessed it."

"Much as my eyes would rejoice," declared Paphnutius, addressing the Christians, "to see the holy cloth—if indeed it be here—you must never reveal it."

Licinius frowned. "You will see it soon enough, old man. But your joy shall be reduced. Pyladeus, enucleate him."

A blond giant stepped behind Paphnutius, forcing a powerful thumb into his eye socket. Paphnutius screamed, as the eye was forced out.

"And now you shall order them," cried Licinius. The bishop was silent. "Listen well, Christians. If you wish to spare this esteemed personage, bring forth the shroud."

His men had ransacked every dwelling, without success. Matthias gritted his teeth. He must not move. His first duty was to the shroud, brought here long ago by an ancestor, Melchi Bar-Azariah. The relic was hidden in his own small house. God help me, he prayed, not to hate.

Licinius was suddenly weary of all this. It seemed so trivial, so boring. Speaking to a guard, he said, "Phoebigena, help me dismount." The emperor reached out, clutching Phoebigena's hand, then threw his body over the helping arm. The guard crashed to the ground, under the emperor's considerable weight. Licinius shouted triumphantly, "You are thrown. I win this fall. No one can beat me." He looked to the other bodyguards, who appropriately howled, "*Hahahae*." Licinius drew Phoebigena to his feet and patted his cheek. The emperor felt better now. "Paphnutius will prostrate himself before his *imperator* and *dominus*."

"The Lord alone is my *dominus* and master," said Paphnutius faintly.

"Adonis," screamed Licinius, "*poplites succidite!* And if he bleeds to death, you pay with your own legs."

The guard, with a face of awesome beauty, pushed Paphnutius to the ground and carefully drew his sword across the hamstring tendons behind both of the bishop's knees, rendering the legs forever useless. Then Adonis, with a boyish smile, bowed modestly to the emperor.

Licinius nodded, feeling another wave of weary disinterest wash over him.

A rider reined in his lathered horse before the emperor. Saluting as he leaped to the ground, the messenger called out that he brought news of Constantine. Licinius had last heard that the Western emperor was quietly bivouacked at Thessalonica with his cavalry and foot soldiers. His son Crispus reportedly rested at Piraeus with his little fleet. But startlingly the messenger reported that the forces of Constantine and Crispus had been sighted thirty miles east of Maximianopolis, less than a week's march away. Licinius felt instantly alive, excited.

His orders were sharp. "Hermes, carry the bishop to the prison at Chrysopolis. I want him alive. I'll deal with these fools and their shroud later. All guards mount up!"

Ansatus cast a last wistful glance at the boy. In a moment the main body of guards was galloping back toward Byzantium, leaving behind the Christians and bloodstains in the dust.

Riding along the Via Egnatia, Licinius considered his plans. The generals from his armies at Byzantium, Hadrianopolis, and Chrysopolis would be awaiting orders. Though events were moving more quickly than he had expected, he was ready. This time, finally, there would be an end to humiliations. Constantine's forces were reassuringly outnumbered. Licinius had 165,000 foot and horse soldiers; Constantine led a mere 120,000. Crispus commanded only two hundred small galleys, a laughable few compared to Licinius's fleet of three hundred larger warships—all triremes with triple banks of oars. He had the chance at last to utterly crush Constantine.

As he swept with his bodyguards through the great land gates of Byzantium, Licinius reviewed his novel idea of burying Constantine, possibly alive, in the shroud. But this small conceit obscured the main fact. Soon either he or Constantine would become sole ruler of the entire civilized world, that vast continuum of lands encompassed by the Roman Empire. And Licinius knew that the victor would be he. The gods were good!

✳   ✳   ✳   ✳   ✳

On the highway from Byzantium to the Danube, in the city of Naissus, there was a popular inn. To it came travelers, military men, merchants, and sometimes secret Christians. It was here, with the sounds of merriment rising from below, and whispered words of Christian prayer above, that Constantine was born.

His mother, Helena, was the daughter of Flavius, the innkeeper. Constantine's father, Constantius, was a distinguished officer under Maximian, co-ruler of the empire with Diocletian. Constantius had halted at the inn while on an official mission to

Persia, in order to be present at his son's birth. His was a marriage of love.

Helena was a handsome, fair-haired young woman, whose cheerful manner concealed a thoughtful intelligence. She enjoyed meeting and talking to the astonishing variety of persons who paused at the Deversorium Flavi. The travelers would leave their mounts and strings of pack animals in the broad courtyard beside the inn, then pour into the tavern to refresh their dry throats with Illyrian wine. At times Helena would serve them.

Her long, questing conversations with Christian wayfarers had led to her conversion to the faith of Jesus. In the happy days of childhood, before Constantine found himself under the unending pressures and stresses which were to mark his way through life, his mother would tell the boy stories of Jesus and the apostles. And there were exciting times when Constantius, much to his wife's misgivings, would take his son to the encampments under his authority in the provinces of Spain and Gaul.

Constantius knew of his wife's clandestine participation in Christian worship. He was of liberal mind and tolerant. One day he told Constantine that he could find no fault in a faith which promoted the ideals of ethical power and love. Its high moral principles were directed toward social order in a world that could well be the better for them. This gentle and moderate man shunned the opulence of the Eastern monarchs. Above all he treasured the hearts of his people. For when he needed them, he could count on their support. Constantine absorbed the lesson.

When Constantius rose to the rank of caesar, Constantine was ordered to the court of the emperor, Diocletian, almost as a hostage. It was a totally different world. Diocletian, unlike previous Roman emperors, followed the Eastern tradition of godlike distance from his subjects, and awesome ostentation. He demanded that all should prostrate themselves before him. His attitude toward Christians was harsh and suppressive, and it was in such an atmosphere that Constantine learned the lesson of prudence.

Constantius's rise required that he renounce Helena and marry Theodora, stepdaughter of Maximian, Diocletian's co-emperor in the West. The emperors sought such family alliances to insure the loyalty of their junior rulers. The divorce was a bitter and shameful event for Constantine, now eighteen. He was a tall and majestic figure, whose valor and skills in the wars of Persia and Egypt won him a reputation which far exceeded his rank. Helena's son had buried his embarrassment in military ardor.

The refinements of the Eastern court at Nicomedia, across the Bosporus from Byzantium, left their effect on him. He perceived the value of Diocletian's aloofness and unassailable dignity. Like his emperor he came to disdain the brash familiarity of the people from Rome. Their easy moral standards repelled him and he seemed impervious to the allure of their varied pleasures. Constantine fancied flowing silk robes and wore his blond hair curled in ringlets across his forehead, in the Greek manner.

When Diocletian and Maximian resigned as augusti, Diocletian to the joys of his beloved cabbage garden, Maximian to dreams of a return to power after his forced abdication, Constantine's father assumed the purple of senior emperor in the West. The caesar, Galerius, became augustus in the East.

Constantine was now pinned under the thumb of a suspicious and jealous Galerius. From Britain, Constantius wrote many letters to Nicomedia, demanding the release of his son. But Galerius, with numerous excuses, would invariably defer permission. One evening, after heavy drinking, the emperor agreed to let Constantine depart. From experience Constantine knew the next day would bring a change of heart, so that night, with his ten aides, he slipped away from Nicomedia. He gathered up all the horses at relay stations along the way, thus preventing effective pursuit. In remarkably swift time he arrived at his father's headquarters in Britain. A year later Constantius died at York, and the army enthusiastically acclaimed Constantine the augustus, Emperor of the West.

*　*　*　*　*

Encamped at Thessalonica, Constantine was prepared to eliminate Licinius. The old Eastern emperor had become notorious for his vices and unspeakable cruelties to the Christians. Constantine was on the alert for Licinius's spies. When an officer of the camp reported that a foreign merchant was vending honey and almond confections and cheap brooches of inlaid enamel,

Constantine smiled. He had been awaiting such an individual. The emperor watched as the man scribed his accounts on a wax tablet. The fellow was reporting the number and readiness of the troops. His wares were obviously Byzantine and his return route was eastward, along the Via Egnatia.

Crispus, his Gallic troops concealed in the woodlands, was alerted. He set forth almost immediately, one day behind the spy. Twelve hours later Constantine's army followed. Licinius would have little time to organize his defenses.

At the Hebrus, Constantine was shocked by the massive army Licinius had gathered. The Western emperor had never lost a battle. But now, surveying the formidable forces across the river, he wondered if he might be facing his first defeat.

The dilemma had been precipitated by his son's eagerness for battle. Crispus, with a column substantially less than his own, was already leading his men across a downriver float bridge his engineers had hastily constructed. A great number of Licinius's Numidian forces stood in the near distance, watching with fascination. Constantine's main striking force was still miles behind. Learning of Crispus's impetuosity, the emperor, thanks to hard riding, had arrived on the near banks of the Hebrus. He was alone, with twelve of his Scholarian Guard. The enemy was ranged on the opposite side, along the plain before Hadrianopolis.

Constantine's uneasiness seemed to have communicated itself to his mount. Patting the nervous horse, he said, "Arion, you have reason to be skittish. My son is a madman."

He had often reflected that this inevitable contest between himself and Licinius would eventually determine which religion would prevail: the Eastern ruler's pantheon or his own Lord.

Christ had come to him years before, his sign a flaming cross in the skies near Rome. That day Constantine had matched his faith in this sign of the Lord's power against his rival, Maxentius, and won. When Maxentius had drowned in the collapse of the Milvian Bridge, Constantine was resolved. Upon his triumphal entry into Rome he turned away from the usual sacrifice at Jupiter's temple. For him, never again the old gods. Henceforth the shields of his soldiers bore the Christian monogram of CHI RHO, the first two Greek letters of the name Christ. He believed it wise not to accept baptism until the final days of his life. Though he now considered himself a Christian, much of his empire embraced the pagan faith of the Romans, so Constantine was ruled by political prudence. On the other hand he had encouraged Crispus to be baptized.

Licinius appeared to be positioning his troops. "Lord be with us. We are fools," Constantine whispered to himself. Then, uttering the fierce cry which had preceded so many victories, he rode in full armor into the broad, swift-running Hebrus. His personal guard followed, while Crispus, with his legionaries, raced across the plain toward apparent disaster.

Constantine had to struggle mightily against the current. For he anticipated the effect ignoring the bridge and crossing in this manner would have on the adversary. Constantine, they would say, is equal to a thousand men.

The emperor's small group led Crispus into the melee. Constantine fought as never before. In the heat of battle he thought only of victory. Seeing him in heroic combat his enemies felt dread, his compatriots fanatic devotion.

All afternoon they battled. Near dusk Constantine withdrew across the bridge, hoping for a cloudless night sky. The moon would be full. So far the engagement had not been decisive.

His troops had begun to arrive. At nightfall a fresh breeze from the south cleared away the clouds and the moon shone with a bright, metallic light over Licinius's sleeping camp. Constantine started back. Five thousand archers were ordered to approach the rear of the enemy soldiers, from a high point above the plain. The forces of the West moved quietly back across the river. Then, with trumpets blaring, and the rough cries of his men, battle-hardened for many years, Constantine attacked. Before dawn thirty-four thousand of the enemy lay strewn about like fallen trees before a great wind.

Exhausted by the fight, Constantine waited neither for daylight nor his son but set off for his villa at Philippopolis. He arrived some days later at midnight. Rousing a few serving women, he had his body bathed and rubbed with oils. He planned on enjoying the deep sleep in his own bed which always followed a victory. But anger with Crispus kept returning to trouble his repose.

Two days passed. First light was touching the ripening pomegranates in his palace garden as Constantine paced furiously along the herb-bordered paths. A courier had just announced Crispus's imminent arrival.

"Father!" The youthful caesar, arms outstretched, hurried to Constantine. He was a blond replica of his father. "I supposed you would be asleep."

With a scorching look Constantine wheeled around. Offering no greeting, he cried, "How dare you initiate an attack without my permission?"

"You are angry with me?"

"I speak of the charge of your inadequate columns against Licinius's army. You knew well our main forces were too far away to join you."

"Why should it matter? We won."

"We won because I raced there and saved you. Now—a full explanation."

"I went ahead because I knew the terrain. It occurred to me that Licinius would never be expecting an attack by only part of our troops. Remember, his spy's last report would have described us as at rest and unready. Moreover, the land around Hadrianopolis was flat and we could advance at full speed to take them by surprise."

"Barely in time. It was one more example of your foolish risk-taking."

"But we won."

"Not such a great success. The prize escaped." Constantine was startled at the force of his anger. After all, his son and heir had helped him to an important victory. Something undefined rankled. He added, "We won because I forded the river to lead your troops. And my night attack made the difference."

Both men paced the garden. Crispus finally spoke. "I have learned Licinius and the remnants of his army are at Byzantium."

"That was to be expected. He must not be given a chance to rebuild his forces. Licinius is dangerous. Don't ever forget it."

Crispus looked intently at his father. "Nor should you forget, Father. Licinius would gladly murder you. He must be destroyed."

Father and son agreed they would prepare a move on Byzantium.

"I am totally confident," said Crispus, "we will triumph, Licinius shall die, and you, Father, you will be master of the world."

Constantine studied the handsome young man before him. Just twenty-two, with all the vitality and youth he had once known. He said, "Then you should rest well at night. It will all be yours one day." Observing the look which flashed in his son's eyes, he felt his strange, undefined rancor return.

A month later the forces of Constantine laid siege to Byzantium. In an unexpected strategic move Crispus engaged Licinius's fleet, which held the Bosporus and seaward access to the city. After a day and a half, aided by a favorable wind, his Greek sea warriors surprisingly destroyed one hundred and thirty of the Eastern ruler's warships. Byzantium was cut off from all provisions. Now Constantine proceeded to raise high mounds before the city walls. On these he erected towers for missile-projecting machines. Below he moved his battering rams into position.

On September eighteenth Licinius's army was decimated. Before Byzantium opened its gates to the besiegers, he escaped to Chrysopolis and his reserve battalions. When the inferior Numidian and Egyptian troops there were attacked by Constantine and his son, Licinius faced another fiasco. His next move was to flee with his wife and guards to the palace at Nicomedia. There he awaited the final chapter in his rise from the peasantry to the throne of the East. The gods had not been good.

Constantine decided he would delay at Chrysopolis. He and Crispus had an important duty to fulfill: the freeing of hundreds of Christians Licinius had incarcerated there.

Among these wretched prisoners were some of the greatest bishops of the Christian church. Deeply affected by their courage in the face of obviously cruel treatment, Constantine attended them personally, ordering that they be brought into the sunlight, clothed in clean robes, and given food and drink.

Paphnutius, the bishop of Egypt, who had been brought from Melantias by Licinius, was lying face down on a shallow pile of straw. The emperor bent over him, holding a lamp close to the bishop's face. "My friend," he said gently, "let me help you."

Though weakened by injuries and imprisonment, the elderly bishop had lost none of his presence. "Emperor, do I understand correctly? We are free? That beast is defeated at last?"

Constantine nodded, and Paphnutius reached out to him. "What a great moment! Emperor, I bless you." Holding up his shackled hands, Paphnutius tried to trace the sign of the Cross.

The emperor knelt beside the bishop while a soldier struck off his fetters. "I am ashamed," said Paphnutius, "that you, with your great responsibilities, should take time for this." The chains fell to the floor. The bishop could now pull himself to a sitting position. "Though I have lost the use of my feet, these old hands will still be of service." He wiggled his fingers.

Sadly Constantine gazed at him. In a tone that seemed almost pleading, he said, "I should like to have many conversations with you. Please let me carry you back with me."

Paphnutius shook his head. "Forgive me, but later, surely. I have been here too long. There is much work awaiting me. And it will be joyous work. You have given us new hope."

Seized by a tender impulse, Constantine kissed the bishop on his eyeless cheek. Paphnutius responded by wrapping his arms about Constantine in a fragile embrace.

Following the release of the Christian prisoners at Chrysopolis and the restoration of their military rank or lost property, Constantine and Crispus rode on to Nicomedia. The trip was leisurely. No more was there need for haste. On the approach road a messenger hailed the imperial party. He bore a message for the emperor from his half-sister, Constantia, wife of Licinius. They had been close, Constantia and her brother. After their father's death Constantine had pledged to protect all of his half-brothers and -sisters. Now Constantia wished to remind him of that pledge by guaranteeing her husband's life.

Constantine sat comfortably on Licinius's former throne. He had been listening to Constantia. Along with his bodyguards Licinius was led in and, sobbing, threw himself prostrate at Constantine's feet. The beaten man wore a shapeless gray cotton garment. In his outstretched hands was the purple imperial gown. Constantine paid no attention to him but listened for some minutes more to Constantia's plea for mercy. Then, noticing the figure before him, he visualized the tragic sight of the tortured Christians at Chrysopolis.

He remarked, "What have we here? A toad who weeps like a man? Or a man who resembles a sad toad? You are right, my sister. This sorry creature can only be pitied. Can it possibly be my mighty brother-in-law who grovels here beyond all dignity?"

"Mercy, for the love of Jupiter," sobbed Licinius.

"But Jupiter brings no mercy," responded Constantine. "Perhaps the name of a better God might come to mind."

"Spare me in the sacred name of Jesus Christus! I offer you for all eternity my purple."

Constantine was silent.

"I am an old man," whined Licinius.

"True, you are very old," said Constantine. "And for what is left of your days, you will be spared, thanks to your wife, to enjoy them under house arrest at Thessalonica. You have my personal assurance of your future safety. You may now rise to your knees, old man, and make a choice among these young men of yours. Whom you reject shall serve Rome. As to yourself, you have no further need of guards. But I shall allow you to retain two of them."

Stifling a sob, Licinius looked at the twenty lined up against a wall. "Only two?"

"Choose," said Constantine.

Hesitatingly Licinius said, "Ansatus and Adonis." Phoebigena's face turned pale. His ivory features contorted into a mask of rage.

"Now be of good cheer, brother. You are invited to my feast in honor of an empire finally reunified under a single leader."

When Licinius had been led away, Crispus turned to his father. "Do you realize what your decision might mean? It exposes us again to Licinius's tricks. And they could be most serious." Never before had Crispus been openly critical of his father's judgment. His attitude angered Constantine.

"You question my decision? No one may dare that," cried the emperor. "Have a care, young caesar. Even you are not above my authority."

"It is you who should have a care. Your compassion is a weakness. We may all pay for it." Not waiting to be dismissed, Crispus hurried from the room.

That night the banquet hall resounded with ebullient voices of the guests: generals, high-ranking officers, tribunes, and praefects. Crispus sat beside his father, both resplendent in their imperial robes. On the other side of Constantine was Licinius, still in his drab cotton gown, morosely downing cup after cup of wine. At one point he began giggling, then laughing hysterically.

"How appropriate that you join in our good cheer," commented Constantine.

"It's the whole ludicrous world . . . life is a joke." Licinius hiccuped and tears rolled down his cheeks. "Yesterday I had a great army . . . I was invincible . . . you were to be buried . . ."

"He's drunk," said Crispus.

". . . a final gift for you . . . the shroud of Christus . . . you would be buried in it. And now, now . . ."

"*What* shroud?"

"It's in Melantias, your Jesus' shroud. I almost had my hands on it."

"Control your mirth, old man, and explain," ordered Constantine.

And then Licinius told of the shroud of Melantias—the surprising details he had learned.

"All this seems beyond belief," said Constantine to Crispus, lowering his voice. "Melantias! An insignificant town near Byzantium. Why there, something of such importance? And when could I ever trust the words of Licinius?"

Crispus looked at the former emperor. His head had sunk to his chest. A final tear hung on his chin. "I believe he spoke in the wine of truth," said Constantine's son thoughtfully.

"Why need he have lied? Yes. Possibly—yes! We must visit Melantias. Make inquiries. The shroud of Jesus; can it be so?"

"Why trouble with inquiries?" Crispus said. "Let me take a detachment, Father. I'll seize it and bring it back to you. Then we'll see whether this object is really what he says it is."

Constantine frowned. "No, I will not steal from my subjects. This is not a matter for force. You forget, we are Christians."

Soon afterward, riding donkeys and disguised as travelers, Crispus and Constantine slipped away to Melantias. They began asking questions in the village and very quickly discovered the inhabitants to be uncommunicative on the subject of the shroud. No one seemed to know anything.

At the inn where they lodged, however, was a young barmaid who discovered an immediate attraction for Crispus. Although she herself knew of no such object, she said, she could direct them to a man who was thought to be a leader of the local Christian community.

The girl led them a short distance north of town and, before turning back, pointed to a small dwelling by a vineyard on the hillside. An old man with a gray beard was hoeing a vegetable garden beside the house. Constantine introduced himself as Julian and his son as Paulus, explaining that they were travelers seeking rest in the shade. The old fellow—his name was Matthias—was stooped from years of labor. He told them they might rest under the trees a short while but added that they could not stay long since he had work to do in his vineyard. Though his tone was kind, there was an unyielding quality to his words.

Constantine came directly to the point. He explained that he and his son were Christians who had traveled far, hoping to see the blessed shroud which they had been told was to be found hereabout.

Matthias's face momentarily grew tense, then assumed a noncommittal expression. He shrugged, declaring that though he had lived there his entire life, he knew nothing of any shroud. Surely their informant was mistaken. He himself would like to see so remarkable a relic. And besides, he said, why should anyone trust strangers claiming to be Christians? Even with Constantine successfully battling the Emperor Licinius, one could never be sure —never be cautious enough. Licinius was tricky and unprincipled. He, Matthias, had seen horrible proof of that.

Constantine felt a surge of anger. He had a brief impulse to reveal himself, but he was not Licinius and he had come in peace. He told Matthias that Licinius was not only totally beaten, but now—he had it from an absolutely reliable source— the ex-emperor was being confined under house arrest in Thessalonica. Christians need fear no more. Constantine was their friend.

"Thanks be to God," said Matthias. "He has answered our prayers." And then he quickly added, "I mean the prayers of all good men who regard the Christians as decent people and Licinius as evil." Whatever was their faith, he said, it was his pleasure to let them rest under his trees. But now he bade them farewell and good fortune in their travels.

Frustrated and wondering if Licinius had been lying, Constantine backed away. Maybe he should come again and bring with him a prominent bishop. Perhaps he should have let Crispus seize the shroud by force. The emperor was unaccustomed to being thwarted. But after a moment's consideration he told his son that they must be on their way.

Before they turned back, Crispus faced Matthias, made the sign of the Cross, and uttered a prayer of blessing. Constantine, too, signed the Cross, and said, "Amen." They had started off down the road when Matthias called them to return. He apologized for doubting their membership in the Communion of Christians.

As he led them toward his house, he told them of the dreadful persecution of the Melantias Christians and the story of Paphnutius, who had suffered so bravely to protect the shroud. Constantine looked grave. His regard for the ascetic bishop grew even greater.

"Truly," said Crispus, "we are Christians. It would be the most blessed experience could we see, even for an instant, the shroud of Jesus."

Matthias said, "We very rarely display the holy treasure. For more than two centuries, since the time of my ancestor Rufus Bar-Melchi and his father, our family has guarded the shroud. Our precaution has become a habit." The small group of Christians living at Melantias had limited their viewing of the relic to but once each year, on the anniversary of the Lord's crucifixion.

"You must be careful, my friends. Do not publicly admit your faith," cautioned Matthias. "Please follow me."

They crossed Matthias's main room. The emperor was impelled to say that Christians had no further need of secrecy now that Constantine headed the entire empire. Matthias responded, "Still, one must not forget his mother, Helena. That one is a collector of relics. A fanatic, I hear. Should she learn of the shroud, she'd grab her son by the ear and order him to send all his armies to Melantias." Constantine grimaced under his disguise and started to protest as Matthias conducted them across a small courtyard. "Now you shall see the sacred shroud."

At these words father and son focused all their thoughts on a small door at the courtyard's far side. Beyond was a hall-like chamber with a long table set below eye-level. Benches were ranged before it. Matthias reached under the table and retrieved a small wooden cross which he placed in a niche on the back wall.

"You must both turn away from me and face the entry door," Matthias commanded. Unquestioning, the visitors reversed their positions on the bench. "Only the descendants of Melchi Bar-Azariah may know the shroud's hiding place."

It was afternoon and when Matthias threw open the shutters on the room's west side, the chamber was flooded with sunlight. Set into the plastered back wall was a wooden cupboard. Its door, partially open, revealed tallow candles and oil lamps. Removing these, Matthias pressed a point on the far surface of the cupboard. A concealed closure swung open. Within the recess beyond lay a pottery coffer from which Matthias withdrew a folded cloth. After closing the hidden compartment, he lightly kissed the fabric and spread it on the table.

"Brothers, behold, the burial cloth of our Savior."

"Look," whispered Crispus, "the figure!" They could make out the pale images of a man—front and back views. They were mottled with dark bloodstains. Constantine sharply drew in his breath; Crispus's heart was beating rapidly.

"It has been told in our family," said Matthias, "that Simon Peter saw this miraculous image of Our Lord when first he came upon the shroud in the tomb from which Jesus had ascended." It was as if they were unbelievably close to the Son of God. The emperor and his son sat with bowed heads and fixed gaze for many minutes. The room smelled vaguely of burned candle tallow. Constantine, profoundly moved, knew he would never take the relic from the old man who guarded it.

His thoughts returned to that moment on the march to Rome: a cross superimposed across the noonday sky, his first sure knowledge of Christ's presence. Others, too, had seen the cross that day, and in the clouds those words beneath it, "BY THIS SIGN YOU WILL CONQUER." His life had been changed by it. Now, again, he felt God had spoken to him. His heart grew full with love and wonderment.

Upon his return from Melantias, Constantine moved with his court to Byzantium. There Crispus and his young wife, another Helena, were reunited at a family celebration given by the emperor and Crispus's stepmother, Fausta. Daughter of an emperor, Fausta had always kept a cool distance from her stepson, who was Constantine's natural son by Minervina, the mistress he had deeply loved. Crispus, for his part, distrusted the arrogant Fausta, and both he and his wife grew suspicious when Fausta began treating him with unusual affection.

"What is she up to?" Helena whispered when, for a moment, the family's attention turned to Fausta's children. Constantine, meanwhile, observed the scene with pleasure. He enjoyed these times of family harmony. To please his wife the emperor was especially playful and affectionate that day when her three young sons, whom he had fathered, were brought in for a romp. Surprisingly their mother scarcely noticed them, so intent was she upon the conversation she had initiated with Crispus. Helena observed the scene with suspicion.

After the women had retired, Crispus and his father were alone, the latter lingering over his cup of wine. "I look forward to more youngsters around here," he said.

An instant of discomfort gripped Crispus. "Helena and I hope one day we may give you a grandchild."

"One day?"

"Father . . ."

"There are no problems between you?"

"No, certainly not."

"You have been married two years, have you not? Is Helena in good health?"

"Yes, of course." Crispus wished this conversation over. "I do not know what is wrong. Perhaps I am away too much. We travel a great deal, Father, you and I."

"That reminds me," said Constantine, "I plan a trip to Palestine and I would enjoy your company."

"But I cannot be with my wife and travel with you at the same time. You must pardon me, Father. I beg you to understand if I decline your invitation." Constantine nodded, concealing both his displeasure and disappointment.

Later Constantine was joined by his devoted friend and counselor, Eusebius, Bishop of Caesarea, a leading figure in Christian affairs. He had been a disciple of the renowned theologian Pamphilus. Having recently completed an epic history of Christianity, he was considered to be the most learned man of his age. The old priest, his snowy hair falling to his shoulders, prostrated himself before the emperor. Embarrassed, Constantine helped Eusebius to his feet. Deference and praise from these high representatives of Christianity left the emperor feeling diffident, uncomfortable.

They spoke of personages whom Constantine had freed from the prison at Chrysopolis. The emperor reported on the condition of Paphnutius; Paul of Neocaesarea, who had been paralyzed in both hands; Eustathius of Antioch, blinded; Spiridion of Cyprus . . . Eusebius's eyes filled with tears. Understanding what his old friend must be feeling, Constantine decided this was the moment to confide a plan he had held in his heart many years.

"Though it cannot be undertaken immediately, Eusebius, it is my intention that before my reign is ended, and if God permits me to do so, Christianity will become the official religion of the empire."

The bishop became so visibly stirred by the information that Constantine stopped talking to allow him to regain his composure. Continuing, he said, "However, the empire—so sadly divided these years—needs now to be united. To accomplish this it is necessary that I also offer a secure future to our pagan subjects. The change to a new religion must come about gradually. But it will come. I plan that Crispus shall succeed me. He has been raised as a Christian."

At the mention of Crispus, Eusebius smiled. "Seldom have I seen father and son so close. It is a blessed thing, Emperor."

The troubling feelings began to gnaw again. Constantine was compelled to confide his doubts. "I know there is much love between us. Yet there is something else, something distressing to my spirit. Crispus is impulsive. He wants too much at once—for the empire."

Eusebius, no fool about people, recognized what lay behind the emperor's words. "Do you not also fear he desires too much for himself?"

No one but he could have made such a remark without arousing Constantine's ire. Morosely the emperor sank deeper into his chair. "I really should not feel as I do. I love my son, as I loved his mother. No one is closer in my affections. Yet I suspect his love for me is mixed with this—this urge to take from me the authority that is mine. It is not yet his time."

"He is young, my Emperor. Have you forgotten the urgency of your own youth? Then a day seemed a lifetime. The caesar serves you well; you must allow for his impetuosity." Pausing, he shot a knowing glance in Constantine's direction. "Impatience is a curse with which many of us must contend."

Catching his meaning, the ruler said, "I did not realize my faults were so similar—or so obvious."

"Ah, Emperor, one could never find you rash. The imperial diadem calls for many quick decisions. But if you are ever uncertain of your direction," said Eusebius delicately, "perhaps we might pray together."

That summer of 325 Constantine involved himself enthusiastically with the affairs of a growing Christianity. Though he refrained from accepting baptism for fear of offending his pagan subjects, he became increasingly dedicated to strengthening the position of the Church. In July he journeyed to Nicaea, near Nicomedia, to preside over a convocation of three hundred learned bishops, gathered to establish a unified doctrine and hammer out a creed acceptable to all Christians. There was much turmoil and dissent among the participants. Some viewpoints were divergent enough to be considered heresies. Finally Constantine took over the meetings and, with Eusebius's counsel, set forth the orthodox concepts which were to prevail.

The following summer Constantine traveled to Asia and Palestine. In the Holy Land he made pilgrimages to those places where Jesus had lived and died.

Jerusalem, now known as Aelia Capitolina, had greatly changed since the days of Jesus. It lacked the spirit and energy of its Judaean past. The city had become a Roman colony and a center for solemn Christian tourism.

After Hadrian had rebuilt the ruined capital, he had forbidden the dispersed Judaeans to approach its outskirts. Any Jew discovered looking at the distant remnants of the walls faced a sentence of death. But by 330 there was a kind of amnesty, and on special occasions Jews were permitted to visit and wail by a rock in the ruined Temple area. Hadrian had built a pagan sanctuary honoring Jupiter on the site of the Temple. He covered the holy sepulcher with earth, paved the entire area, and erected a shrine to Venus. When Constantine ordered the shrine to be cleared, Jesus' tomb came to light. The emperor directed that a church be built on the site.

Sitting alone in the garden of Gethsemane, Constantine reviewed the edicts he had issued which particularly pleased him. Long ago the emperor Maxentius, indifferent to the rights of Romans, had bestowed their estates upon his Praetorian Guards and given them the wives and daughters of upper-class citizens. Sophronia, a Christian matron Constantine had greatly respected, committed suicide rather than succumb to Maxentius's demands. Constantine ordained the most severe punishment and execution for seducers and rapists. He provided monetary assistance for unwanted children and orphans who in those harsh times had been allowed to die. Humane treatment was mandated for slaves and prisoners.

One thing that offended his sensibilities was the Romans' excessive fondness for sausages. At such pagan revels as the Floralia and Lupercalia, sausages not only served various obscene us-ages, but were devoured by the celebrants in joyously crazed abundance. Constantine banned sausages. Subsequently an underground sausage trade began to flourish.

As he rested there in the quiet garden, a great and sudden peace came over Constantine. It was as if the weight of all his years of struggle had flown away. There was no more stress. He felt his whole person grow slack and relaxed in a deep tranquility he had not known since childhood. It came to his consciousness that he had triumphed over adversity, and finally could face the future with trust and equanimity.

It was in such a gently euphoric state that the emperor received shocking news: Licinius had been assassinated at Thessalonica. And there was more, a rumor that the deed had been done by Crispus.

Rome was a city Constantine did not much enjoy or approve. However, his wife preferred to live there. Now, in helpless distress, he sped to her, anxious to learn the truth of Crispus's reported treachery.

Fausta was waiting. "My dearest," she said to the agitated emperor, "Crispus is not here. He went to Pola on holiday with Helena." Constantine questioned her about the assassination.

"I know all about it, husband," responded Fausta smoothly. "I have my sources."

Constantine had no reason to doubt Fausta. She had saved his life at the expense of her own father. When Fausta had informed him that their houseguest, Maximian, now a bitter and official nobody, planned to murder him in his sleep, Constantine had placed a servant in his bed. The domestic thus honored received a knife in the heart from the ex-emperor. Maximian was allowed to hang himself.

Yes, Fausta was to be trusted. Her husband treated her with the respect and affection she merited, showing her great deference in public. The world thought him truly in love. And doubtless he was, though the relationship lacked that certain sweetness he had known with the woman who bore Crispus.

"Why, Fausta? Why should he do it? Crispus fully understood my decision concerning Licinius. He has countermanded my specific orders. I gave my word to Constantia that her husband would be spared."

Gently Fausta caressed him. "Do you remember how distressed you were with Crispus after the battle across the Hebrus? How you believed he risked much without your authority to satisfy his personal impulses?"

He wished she would leave that subject alone. But he had always felt it necessary to discuss with Fausta the things which troubled his feelings. She could explain his inner workings so much better than he. Sighing, he realized he should be grateful.

"Why are you surprised? It's simply the nature of your son. You have often complained to me of his wilfulness, his impetuosity." Fausta continued, "After that battle, you might remember, dearest one, how attached to me he became? Do you recall that night of the family celebration, that Crispus paid so very much attention to me?"

But before he could think about what she was saying, Fausta returned to his original question. "Your son killed Licinius to assure his own position in the succession." Lacing her arms around him, she said, "So long as Licinius lived, Crispus could never be entirely secure. Regardless of what he tells you, Crispus murdered Licinius. I know this to be true, without question." She paused. "Dearest Constantine, there is something else you should understand. I have long hesitated to discuss it with you for I always wish to spare you pain."

A horrible apprehension seared through his mind.

"That night in Byzantium was the first of many such nights. During your absence Crispus would come to me and confide his thoughts. Once, after much drinking, he revealed his true intentions."

Constantine resisted an impulse to flee Fausta's quarters.

"Your son intends to do away with you and marry me. Doubtless that is the reason he did not accompany you this summer on your travels."

With a violence compounded of fury and heartbreak Constantine raged about his wife's rooms, ripping silken wall hangings, smashing pottery. Silently Fausta watched his frenzy. Exhausted at last, he collapsed into a chair, his face hidden in his hands.

A reserved man, Constantine permitted himself closeness and warmth only with the members of his immediate family and a few bishops. His affectionate trust in Crispus seemed a natural part of his very being. Now, in one terrible instant, that trust had been fractured. Something within had torn away, leaving him defenseless against his overwhelming emotions.

Constantine summoned his secretary. Rapidly dictating, in Fausta's presence he set forth his son's death warrant. Then he initiated a new order of succession, naming his three young sons by the empress.

Fausta concealed her jubilance. Following the astonished official's exit she proffered an extract of the poppy to her husband. Mindlessly he gulped it down. By the time he awakened, Crispus was dead, run through with the executioner's sword. It was whispered he died bravely, protesting his innocence, his deep love and admiration of his father. Yet no one dared report this to the emperor.

However, one who would not be silent was Crispus's widow, the young Helena. When she arrived from Pola, she refused to be detained by guards and went straight to Constantine. Weeping, she threw herself at his feet.

"There is something you must hear. My husband adored you. You should be aware how greatly he wanted to present you with a grandson. While you believed him to be at Thessalonica murdering Licinius, we were together at Pola trying to have a baby." Wasting no time, she produced witnesses, Christian friends and servants who swore to having been with them that fateful day. "I have just learned of something that may be related," continued Helena. "A former bodyguard of Licinius, someone named Phoebigena, was found in Licinius's garden, fallen on his own sword."

At last Constantine discerned the truth. Fausta! Fausta—ambitious, unprincipled, mother of three boys who had no hope for power with Crispus in the way.

Going swiftly to his wife's apartments, he confronted her with what he now perceived. She shrugged. "So, what was he? A bastard. And his mother, who was she? Certainly not the daughter of an emperor."

Wrenched by grief and fury, Constantine bellowed, "His

mother was a woman I loved far more than I ever loved you. Crispus was born of that love. He was my pride, a decent man, a brilliant leader. Who can replace him? Those weaklings of yours?"

Never before had he struck a woman. Now he grabbed the cowering Fausta and slapped her till she collapsed to the floor. Reaching down, he tore away a great handful of her ebony hair; then stamped on her fingers. Fausta's screams of pain followed him back along the colonnaded halls.

Constantine entered the apartments of his daughter-in-law. "I understand now," he said brokenly. "It was that lying Fausta." The grieving widow stared at him. "You will never forgive me, nor can I forgive myself. But there remains her punishment." Helena's face showed a fierce eagerness. "I have lost a son, but you, Helena, are deprived of much more. I offer you what I may not allow myself—blood for blood." Wordlessly she nodded.

Helena carried out Constantine's command. Waiting until Fausta was in her steam room, Helena entered the chamber. Concealed by clouds of vapor, she approached the naked empress. Then, with a scream of rage, the younger woman seized Fausta's hair and tightened it around the empress's neck, strangling her.

The emperor seemed to grow old overnight. He resolved to turn his face away from Rome, the city so detested by him, and put into effect a plan he had often discussed with Crispus. The founding of a new city, a Christian city. It would be called New Rome and was to be built upon the site of Byzantium.

About to quit the Imperial City forever, Constantine, despairing, wavered a moment in his faith as he desperately sought some remission of his guilt. Unattended, he went secretly to the Temple of Apollo on the Palatine Hill where he consulted priests of the ancient religion.

"Will your gods forgive me the death of my son?"

Seated upon the sacred tripod, an oracle of the college *sacris faciundis* drank fresh blood from a lamb the emperor offered in sacrifice. Falling into a trance, she muttered that his answer awaited him where death would speak of life.

Dissatisfied, he moved on to the house of the haruspex. After carefully examining the entrails of another sacrificial animal, the haruspex, an esteemed seer of Etruscan ancestry, seemed uncertain to take upon himself so great a decision. Saying that the entrails were that day silent, he advised the emperor to seek help from the greatest of the augurs, chief priest of the Roman college.

"We must look to the sky for a sign of Jupiter's will," advised the ancient augur in a screechy voice.

On that moonless night of bright stars the priest, wearing a toga of scarlet stripes and purple border, led Constantine to the top of the steep hill, southwest of the Palatine. There the two pitched a tent.

"I shall mark out and consecrate a space on the earth and in the sky above, within which the decision shall be given." Waving his crooked staff, the augur set the boundaries. Then, covering his white locks with a mantle, he prayed the gods for a sign.

All night they waited. Near dawn the ancient one let out a cry. "There it is!" A bony finger pointed upward. Constantine looked in time to catch a fiery streak in the western sky.

"A star, a falling star!" The priest was trembling. "The omen occurred in the west. Jupiter looks unfavorably upon you."

For a moment Constantine considered killing the old man and leaping to his own death from the precipitous height. But then, thinking of the absurdities he had witnessed during three days of this pagan nonsense, he exploded with laughter. Quickly rising to his feet, he smashed the blue tent, pinning its occupant beneath it. Scrambling back down the hillside, between paroxysms of laughter, Constantine saw that his blinding desperation had led him to these ministers of paganism. Never again! He would now issue an edict banning all pagan symbols from the Empire's coinage.

Crispus had died in July. By November the emperor had laid the cornerstone of his new city.

Chapter 10

New Rome (Constantinople)—Melantias, 333–336 A.D.

Four years of energetic construction and Constantine's city, New Rome, was nearly complete. Trying to forget his misery, the emperor worked tirelessly with his architects and builders.

Covering five hills, New Rome was filled with art and statuary created by masters of Greece's Golden Age and brought by Constantine from throughout the world. Among the city's magnificent buildings were a school of learning, a circus, two theaters, eight public and one hundred and fifty-three private baths, fifty-two porticoes, five granaries, eight aqueducts, four senate halls, fourteen churches, and as many palaces.

Troubled by the emperor's emotional state, Bishop Eusebius remained close by, whenever his duties in Caesarea would allow. Prompted more by sympathy than caution, Eusebius avoided any reference to Crispus or Fausta. The emperor never discussed his personal tragedy with anyone. However, the grief reflected in his eyes was unremitting. It was the bishop's belief that baptism alone could free the ruler from his anguish. When the two were inspecting the nearly finished Church of the Apostles, in which Constantine planned to house his burial monument, Eusebius determined to raise the subject.

"My Emperor, there is a serious matter I have long wished to discuss with you." Constantine's expression became guarded. "I wondered whether you had given any further thought to your baptism. It is most sad that you may not receive the Holy Eucharist. But avoidance of baptism, which would cleanse your soul, is the more pitiable."

Adding to the political justification, Constantine now revealed the impediment of his conscience. "I think not, my friend. The Lord isn't interested in so blackened a soul as mine."

"Ah, but he is—yours above others. The Lord is more merciful than you believe. Your life shines with virtues and charity. And you have done so much for Christianity. Our Lord Jesus must hold you very dear."

Constantine's voice became harsh. "Eusebius, you speak like a fool. Nothing can cleanse my soul. What I did—" He broke off and walked away. Eusebius shuffled after him.

"Emperor, God forgives all sins."

"Leave me, Eusebius. We shall speak no more of this."

"But, Emperor."

"Go! Leave me!" He shouted the command, and for the first time the bishop felt the full intensity of his friend's torment.

"I meant no harm," he cried in a tremulous falsetto. So shaken was the old man by the encounter that Constantine sent him back to the palace with an escort.

Quitting the Church of the Apostles, Constantine wandered to the forum beside the recently completed Hippodrome where workmen were placing a statue of him atop a great pillar. An old Greek Apollo had been appropriated, its head replaced with his own, wearing the seven-rayed nimbus.

Struggling to raise the huge figure, the workmen did not notice the object of the statue's glorification.

Eusebius had gone too far, he thought. All references to the tragedy were forbidden. As emperor he would continue to protect the Christian faith, although, in his fixation on his guilt, he believed God's redemption to be hopelessly distant.

Then he thought of the miraculous shroud resting in Melantias. It had been a magnificent experience shared with Crispus. He could remember their indescribable awe when they saw the holy image.

Was the relic still safe? He had guarded his knowledge of the shroud even from Eusebius. Once his mother, the saintly dowager Helena, had inquired about it. She had heard rumors. Now she was dead. Added to Constantine's agony was the lancinating awareness that grief over Crispus had hastened her end.

Constantine knew he must visit his friend Matthias. Perhaps the shroud could heal his inner wounds.

Once more dressed as a traveler, the emperor set forth for the village, fearing he was not worthy to look upon the shroud. He went directly to Matthias's house.

"Julian, it's you!" cried the old fellow. "How good of you to visit me again."

Seated outside in Matthias's garden, Constantine watched the River Athyras flowing toward the ultramarine waters of the Propontis. For moments, in his disguise, Constantine could feel that even his guilt was hidden and he was another person. Matthias and the emperor conversed as if from similar backgrounds. They shared an easy sense of comradeship. Constantine thought of revealing his identity, but reflection stayed him. As emperor he could have no real friends.

The two talked casually of ordinary things: that season's vintage, the local innkeeper who finally married off his homely daughter, a new cistern Matthias was building.

"The shroud," said Matthias, "is comfortingly near, as always. I tend it carefully; it is in perfect condition. My friend Julian, will you see it now?"

Constantine hesitated, unsure of himself. He declared that this trip was undertaken solely to renew his friendship with Matthias. On his next visit he would view the shroud. But his own words somehow shamed him; he dropped his eyes.

Matthias nodded. "As you wish." He offered some new wine and, after discussing its merits, posed the question Constantine had been dreading.

"How is your son? You should have brought him again. A truly amiable young man."

Had a courtier uttered these phrases, the emperor might have ordered him punished. But here in the shelter of anonymity, he could talk freely. "I have killed my son. It happened because of a tragic misunderstanding. A terrible mistake. At the moment it appeared justifiable. There seemed no other choice. Now my soul is blemished and my heart broken. I cannot bring him back; I cannot forgive myself." Never before had he been able to speak of it.

Matthias squeezed his eyes tight in a moment of shared anguish. He gripped Constantine's arm, saying, "Dear Julian, we shall pray for your son's soul, and for yours. It is almost too sad to think upon." Then he was silent, pondering something. "Yours is much like the story of our emperor." He shook his head. "But his tale seems the more piteous. That such tragedy should befall so good a man. Constantine has been touched by God Himself."

The emperor, again, was close to full revelation. He urgently needed to confess everything to one whom he could trust in full conscience. But his accustomed caution still prevailed. He said, "Because of my constant travels, I have heard little news. What are the people saying . . . about the royal murders?"

Matthias slapped his knee. "Ah, they know! The people know! It was that Fausta's doing—a bad woman. The emperor loved her. When a man loves, he is easily deceived."

So, people had perceived something of the truth. This, at least, is to the good, thought Constantine. False stories were being leaked by certain pagan elements and a few scribes. They had added substantially to his woe.

As he got up to depart, Constantine embraced Matthias in a rush of feeling. He prayed silently that one day God might again deem him worthy to look upon the shroud.

The year 336 marked the emperor's Tricennalia, anniversary of a thirty-year reign. Constantine was sixty-two, with much still to accomplish. Since the glorious victories shared with Crispus, he had lost the heart for battle, even to oppose the Goths, whose ruler, Irminric, now menaced his borders. He had not the will to deal with the Persian threat, nor with his three sons whose avaricious natures, inherited from their mother, would doubtless lead to civil war. But the new city delighted him; it was his mistress and, since Crispus's death, his only source of pleasure. He invited many Romans of good family to move to New Rome—some were already calling it Constantinople. There he built them villas, replicating their former houses, and gave them large, lucrative estates beyond the city. He was further comforted by the presence of the Christian bishops, survivors from Chrysopolis, who gratefully attended him as their duties allowed.

Chief among them was his dear Bishop Eusebius. It was proper at celebrations marking the Tricennalia that the bishop should make a laudatory address.

The emperor extended the invitation in person. "But, Eusebius, I fear we may be taxing your health. Please answer frankly. If, in any way, it should be inconvenient for you to speak, we shall understand." With a fond smile toward the bishop, the emperor added, "Though it would indeed be a sad loss not to hear the greatest orator of our times."

Eusebius's pale cheeks colored. "I dare even you, my Emperor, to keep me from it. I shall take a course of hot and cold baths so as to return to full vigor. Should my voice then waver, it will be from emotion, not weakness."

The celebration was to last two days. A brilliant gathering of court officials, bishops of the church, and citizens crowded into Constantine's Church of the Apostles to honor him.

A murmur spread through the crowd as the imposing ruler, robed in purple, moved down the center aisle. Encircling his brow was a narrow pearl-and-gold diadem. When he was seated on a gilded throne placed to one side of the great altar, the church erupted with acclamations of love and admiration.

Looking toward the rear of the church, Constantine sighted an unexpected visitor, Paphnutius. The crippled, half-blind Bishop of Egypt. He had not expected the disabled man to make the long trip. But there he was, refusing all aid, rising from his litter and dragging his body down the aisle toward the other bishops.

Constantine sprang up and moved to the great man's side. He kissed the bishop's cheek below the sightless eye; then, lifting his frail body, he carried Paphnutius in his arms to a place near the throne. "You honor me by your presence," he whispered to the protesting bishop.

Constantine's tender gesture so moved Eusebius that it was several minutes before the old man could begin.

His speech had been delivered once before at Jerusalem. Considered to be the finest oration of the age, it was now expanded and embellished. Though spoken in a quavering falsetto, Eusebius's words flowed from deep springs of feeling which ordinary men had not the talent to express. Those listening that day would never forget what he said.

"We have come here in celebration of the Supreme Sovereign, coruler with the Father in ages which have neither beginning nor end. The earthly sovereign we see before us has been honored by this All-Knowing God with the most praiseworthy reign of any who have ruled the Empire of the Romans. . . ."

Hearing Eusebius's words, Constantine felt ashamed. He had known and served four previous emperors, had founded a great city, freed thousands of Christians, seen Golgotha, and never lost a battle. Yet he had killed his son, his wife, and had been associated with the death of three of those emperors. The bishops regarded him as a Christian. But in his continuing sense of unworthiness he had never accepted baptism or confessed his sins.

Eusebius went on, "Our magnificent emperor, friend of an omniscient God, has gained his wisdom from a greater Wisdom, his goodness from Higher Good, his justness from the Eternal Judge. . . ."

That divine moment, thought Constantine, a cross in the sky near the Milvian Bridge. Would God ever again speak to him? Now more than ever he ached for a sign. A sign of forgiveness for the blood of an innocent son. And his own death? He welcomed it. But first, Lord, a sign!

Eusebius was tiring; his address was long. But in a final effort of will he began his conclusion: "The Supreme Sovereign, God Himself, shall stretch out His hand to him, proclaiming him victor over pretender and aggressor alike. . . ."

The next day at his beautiful Golden Palace, Constantine spent long hours listening to petitioners. As a special gift on his Tricennalia the emperor had offered to hear their requests. Early that morning people had already gathered outside. By the time the ruler took his place in the vast audience hall, the jostling crowd had swelled to enormous size. By late afternoon he was weary. He had sat listening, counseling, and granting favors since daylight. But still they came. The needy young woman with eight children whose husband had abandoned her; a peasant wanting replacement of a dead horse; a youth seeking palace employment . . . Advisors urged the emperor to rest, but he would not. Did God understand how much Constantine himself was a petitioner?

Then, at the back of the hall, he spotted a familiar face. The graybeard from Melantias. Constantine motioned for the room to be cleared and Matthias brought forward. His emperor would receive him alone.

As Matthias approached the throne, Constantine watched for the old man's astonishment when he recognized his friend "Julian." The emperor descended to stand beside Matthias. "Are you surprised, good comrade?"

The man seemed unperturbed. "No, my Emperor."

"Then you recognized me before?"

Matthias said nothing. Constantine saw he was carrying a bundle.

"Have I changed so much?"

"No, Emperor."

Constantine studied Matthias, and understood. The man from Melantias simply wished to spare him embarrassment. The revelations about Crispus's death. Matthias had realized the courage required to expose such painful memories. "So you knew all along who I was."

"Yes, Emperor. It was the story about your son. Forgive me."

Constantine put an arm about the bent shoulders. "There is nothing to forgive. I am grateful for my moments with you. They helped ease a very great burden." The emperor's eyes kept returning to the bundle Matthias was carrying. Could it be? "Let us walk a bit."

"Pardon this intrusion, my Emperor, on such an important day. I have come with a gift."

Constantine took Matthias's arm as they slowly circled the huge room. "But today everyone was here to ask *me* for a gift." The emperor sensed a strong pulsing in his temples.

"Not I. Jesus gave us Christians life eternal; you assured us of life here on earth. I have come to honor and thank you."

Constantine shook his head. "I am not deserving of your honor. You, more than many, must be aware of that."

Matthias halted and faced the emperor. "When you came to Melantias and I showed you the blessed shroud, though you were the most powerful ruler on earth, you did not compel me to give it up to you. You are my friend and the friend of all Christians. I beg you to accept it. It is yours." He held out the bundle. "Though this has remained with my family since the very beginning, it belongs to the world. And you are the world."

With unsteady hands Constantine took the roll of linen. Slowly he opened it and spread it across the marble steps that led to his throne. There it was. The faint, sepia-colored image of a crucified man, the Savior. So absorbed was he in examining the relic, Constantine was unaware that Matthias had left. Quickly he had him recalled. The emperor reassured Matthias of their continuing friendship and asked him to bring his family—his son and grandson—to live at court where they and their descendants could forever be near the shroud Matthias had so generously given.

Finally Constantine was alone with the relic. In truth it was a gift from God to him. The sign for which he had prayed. It was the expiation Rome's pagan priests had denied him, but which he had never stopped hoping Christianity would offer. This personal message from a merciful Lord that even the gravest sin might be washed clean by the petitions of a repentant soul.

Now the dark corners of his mind were flooded with light. He felt purified, sanctified, in touch with a mystery that knew no expression save rapturous feeling. Sinking to the steps and laying his head on the cloth, the emperor wept.

Chapter 11

Venice—Constantinople, 1200–1205

After Constantine's death the Christian city he had founded grew powerful. Constantinople's citizens believed theirs to be a "God-guarded" city. Because of its great wealth and preeminent position in the Christian world, Constantinople had been able to acquire most of Christendom's great relics: the drops of Christ's blood from Gethsemane, pieces of the True Cross, Moses' rod, Jacob's stone pillow, and—most awesome of all—the shroud of Jesus.

The shroud given Constantine by Melchi's descendant Matthias had been moved to several locations in the city. And with it moved the descendants of Matthias. The family had become part of the legend of Constantinople, revered as venerable figures. Wherever the shroud was housed, a branch of the family would be installed nearby, to live in luxury, dispensing good works.

At first the great relic remained where Constantine had placed it, in his Church of the Apostles. Later it was taken to the Pharos Chapel of the new palace. In 718, after a second serious threat to the city from marauding Saracens, it was secreted in a church at Blachernae, the city's most protected area.

No place in Christendom could equal Constantinople. Located at the juncture of East and West, it commanded a strategic commercial and political position. Its huge walls protected it from land attack. Incursions from the sea were virtually impossible because of immense seaward walls, a dangerous current, and the huge chain, on many floats, which denied access to its harbor. The iron links of this chain, each the length of a forearm, reached fifteen hundred feet across the Golden Horn. A traveler approaching from the north immediately sensed the city's allure. Its palaces and churches, gleaming with gold and mosaics, sprawled over seven hills. Long before reaching its gates, the visitor would be attracted by the faint odors of spices and floral essences carried inland on sea breezes.

Although it had several times been seriously threatened, the city had never been taken. Constantinople's citizens rested confident and complaisant.

Venice, their neighbor to the west, jealously guarded its position as Europe's leading sea-power. For centuries the Venetians had coveted Constantinople's far greater share of the world market. And since 1171, when Venetian traders living there had been massacred, Constantinople had been regarded as the Republic's mortal enemy. Yet no war had been declared; Venice was not yet strong enough to challenge such a rival.

During the week preceding Lent, in the year 1200, Venice's powerful Doge Enrico Dandolo saw the main chance. It was not obvious to others, but the elderly statesman, ruling the Republic as a great corporation and he its chief executive officer, was a man who enjoyed discerning those subtle possibilities not readily apparent to ordinary men.

Presiding in the impressive expanse of the Ducal Palace Collegium, Dandolo and the half-dozen members of his Inner Council received a delegation of six knights, representing some powerful barons of France and Flanders. The northern envoys were proposing a fourth Crusade to the Holy Land and wished to negotiate a contract with the doge. For a price to be agreed upon, they asked the Venetians to build and outfit a fleet. It would include sufficient vessels to transport forty-five hundred knights, nine thousand squires, twenty thousand foot soldiers, plus their equipment and horses.

Dandolo's wrinkled features and frail body belied his underlying vigor and sharp intelligence. An octogenarian, nearly blind, he was, nonetheless, a shrewd and effective manipulator. Addressing the group's spokesman, Geoffroy de Villehardouin, he invited the six envoys to stay the week in Venice as his guests. During that period he hoped to accomplish two objectives. First, to give his counselors time to become enthusiastic about the idea, which he favored. Second, to let the Franks cool their heels, thereby increasing their desire to accede to the price he would demand for such an extensive enterprise. He estimated that the endeavor would occupy virtually the entire state for a number of years. He calculated it was likely the barons might eventually be unable to meet their financial obligation—a situation which could be turned to his benefit.

Following the first meeting with the Frankish knights Dandolo devoted the rest of his day to a personal matter. Andrea Grimani, the young nobleman who served as his secretary and trusted confidant, was to be married. The doge had himself arranged the wedding festivities, to take place at the Ducal Palace. Andrea, a short-statured, serious-faced man of twenty-nine, planned to marry Pala dal Brusà. At sixteen Pala was one of the city's most beautiful young women. The markets of Rialto and the Merceria were alive with gossip concerning her surprising choice of young Grimani over the doge's own son, Rinieri. Ignorant of her early years, people were baffled.

When Pala was no higher than the purse which hung from her papa's belt, she had been taught a little game. Her father, Pietro, a widower, would open his strongbox and ask his only child to pile the gold and silver coins in stacks of ten. Checking her accuracy on her fingers, little Pala was always correct. Delighted, Pietro would cover her face with kisses or award her a sack of sweetmeats.

By the age of eleven she had virtually become dal Brusà's accountant and treasurer. She loved to finger and count the money which poured in from her father's extensive mercantile ventures: gold bezants from Byzantium, Sicilian ducats, Swiss bracteates, silver florins from Florence, the mintages of Savoy and Germany, Arab coins struck by the Crusaders, and, of course, Venice's piccoli, marcucci, and splendid silver grossi.

After a day's efforts his daughter would glow with pleasure from Pietro's invariable compliments.

Dal Brusà was the quintessential Venetian in his love of trade and profits. He would sit long hours with Pala, instructing her in his concepts of finance and business. He explained to the attentive girl that great profits came not from the usual unimaginative investments, but from more speculative risk-taking. It was the perception of newer markets and the undeveloped stuffs of trade which brought the highest returns. "Look to the future possibilities, rather than the past," he would say.

Misfortune struck the dal Brusàs when Pala was thirteen. It was reported that Pietro's two galleys, which carried highly valuable cargo from the East, had been taken by Saracen pirates. Pietro, aboard the lead ship, was killed during the attack. Having had bad luck during the previous two years, he had chosen to assure the renewal of his dwindling fortune by personally overseeing purchases of merchandise prior to the fateful return voyage.

The orphaned Pala moved to the modest palazzo of her father's sister. The woman, jealous of the girl's good looks and inheritance, proceeded to appropriate for herself the money which had accompanied Pala.

In choosing Andrea over Rinieri, Pala was guided by her father's past counsel. True it was that Rinieri Dandolo was the son of an affluent doge. But Pala saw him squandering much of his fortune on gambling and his large collection of expensive religious relics. In fact, with his indifference to trade, politics, and the advantages of his position, in time Rinieri would doubtless grow poorer, if not bankrupt. Andrea, with his close connections to the center of power, and his boundless promise, was the future. He offered the greater opportunity. Both men adored her. Though she preferred Rinieri, Pala elected not to vote with her heart, but rather her business sense.

Enrico Dandolo, wearing the vermilion mantle of his office, secured by a golden brooch, stood by the palace portals, awaiting the bride and her party. Onlookers, craning from tower windows or crowded onto balconies, cheered as the bridal barge, draped with cloth of gold, moved slowly down the Grand Canal. It was followed by a procession of gaily decorated *gondole* which bore the sixty female bridesmaids who would attend Pala's nuptials in the basilica of San Marco.

As the bride was helped onto the landing, a hundred white pigeons were released from atop San Marco. They circled in a pale flurry above the Piazza as the crowd sighed audibly. Pala, her ivory complexion flushed with excitement, was wearing a wedding gown of white silk, embroidered in gold and studded with pearls. Her long, sable-colored hair flowed loosely from beneath an ornate diadem. The bridal attendants, colored ribbons in their hair, wore silks in varying shades of blue, green, and violet.

"Today, more than any other," said the smiling doge, taking Pala's arm, "I wish for the gift of keener eyesight. You are lovely, my child." He patted the bride's hand as he led her past a band of fifes and drums toward the festooned entrance to San Marco.

In a city famous for its festivals and spectacles, the event brought fresh delight to the massed crowds. There was their doge doing exactly what they did: attending a wedding. And then there were the pastries! The spectators kept a hungry eye on the mountain of wine casks and nut-topped cakes awaiting the sound of San Marco's wedding chimes. All the cakes contained coins; most were copper, some silver, and a few gold.

From across the Piazza rode the bridegroom. His thin, intelligent face bespoke the scholar. Behind, leading a suite of eighteen friends of the groom, rode Rinieri, the doge's son. This day Rinieri, a handsome fellow Grimani's age, concealed his distress. His father had demanded he accept Andrea's invitation to serve as one of his groomsmen. All Venice knew the two had been close since childhood. Recently, however, they had followed widely divergent paths. Andrea, fluent in Latin and Greek, served the doge in all things, even advising him, when requested, on matters of state. Rinieri lived the life of a rich dilettante. The doge's son dispatched agents throughout the Mediterranean world and beyond, seeking costly holy relics from saints and martyrs to adorn his palazzo. They included such items as a tooth of St. Emerentineus and diminutive skulls from Herod's massacre of the Innocents, fresh from some Arabic cemetery.

From under his heavy-lidded eyes Rinieri studied the man who had stolen Pala from him. Despite the camaraderie, there had always existed, for Rinieri, a certain rivalry. Though the serious-minded Andrea was not a collector, it seemed to young Dandolo that his friend surpassed him in everything else.

Certainly Andrea saw more of his busy father than he. Rinieri yearned to spend time with his preoccupied parent; he admired the old man. And he felt growing resentment that Andrea's work allowed him to be so constantly in the doge's presence.

After the wedding ceremony a great banquet was held in the Ducal Palace, presided over by the elder Dandolo. Though the celebrations would extend over many days, none would exceed this event. The palace courtyard was bright with torches held by brilliantly costumed pages as the wedding party, family members, and attendants were welcomed by the doge and his son.

As Pala and Andrea proceeded up the staircase to where Rinieri stood, the doge's son moved forward, lost in his private thoughts, and stumbled, clutching his father.

"Are you ill?" asked Dandolo.

"I'm quite well, but it has been a very long day."

The doge was amused. "Remember, Rinieri? *I* am the old man. This morning I had a long meeting with envoys from the northern barons. Then I attended Andrea's wedding. Now, at this late hour, I am the host at a great banquet. Shouldn't I be leaning on you?"

Rinieri straightened and tried to smile. "Of course, Father. Please, take my arm."

Later it was proper that Rinieri should follow his father in publicly wishing the newlyweds well. The young man's words seemed halfhearted. "For Andrea and his bride I pray a long life." He failed to add the word "happiness."

Andrea, holding Pala's hand, wondered how his friend felt. Rinieri, also, had sought Pala in marriage. Fleetingly Grimani pondered why she had chosen so ordinary a fellow as himself.

While the guests feasted, the doge excused himself, pleading exhaustion. Quitting the dining hall, he paused beside Andrea and whispered something. Rinieri noted the exchange.

Later the doge's son decided to pay his father a good-night visit. It was something he had done as a child.

The old man was seated upright in bed, his gray locks covered with a white linen nightcap.

"Father, it is I," called Rinieri from the doorway.

"Oh, son," said the doge. "I thought you were Andrea."

Rinieri felt hurt. Why couldn't his father show some affection? "I simply wanted to say good-night. Remember, I used to do that when I was little?"

"Yes, I remember." Dandolo smiled. "Tell me, did you approve of my arrangements for the wedding festivities?"

"The day was perfect, Father."

"That is my impression." Dandolo yawned. "I am truly tired."

"I shan't stay any longer."

"You were kind to come and see me, my son. I am expecting Andrea any moment now. If you see him, tell him to hurry. I am eager to speak of something with him."

Scarcely concealing his irritation, Rinieri quit the bedchamber.

Shortly after young Dandolo had departed, Andrea arrived in the doge's apartment. He apologized for his lateness, saying the banquet had just ended.

Doge Dandolo queried his confidant about the Frankish diplomats' proposal.

Andrea nodded. "I feel favorably toward it. Excellency, the building and outfitting of these ships would involve every man in the Republic. But with your prestige and knowledge I am certain you can accomplish this formidable task. How much are the Crusaders prepared to pay?"

Dandolo flashed his guileless smile. "It is my impression they will pay whatever we ask. More than thirty thousand, so they say, will take the Cross and become Crusaders. To me that seems scarcely possible. But should the barons be unable to pay the full sum, there are other services they could render us.

"There is something else I wish to tell you, my boy," continued the old man. "Should this project get under way, I plan to offer myself as leader of the Crusade."

Stunned, Andrea protested. "Excellency, you must not. Your age, your eyesight . . ."

"Let's hear none of that. As to my age, I was elected to the dogeship as, well, not a young man. And I can feel my energy. It equals that of three men half my age. You should know that. As for my eyes . . . what can I say? My failing vision troubles me far more than the matter of my years."

Grimani had heard tales about the doge's blindness.

"Do you know how this happened?" he said, pointing to his face. "Long ago, when I was on a peace mission in Constantinople, the most terrible man who ever lived, Emperor Manuel, attempted to blind me. That wretched Byzantine feared that when I became doge, I would move against him. Here, only seducers of children and robbers may be blinded.

"One morning, when I was walking alone, Manuel's guards seized me. Holding me down and opening my eyelids, they forced me to look into the bright sun. That's what did it." His face became pained with the memory. "I wanted to declare war that instant. But at the time, we lacked sufficient monies to assure a victory. My sight is a reality with which I must live. Now —I have one more thing to say." He yawned.

"If you are tired, Excellency, perhaps it might wait?"

Dandolo laughed. "Could you possibly wish to be somewhere else? I know, I was young once."

"There is nothing else," quickly responded Grimani. "Your concerns are my prime interest."

"What I want to say is this: when I take the Cross and leave for the Holy Land—should we complete the pending arrangements, of course—I shall want to appoint you vice-doge."

"Excellency. I am only a secretary. It would be unthinkable."

"I can trust you. You are familiar with the operation of the State. It shall be as I wish."

"But what of Rinieri, Excellency?"

Dandolo shook his head. "Rinieri? A good lad—charming. But he is too inexperienced; simply not qualified. Rinieri is interested only in his own affairs."

"It might easily seem so to one who knows him less well than I. Excellency, your many duties have understandably kept you from your son these past years. Rinieri is a bright and capable man. I have seen evidence of that. I respectfully suggest you give him a fair chance to prove himself as vice-doge. I am confident you will not be disappointed. And wherever your future takes you, my place should be at your side."

As Andrea pleaded Rinieri's case, a vision from boyhood sprang to mind. Rinieri and he were participating in the popular sport *forza d'Ercole*. Andrea was climbing to the top of a five-tier pyramid of youths balancing on poles fixed between two canal boats. While Grimani carefully mounted his friend's shoulders, Rinieri's father shouted from the crowd, "Come on, finish it, Andrea!"

Imperceptibly Rinieri twitched an arm, and Andrea plunged into the water.

Now Andrea mused: vice-doge? The top of an even more critical pyramid? But one should be fair. "Yes, Excellency, it is proper that you appoint your son."

Nodding, Dandolo responded, "Let me think about it. Perhaps you are correct."

Pala awaited her new husband in their bedroom at the small palazzo Grimani had recently inherited from his father. She had been crying. "Does our wedding night mean nothing to you? I have been lying here for hours."

Andrea rushed to embrace her, explaining his delay. When she understood that the doge had summoned him, Pala grew suddenly calm. "Tell me what was so important that it could not have waited until tomorrow?"

At the mention of Dandolo's invitation to serve as vice-doge during the Crusade, Pala threw her arms around him. "Oh, Andrea, it's what I hoped would happen. At last you will have the importance and influence you deserve. It will be a first step toward the dogeship and great riches."

Grimani told her he had turned down the offer, suggesting Rinieri in his place. Pala looked incredulous. "You—turned down the offer? How could you? Are you out of your mind?"

"Pala, Pala," Andrea cried, shocked by her reaction to what seemed so right. "I had to be fair to Rinieri. Think, darling, we have our love for each other and the promise of much happiness ahead."

She gazed at her husband despairingly. "Maybe it's not too late. Go to him. Tell him you have changed your mind. The doge might reconsider."

Shaking his head, Andrea responded, "I am simply not that sort of man. It is out of the question."

Pala collapsed in a fit of weeping. "You have wasted our life. I should have married Rinieri."

On the balcony of his palazzo a disconsolate Andrea stared out at the dark shapes of elder trees lining the canal before him. What have I done, he thought. My marriage is already failing. As if in response came the somber Rialtina, tolling the curfew.

Within a week the envoys from Flanders and France were again summoned to the Collegium. Doge Dandolo informed them he and his advisors were in accord. Venice would build the Crusaders' fleet for the sum of eighty-five thousand silver marks. After reviewing the proposition overnight, the knights agreed.

Two years passed, during which all of Venice labored on the enormous project. Personally inspecting the 480 vessels in preparation, the calculating Dandolo came to some conclusions he kept to himself.

Finally, at the beginning of the year 1202, all was ready. The Crusader leaders were received in Venice. Shortly after their arrival, the powerful Baldwin of Flanders and several others paid a visit to the doge. Informing him that only a third of the knights expected had joined the Crusade, they explained their available funds would fall far short of the stipulated eighty-five thousand marks.

Dandolo, who had expected from the outset that the Franks could not meet his price, now saw his opportunity to set into motion the first stage of the plan he had long been hatching.

Turning his back to the barons, he shrugged. "I have completed my part of our arrangement. How will you fulfill yours?"

"Your Excellency," said Boniface of Montferrat, "we are prepared to pledge our personal funds. And others will do the same. But even so, the full sum cannot be raised."

Baldwin, a young man of intense energy, added, "We can devise no further plan beyond our own pledges. However, there will be great conquests. Then, be assured we will meet our obligation to you."

This was the moment for which Dandolo had been waiting. He turned and faced the anxious barons. "There is a port on the east coast of the Adriatic, Zara. For many years Zara existed under our protection. But now, alas, the King of Hungary claims it." He raised his voice. "Though we are a powerful nation, we have been unable to regain our rightful possession. Perhaps, with your help . . ."

The towering, white-haired Boniface interrupted. "But Your Excellency, Zara is a Christian city. We are embarked upon a holy Crusade against the Infidel."

Dandolo smiled slightly. "It was merely a thought. For your assistance in returning Zara to us, we would be willing to postpone your obligation. I know in proposing this I speak for the Great Council of the Republic. Later you could continue on to Jerusalem and pay us the monies owed when God grants you rich conquests."

The barons had been snared and they knew it. There was no choice but to agree. However, such a bargain stuck in their throats. Facing the prospect of attacking a Christian city, many knights returned home.

The doge's private plan, which had been revealed only to Andrea, was publicly announced a month before the Crusaders were to set out. Prior to a great Mass held in San Marco for both Franks and Venetians, Dandolo spoke affectingly from the pulpit of the great Crusade and of the barons who would risk lives and fortunes for God's glory. Then, kneeling in front of the altar, he faced his people.

"I am old and frail, my eyes are dim, and I should be taking my ease. But before I die, it is my hope to truly serve Our Lord. Therefore I beseech these great and good nobles to let me be the first citizen of this Republic to take the Cross. I shall go to Jerusalem; I shall lead the Crusade. We will conquer!"

A stunned silence followed. Sensing the moment, Baldwin of Flanders leaped forward. Tearing two small white strips of cloth from his tunic, he made a cross and placed it on the doge's red cloth cap. Waiting trumpeters saw Dandolo's slight nod and sounded a brilliant fanfare. The basilica erupted with cheers. Venetians flocked to the altar to take the Cross and follow their doge to Jerusalem.

Boniface and Baldwin, watching the pandemonium, and suddenly aware of the power of this charismatic leader, found themselves, like the others, cheering the old doge. How could they foresee what Enrico Dandolo's presence was to mean to their future and to the future of all Christendom?

On a crisp morning in early October the Crusaders were ready to depart. Each noble commanded a ship and transport. The doge controlled an armada of fifty galleys. Brightly blazoned shields of the northern knights hung from their ships' bulwarks. The barons' banners flew aloft.

Enrico Dandolo's vermilion-sided ship was in the lead. As he came on board, from atop ornamented wooden castles fore and aft rose the strains of a hymn, "Veni Creator Spiritus," sung by a great chorus of clergymen. A smart wind whipped the Adriatic waters as sails snapped open. Over the dull, rhythmic boom of gongs which maintained the stroke of the rowers, crowds onshore shouted emotional farewells. One hundred silver trumpets sounded a fanfare. They were under way.

In Zara, after a mere five-day siege, Dandolo achieved an astonishing victory. The Crusaders elected to winter there before moving on to their objective, Jerusalem.

During that time Boniface of Montferrat, who had traveled north, met Prince Alexius, deposed heir to the throne of Constantinople. Emperor Isaac Angelus, Alexius's father, had been blinded and removed from the throne by Isaac's brother, who now ruled the Byzantines as Alexius III. The former emperor was being held in a Constantinople prison but his son had managed to escape to the northern land of Swabia. Offering very attractive terms, the young Alexius invited Boniface and the Crusaders to make another detour. He promised two hundred thousand silver marks if the Crusaders could deliver the throne to him.

The offer was altogether tempting. Though Boniface had no

liking for the young fop, he resolved to plead his case. Returning to Zara, he discussed Alexius's offer with Dandolo and the barons.

Later Dandolo dined alone with Andrea. The doge was unusually excited. Grimani, who had already learned of the offer, hardly expected Dandolo to acquiesce. After all, Constantinople was the most powerful place on earth, center of the Eastern Church.

"You have eaten nothing, Excellency. Does your stomach trouble you?"

"Not at all. You know I never eat while I'm thinking, Andrea."

"The proposal from the Byzantine prince?"

"At last, Andrea, it has come. The opportunity to make our Republic the greatest state on earth. Think of it. The wealth of Byzantium!

"Have you heard of the Holy Shroud, my friend? Once I saw it displayed in one of their churches. That was before they tried to destroy my sight. Not only shall I have my revenge for that but the shroud of Jesus will be ours."

Horrified, Andrea broke in. "Your Excellency, never before have I questioned any of your decisions. You are the greatest man I have known. But now I must argue with your reasoning. A great leader such as you should not, must not, act out of personal vengeance. What you are contemplating cannot be justified."

Harshly, Dandolo said, "You are naive. I do not make decisions of state for personal reasons. Yet, think. This Alexius, he would be our creature, our puppet. At last we could have control of the greatest power on earth."

"But to put this, ah, creature on the throne requires war."

"Of course."

Andrea was quiet. He felt only revulsion for Dandolo's reasoning.

"You say nothing, Andrea. You do not approve of me?"

"I have loved you like my own father. And I shall never leave your side. But how can I condone this decision? Nor, I believe, would Our Lord."

Dandolo laughed. "Ah, so you think you speak for God. Well, maybe so. But should I be required to give up my soul for the good of the Republic, I surely will. This is the course responsible leaders must choose."

Andrea was deeply troubled by what he perceived was to follow. Yet he said nothing more. All that he felt was penned in the diary he had kept since his difficult marriage to Pala. Andrea's personal journal often seemed to be his only comfort.

As the fleet prepared its detour to Constantinople, again many disillusioned Crusaders deserted. One of the most important of these was Simon de Montfort. And with him went a young French knight, Andrea's new friend, the handsome and devout Denis de Croissy. Denis was a year older than Andrea. He had first served de Montfort as squire and now was his second in command. Denis and Andrea had been drawn together because of the special idealism each recognized in the other. Grimani's despair over the pragmatic doge and what he feared Venice was becoming could be expressed openly to his friend. De Croissy had been distressed by the outrage at Zara. After the decision was reached to go on to Constantinople, the young knight confided his plan to return to Paris.

"So you will not follow de Montfort to Syria?" asked Andrea. The two were seated on Zara's broken battlements. It was a fine day in early spring; the sea a gemlike blue. "I understand the baron will travel there with others to await an additional force of Crusaders."

"I doubt it. For myself, this whole business has been sickening. Do you know of the Knights Templars? They are a great and holy Order, with many members and chapterhouses throughout Europe. I plan to join them." Struck by an idea, Denis clutched Andrea's arm. "Come with me, Andrea. We will go to Paris together and become Templars."

Andrea smiled sadly. "I have a wife."

Denis persisted. "Yes, but the Order accepts married men. You could serve for a limited time, spending, say, two years with us."

Thinking how disappointed he was with his marriage, Grimani was tempted to say yes. But suppressing the impulse, he resolved to proceed with the doge.

"God go with you, Denis," he said. "You will always be my friend." The two clasped arms, then embraced.

"Andrea," said Denis, "in the event you should ever need me, contact the Templars at Paris. I shall never forget you."

With the arrival of the Byzantine Prince Alexius, Dandolo and his forces moved on to Constantinople. Observing the prince's behavior, Andrea was even more appalled by the doge's decision to back him. Alexius strutted the deck in garish silks, nibbling slabs of honeyed panforte, and from time to time disappeared below with certain sailors. At other times the prince would guzzle wine until he collapsed, snoring, on a coil of rope. Though the eccentric Alexius seemed a curious candidate for ruler, the doge recognized he must serve as the justification for what was to come.

At the end of June 1203 the Crusaders at last beheld the golden city. Beyond the harbor entrance they could see the gleam of imposing towers and above them all the mighty dome of Santa Sophia, afloat like a shimmering bubble.

As they dropped anchor, the Crusaders decided to openly make known their intent: the return to the throne of the state's rightful rulers, Prince Alexius and his imprisoned father, Isaac. Galleys were to be rowed as closely as possible to the city's high seaward rampart. Alexius would be stationed at the bow of the doge's lead ship, displayed for all to see.

Hundreds of Constantinople's citizens crowded onto the walls to watch the odd procession. As the ship carrying Alexius sailed by, trumpeters sounded a call and heralds proclaimed the arrival of the Byzantines' legitimate ruler. Then the prince, in his unctuous voice, called out, "People of Constantinople! I am come, at last, your true emperor!" Stretching out his arms, he gazed beatifically at the crowded battlements.

Faced with this bizarre personage, people began laughing and hooting. "You, our emperor?" shouted one citizen. "We never heard of you."

Others called, "Go home to your mother!" Turning their backs, several men contemptuously dropped their breech-clouts. Observing this show of bare buttocks, Alexius's face betrayed a mixture of high pique and low desire.

Seeing the collapse of their theatrical plan to return Alexius without a struggle, the Crusaders knew they must now take

Constantinople by force. Their first objective was the heavily guarded Galata Tower, terminal point of the great harbor chain. After a fierce fight the Crusaders won the tower and released the huge windlass controlling the chain. Venetian galleys rowed unhindered up the Golden Horn.

Eventually the effete citizens of Constantinople proved no match for the invaders. The city fell; Alexius rescued his father from prison, and together they assumed the throne as co-rulers. But Alexius's promise of two hundred thousand silver marks for his protectors had been a deception.

The Franks soon learned they were not going to get their money. Added to this was a resentment that long had simmered between the Western and Eastern Churches over papal jurisdiction and the Byzantine manner of worship, as well as Byzantium's close ties to the Islamic world. Moreover, the Frankish rank and file, with their brutish ways and total contempt for the finer amenities of life, resented Constantinople's exquisite culture and refinement. Storming the city a second time, the Crusaders could not be restrained. Surging through the streets, drunk and shouting their battle cry, "Holy Sepulchre," they began three days of looting, burning, and raping. Even nuns in the many convents were not spared. Crashing into houses and churches, they smashed altars and furnishings to obtain gold and gems. Loot was carried to three churches and heaped in gigantic piles for eventual division among the leaders. But much more was secreted and stolen.

Andrea and the doge followed the sack from atop a roof of the palace they had occupied. As Andrea, in a choking voice, tried to describe the horrible scene, Dandolo could hear the screams of women being assaulted, the neighing of frightened horses, the howls of men drunken with unrestricted license and Byzantine wine. He wept.

"Oh, my God, I could not control them; forgive me. Andrea, you, too, must not blame me; it is the price one must pay."

Grimani said nothing. "I would rather be dead," bemoaned the doge, "than part of such a thing. The Franks are beasts." Then he remembered the shroud of Jesus, the relic he had come here to obtain for the people of Venice. Even now it might be destroyed. Dandolo recalled having seen it at a small church, St. Mary's, in the suburb of Blachernae. He begged Andrea to go there at once.

Moving northward through debris-filled streets, Andrea encountered bands of carousing knights, blood on their clothing, laden with plunder: chalices and icons from churches, jewels and plate from private homes. Passing Santa Sophia, he noticed its silver and gold doors had been hacked to pieces. Mules were being led in and out to carry away the booty. The bawdy songs of a whore resounded from within its sanctuary.

Nauseated by the stink of smoke which was everywhere, Andrea finally arrived at Blachernae. Its great palace was being plundered by a contingent of Flemish archers. But oddly enough, upon entering nearby St. Mary's, he saw the place was deserted. It had not been touched. Standing in the flickering light of altar lamps, he could only faintly hear the tumult outside. All sanity and peace seemed to have fled the world and settled in this quiet place. Andrea knew the shroud must still be here. He had to find it; no time could be lost. At any moment those drunken madmen might burst through the doors.

Moving behind the richly decorated altar, Andrea began his search. In the darkness he groped for a closet or a niche where the reliquary might be secreted. Suddenly he tripped over something.

The "something" wailed, "Don't hurt me! Please don't hurt me!" It was the voice of a young boy speaking Greek. One of the Byzantines.

Responding in the same language, Grimani said, "I shall not harm you. Don't be frightened." A small figure came to life, rising slowly. In the deep shadows Andrea could not make out a face.

"What were you doing down there?"

The youngster was so afraid he could say nothing intelligible.

"Come now," Andrea said, "you are safe here. I have other business than frightening children." Gently he led him to the half light of the sanctuary. Now Grimani could see the dark-complexioned youngster. His eyes seemed far too large for the classical lines of his face. He was about ten.

"What is your name, lad?" Andrea spoke softly.

"Theo, your lordship, Theo Metochites."

"Theo, you must leave this church. The situation is perilous. It is best that you come with me." He would protect this child. Though such a kindness meant little compared with the carnage taking place in this city, it eased Andrea's conscience.

"I cannot leave here, your lordship."

Andrea said, "I have come to rescue the shroud of Jesus. Do you know where it is kept?"

Theo stammered that he did not know where it was.

"Theo, the Doge of Venezia wishes to take the shroud to safety. If you do not help me find it, the rabble on the streets are sure to storm in and burn it."

Starting to cry, Theo sank to the floor and clung to the Venetian's legs. Andrea patted the youngster's head.

"I promise I will not harm you, Theo. But be quick. It must be found now."

Theo looked up at Andrea. "If I show you the relic, will you let me stay with it? My family has always been near it—since long, long ago."

Grimani realized this child must be an important link to the great relic. "What happened to your parents?" he asked.

"My mother died when I was little. Those terrible men murdered my father in the street." He sobbed. "When I ran here, the priests took me in. But they were killed defending the quarter. Now *I* must guard the blessed relic."

Andrea gently reassured him that the shroud would be safe where it was to be taken. The Doge of Venice planned to house it in the great basilica of San Marco.

"But may I go there, too—to Venezia? It is part of the legend: if we abandon the shroud, bad luck will follow."

After Grimani promised Theo he would be allowed to stay with the relic, the boy led him back behind the altar.

"There." He pointed to the marble floor. "I was trying to hide it."

In the dimness Andrea saw a silver chest. The boy had been huddled over it. No time could be risked to check its contents. Andrea lifted it and hurried out of the church with Theo.

In the smoke and confusion of the streets no one paid attention to someone carrying a mere silver chest. The Crusaders were now at work chopping up the huge Greek bronzes brought centuries before by Emperor Constantine for his new city.

"Why are they doing that?" cried Theo, watching men with battleaxes hacking away at an enormous statue of Hercules.

"They will melt down the bronze and sell it later," said Andrea regretfully. He remembered the doge once telling him that every householder of Constantinople was, by law, entitled to his own view of a statue or monument.

Dandolo wept when, at last, he fingered the linen of Jesus' burial garment. With his failing sight he was unable to see the image of Christ. But young Theo described it, then recounted some of the legends which connected it to his family. Dandolo directed Andrea to treat the boy well. "Theo shall stay with Pala and me so long as he wishes," promised Andrea.

After secreting the cloth, Grimani assured Dandolo that should the old man die before returning to Venice, the shroud would nevertheless rest on the altar of San Marco. He would see to it. And he would proclaim it to be the doge's legacy to his people.

Within a week the rape of Constantinople was complete. Enrico Dandolo, compelled to remain and assist the Crusaders in the struggle to consolidate their conquest, fell gravely ill within the year.

Two weeks before his end, concerned that the shroud and some other valuables might fall into the hands of the Franks, the doge dispatched Andrea and Theo, with three galleys, back to Venice. Upon his arrival Grimani discreetly smuggled the shroud from his ship.

After a brief reunion with Pala, Andrea went directly to Rinieri's apartments in the Ducal Palace. Drawing Rinieri aside, Andrea reported that he had brought back the miraculous shroud of Jesus, and further, that it was Doge Dandolo's precise wish that this relic belong to all the people of Venice. It was to be presented by his son to the basilica of San Marco.

Stung by the implied rejection, tears came to Rinieri's eyes. He angrily declared Grimani to be a liar. Without question Dandolo intended it as a gift for his own son whom he dearly loved. It would be the crown jewel of Rinieri's private collection. The vice-doge's assertion was made with force and implicit threat.

Confronted by this dilemma, Grimani quickly apologized, saying several days would be required to recover the relic from its place of concealment in the heavily laden hold of the ship. Rinieri impatiently ordered his friend to be quick about it but did agree, after much debate, to expose the shroud, once, at a Mass in San Marco.

From his palazzo Andrea summoned an artist he had retained in the past to paint a miniature portrait of Pala. Told to study the shroud, the man was then given a couple of silver grossi. Andrea directed him to assemble his art materials and buy a linen length of similar weave and dimension from a cloth merchant along the Merceria.

Returning the next day with a long bolt of fabric which was of virtually identical weave, the artist set about the unaccustomed work of replicating the shroud image. It required painting on a far larger scale than he had ever attempted before. Andrea, always present, required the man to remain at the Grimani palazzo during the duplication process. Everyone was barred from their work chamber; no one could guess what was going on.

The artist's first effort seemed all wrong. It failed to reproduce the original's mysterious quality, and the rivulets of painted blood lacked authenticity.

While they were discussing their next attempt, Andrea received a scorching letter from Rinieri, reiterating his contempt for Grimani's lies and reasserting the vice-doge's argument that the shroud was rightfully his possession, but, as promised, would be displayed once in San Marco before the year was out. He was growing tired of the delay, he wrote, and expected prompt delivery of the relic or Andrea would regret it.

The artist's next effort, although a great improvement, failed to reproduce the original's ancient look and the matter of the bloodstains remained a problem.

Drawing his stiletto, Andrea made a small cut across a vein and allowed his blood to run into a glass vessel. It would serve as a more authentic pigment. But the shroud still seemed too new.

With some trepidation they decided to bake the counterfeit linen lightly in an oven. The task was accomplished during the nighttime hours while the kitchen domestics slept. By inspecting their handiwork every other minute, they were able to pull it from the oven at the precise moment when all the colors were just right. The result was remarkably similar.

Andrea paid the artist for his labors, enjoining him to perpetual silence. He would be the recipient of severe treatment by the Church if the truth were ever to be disclosed.

In order to mark the genuine from the copy, Grimani wrapped the true shroud in red silk, hiding it with the other in a heavy *forziere*. Then he returned to the vice-doge and explained that after much reflection, he would not reveal the relic's whereabouts until Rinieri promised to abide by his father's request.

In an explosion of fury and chagrin Rinieri ordered his former friend arrested. Imprisoned in a dank cell at the lowest level of the palace, Andrea was deprived of all food except for an occasional piece of bread, and allowed only a daily ration of water. Each afternoon for three days Rinieri visited him. Carefully watching the imprisoned man, he would eat a leg of steaming chicken or wave a piece of hot roast meat before him.

"Tell me where it is and you are free. I promise you a feast."

Andrea was convinced he must endure this torment awhile longer, to make his plan fully credible. A week later Rinieri arrived with tears in his eyes and told Andrea that his father had died in Constantinople. "He has left me a token of his love—the sacred shroud. And I shall have it!"

Now that the doge was dead, Andrea feared Rinieri would use harsher methods to force information from him. The vice-doge must soon relinquish his office, since the dogeship was not hereditary. Andrea gave the jailer all of the silver coins he had concealed in the lining of his jerkin to smuggle Pala into the basement prison. The time had come to put his plan to work.

It was obvious that Pala did not relish entering such a depressing place. The jailer left her a lantern, and in its light she confronted her weak, sunken-eyed husband. She cried, "I cannot believe Rinieri would do this to you."

Though talking now tired him, Andrea slowly explained his scheme to her. "I have a friend in Paris, one of the Templars. His name is Denis de Croissy. You must immediately sail with the true shroud to France. You are to leave the relic with Denis and the Templars for safekeeping. I trust de Croissy. After the Council holds an election and Rinieri steps down, Denis will return the relic to us. With a new doge it can at last be safe in San Marco. Please, don't delay. I cannot hold out much longer." And he told where the strongbox key was concealed.

As soon as Pala sailed, Andrea would surrender to Rinieri's demand and reveal the shroud's location—the false shroud. He felt sure the vice-doge would then release him. Pala therefore must not fail to send word of her departure through his jailer.

Telling him not to worry, that she would do as he directed, Pala hurried back to their palazzo and went immediately to the chest where the two shrouds were hidden. Carrying both to her bedroom, she closed the door. Tossing the red silk that covered one of them to the floor, she unfolded both pieces of linen. Amazing! Identical in every detail. She remembered what Andrea had once told her: this relic was the most valuable object on earth. But what did he know about values? Idly Pala wondered what sort of price it would fetch on the open market. She studied the two shrouds. So perfectly similar were they that when it came to refolding them, she could not decide which cloth was genuine. Frantically she unfolded them again, examining each minutely. It was hopeless. But what was the difference? They were the same. Arbitrarily Pala chose one, wrapped it in the red silk, and called for Theo. She would take him with her to Paris.

Everything went smoothly. Pala quickly located the captain of a merchant vessel who took the purse of grossi she offered. According to their deal he cast off within twelve hours after Andrea's jailer had been notified. The ship was bound for Bruges via Almería, Lisbon, Bayonne, and Portsmouth. From Bruges she would go by road south to Paris.

But was Pala carrying the true shroud? From that day on no one could ever be sure.

Chapter 12

Venice—Paris, 1205

As soon as his jailer reported that Pala and Theo had left port, Andrea asked to be taken to the vice-doge. Begging Rinieri's forgiveness, he revealed where the shroud could be found. Rinieri immediately sent a courier to the Grimani palazzo. When the man returned with the linen cloth, the vice-doge set Andrea free.

To honor his father's last request Dandolo displayed the relic in the basilica of San Marco at a great Mass attended by most of Venice. After the ceremonies Rinieri locked the relic in a gold-inlaid chest which he kept in his private suite at the Ducal Palace.

So greatly did the Venetians respect what was believed to be the old doge's wishes, that no one questioned his son's possession of the shroud.

Rinieri had convinced himself that the shroud was part of his inheritance, given him by a father who had loved him very much. At night, thinking of the old doge, Rinieri would sometimes arise and remove the shroud from its container. Looking at it, he would feel comforted.

Seven weeks later, after an uneventful voyage, Pala reached Paris. Unlike the narrow, angling pathways bordering Venetian canals and marshes, the vistas of Paris were open. Visitors gained an immediate sense of a great city, alive with people who bustled through its streets alongside a rattling traffic of carts and wagons. Pala found the atmosphere exciting, and resolved to see everything.

She and Theo settled at an inn close by the Temple walls. Their room fronted on Rue de la Corderie above a ground-floor tavern. Her four servants were lodged in the attic.

The morning after their arrival Theo was sent to contact Denis de Croissy. Understanding that Templars held themselves aloof from women, Pala thought it best to let her young companion initiate the temporary transfer of the shroud.

The religious and military Order of the Temple occupied an entire fortified quarter of the Seine's right bank. Ringed by a ditch and a high wall, the Paris Temple formed an autonomous unit, free of Crown taxes, having its own jurisdiction, wharf, and armed guards. Its great tower, flanked by four smaller towers, could be seen for miles around.

The Templars, answerable only to the pope, were fierce Crusaders and protectors of the Holy Land, but they had also achieved a reputation as the world's leading bankers and money-lenders. France's royal treasury was secured within the citadel.

Knights of the Order cut their hair short and allowed their beards to grow untended. After their initiation they did not drink, gamble, or hunt—except the lion, which roamed those far-off lands where they fought the Infidel. They dined simply and undertook their rituals in secrecy. By 1205, nearly a century after their founding, the Templars were known throughout the world for their power, honesty, and vast wealth.

Stopping at the Temple's main entrance, Theo called out in the French he had been taught by his ship's captain, "I seek the knight Denis de Croissy. I bring an important message from Venezia."

One of the guards, dressed in a brown mantle with the red Templar cross upon breast and shoulder, disappeared into a sentry house, reappearing at the open portcullis grill. "I am not familiar with this member of the Order," he said. "There are two thousand of us here. We can't know everybody. So wait, boy. I shall send for someone who may help you."

Since the guard made no move to raise the portcullis, Theo settled against the wall of a large townhouse across the street. Suspending his curiosity about the world beyond the Temple walls, he found himself turning to thoughts of Venice. Theo silently prayed that Andrea would be released from imprisonment.

"You, boy!" shouted the guard. "Come here."

Theo walked back across the drawbridge. The guard had returned with an aging official, who carried a thick sheaf of parchments. After reassuring himself of the seriousness of Theo's mission, and verifying the name of de Croissy, he searched through his lists. Finally he called through the bars of the portcullis. "I regret that you will have to inform whoever seeks him that the knight Denis de Croissy is not with us at present."

"Then where can I find him?"

"It is not so much a question of where, but when. It is noted here"—he scrutinized his roster—"that de Croissy was dispatched to our headquarters—Cyprus—ten days ago. It looks to me like he was delivering our quarterly reports. The answer to 'when' is probably in the next ninety days. I ought to know; I used to make the trip myself."

Theo was advised to await de Croissy's return with patience.

Pala was absent when he returned to the inn. Eager to see more of Paris, she had gone out to stroll the nearby streets carrying the folded and wrapped shroud with her. Her father had told her that risk-taking should not preclude a certain prudence. Pala never forgot.

Peering into workshops of the quarter's market area, she was disappointed to find all were devoted to things which did not interest her: ropes, harnesses, saddles, nails, and barrels. And, unable to speak French, she could not locate any of the hat makers, dressmakers, or fabric dealers whom she had hoped to visit.

As she neared her lodgings, exasperated, Pala uttered aloud the words, "Oh, to speak French—how maddening!"

A rich, low voice with, she thought, a Genoese accent addressed her in heartening Italian. Pala turned to face a handsome man in his twenties who was dressed in high style, *alla spagnuola*. He was wearing a close-fitting red cap and short red jerkin, under which he sported such tight-fitting pink silk hose as to seem positively immodest. His curled brown hair fell to the shoulders; his chin was dimpled.

"Ah, her language is as fair as her face," he said, flashing his even white teeth.

When Lorenzo della Comba introduced himself and told her he was staying at the same inn, Pala accepted his invitation to a tumbler of wine in the tavern. They chatted pleasantly until midday. She learned that Lorenzo, from Genoa, was a merchant-trader, a man of commerce just like her father. He was, further-more, unmarried—a widower.

In his easy, self-assured way, Lorenzo discussed the market for red damask, the demand for cloves, the price of slaves and grain, how Russian furs could be bartered for cotton from the Levant. He had a quietly confident manner and, to Pala, seemed all knowing. She wished Andrea could be just like this lovely man.

Pala found herself laughing delightedly at his observations on the wide, exotic world he traveled. Looking intently into his long-lashed brown eyes, she prayed he would not soon depart Paris.

Della Comba, in turn, was astonished by this handsome young woman who was not only interested in mercantile matters, but could discuss them intelligently, with zestful charm. Quite unlike the ladies of Genoa, who invariably limited themselves to local gossip or details of social gatherings and festive dinners.

He knew a tavern near the Seine, famed for its excellent sea-food. Pala gaily accepted his invitation. But before leaving, she asked the tavern owner to send some food to Theo and instruct him to go to bed early. Lorenzo, learning that Pala was childless and the lad merely a kind of errand runner, insisted on paying for Theo's meal. He added a large beaker of strong ale, asserting that the child should enjoy some Parisian brew.

Watching the riverboats with their cargoes of foodstuffs and merchandise, the two talked on into the afternoon. Pala realized that to her fascination with Lorenzo was now added a certain deeper feeling, and she felt suddenly depressed when Lorenzo informed her that he planned soon to depart for Bruges. He held an option to buy a fine ship moored by the nearby inlet, no later than month's end.

To shift the subject Pala remarked, "You probably are wondering what is contained in this package I have been carrying." Lorenzo smiled politely. "It happens to be," she said, "the shroud of Jesus Christ." Lorenzo's wine spilled across the remnants of a large langouste.

"Would you be gracious enough to repeat your last remark?"

Pala told him of her mission to Paris. Incredulously he asked whether he understood correctly that her husband—it was already clear she was desperately unhappy with him—was actually intending to *give* the shroud away to San Marco?

In the course of his ventures, he said, he had occasion to purchase a holy relic here and there. In fact, the ship he intended to buy would be financed, in some part, from the sale to a Flemish archbishop of assorted bones of Saints Felicity and Felicissimus. Those desiccated old ribs and fingers were worth their weight in gold, a thousand times over. Did she realize the Templars actively sought important relics for private veneration and to further enhance their already great public prestige? What was more to the point, they could afford anything. The woman of commerce in Pala was heard to gasp.

As darkness descended over Paris, Pala and Lorenzo lay together in his room. She had, for the first time, fallen in love. It was like a miracle. And Lorenzo had finally met the woman of his life. But he could not delay his trip to Bruges much longer; alas, business was business. He whispered tenderly in her ear that their love could never end. Somehow they would find a way to be together—forever. "Every problem has a solution," he murmured. "One has only to think of it."

Theo awakened groggily near dawn, as Pala was sliding into the far side of the bed. He told her the bad news. Denis de Croissy was in Cyprus and no one could be absolutely certain as to the date of his return.

"Go back to sleep, darling," said Pala dreamily, closing her eyes.

It was a little past sext, the canonical noon hour, when Theo, carrying the shroud bundle, led Pala to the Temple portcullis.

He announced through the bars that his mistress, recently arrived from Venezia, requested an audience with the Master of the Paris Temple. The matter concerned an important holy relic.

They were escorted to a manor house immediately beyond the gate—the farthest point a female could approach within this all-male domain.

As Philippe de Plaissiez, bald, bearded, and formidable, entered the manor salon, accompanied by two giant Knights Templars, the guard attending Pala and Theo snapped to respectful attention. De Plaissiez, whose voice was an unvarying growl, demanded to know what trivial matter was this which distracted him from the affairs of the Order? Pala motioned to Theo to speak. After some minutes of incomprehension one of the knights said that the boy spoke his hideous French with a Greek accent. With the master's permission, the boy's meaning would be much clearer if he talked in his mother tongue while the knight translated.

Starting with a history of Theo's ancestors and continuing to the taking of Constantinople, the story of the shroud gradually unfolded. No one interrupted. Pala asked Theo to open the package. The master, his knights, and the guard stepped backward as the shroud was laid out over a large Syrian rug. All froze. Then de Plaissiez, followed by his retinue, dropped to his knees before the image of the man of the Cross.

When at last de Plaissiez spoke, his voice rose an octave higher. "Madame, at this moment I have no words with which to express my emotions." He coughed and rose, still gazing at the relic.

Then, regarding Theo fiercely—his growl had returned—he demanded the boy's name. Addressing him while the knight translated, he said, "We heard in Jerusalem of this blessed cerement. Until now it had eluded us." He paused, and a faint note of suspicion crept into his voice. "Is it not strange there is no word of the linen's image in the Gospels of Matthew, Mark, Luke, or John?"

Said Theo, "There has always been the legend in our family that Saint Peter himself brought the shroud out of Judaea to Rome. And that, I have been taught, was before the Gospels had been recorded. After Peter was crucified, my ancestors fled with the shroud to Byzantium."

"Do you now swear, Theo Metochites, before God and all the Saints, that every word you have told me is precisely the truth?"

"I so swear," said Theo, adding, "I further swear what I say to be true upon the very image of Christ."

De Plaissiez cleared his throat. "Madame, what is your intention regarding the shroud?" The towering knight-linguist repeated the question in Italian.

"It is my husband's wish to leave the shroud in the care of Denis de Croissy until—"

"De Croissy!" The master fairly shouted the name. "Holy Sepulchre, why de Croissy?"

Pala explained that it was Doge Enrico Dandolo's wish to donate the shroud to San Marco's basilica, but certain circumstances at present prevented—

Said de Plaissiez, "Madame, Dandolo is dead. Which, of course, changes things. The shroud belongs here in the hands of the most powerful Order on earth. We have humbled kings. What price will you take for this relic?"

"I had not considered," said Pala, her thoughts in turbulent disarray. What would Lorenzo advise?

"We will pay two hundred thousand silver marks. Or its equivalent in gold coin, should you prefer."

Pala's mind became sharply clear. That was enough to build a duplicate Doge's Palace on the other side of the Piazza! It was more money than Andrea could earn in countless lifetimes.

"Double your offer and I accept," she said.

Theo did not understand immediately. And when he did, his face went pale.

"Done," said de Plaissiez with finality. "Silver or gold?"

"Gold," said Pala. With such riches she could return to Venice; invest the money for Andrea. Buy ships. Cargo. Double it again. Triple it. Her pulse was accelerating.

"Make out duplicate contracts, de Gaillac," said de Plaissiez, addressing the linguist. "And order our bursar to deliver the gold here." He assured Pala the money would be available within the hour.

Turning to the boy, who was silently weeping, he said, "Theo Metochites, will you remain at the Temple with the shroud? You, who are so close to the relic, should continue to serve it. Our Order requires your presence. And you will have a good home here always. This is our wish."

The master's wish conveyed a quality of command. Theo looked toward Pala beseechingly. "I must stay. Please understand, mistress."

She gazed at him for an instant and nodded. An ages-old smile composed itself on Theo's youthful Grecian features.

Shortly several younger knights entered with a fat knight-bursar. The young Templars carried small, heavy leather sacks. Then they went off to fetch still more. The bags of gold began to form a sizable pile on the rug. Opening one, Pala found it filled with shiny bezants. De Gaillac returned with a clerk bearing two documents and implements of his office. As Pala watched, the bursar weighed each sack on a large brass scale and called out the weights. The clerk entered the figures in an account book. De Plaissiez signed the documents, followed by his knights as witnesses. Then Pala took up a plume which the clerk offered her and, after reading the parchments carefully, added her signature. The clerk melted wax and impressed large red seals on the contracts.

"Brothers, remember this day well," de Plaissiez said. "It is a moment to be equalled only by our reconquest of the Holy City."

All she needed was time, Pala thought. Sufficient time to begin a vast new business for her husband. Then what would it matter? Andrea could give some part of the profits to San Marco. Even a very generous donation would scarcely make a difference in their wealth. It could begin a splendid and better life.

She felt dizzy with exaltation. De Plaissiez was saying, "I shall arrange for all Paris to behold the Templar shroud before the altar of Notre Dame on the Feast of All Saints." The import of the Temple master's words slowly came into focus, and Pala was transfixed with terror. All Saints fell on the first of November. There was no time for anything. What had she been thinking of? How could she justify her actions? It had all been madness. Both Rinieri and Andrea had access to Venetian commercial agents returned from Paris. Word of the Notre Dame exhibition was certain to reach them. Could her husband explain? And if he did, how would Rinieri react?

She saw them both as implacable, unforgiving. Without a doubt Andrea would have her immured in a convent for the rest of her life.

Then thoughts of Lorenzo rushed into consciousness. Of course, she must run to Lorenzo. He alone could help her.

De Gaillac said that if Pala chose, her money could be held at the Temple until she required it. After all, the Templars guarded the wealth of the king of France. Pala nodded and, holding her document, left the mansion. A guard ran to escort her to the citadel gate.

De Plaissiez told Theo to take the shroud and follow him.

For Theo life was a series of rapid changes. Bearing the folded shroud, he followed de Plaissiez, de Gaillac, and the master's other aide, de Saintonges, an unsmiling man with a scarred face, to a small, guarded room in the keep. The tall knight unlocked it with a key which hung from a chain around his waist. Within the chamber lay many reliquaries, assembled on a broad table. De Saintonges chose the largest for the shroud, a jeweled silver casket, and placed its contents in an empty coffer.

"You should rejoice that the shroud will remain with us," the master told Theo. "Nowhere else would the relic be safer than in our keeping."

"Then I wish to become a Templar," Theo said.

"You are too young to become one of us. In time we shall see. For now, we can offer you work here."

Theo thanked the Temple master, who patted the boy's head.

The youth was given employment in the Temple bakery. And each Friday he was required to carry out a special task. After de Saintonges opened the reliquary room for him, Theo polished the shroud's container by the light of his lantern. Then he brought the shroud to a larger chamber, which had a specially built long altar where he stretched out the cloth for the Templars' newly devised ceremony of veneration.

During those early months Theo was eager to experience the life of a Templar. He tried to maintain the Order's discipline, though it was not an obligation. He slept in a bare cell and, with the others, rose twice during the night for prayers. He kept strict silence throughout meals, listening to a reader who recited in Latin, which he did not understand.

Soon this discipline became oppressive and he pleaded with the master to be allowed more freedom. Having made no formal commitment, Theo was permitted to come and go as he pleased, so long as he fulfilled his Friday duty. For this he was paid a generous wage.

He found a friend his own age in Remi, son of a miller who daily drove wagonloads of flour to the Temple bakery. As an escape from the Order's dreary meals Theo began to dine with Remi's family. They lived in a Templar-owned house, with an undershot mill wheel, below the Grand Pont.

Theo's visits to the jovial clan always left him in good spirits. In addition to Remi, the miller and his wife had three daughters. When Theo was sixteen, he married Lorette, the eldest. She was plain looking and witty; a loving companion. The youthful couple lived with the miller's family.

Because he and his wife had only girls, Theo was compelled to continue his Temple visits in attendance on the shroud.

Theo's first daughter married a young miller named le Meunier. In his old age Theo had the satisfaction of seeing his grandson, Henri le Meunier, an apprentice miller, caring for the shroud on Fridays at the Temple.

Lorenzo had been napping when Pala knocked. Tearfully she rushed into his arms. Upon learning that the shroud had been sold, he remarked, "Pala, love, that was a fair price. All things considered, you did quite well." He began to kiss her, but kisses were no consolation.

Pala recounted the story of the duplicate shroud and her fear that what she had done would all too soon be known in Venice. Lorenzo soothed her, saying not to worry; he would think of something.

She wailed that he did not understand. The Venetian merchants returning to Paris were certain to report details of the Notre Dame exhibition. And to make matters worse, there was de Croissy. Surely, whenever he returned to the Temple, he would write to Andrea. Pala begged Lorenzo for counsel, declaring how frightened she felt.

Lorenzo urged her to rest, and helped her to his bed, while he thought about the problem. As he stood regarding her, he suddenly clapped his hands, shouting, "I have it! A plan which cannot fail. But tell me, my darling, do you trust me?" Pala answered yes, many times. "Then listen," he said. "Return to Venezia. Tell your husband the shroud is safe in Paris."

Pala said plaintively that she dared not go back. She only wanted to stay with him.

Lorenzo assured Pala that his plan depended on their being together. But first she must visit Venice—briefly. His ship would be waiting beyond the Venetian lagoon, one week after her return. He could calculate the time with fair precision, based on her sailing date. A seaman from his vessel would be sent ashore with a message telling where the ship was anchored. She was to join him at once. That would be long before anyone in Venice learned the truth.

There was a reason why his ship would be lying so far offshore, Lorenzo told Pala. He once had a little trouble escaping the armed guard boat of the Venetian contraband patrol. A minor matter involving the salt cargo he was bringing in from the Barbary. Doges were obviously oversensitive about their lucrative salt monopoly. And anyhow, it was wiser that she not be seen boarding his vessel.

He invited Pala to visualize how fine it would be when they were at last together, never again facing separation. They would be rich and happy in Genoa. In fact, with this new affluence it might not be very difficult to obtain a papal annulment of her marriage. Then they could be wed.

Pala sat up in bed. Yes, an annulment seemed altogether reasonable. Andrea and she had hardly made love at all. Just a very few times. It was not fair that those few should count. And honestly, she had experienced scarcely anything.

Lorenzo interrupted. "Yes, with the shrouds sold . . ."

"Shrouds, did you say?"

"Of course. That is why you must return to Venezia. You sold one shroud which may be false, why not the other? Two are better than one."

He reminded her that the doge's son had once adored her. When the seaman notified her, Pala was to go immediately to Dandolo with a gift of flavored spirits, lavishly praise his collection, and ask to see the shroud. She might kiss Rinieri, if the situation demanded, but before anything she must pour him some of the spirits. Tomorrow Lorenzo would seek a Parisian apothecary and buy a sleeping potion to be added to the gift.

Lorenzo assured Pala that the rest was easy. She need only roll the Dandolo shroud in some cloth and hire a barge. He would be waiting aboard the galley to carry her to Genoa and their rightful destiny.

"And the gold?" she queried.

Lorenzo volunteered to guard it until they met.

"It would be better if I held it until then," replied Pala, the woman of commerce. "But for you, Lorenzo, I shall do all else," added the woman in love. And she motioned him to the bed.

By his last day in Paris della Comba had contacted the commander of a Venetian galley and arranged passage for Pala and her servants from Bruges to Venice.

The two lovers left for Bruges together. As she and Lorenzo rode their horses northwest, followed by armed servants and a heavily loaded wagon, Pala reviewed the recent past. She regretted not at all having failed to see everything in Paris.

Pala sat at the stern of the *Santa Marina,* looking backward along the galley's wake. It had become a ritual since her farewell to Lorenzo—as if she were still connected by this watery path to the man and their tender past. She was not yet ready to stand by the prow and face the future.

Behind her, at a midship dining table, the off-duty rowers were collecting small coins to pay for the daily meal of St. Phocas, protector of seamen in stormy weather. Later the monies would be distributed to the poor.

The good-hearted young *scapoli* were well-paid and pleased to enroll for the service of the oars. They were privileged to bring on board a certain amount of duty-free merchandise for overseas trade. Their rations of bread, meat, and wine were the strict responsibility of the captain.

Capitano Mocenigo, his eyes perpetually narrowed as if he were studying some distant object, stood with legs planted wide on the gently pitching deck, discussing the last port of call at Mallorca. With his Venetian inclination to foul language he reviewed a detail of the recent cargo bartering. The mariner stationed by one of the ship's two rudders, attached to the vessel's sides, nodded understandingly. Actually Mocenigo was annoyed because he was duty bound never to leave the ship during its voyage. From the quay a particularly desirable Mallorcan lady had cast long and inviting glances toward him. The sea always did something to a sailor's blood.

Heading out of Naples, the galley rounded the heel of the Kingdom of the Two Sicilies, off Otranto, and made its way northwest toward Venice. That day Pala came forward to the bow.

She spent the hours going over every move which would be required to carry out her enterprise. She watched the strong, smooth strokes of the *scapoli*, as the galley, its sail now lowered, stood in to the cove for a safe night at anchor. A thought occurred to her. Part of her task called for a long period of rowing.

By the door of her cabin two of her servants were standing the alternate watch, guarding the stack of moneybags which lay within. They were armed with swords and stilettos. Like her other two employees, these young men had served primarily as bodyguards during her journey. It was time to initiate them into their forthcoming assignment.

Pala asked whether they had ever had any practice in the use of oars. This pair, like the other two, responded affirmatively. All had employed single oars to leisurely scull along the canals. This was not what Pala had in mind. She announced that the following day they were to request a turn at the rowers' bench. It would strengthen their muscles.

The callus-handed *scapoli* were highly amused, particularly when, next morning, the beat was slyly speeded up. In a very few minutes the sweating novices were grunting in pain. Their hands were reddening and blisters had begun to form. Learning of the problem, Mocenigo rubbed the servants' afflicted palms with fragrant balsam of the spicebush, benzoinum, and sprinkled them with powdered pine resin. He then wrapped them in strips of linen.

Some days later, as a pair of her men stroked into the lagoon of Venice, Pala was satisfied.

The most competent of the servants was sent ashore to hire a sturdy barge, powered by six oarsmen. When he returned, the gold was loaded on the craft, normally used to transport goods through the canals. It was her dowry, Pala explained. The boatmen were dismayed when their barge sank quite low in the water. She promised to pay them much more than the usual fee and to retain them for a week.

Accompanied by her servant-guards, she directed the rowers to the far northeastern side of Venice. The barge surged sluggishly through the placid lagoon waters, arriving finally at the quay of an empty warehouse which had once belonged to her father. It was located in the Castello district of the city, an area between the crumbling castle of Castrum Olivoli and the Arsenale Vecchio, the shipyard where the Crusaders' galleys had been built.

Inhabited by workers, it was a desolate and foul-smelling place among the marshes. Pigs nosed about in the grass. Slops from rickety houses ran down the narrow, unpaved streets. Pala's father, who had built one of the town's first private drainage systems, used to complain that its citizens had made all Venice into a sewer.

The gold was installed in the warehouse and, again, a watch set up, this time behind barred doors. Pala was rowed up Rio di Castello into the Canale di S. Marco. In a few minutes she was home.

Andrea expressed delight on seeing his wife but wanted to know immediately about the shroud. She told him it was safe in the Temple and he could rest assured. To his next question she responded that de Croissy was in excellent health, and he looked forward to seeing Andrea again when he returned the relic. Andrea complimented Pala for her achievement, then kissed her forehead. He would soon dispatch a letter to Denis.

With Rinieri no longer in authority, it was finally safe for the shroud to return to Venice. Dandolo had been displaced by the newly elected doge, Pietro Ziani. Andrea understood that Rinieri idled away his time these days in his palazzo, gambling with associates and arranging to purchase new acquisitions. He had ceased to collect holy relics. He was currently interested in ivory carvings, fine mosaics, and like objects of artistic merit. This was fortuitous, thought Pala.

Andrea told Pala he had been released from imprisonment the day of her departure and, happily, was now feeling very well. He looked forward to spending much time with his pretty wife.

Claiming deep fatigue, Pala declared she could sleep for a week. Andrea must forgive her; she looked forward to a quiet period of recovery from her time at sea.

Six days later Pala was summoned to the palazzo's boat landing. A bearded seaman handed her a sealed message and rowed away. Lorenzo's ship was anchored in the Adriatic at Porto Curtelatio, off Iesulo. It was time to act.

Her two servants took her already-packed clothing down to the Grimani gondola. With a small silver coin Pala dismissed the *gondoliere*. Holding the package Lorenzo had given her, she stepped into the gondola and was sculled away toward the hired barge which waited each day at a mooring around a bend in the canal. She transferred to the much larger craft and directed the oarsmen to the Dandolo palazzo. A light breeze from the west gently rustled the dry autumn leaves of trees lining the canal bank.

Pala was wearing her favorite costume: an open blue cloak with a long ermine collar which fell from her shoulders, revealing a blue silk embroidered gown, drawn in at the waist by a white girdle. A blue mantle poised gracefully over her dark hair. Around her throat hung a necklace of tiny gold rings.

Rinieri's doorkeeper led her across the terrazzo-paved floors, through a mosaic-lined vestibule, and into the quietly tasteful reception room.

It was decorated with molded plaques depicting griffins, lions,

and peacocks, interwoven with tendrils of foliage and pomegranates. Horseshoe-shaped chairs, covered with pale, orange-
colored velvet, were placed gracefully about the room. A stone-
carved fireplace ascended the back wall, flanked by two tall
wrought-iron candelabra. Off to one side Pala could see a gaming room. On an inlaid ivory table were a scattered pack of playing cards, dice, and colored tip-sticks among a little squadron of
silver wine tumblers.

With hurried steps Rinieri entered the reception hall. "Pala! I
did not believe my doorkeeper when he informed me you were
here. By San Marco's blessed nose, you look more beautiful than
I had remembered."

Dandolo's skin was sallow, his face puffy. And obviously he
was not yet bankrupt. Maybe he was cheating at cards.

"Five long years," said Pala.

"It's been that long."

Pala gazed into his somewhat bloodshot eyes. "I've been to
Paris. That city's great elegance made me think of you, as I have
before—many times."

"And I have thought of you," he said, his lips forming a dole-
ful smile. He begged her to be seated. Pala did not relish what
must follow. Burying her face in her hands, she started to sob.
Her package dropped to the floor.

"Oh, dear, dear Rinieri, it is so terrible what the physician in
Paris said."

"The physician in Paris?" he repeated.

"I am dying. That is why Andrea sent me to Paris. It seemed
my last hope to visit the famous Saintonges de Plaissiez."

Rinieri believed he had heard of the man.

Then, amid sobs, Pala explained that for the past several years
—since the marriage, in fact—she had suffered from a fearful
malady. She would grow faint and lose consciousness. For days
she languished as if in sleep. Then, for brief periods, she recovered. Like now. But the illness had been growing worse. De
Plaissiez had examined her at length, regretfully announcing she
had not many months to live.

"Oh, Rinieri, too soon I shall be dead! Perhaps God is punishing me for ever turning from you. I have been a foolish woman.

But maybe it is not too late for a moment of true happiness. I want to pass my last days on earth with you."

Rinieri came to her with tears and words of comfort. He kissed her gently.

"But let us speak of more cheerful things. I have brought you a gift." She handed him a package wrapped in cloth of gold. It was an exquisite, enameled flagon of finest Byzantine craftsmanship: blue and red, with a golden stopper; small gold circles enclosed tiny figures.

Rinieri examined it appraisingly. Lavishly thanking her, he declared the flagon to be a veritable treasure for his assemblage of precious objects. Pala insisted upon viewing his collection. With his consummate taste, she said, it must be the Eighth Wonder of the World.

Carrying the flagon, he conducted her to a long gallery which was lined with tables displaying hundreds of marvelous things: relics and Grecian bronze figures, archaic friezes, and intricately carved ivories. Over one wall hung the shroud.

As she looked at it, Rinieri explained to Pala that, after his acquisition of the sacred linen, it made no sense to collect further relics. This one holy object could never be surpassed, so he had turned to other things.

Pala now explained that the flagon was filled with a rare, new elixir, recently devised by the great French alchemist Arnaldus de Villa Nova. With his alembic he had distilled strong spirits from a priceless wine, spirits flavored with angelica and honey. Rinieri must try it at once and make a pledge to their future—a future she would spend with him.

He found the elixir delicious and urged her to sample it, but Pala declined, declaring it was all for him. After some minutes he murmured, "Amazing, it reaches the soul." Falling back in his chair with a blissful expression, Dandolo closed his eyes. Not long after, he was snoring.

Lorenzo was right. It had been easier than she'd dared imagine. Pala detached the shroud from its supports and rolled it. Removing a fabric covering from under a row of Tanagra statuettes and a figured Corinthian amphora, she quickly wrapped the relic and left the collection gallery.

At the warehouse it took some time to load the gold sacks into the long, narrow barge. Along the shores dry leaves and small twigs were in constant motion; a delicate ripple spread across the lagoon. Again the barge lost much freeboard: the gold's weight had lowered the waterline nearer the gunwales.

Pala announced to the six oarsmen that four of them must be left behind. She was replacing them with her servants, competent rowers all. The boatmen protested but when she dropped large silver grossi in their hands, all protest ceased. Already they had earned sufficient payment for many weeks of service.

The barge headed east, toward the elongated islands which sheltered the lagoon. The craft slipped between them at Porto Rivoalti. The gold was stacked amidship. Pala sat at the bow, straining to catch sight of her lover's galley. She held the rolled shroud securely with both hands.

The west wind was rising in strong gusts. Whitecaps leaped across the Adriatic. Boatmen of the gentle lagoon were not sailors of heavy seas. As they rowed north toward Iesulo, the blow was driving them eastward off their new course. The boat was shipping water.

The two boatmen began singing a hymn to St. Phocas. Suddenly one shouted they must turn back.

"Never!" cried Pala. "Keep rowing!" She tossed some gold bezants to the men as puffs of spume struck their faces. The coins lay untouched.

The galley of della Comba came into view. Streaming from its mast was a long orange-and-black pennant. Lorenzo had told her to look for the pennant.

Now the barge, attempting to make good a northerly course toward land, was becoming swamped. It wallowed, almost parallel to the waves.

"The gold!" cried a boatman. "It's our only chance. Throw it overboard!" The two rowers yanked in their oars and began to jettison the bags into the roiling sea.

"No, stop them!" screamed Pala to her servants. The four rushed to the boatmen and started grappling with them. They were joined by Pala, the shroud clamped in one hand.

The barge, full broadside to the gale, broached to in the fast-running sea. All the gold slid to one side. As the boat capsized, Pala, tightly clutching the relic, was pitched over its side, followed by an avalanche of gold. She sank beneath the waves, the shroud still locked in her grip.

One of the boatmen, a strong swimmer, was washed, half drowned, onto Litora Heradia.

Andrea would never talk of the tragedy. The actual details were self-incriminating. The humiliated Rinieri proclaimed that according to his doorkeeper, Pala dal Brusà had entered his palazzo under false pretenses while he was away, and absconded with the shroud. The citizens of Venice thought the surviving boatman's tale of the many sacks of gold to be a gross exaggeration, and they deeply mourned the loss of what they believed to be the true shroud of Jesus.

Chapter 13

Venice—Turin, 1978

Molly and Nico traveled to Venice by train. Surprisingly it was her first visit. From the moment of stepping onto the spacious paving of Piazzale Roma, she was seized by an unexpected burst of joy. Venice instantly seduced her senses.

There, shouting in many languages, waiting for the *vaporetto*, hailing water-taxis and gondole, was a profusion of visitors: hardy, blond Swedes, camera-bearing Japanese, Germans in socks and sandals, French nuns, backpacking American students, along with manically gesticulating Italians.

Nico leaped into action, commandeering a *motoscafo*. Small waves slapped against the boat's sides as Molly's suitcase was loaded. Nico helped her to a seat at the stern.

The motor launch shoved off, distancing them from noise and bustle as it cut through the waters into the reverse S of the Grand Canal. It was a tour for the eyes, and Molly's swept the scene in endless delight. Ornate mansions, palazzi, with their colonnaded windows, came in delicious colors: ochre, blue, yellow, and pink. Along their landings, groves of tide-stained poles and brightly striped moorings swayed gently in the craft's wake. Gardens and flowering vines on flat rooftops claimed their share of Venetian sunlight. Everywhere there was movement and vitality: people shopping along the canal banks, chatting in the little squares, turning under azure restaurant umbrellas to watch the water traffic, while those afloat craned to stare at the people on shore.

That façades were weathered and peeling, that houses, crowded upon one another, seemed overaged, their staircases half-drowned, became, at once, not a blemish, but rather something elegiac and a declaration of continuing life in this very ancient but perpetually youthful city.

Soon, after passing under the familiar arch of the Rialto Bridge, they arrived at the Palazzo Sforzini. Poised in decrepit grandeur, the palazzo's Renaissance façade appeared in need of repair. However, its interior was richly elegant. The walls of the reception room were lined in pale blue silk. Tall windows watched over the canal. Though some of the halls of the lower floor were partially lost in shadows, they were paved in unsolemn, multicolored marble, below delicate chandeliers of Murano glass.

Molly was welcomed effusively by Nico's two sisters and their husbands, who occupied apartments in the palazzo's upper stories. She immediately found a warm rapport with the count's siblings. The elder of the sisters, an intelligent but plain-looking young woman, worked as a curator at the Guggenheim collection. Her husband was a banker. Nico's other sister, more attractive, was hugely pregnant with her first child. Her husband, who owned a construction business in Mestre, was forever helping his wife in and out of chairs and inquiring about her comfort.

Nico explained that his mother was taking her afternoon nap, but looked forward to greeting Molly at dinner. It was clear from Nico's deference and the sisters' frequent references to their mother, that Contessa Sforzini was a powerful presence in their lives.

Molly expected someone with a more formidable appearance than the small, silver-haired person who entered the drawing room as they were having cocktails. The contessa extended her hand. "My dear, how very delightful that you will be our guest." Her movements were precise and quick, like Nico's.

As the evening progressed, the contessa asked Molly question after question about her background, work, and ideas. Molly felt uneasy under the relentless press of the old lady's interrogation.

Nico observed her discomfort and referred to it later when he and the contessa had a moment alone.

"Mother, why did you find it necessary at dinner to plague Molly with so many questions?"

"Because I want to know her."

"There are less obvious ways."

The contessa smiled and touched his cheek lightly. "Oh, my darling, there you go, criticizing me. I believe I was gracious to be so attentive to your new friend."

"You know well what I mean. And I can say this for Molly, she certainly answered you most candidly. Good heavens, Mother, I have not asked her to marry me. I merely invited her to be our guest for the weekend."

Looking her son straight in the eyes, the contessa winked.

After dark Nico took Molly to Piazza San Marco, where young people in the crowded square were amusing themselves with a new toy. An imaginative inventor had devised a way to light up the old-fashioned yo-yo. The resultant "*yo-yo luminoso*" had become the rage that year in Venice. The piazza danced magically with tiny green and pink lights, oscillating in the air like drunken fireflies.

Molly and Nico sipped espresso under one of the arcades, while an antique string orchestra played musical-comedy tunes of the twenties. Nico loved chatting about Venice and the Sforzini family's years along the Grand Canal. Wherever they walked, he received nods and greetings from passersby. It was evident that Nico and his family were highly regarded.

They strolled along the city's shadowy back streets, pausing on small bridges to watch the gondole, each lit by a small lamp, glide through silent canals. Now and then they heard the *gondolier*'s warning call as he sculled under an arch or toward a bend.

Nico turned to the search they were to make next day. "Are you aware of the full story of Vittorio's discovery, Molly?"

"Not completely. I'd like to know exactly what we're hoping to turn up."

"I am not sure about that myself. As you know, Vittorio came across a reference to two shrouds in a book in the Torino university library. Yesterday I checked the book myself. The reference is merely a footnote, and rather inadequate at that. The author states one of his sources—he does not give it—was found here at the Marciana. He says it confirms that a shroud with Jesus' image on it was displayed before the altar of San Marco in the year 1205. That is just one year after the Venetians aided in the sack of Constantinople during the infamous Fourth Crusade.

"This author, Carpano, claims he has also seen a document which establishes that during the same year, 1205, the shroud was displayed in Paris as the possession of the Knights Templars. And that I believe to be true. Vittorio has a Jesuit friend in Paris who wrote him in answer to his query about the Templar shroud. Father Paul Ignace Peyriac found the information in the Archives Nationales. It was an order signed by the Templar grand master, Philippe de Plaissiez, authorizing 'our holy and blessed shroud' to be moved to Notre Dame cathedral for a Mass of thanksgiving. The parchment was dated September 15, 1205."

"The idea that there might have been two shrouds would seem inescapable then. Of course, *one* of them had to be fake. That is, if the other one was authentic." Smiling, Molly continued. "I remember when I was working at the AP Rome office in seventy-three seeing a very good fake. Actually, it was a quite legitimate copy which the Italian radio and television network, RAI, prepared for a documentary which followed the first TV showing of the Turin Shroud."

Nico, in Israel at the time, had missed it. Molly said now that she had actually studied the Shroud of Turin, she realized the modern copy was very convincing. She understood that the image had been painted on an exactly scaled duplicate cloth using tea as the pigment.

Before turning in, Molly was given a tour of the Sforzini residence. With special pride Nico showed her the cavernous library, its shelves lined with rare volumes. On one wall was an exquisite painting of a woman's head, long gold hair gleaming on bare shoulders.

"That is a Leonardo," explained Nico. "An ancestor commissioned it when the house was new." He laughed. "The government does not permit us to move it. This room has been declared a national monument."

Molly's own bedroom was pleasantly overstocked with antiques. Surprisingly the bed, a canopied marvel, managed to be comfortable. Standing alone on her balcony, looking out at the Grand Canal, lively even now, and at the lighted city beyond, Molly contemplated Nico's glorious Venetian world. Every facet of it offered one a feeling of faded centuries, but also a sense of the familiar, perhaps because of its paintings from Canaletto and Guardi to Turner.

Friday morning Molly and Nico began their search at the Marciana Library, across from the Palace of the Doges. At Monti's suggestion Nico chose to begin with the papers of the thirteenth-century doge Enrico Dandolo. Then he planned to go on to those of Dandolo's son, Rinieri, who had briefly ruled Venice as vice-doge while Dandolo was waging the Fourth Crusade at Constantinople.

One of the librarians, an officious little man, approached them as they entered the reading room. A few words from Nico had him smiling and bowing obsequiously. However, there must have been some difficulty in locating the Dandolo papers. It was a long wait before the man returned carrying a dusty case. Reminding them to handle the material with the greatest care, the librarian then placed himself on a high stool at one side of the room, observing their every move.

The case was stacked with documents and correspondence. Many of the papers were faded and foxed, almost illegible, and it was difficult to read the spidery handwriting of Dandolo's secretary, whose name, they learned from references in the letters, was Andrea Grimani. Even so, Nico was able to scan the Latin and medieval Italian at a fair pace, while Molly took rapid notes; but it was still three hours, and time for midday closing, before they completed the material.

They had found nothing. They returned later to study the less voluminous papers of Dandolo's son. It was almost closing time, and the little librarian was impatiently awaiting the return of his dusty container, before Nico indicated he had discovered something.

It was the first page of a letter. In an upper corner was the word *"exemplar,"* a copy. Rinieri—or more likely, his secretary—had written of a shroud which the vice-doge planned to display in San Marco during the year in which the letter was written, 1205. Since part of the page was stained, Nico could not make out to whom it was addressed. But he could tell, from the body of the letter, that it sought to establish Rinieri's ownership of the relic. It went on to excoriate the recipient of the letter for his lies. The succeeding pages were missing.

Nico and Molly were curious to know more about the "lies" Rinieri had ascribed to his correspondent. They sensed they were onto something significant.

The next morning they were back again, going through other cases containing assorted correspondence from Doge Dandolo, Rinieri, and their Venetian contemporaries. They spent the entire day sifting through dusty files. Nothing turned up. Toward closing time they were discouraged and had had enough. As they were about to leave, the officious librarian inquired whether they had had good luck. Their faces told the story.

"Wait," he said, small eyes gleaming. "There remains one final place, our *'cestino per rifiuti'*—the rubbish basket. It is essentially worthless, but who knows?"

He returned with a larger box. Throughout its depths were oddments and scraps, uncatalogued fragments which had found no other home. The weary researchers regarded it with little zest.

"We should give it a try, I suppose," said Nico rather half-heartedly. Molly took a deep breath and they plunged in. After sifting through the box's contents for some time, Nico uncovered a sheaf of crumbling papers, tied by a disintegrating cord. The torn label bore the word "—rimani."

"That could be Doge Dandolo's secretary!" he said, his voice rising.

He delicately opened the packet. A few yellowed fragments fell away. As the leaves separated, Molly's attention focused upon an assemblage of small parchment pages, bound together. Nico slowly spread it open. Its cover bore the faint words *Commentarii Diurni*—a diary. Anxiously he began to read. There, in clearer script, was the name "Andrea Grimani" and the dates "1200–1205." Molly could feel a shiver along her backbone.

Nico translated aloud. Entry after entry dealt with Grimani's relationship to the old doge during the Crusade; and with the details of an unhappy marriage.

Then they saw it. A paragraph about the shroud; how Grimani had brought it to Venice from Constantinople. Here was proof that the shroud had a history dating back more than a century and a half earlier than was presently known. A few pages later they found what they had sought. Grimani wrote of having a copy made, "to protect our precious relic for all the people." Why he had needed to do so, or what had become of the two shrouds, was not revealed, for the diary broke off at that point.

"Do you imagine the shroud Rinieri displayed in San Marco was the original?" Molly asked Nico.

"Only the scientists can tell us now," he replied thoughtfully.

Molly and Nico were both elated by their find. It would add importantly to the relic's provenance. Yet as they walked along Nico's favorite byways and bridges, they were concerned about Vittorio's reaction to their discovery. This verification of a forged shroud could be a serious setback for him. Before, it had been only a conjecture; now it was fact. Molly also thought of Richard's neatly worked-out theory.

On Sunday, their last day in Venice, Nico planned an afternoon at the Lido. Cutting across the lagoon in a *motoscafo*, Molly reviewed the events of the last two days. In a personal way she had become thoroughly intrigued with the ancient detective story unfolding in Turin. She had also truly enjoyed this visit with Nicolò Sforzini. More, perhaps, than she wished to acknowledge.

The boat operator tied up at the Lido pier. Nico helped Molly onto the dock leading to the Hotel Excelsior Palace. Watching a few bathers sampling the September Adriatic, they lunched on the terrace of the famed old watering-place. Nico described his work in Israel, excavating near Masada. "I am uncovering a first-century Roman military post between Masada and Ein Gedi. Most fascinating. There are several seasons to go before my dig is completed." He paused a moment, considering something.

"Last spring I made an interesting find one kilometer west of my excavation." He told her of a gold ring with three trees in intaglio still encircling the finger of a female skeleton he had found in a small cave. After some research he had concluded that the crest of three trees was that of the family of Flavius Silva. *Silva* in Latin meant "a wood." Silva had been governor of the region and commander of the Roman forces at Masada. "But what this ring from a Roman general was doing on the finger of a lone woman in the Judaean wilderness will forever elude me. She might have been a Jew."

Molly asked whether Nico had held out the ring for himself. Looking somewhat embarrassed, the archaeologist admitted he had. He hoped that, one day, it would grace the finger of another, the woman he married. "It could have been for Livia," he said, reflectively. "I was engaged to her but something unfortunate happened between us, and we have never seen each other since. It is finished."

Molly admitted that she, too, was no stranger to love which simply faded away.

"Ah, Lorca," smiled Nico, quoting the Spanish poet. He began, "*Ay, amor . . .*" then switched to English, "Oh, love, that disappeared through the air."

Molly studied the empty horizon. "The man whom I accompanied to Monsignore Monti's reception, Richard Coolidge, once meant very much to me. Our relationship ended rather cruelly." She laughed. "To rephrase Christopher Marlowe slightly, 'That was in another country, and besides, the *wrench* is dead.'"

She realized she was becoming increasingly fond of Nico. Of course, the gap between their religious viewpoints seemed very wide. But why think of that now?

As light failed, Nico led Molly to the hotel's ballroom. In times past he had come here for dances and soirées. It was a place of good memories.

The long expanse of room was deserted. Gilded chairs leaned against pink-clothed round tables. Molly could imagine how it must once have looked, brilliant with jeweled elegance, men and women fresh from the exclusive coteries of Europe, waltzing under the massive crystal chandeliers. French windows, stretching the room's length, faced the Adriatic. Molly and Nico strolled past the long glass façade, their voices echoing softly across the emptiness.

Bowing, Nico asked Molly to grant him a dance. Entering his fantasy, she moved into his arms. She hummed all the waltzes she could remember as they glided over the polished parquetry. "Tales from the Vienna Woods," "The Blue Danube," passages from Ravel's "La Valse," the ultimate dream dance.

As they watched the last light fade on the darkening sea, Nico brought his lips against hers. She returned the kiss, lightly. They stayed there, arms clasped, looking out the window until all was darkness.

Returning in their motor launch toward the brightness of Venice, Nico held Molly in the sheltering arc of his arms. Her head rested against his shoulder. They spoke little, enjoying their closeness. At the palazzo they paused on the boat landing as the *motoscafo* chugged away. Nico took her face in his hands; they kissed long and ardently. "My beautiful darling," he whispered. "These moments have been so sweet; there must be many, many more."

As they kissed again, Molly was aware of something she had not known for a long time. It was an inner lightness, almost a giddiness. She told herself she must still be feeling the excellent wine they had had at the Lido.

Richard Coolidge had just finished posting a small packet to the States. In his covering letter he asked Nordlinger to cable as soon as he knew anything. It would take at least a week to get there. Scott would have to reserve time on the accelerator. And add a day or so to obtain a result. Richard had avoided giving Nordlinger any details. However, his friend would not think to question the matter. Richard had shipped old textile specimens like this before. He had made clear that this was a rush job. Scotty would come through.

The telephone rang. It was Camillo Acciaro, inviting him for dinner. Richard accepted, glad for the opportunity of seeing Acciaro again. He only half believed the man's words about funding the Institute. But it could be. There were a lot of rich eccentrics around. In any case he and Camillo shared a fundamental interest and Richard felt certain some worthwhile publicity would come of the association.

Acciaro expressed pleasure when Richard announced he already had established a relationship with one of the scientists who could be counted on to relay the desired information as soon as it became known. But curiously, he was not particularly interested when he heard the age-dating would probably be postponed. Why would Acciaro's book necessitate such precise details of the tests? "Shouldn't you ask the scientists yourself?" Richard queried.

"Because I am the iconoclast, and while they appear to maintain an apparently unbiased attitude, these scientists want to prove the relic is genuine."

Richard disagreed. He knew scientists. In a way he was one himself. His impression was that they were hell-bent to uncover a forgery, but in any event they would be completely objective— though none could actually suppose the thing to be authentic. "I agree this investigation is unwarranted. Probably secretly cooked up by the Vatican to generate publicity. I can't help being cynical."

Richard felt impelled to hint to Camillo that he also was involved in some shroud testing. The result would surely be pleasing to them both. Though even as he spoke, he knew he would never disclose the truth to the Italian. It was his own affair.

In addition to wanting a list of the tests to be performed, Acciaro had one other request for Richard. He wished to know the precise time, down to the minute, when each experiment would take place. When Richard asked of what possible use such information could be, Acciaro replied, "Just consider me a very thorough researcher. Now, shall we talk more about your splendid Institute? I have taken up the matter with my associates."

Vittorio Monti drove his small blue Fiat, with its silver stripes, northwest toward Aeroporto Caselle. He was very proud of the car. It had belonged to a son of his housekeeper, Serafina. Except for a few dents the car was in excellent condition. Accelerating in short bursts, the priest wove in and out of the heavy traffic. It was up to him, as Keeper of the Shroud, to welcome the American scientists to Turin. They would be arriving with their wives and children on a single plane. Landing separately would be seventy-two crates—four tons of equipment. It was hoped that any difficulty could be avoided passing it through customs and on to the Royal Palace, where a large hall, formerly used for greeting foreign dignitaries, was to be transformed into the laboratory.

About twenty scientists in the group were from the United States. American scientific institutions had also loaned or donated most of the equipment. As an economy measure the investigators planned to employ their wives as directors of logistics.

Vittorio still secretly hoped something would happen to forestall the experiments. Official permission from the shroud authorities had not yet been given. He could not avoid distrusting these scientists and their formidable machines.

When the Americans finally were settled in a bus which would take them to their hotel, the Sitea, Monti was relieved. That much was over, and now he need have little association with them during this week before the testing. The archbishop had designated others to assist in arrangements. Monti watched the bus pull out of its parking area. So, here they were, a congress of executioners.

Returning to the security of his beloved auto, Monti tried not to focus upon the anger and fear now roiling inside him. However, the scientists' arrival was only the beginning. On the following day Nico returned from Venice.

"I have less than happy news to report, Vittorio," he said.

"Go no further. I can guess. You found written evidence that there was a duplicate shroud."

Nico discussed Rinieri's letter and the diary of Andrea Grimani. Probably it was the Rinieri letter to which the author Carpano had referred. But the excerpts from Grimani's diary offered far more troubling detail. Nico elaborated. When he had finished, Monti shrugged helplessly. "My son, what shall we do?"

"I do not know, Vittorio. It has to be your decision. However, at this point I believe only science can give you an answer."

The monsignore poured a glass of one of the Piedmont's fine

wines and handed it to his friend. "Until now our blessed shroud has brought me the greatest comfort."

"What you accept as the shroud's fundamental statement can never change, regardless of our determinations."

Monti shook his head. "I am not young, Nico. A man must reach the last days of his life believing that what he has done has been worthwhile. You have met my friend Carlo, the bricklayer. For fifty years he built foundations and walls all over Torino. He can look at his work and know how secure it is, how real. Carlo is respected. I, too, have been respected. For hundreds of years my family has served the holy cloth with honor. Where would I go if the shroud is not what we believe it to be? My superiors will send me away. A miserable parish in Sicily. A mountain hamlet in Calabria. I should soon perish in such a place."

"But, Vittorio, you are a priest."

"And yes, shall I confess it? I am guilty of the sin of pride. Pride is in my blood, Nico. *Mea culpa.*"

"Vittorio, God will not desert you. Nor I. Do not be so hard on yourself." Nico walked to the window and stood for some minutes with his back to Monti, his thoughts now on another matter. "Vittorio, what do you think of the American journalist, Molly Madrigal?"

Somewhat bemused, the priest assured Nico she had favorably impressed him.

"She came to visit me and my family at Venezia. We had a glorious weekend. I believe I am in love with her."

Vittorio focused his attention on the younger man. Had this been God's answer to his prayers? This American woman, was she good enough for Nico?

"Have you told her how you feel?"

"Maybe she guesses. But I am uncertain of her sentiments toward me. She was once involved with Richard Coolidge, the American who is trying to discredit the shroud."

Monti thought, one mark against the pretty journalist. Coolidge seemed arrogant and sardonic. How could this woman have ever loved him, and also be attracted to a wonderful, positive person like Nico? But then he challenged himself: Who am I to raise such a question? What do I really know? He would pray for a happy resolution of the matter. Meantime his young friend needed support.

Patting Nico's shoulder, Vittorio said, "A little valor, *cavaliere*. Think of this as another Gran Premio race that you are out to win. From what I could see, your Molly is a bright and sensitive young woman." He took Nico's hands and held them a moment. "Whatever is decided, you both have my blessing. By the way, does your mother know about this?"

"Of course. She knew before I did."

Later it occurred to the priest that because Molly Madrigal had been in Venice with Nico, she must now understand much about the two shrouds. The fact alarmed him until he recalled her telling him the *View* story would not be run for several weeks. By then the matter might already be decided. Still, Monti was unable to shake off something which weighed forcefully upon him: the growing terror that matters concerning the shroud were fast moving beyond his control.

Deeply troubled, he wandered over to the Duomo. Standing inside, he watched the thousands of tourists and pilgrims waiting patiently for their moment near the relic. It was early afternoon, two days before the exposition's close. On Sunday, at midnight, and for five days and nights thereafter, the shroud would belong to the scientists.

Monti studied the crowds of visitors, smiling and eager, and he was afraid. What would happen to their faith in Christ if those scientists announced the figure on the cloth was mere trickery? What would it mean to him?

Staring up at that precious linen, Monti came to a decision. He would reveal Nico's findings in Venice to no one, neither the archbishop, nor the scientists. And from now on, whenever the issue arose in the commission, he would oppose radiocarbon testing.

Let the scientists do what they would. Without carbon dating one could never be sure. What he had already established of the shroud's history must suffice. He thought about the great congress on the shroud, scheduled to begin next morning and continue for two days. Shroud scholars, proponents and opponents, from all over the world were scheduled to present results of their research and conjectures to date. Although invited, he had not submitted a topic. This information, this Venetian problem he had blundered upon, should, in all honesty, be announced during the congress. The delegates had a right to know.

Kneeling in the cathedral shadows of San Giovanni Battista, Monti asked God to forgive him for lacking the courage to let things take their course. However, the Lord had put him in a position to influence events, and he reasoned that he must exercise this right.

The Second International Congress of Sindonology—shroud scholarship—entitled *"La Sindone e la Scienza,"* was held in a large conference hall at the Istituto Bancario S. Paolo. Thirty speakers had been scheduled, two thirds of them Italian. Each was allotted fifteen minutes, to be followed by a five-minute period of questions. There were simultaneous translations in French, Italian, and English. Both Monti and Molly attended the sessions.

The report of an eminent forensic pathologist from the United States was a highlight of the meetings. An exacting medical examiner, the American had undertaken an extensive study of anatomical and traumatic aspects of the shroud figure.

The pathologist, who had served as coroner in a major American city, observed that there appeared to be puncture wounds about the figure's scalp: nineteen frontally and thirteen on the rear image. They might have been caused by one-inch thorns, bound to the head like a cap. A Holy Land plant, *Zizphus spina,* could have been used. Further, the blood rivulets from these injuries flowed in a direction consistent with gravity, as did the wounds on the wrists. There the blood flowed down the arms in two distinct directions, consistent with the victim thrusting himself upward. Crucifixion, an especially slow form of death, compelled the sufferer to raise himself by his nailed feet in order to draw more air into his constricted lungs and ease his difficulty in breathing. Though the legs were often broken to hasten death, the practice was not followed in this instance. It had been already concluded that a frequent cause of crucifixion death was asphyxiation.

The pathologist went on to note that a marked contusion on the right cheek and a possible cartilage separation on the nose could have been caused by a strong blow to the face. Also, both shoulders evidenced abrasions which seemed to have been caused by the bearing of a heavy weight, about eighty to one hundred pounds. Such an object as the crucifixion crossbeam would have effected these injuries. The crossbeam was ultimately attached to a permanent, upright beam. The assembled cross, as traditionally depicted in medieval art, would weigh several hundred pounds, and would doubtless be too heavy for a man weakened by scourging to carry. There appeared to be abrasions on each knee, possibly from a fall while carrying a heavy object.

Neither thumb was visible on the image. Contact by a spike with the median nerve in the wrists would explain the thumbs' contraction.

The pathologist also noted the more than one hundred lash marks from shoulders to calves, whose terminal dual markings were possibly caused by a Roman *flagrum,* the double- or triple-thonged whip ending in small dumbbell-shaped pieces of bone or metal. Positioning of the marks indicated the man's arms were lifted over his head during the flagellation. Earlier study had concluded that the scourging was applied by a man moving to each side of the prisoner, or by two Roman legionaries working in unison, and historical evidence confirmed that this scourging was far more severe than that usually given to prisoners about to be crucified.

Substantial bleeding had occurred from the figure's right side, as the result of an apparent lance thrust. Though dead bodies cease to bleed, the dislodging of a blood clot could have caused residual, pooled blood to have oozed out. The "water" that was said to have poured out after the lancing would have been pleural fluid, accumulated during the brutal beating. The variously directed rivulets of blood associated with the chest wound could have been caused by the body's having been moved after it was lowered from the cross.

The heels showed abrasions, perhaps from the corpse having been dragged across the ground.

Listening to the pathologist's careful recitation of this torture-racked death, Monti experienced the sadness he knew each year on Good Friday. And then he felt elation, for this objective physician appeared to be confirming that the image could only be that of Jesus Christ. Furthermore, there were many details which Vittorio found to be a sure denial of the possibility that the original shroud image had been created by some medieval forger. Perhaps, he thought, as he left the auditorium, there was hope after all. He was glad he had not reported on the Venetian matter.

When Molly returned to her hotel room, she put her opened notebook on the little writing table beside the Jerusalem Bible she had purchased. There were numerous slips of paper between certain pages of the gospels. She began to compare the pathologist's findings against the words of New Testament men who had written of Jesus' ordeal.

Though the Gospel accounts repeated details of many of the same incidents, she opened first to Mark 15:16–19—"The soldiers led him away to the inner part of the palace, that is, the Praetorium, and called the whole cohort together. They dressed him up in purple, twisted some thorns into a crown, and put it on him. And they began saluting him, 'Hail, king of the Jews!' They struck his head with a reed and spat on him; and they went down on their knees to do him homage." John 19:1 and 3—"Pilate then had Jesus taken away and scourged; . . . and they slapped him in the face."

This was consistent with thorn injuries to Jesus' head, the broken nose, the swollen cheek, and the marks left by the scourging.

Luke 23:26 could reasonably explain the abrasions to Christ's knees. "As they were leading him away they seized on a man, Simon from Cyrene, who was coming in from the country, and made him shoulder the cross and carry it behind Jesus." Why should Jesus have been relieved of the cross burden unless he had fallen and was unable to go on? It seemed a fair inference.

It was also implied here that the shoulder injuries had been inflicted by the weight of the crossbeam.

And what about Jesus' lance wound? John 19:33–34 told the story. "When they came to Jesus, they found he was already dead, and so instead of breaking his legs one of the soldiers pierced his side with a lance. . . ."

It all seemed to check out. Her eyes drifted down to the account of the apostle Thomas, who demanded to put his fingers into the revenant Christ's nail holes and lance wound before he could believe. Then he felt the wounds and acknowledged Jesus. Molly thought, if only I could believe. She could not quite say why—but she felt it would make things better.

With a weary expression Camillo Acciaro faced his two confederates, Strà and Rozza. "Gentlemen, until that dim-witted Church makes up its mind to allow the testing, my American professor obviously cannot relay any critical details to me. We simply must wait a little longer. Now there is another matter. I will require an automatic weapon. Perhaps one of you gentlemen might advance me sufficient funds to acquire one."

"Camillo, I paid for your deluxe dinner last week," commented Rozza. "Why not buy something you can afford, like a six-millimeter Beretta?"

"That baby gun is guaranteed to hit the target if you push it hard into someone's belly," jeered Strà.

Reflected Acciaro, "The Beretta could be the answer. Firstly, I don't plan to kill anyone, and secondly, I have never fired a gun in my entire life."

Strà exploded with a short, barklike laugh. Above all else, Acciaro hated to be laughed at. Drawing himself upright, he said, "You had best bear in mind, and never forget it, that soon you will share in the most ingenious, the most lucrative, and—yes—the greatest adventure of anyone who ever dared to contravene both the Church and the state."

Chapter 14

Paris, 1306–1314

"Hang the king! Hack off his head!"

A screaming mob of Parisians streamed toward the royal palace. Enraged by King Philippe's debasing of the currency—depreciated to two thirds of its former value—the outraged crowds had found themselves in much the same position as if they had been robbed by brigands.

A woman standing by a doorway shook her head as she said to a friend, "Yesterday I watched soldiers at the pork market boiling a counterfeiter in lard. The poor, honest counterfeiter did less to harm our money than the king. It's Philippe who should be fried."

The other woman grabbed a kitchen knife. "You're right, Hélène, let's join them." Running to catch up, the townswomen headed for the Grand Pont.

The object of all this fury, France's King Philippe IV, cowered behind the walls of his sumptuous residence. The crowd now threatened to storm its gates. Aware of the imminent danger, Philippe knew he must escape his palace on Île de la Cité. Only one place in Paris could hold back the rioters: the fortress of the Knights Templars.

Philippe sent an urgent note to his good friend, Hugues de Payraud, one of the Order's highest officials. Hugues instantly

offered Philippe refuge. But how was he to reach the fortress un-detected? De Nogaret, the king's chief advisor, conceived of a ruse. A messenger was sent off again, returning with one of the Templar mantles. It was white with a large red cross on the shoulder. Its deep, matching skullcap could conceal one of Phi-lippe's highly recognizable features—his wavy blond hair. Since the king, known as Philippe the Fair, possessed a familiarly handsome face, it, too, had to be concealed. Philippe had an idea. The Templar knights wore untrimmed beards. One of his grooms possessed such an adornment. The groom's heavy beard was carefully scissored off and attached to the king's face.

Philippe's messenger had also been given one of the Templars' piebald banners. Carrying this banner and riding alone, the frightened king made his way through the mob toward the Grand Pont, which connected Île de la Cité to the Right Bank. He had to fight the impulse to spur his charger into a gallop.

Upon reaching the safety of the fortress, Philippe was given comfortable rooms and Templar servants to attend him. So great had been his anxiety that it was several days before he felt sufficiently relaxed to move outside his quarters. He had never visited the Templar precinct before, though he had once consid-ered joining the Order. Now he had other thoughts about the knights and their wealthy establishment. Certain rumors in-trigued him.

For two decades following their acquisition of the holy shroud, and unaware that it might be a copy, the Knights Tem-plars staged exhibitions in Paris for public viewing of the cloth. But the Venetians were unimpressed. They assumed their true shroud had been stolen by Pala dal Brusà and lost at sea. And, for private reasons, neither Andrea Grimani nor Rinieri Dandolo ever revealed what each believed to be the actual story behind the shroud of Venice.

During the year 1225 the French king, Louis VIII, resolved to become possessor of the Templars' shroud. As he was in the pro-cess of planning a Crusade against a powerful and heretical religious sect of southern France, the Albigenses, he determined that his battalions would also storm the Templar citadel and cap-ture the relic for France.

Alerted, the warrior monks hid their venerable possession in a secret place within the walls. The story was circulated that they had taken it to Castle Pilgrim, their headquarters at Acre, near the Holy Land. There, so they announced, it awaited the return to Jerusalem, which, in 1187, the Templars had lost to Islam.

Now the shroud could be viewed by only the Order's *grands dignitaires*. No others knew of it, except the direct descendants of Theo Metochites. Because of their association with the relic's past, a custom arose that successive Grand Masters of the Temple would contribute to the support of this family, whose name at this time was le Meunier. Legends, reaching back to Jerusalem, were passed on by the le Meuniers, but with each successive generation details became altered or forgotten.

Some months before his uneasy stay as a guest of the Templars, Philippe discovered among his personal bodyguard a distant relative of the Metochites family. He had once served the Order. When the king began to form a plan concerning the Templars which would, among other things, solve his financial woes, this man proved useful. Though never a knight, he had been aware of much that went on. During questioning by Philippe, this guard repeated the rumors of a strange ritual which took place Fridays after midnight prayers in a secret chamber deep below the Temple keep. Only the Temple hierarchy were permitted to be present. Odd shouts and cries could sometimes be heard emanating from the chamber.

During his visit with the knights Philippe came upon the secret location of this sanctuary. He had asked one of the servants assigned to him, an unsuspicious fellow, to point out those areas which must be avoided by outsiders to the Order. The man led him directly to what he sought.

Late one night, sneaking about the passages below his rooms, Philippe found a means to enter the forbidden sanctuary. A tiny balcony, where singers or psalm-readers might stand, was located at an upper corner of the room. One could crouch unseen below its railing.

That Friday, during matins in the nearby Temple church, Philippe stole away and hurried onto the small balcony. The sanctuary was still deserted and darkened. Soon, however, one of the knights entered, accompanied by a young man who did not wear the Templar robes. Philippe recognized the knight. He was Geoffroy de Charny, the Order's Master of Normandy. Torches were placed in sconces; the youth polished a silver coffer by the altar.

In silence others entered until about twenty had gathered. More torches were lit. The light was brightest at the room's center where a long altar was placed. Philippe heard a guard being stationed outside the narrow balcony door. He was certain this must be the rumored secret ceremony and was seized both with fear and excitement.

The knights grouped themselves in a semicircle around the altar. The youth opened the silver casket, reverently removed a folded length of ivory linen, and draped it across the altar. Then he left the chamber.

The cloth was faintly marked; Philippe strained to see. By Our Lady! Could that be the shroud? The shroud of Our Lord, Jesus Christ? For decades the Capetians, including his grandfather, the beloved Louis IX, had tried to get their hands on this relic—if this was truly it. Jacques de Molay, the Order's grand master, had mentioned to Philippe that the shroud was now on Cyprus. Jacques, that liar, was godfather to one of the king's sons.

The ceremony began, and Philippe pressed his face against the cold stone balustrade.

At a signal from de Charny the twenty high-ranking knights prostrated themselves on the floor. Next they rose and, swaying, shouted an unintelligible word in what seemed to be a foreign tongue. The chant and the room's brightness were hypnotizing as the knights moved in a rhythmic motion around the altar twelve times. After the recitation of a long and solemn prayer the ceremony came to an end. One of the knights pounded the chamber door. The young man reentered and carefully replaced the linen in its receptacle.

When he heard the door guard march away, the king cautiously returned to his suite. It was then that he began calculating how to get the relic for himself. Philippe concluded that first he must devise a plan to suppress the Order. It was said that the Templars owned nine thousand manor houses located in every Christian country from Denmark to Castile, Ireland to Cyprus. They had become far too powerful, bankers to the world, possessing vast, far-flung holdings. No, they could not be allowed to continue amassing riches. Here in Paris they were thought to be more powerful than he. And so they are, the king thought bitterly. Here I am, seeking refuge with them. But, by possessing the shroud . . . His pale eyes narrowed. De Nogaret. He was the man to formulate a scheme. Then, soon enough, the relic, and an incalculable fortune, would rest in Capetian pockets.

The following summer thirteen-year-old Jean de Charny arrived in Paris. Jean was an earnest, brown-haired youth, of athletic build and dark romantic eyes. He was serving as squire near his home in Anjou and had traveled to the city with his patron, who was to participate in a tournament. Jean looked forward to visiting his uncle, Geoffroy de Charny, a Templar *grand dignitaire*.

This was young de Charny's first visit to Paris. It made an astonishing assault on his senses. There were coiling streets with workshops and stores, straight paved avenues, palaces and sumptuous mansions. Above all soared a profusion of church spires.

The sounds of the city. The voices of the crowds. Rattles clacking from a passing band of lepers. Vendors hawking their wares. Street signs of all manner of artisans clattering in the wind: giant gloves of the glovers, the bullhead of the butchers, signs with swords, signs with hats, signs with rolls of cloth, enormous pots hanging from hooks, all competed in a vital, turbulent cacophony.

And the people. Apprentices hurrying with bales of material, lovers wearing the colors of their sentiments, fat churchmen, money changers, prostitutes in *clapier* doorways, minstrels, gypsies, boats in the Seine freighted with bright vegetables, toll collectors on bridges shouting *"Holà, que passez?"* Students from the University of Paris staggering, drunken and singing, to shabby quarters.

The odors. The deliciousness of *charcuteries*, the incense from open church doors mixed with the stink of gutters where pigs rooted, and the stench of poverty and sickness from the Hôtel de Dieu and the poorer quarters. A noblewoman with her servants, passing in a perfumed cloud of roses and jasmine.

And throughout the day the bells of Paris rang the canonical hours and the curfew, chimed the marriages, and tolled the deaths.

Geoffroy de Charny was happy to see his young nephew. His brother's second son, Jean had always been his favorite, the child denied him by his vows as a Templar knight.

"Well, Jean, my son, what brings you to Paris?" he asked briskly.

Awed by his uncle's great stature, long silver beard, and booming voice, Jean took a moment to find his tongue. "I wanted to be sure that you were in good health. The riots—we heard many persons were killed."

"Even the king feared for his life. As well he should," Geoffroy added darkly.

They were sitting on a small rug which covered the stone floor of de Charny's cell. A single lamp, suspended from the ceiling, cast an anemic light. The hour was late. Thomas, another knight, had moved out of the room he shared with the Master of Normandy so that Jean might stay the night with his uncle. He would sleep on a straw pallet which was one of the cell's sparse comforts.

The Templar began questioning his nephew about his life as a squire. Had he found good companions? Did he understand the spiritual and moral obligations of knighthood? Did he perceive those qualities in the knight he served? For it was important always to be shown a good example.

"You have been my example," replied the boy, eyes glowing. "I admire no one more than you, Uncle."

Geoffroy affectionately patted young Jean's cheek. He was remembering his exemplar, with whom he had served many years on Cyprus. However, there was not so great a disparity in age between him and Jacques de Molay. Three years, only. Not so much a father-son relationship, either. More brotherly, perhaps. No, deeper than that. Thinking of Jacques, Geoffroy felt a nostalgic warmth. This was the grand master's first visit to Paris in two years. Geoffroy had been delighted to welcome him again. Since de Molay's arrival in June, they had had many wonderful talks.

"Uncle, I am so glad to be with you here at the Temple. I have a secret to confess." The young man blushed. "I am considering joining the Templars when I reach eighteen."

Geoffroy was not surprised. He had expected it. Yet he felt it necessary to hide his pleasure for the moment and play devil's advocate. "Do you not wish a more normal life for yourself, nephew? A wife, children? You know, as a married man you could still associate yourself with us for periods of time. Wouldn't that be enough?"

"I could not wear the white mantle and the red cross and become a knight like you."

"It is a hard discipline, Jean." Geoffroy reflected a moment. He had occasionally yearned to know his brother's happiness. But, of course, those years with Jacques on Cyprus, both of them sharing the same life, the same ideals, had been deeply fulfilling. Then his friend had risen in the Order, been sent to England.

"Nonetheless I seek it, with all my soul."

They were quiet a moment. Geoffroy smiled happily. "So, we shall soon be brothers. Now it is time we retired. I hope you won't mind sleeping with the lamp lit. It is one of our rules. And we are roused twice during the night for devotions. Since you plan on joining us, Jean, this will give you a taste of our discipline."

Settling as best he could on the crackling pallet, Jean knew he could not sleep anyway. The excitement of being in the Temple, in Paris, heart of the world, surrounded by men he admired, sent a thousand thoughts careening through his head. Soon he could hear his uncle's rough snoring.

At midnight he accompanied Geoffroy to matins. In the dim chapel he remembered a curious bit of gossip about the Templars. Before Geoffroy dropped off to sleep again, Jean brought up the story he had heard about a strange idol, a head some said was called Baphomet, worshiped in secret ceremony by a select few. He supposed Geoffroy was one of them.

Angrily Geoffroy grunted. "By the blood of the Lamb, we

have no pagan idol! Baphomet? Where do you learn such things?"

Chastened, Jean said, "Some speak of it."

"Let them talk. There is no truth to it. My vows as a *dignitaire* forbid me to explain further. Go to sleep."

"Uncle, I hear dangerous talk in the streets. Talk against the Templars. It is said you consort with the devil."

Geoffroy was aware such rumors were being spread everywhere. That was why Jacques, as Grand Master, had been summoned from Cyprus. Pope Clément V demanded answers. De Charny knew, however, the rumors had come from King Philippe. If this was some part of the king's scheme to discredit the Templars and take over their possessions, it would never succeed. The Knights Templars were more powerful than Philippe. Geoffroy yawned. "We shall be awakened again at lauds in three hours. Get some sleep, nephew. This is nothing for you to worry over."

Yet, indeed, de Charny and de Molay, when they weren't reminiscing, talked of nothing but their fears for the Order. Following Jean's departure de Charny met with the grand master. Since the August day was sunny, they walked in the fortress garden.

Though both were of noble birth, Jacques de Molay, in appearance and personality, was his companion's opposite: short and stocky whereas Geoffroy was tall and imposing. De Molay, a shrewd and thoughtful man, possessed a deceptively simple and direct personality. He enjoyed teasing de Charny about Geoffroy's interest in books and learning. De Molay had no use for intellect. "Brawn, daring, moral courage, and devotion to Our Savior make a Templar," he liked to boast. The grand master was passionate in his dedication to the great Order he headed. Unofficially the Templars were considered the pope's army; a vast international network of Crusaders who had distinguished themselves in the mighty struggles to regain the Holy City. De Molay had lived his life in their service. He neither knew nor cared for anything else, except his learned friend de Charny, whom he long ago had elevated to high rank in the Order.

"There is trouble," said Jacques. "I had suspected it, but it has now been confirmed. We have an informer in the employ of Guillaume de Nogaret, the king's propagandist."

"You mean the king's liar?"

"Yes. A base man, de Nogaret. Have you met him?"

Geoffroy had not. De Molay recounted some of the charges de Nogaret had prepared for presentation to the pope. Monstrous accusations against the Order which, because of the secret nature of Temple proceedings and the Templars' enviable wealth, easily found believing ears.

"Witchcraft, outrages against Our Lord and His worship, crimes against nature, bestiality, homosexuality. Of all these and more, some believe us guilty."

Contemplating this last charge, Geoffroy felt shame. Fatherless from a very young age, he had joined the Order at sixteen and, shortly after, met de Molay. They had formed a close friendship. For some years during his youth Geoffroy had been troubled by a strong physical attraction for Jacques. Often he would want to express his devotion by caressing and embracing the slightly older man. But de Molay was a person of extraordinary spirituality, completely dedicated to the ascetic Templar ideals. Across the forty years of the relationship their friendship and affection had deepened into something, de Charny felt, which went beyond mere feeling, something more of spirit than flesh.

Cutting short the stroll, de Molay turned to Geoffroy. "Philippe is determined to destroy us," he said.

De Charny was appalled. This was unthinkable. Were they not protected by the papacy, answerable only to the Holy Father himself? Was a king of France prepared to defy the pope?

As if reading his mind, Jacques said, "Pope Clément summoned me from Cyprus, as you know. I told you how I traveled slowly, under heavy escort from our own knights, carrying ostentatious cartloads of gold and silver. These preparations were not made without great deliberation. It was necessary that the people be reminded of our wealth and power; that the Templar Grand Master was now resident in Paris. Perhaps our young ruler will consider more carefully before undertaking any rash moves against us. Nine thousand manor houses throughout the world, my friend—nine thousand!" Pride lit his fierce warrior's face. "Well, it is time I pay a call upon Philippe the Fair. I can assure you he will treat me most cordially. But he is planning a blow. My informants tell me that; my instinct tells me that. Where? When? I am dueling with shadows."

France's king had just returned from a hunt which began at dawn. He was pleased with the day, having taken four roebucks. At the palace portals he was met by Guillaume de Nogaret, who presented him with the document they had been discussing for weeks.

Alone, he eased into a chair and began to read it. If he approved this draft, within a month all *baillis* and *sénéchaux* throughout the kingdom would receive a sealed copy. The strict instructions were not to open it until a specified date. One week later, in a coordinated stroke, the blow would fall. Philippe read slowly, carefully, nodding his head at certain phrases. "Detestable crime," "execrable evil," "almost inhuman." Yes, he decided, Guillaume had followed the instructions perfectly. He, Philippe, was masterminding the operation. But de Nogaret had done his part well. Through clever propaganda he would enlist the sympathy of the people.

Philippe stared at the parchment. A bold stroke. Yet possibly a foolish one. Pope Clément might be unpredictable. Though Philippe had aided his ascension to the pontifical throne, the pope was not always to be counted on. The plot could fail; excommunication might follow. Philippe's pious heart began to beat heavily. Then he remembered the shroud; de Molay marching into Paris flashing all that gold and silver.

"Sire?" It was one of his pages. "The Templar grand master is here. He wishes to know whether you care to receive him."

Guiltily folding the draft with a quick gesture, Philippe said, "Of course. Let him enter." He got up and began pacing beneath a small window. Upon arriving, de Molay faced the king's back. The grand master dropped to his knees and remained there for what seemed to him an inordinate amount of time. Having recovered his composure, Philippe turned from the window. He moved quickly to de Molay and drew the old man to his feet.

"Jacques, my friend, what a delightful diversion. The hunt this morning was pleasant, but upon my return an advisor was waiting with all kinds of disagreeable matters. Now you have rescued me." He smiled affectionately. "Come, be seated."

De Molay thought once more what an engaging fellow this was. Tall and handsome, Philippe possessed extraordinary qualities. His intellect, piety, and good deeds were known to many. Moreover, he gave off an aura of warmth and sincerity which made it easy to like him.

Though de Molay perceived the king as a highly dangerous individual, it was hard, at times, to keep in mind that he was an antagonist actually plotting against the Order. Jacques told himself to keep on guard.

"Your Majesty, much time has unfortunately passed since last we talked. I should like to inquire after the health of your sons, my young godchild, Charles, in particular."

"Jacques, you are sitting too far away. Come closer, beside me. My children are all well and really quite grown. Charles is an excellent huntsman."

"The truth is, Sire, I am concerned with the strange rumors flying about. A young friend of ours reports that he has heard talk against us in the streets."

The king blithely continued, "Jacques, I was asking about you. How is your health? What gift might I offer to make more pleasant your stay in Paris? Perhaps one of the stags I killed last week. It has been hanging and should be excellent by now."

"There is only one gift which would satisfy me: an end to the charges against our Order. They are base and vile and totally without substance."

"But, my good friend, what have I to do with all this? How could I stop such street rumors? It is impossible to trace where they begin."

De Molay felt sour disgust rising in his throat. He could have challenged Philippe's statement, but caution and thoughtful deliberation were his only allies in this game of wills. For the moment Philippe held all the cards.

The king continued solicitously, "You know as well as I the greed of people. Your power, your wealth, provoke envy. Your Temple is a state within a state. Foreigners and even fugitives from our justice find refuge there. . . ."

Jacques interrupted, "Even you, Sire, once found haven with us."

"Indeed so. And you must believe my sincere gratitude. But that does not alter the truth of what I am saying. And there is the matter of your secret ceremonies . . ."

"They are beyond reproach!"

"But who is to know that, Jacques? Even I, who once hoped to wear the cross of red, am a stranger to your secrets." Deftly, then, the king turned his conversation to other subjects; his hopes for a new Crusade, his continuing grief over the death of his wife, Jeanne. The old Templar soon found himself offering advice and sympathy. But later, upon leaving the royal palace, he noticed his hands were shaking badly as he reached for his horse's reins.

The blow de Molay feared was not long in coming. During the early hours of Friday, October 13, 1307, a small contingent of several knights and king's serjeants appeared at the Templar gate. Guillaume de Marcilly, in charge of the group, called out, "You, there, open up."

A Templar guard looked down from a bartizan. "What's this all about?"

De Marcilly waved a document about his head. "The king commands that certain monies must immediately be withdrawn from the royal treasury funds you hold. It's an emergency. Open up." The drawbridge was lowered, the portcullis was cranked up; the group casually rode in. As the Templar officer reached for the document, de Marcilly thrust his hand forward, the dagger below the document plunged into the Templar's heart. Instantly the others raced to the drawbridge and portcullis control points, neutralizing the Templar guard. From behind a mansion across the square galloped a battalion of king's knights in armor. They surged through the open gates, engaging and easily overpowering all resistance.

Earlier that evening the grand master had not been able to sleep. Pacing the Temple grounds, he reviewed the fragmented intelligence reports. Coupled with his intuition they spelled imminent threat. Wheeling around, he raced to Geoffroy de Charny. Quickly they reviewed their emergency plan and decided to act. The key element was Guy le Meunier, a young miller who lived a short distance from the precinct walls. Guy and his widowed father, descendants of Theo Metochites, milled flour for the Order. Guy's Friday task was tending the shroud.

"How may I serve you?" asked Guy sleepily, after Geoffroy had brought him and his father to the fortress.

Said Geoffroy, "There is no time to explain fully. We expect the king will send soldiers to confiscate our wealth. And the shroud."

De Molay interrupted, his voice trembling, "The gold be damned. But the shroud, it must be hidden at once."

"I can do it," said Guy, suddenly awake. "I'll run away with it, to the countryside and . . ." Lamely, he stopped, realizing his idea was foolish. The king's agents were surely on the alert everywhere.

"There is a way," said Geoffroy calmly. Then he outlined the plan he and de Molay had devised.

De Molay nodded. "It is our only hope. Guy, we're asking you and your father to share our secret. You both must leave at once with Geoffroy. Never mention your association with the Temple. I shall not tell you where we secrete the shroud. The place is already prepared. Should our enemies learn of your connection with it, they would rack the information from you. But know this. At some time in the future, when things are clearer, no matter how long it takes, we will contact you with further instructions. You will act as our agent, delivering the relic where we direct."

Together they descended to the room of the secret ceremony. Following de Molay's instructions, Guy lifted the shroud from its reliquary. Guy's father felt a lump in his throat, seeing the precious linen for the first time in years. It was then rolled and tied in a leather sheath. They continued to a room unfamiliar to Guy. It was piled with shirts of mail, rusting armor, and helmets.

Pushing the heavy equipment aside, Geoffroy revealed an almost invisible trap door. When it was opened, a stale, earthy smell rose to their nostrils.

Said de Molay, "Geoffroy will lead you to safety and a new life." Guy observed that Geoffroy was holding a small, heavy sack in his left hand; in his right he carried a lantern.

De Molay continued, "Now, you must both swear never to reveal a word of this conversation."

"Master, I swear it on my life." Guy's father repeated the vow. Jacques de Molay made the sign of the Cross as he wished God's blessings upon them.

The way along the narrow underground passage was dark and eerie. Geoffroy's lantern played strange shadows on the wooden beams which braced the tunnel. They walked single file—it seemed for a timeless interval. Guy's voice sounded suddenly too loud as he broke the silence to marvel at the tunnel's construction. Geoffroy explained it was the work of an early Templar, his name now lost. He had been an engineer and a specialist in the undermining of besieged city walls. After a broad tunnel beneath the wall was complete, its beams would be set ablaze, the tunnel's cave-in collapsing the wall above.

They arrived finally at a barred door. As it creaked open, and Geoffroy pushed aside a thick drapery of fishing nets beyond, Guy could see they were alongside the Seine, at the Templar wharf. Behind them was the Petit Temple, a small riverside building.

Geoffroy blew out the lantern and untied a boat. Straining through nighttime mist, he directed their course. The boat ran aground on the Left Bank near the monastery of the Grands Augustins. Speaking softly, the Templar said, "First, I give you this map, a key, and this sack of silver and gold coins. There is more than enough to repay the loss of your business and keep you both in comfort for many years. The map will lead you to a little house we own. It is to be found by the old Roman Thermes de Julien, facing the Sorbonne. The house is yours. A title to it is properly inscribed on the other side of the map. The key opens its door. There is an empty shop in the front.

"Never, never return to the mill; it must be forgotten for your safety and the future well-being of the shroud. Live quietly, and God protect you both." He embraced them, took the shroud from Guy, and returned to the boat. They watched as he disappeared into the mist.

Shortly after de Charny made his way back via the underground passage, the Templar guard surrendered. Thrown into one of the fortress dungeons, Geoffroy surmised that de Molay was being held nearby. But they did not see each other until one week later when both were brought before Guillaume de Paris, Papal Grand Inquisitor of France.

In a suave tone Guillaume declared, "You, Geoffroy de Charny, Master of Normandy, and you, Jacques de Molay, Grand Master of the Poor Knights of Christ of the Temple of Solomon, are accused of heinous crimes against Our Lord, His church, nature, and all mankind." The inquisitor slowly recited a list of eight charges, exhorting each man to answer "yea" or "nay" to each. Geoffroy was unable to believe what he was hearing: that the Templars had betrayed the Holy Land, worshiped the devil, spat and urinated on the Cross, murdered members who tried to expose the Order, practiced idolatry . . . He denied them all, as did Jacques.

"And you, Geoffroy de Charny, and you, Jacques de Molay, are accused, further, of requiring novices to perform 'the kiss of shame.'" Guillaume's voice droned on dispassionately. Geoffroy's spirit was seared with grief. "They must bestow this kiss upon your buttocks, your penis, and mouth. Moreover, you are accused of committing unnatural acts upon each other, the crime of sodomy . . ."

Their private relationship in question? This was the final blow. Geoffroy felt drained, unable to speak. Then he glanced at Jacques. The old warrior was looking into his face, radiating back the courage that had momentarily fled. De Molay turned to the inquisitor. His voice rang out. "Though you and all the authorities of the Church think yourselves safe from the wrath of poor prisoners like us, beware of God's wrath for your lies."

De Charny, his mettle restored, shouted, "By all that is sacred I deny these charges!"

Abruptly the two were hustled away. Never again did they appear together before the inquisitors.

Geoffroy de Charny did not forget Jacques's noble defiance that day. It sustained him through the ominous threats, interrogation under torture by Philippe's knights, and the silent horror of being shut away in darkness.

Repeatedly Geoffroy denied the charges put to him. But finally his jailer confided the unthinkable: the grand master had broken. Jacques had confessed to the worst of the allegations: spitting at the Cross, and denying Christ. Geoffroy refused to accept the report. But soon doubt set in. One morning he awoke from terrible nightmares and began beating upon the heavy door of his cell. Screaming and pounding until his knuckles bled, he collapsed exhausted to the stone floor. It was not long before he was dragged once more before Guillaume de Paris. Again the questions were put to him. Ill and disheartened he nodded as each of the eight charges was repeated. Satisfied, the grand inquisitor produced a frosty smile. Geoffroy prayed for a sword. Such men did not deserve to exist.

More than ninety Templars had died at the stake. Some had succumbed to torture or the terrible conditions of their imprisonment; others had killed themselves. Geoffroy, too, pondered suicide. He knew Jacques would never consider such an act. It would be risking eternal damnation. However, his friend might already have died of ill treatment. Who, then, would be left to reveal where the relic was hidden? Geoffroy resolved to stay alive.

For seven years de Charny and Jacques de Molay, who had managed to survive, languished in the Temple dungeon. Meantime Philippe IV scoured France for the missing shroud. The ruler was, however, most discreet about questions relating to the cloth. Should others learn what he sought, they might find it first. Only a small group of his most trusted men were privy to his secret search.

Geoffroy de Charny, during his confinement, awaited one thing only: a chance to contact Guy le Meunier. Neither he nor de Molay had anticipated long imprisonment. The Templar cared little for himself. With the Order's disgrace life for him had ended. Now he concentrated upon saving the shroud. It must be kept from Philippe's hands. The royal treasury was no doubt bankrupt, the king having constantly mishandled the realm's currency. Should he be permitted to get hold of the relic, Philippe would surely sell it for a fortune. Now only le Meunier could save the situation.

Years before, de Charny and de Molay had worked out their plan. Since the grand master had no sons and Jean de Charny, Geoffroy's devoted nephew, had once planned to become a Templar, it was agreed that Jean should be the recipient of the shroud. The two leaders even speculated that eventually the younger de Charny might reestablish the Templar Order. Geoffroy's every waking hour was spent praying God would give him the chance to set his plan in motion. But first Guy le Meunier must come to him.

Chapter 15

Paris, 1314

Since their escape with de Charny the night the Temple fell, Guy and his father had rarely left their new house. Not until the king's agents—at first they seemed everywhere—could no longer be spotted did the two feel safe.

In February of their second year on the Left Bank, Guy's father died. Several months later Guy married Clotilde, daughter of one of the quarter's bakers. She was a superb pastry cook and a good wife. Clotilde opened a little bakery shop in the front of their house which soon became a neighborhood favorite. Guy's first son, Matthieu, was born the following year.

True to his vow, Guy never spoke of his role the night the Temple fell. Seven years later he was still waiting for word from de Molay or de Charny. In the streets he heard occasional rumors about the Templars and their ordeal. It was said that many had been burned at the stake, but Guy learned that the two leaders were confined in their own fortress. Still no message arrived.

In recent days Paris gossip centered on a critical decision made by the king, though precisely what, was not clear. It was to be Philippe's final solution to the troublesome problem of the Templar leaders. With trepidation Guy wondered whether Philippe might be considering murder. Some believed the king would do anything to rid himself of the problem, for it troubled his conscience. Besides, Philippe feared that Pope Clément might reverse himself and the Order would spring back to life. Should that happen, laughed the wags, King Philippe's crown would teeter precariously upon those blond locks.

Guy believed in following orders. De Molay's last words were "When things are clearer, however long that takes, we will contact you with further instructions." But seven long years had passed without a summons. If he were ever to help, the time was now. After all, the shroud was his affair as well as theirs. It was time to act.

In his palace near Notre Dame, Philippe IV spent long hours mulling over his spectacular coup. It seemed a hollow victory. Though in one night he had completely destroyed the Order, his success had not yet brought him any material benefits. If ever the papal commission could be pressured to rule that the charges against the Templar Order were true, their assets would be his. But Philippe's ultimate objective was still unrealized and he was consumed by frustration.

Another matter plagued him: nowhere had his men located the shroud. After thoroughly searching the fortress, they had found nothing.

Furthermore, Jacques de Molay's years of imprisonment made Philippe increasingly uneasy. His conscience pricked him about the man who had been his friend, head of the Order which had once saved his life. There was something about the old knight—a purity of purpose. Even now Philippe rather admired de Molay. Although the king had convinced himself that suppressing the corrupt Templars was a holy act approved by God, he still sought the grand master's acquiescence to what had been done. Moreover, he needed something important from de Molay. One day, seven years after the arrests, he finally compelled himself to face the Templar.

Philippe was taken aback by what he saw. This trembling shadow, this filthy scarecrow—Jacques de Molay?

As the king came nearer, Jacques drew away, shielding his eyes from the unaccustomed light.

"You have had a bad time."

Grunted Jacques, "No doubt better than some. At least I'm alive." His spirit had lost none of its fire. The king was uncomfortable.

"We are relieved to hear you have confessed your sins, Jacques. Your soul must be the better for it."

"I never feared for my soul. But what of yours?"

"Mine? I sleep well at night." Philippe's voice had risen. "I have nothing to confess."

"Nor I, and you know it." Jacques pulled aside his soiled robes. "These are the marks of my guilt." His body was scored with burns and ugly scars. "Here is your truth!"

The grand master collapsed into a chair and gazed steadily into the face of his adversary. Uneasily the king said, "This visit need not be long. Soon you can return to your—"

"Cell? I have learned to value it. It feeds the soul. By the time you put an end to me, I shall be quite holy."

"Jacques, I do not plan your death. I may even decide to set you free in return for some information which I know you possess." He paused, then continued a bit nervously. "The shroud of Jesus—I saw it once, in your chapel."

De Molay looked surprised, but said nothing.

"My men have combed the citadel; it seems to have vanished. It must be found for the benefit of the people."

"For the benefit of your treasury!" growled the grand master, with unexpected ferocity.

Philippe flinched. Annoyed with himself, he said menacingly, "You shall be further punished for this insolence, de Molay. Remember, you speak to the anointed king of France."

De Molay added, "Also a baptized child of Our Lord God. Have a care for your soul."

"Where is the shroud, Jacques? You can tell me."

De Molay stared ahead.

"I will find it, old man. The Templars are nothing. You have no power, no wealth. You have been swept up like rat droppings."

Jacques's expression softened. "I am what I have always been, God's most humble servant. I love Our Lord. Death in His service is the ardent wish of all Templars." He pointed a finger toward Philippe. "Your Majesty, I have known you to be a pious man. What happened to change such a devoted spirit? Once you begged to wear our robes. Let me believe it was not you but others who provoked these cruelest of deeds. You must still be a good and worthy servant of Our Lord. My instinct tells me so." Philippe managed a twisted smile.

The Templar continued, "Though mine is a simple mind, it sees things clearly. I understand exactly what you did and why. To understand all is to pardon all." He shrugged. "My life is nothing." Unsteadily he stood up. "Now, Your Majesty, if you would permit, I shall return to my rathole."

Though somewhat shaken, Philippe had not forgotten his purpose in summoning de Molay. "And the shroud?"

Jacques managed an uncertain bow. "The shroud?" Reaching the door, he looked a long moment at Philippe. "Sire, please deliver to my godchild, Charles, all love and blessings." With head erect the grand master backed into the arms of his jailer.

The king had been sipping wine. With a ferocious oath he hurled the goblet against the closing door.

Crossing the Petit Pont, Guy walked through the streets of Île de la Cité until he reached, via the Grand Pont, the shores of the Right Bank. He carried a small lantern and clutched beneath his tunic a flattened bar of iron, purchased at a smithy. Paris was dark, deserted, and silent. Only a few lights could be seen at distant crossroads. Some time before bells had rung the matins.

He made his way along the quay until he spotted the Petit Temple in the moonlight. Beneath it was an old stained wall, part of which was covered with festoons of rotting fishnet. They fell apart as he pulled them aside. The ancient wooden door was still there. As he had supposed, it was locked from the inside. Guy forced his iron bar into a space between door and wall and pulled hard. The sound of the door bursting open exploded into the nighttime stillness. Motionless, Guy waited in the doorway. He was unchallenged. The door made a groaning sound as he closed it behind him.

Passing through the long tunnel, he had to wade into pools of water from the dripping roof and duck under beams that had partially collapsed. He mounted steps at the end of the passage and tried to raise the trap door, but it would not budge. Straining mightily, he began to feel it give. He could hear metal sliding away on the other side as, with tremendous effort, he pushed up and at last was through.

Guy had a general idea of the prison location in the Temple keep. He gripped his iron bar, expecting trouble at every turn, but he found the cells without mishap. A few torches burned smokily along the dungeon passageways. The place stank of feces and human rot. Cautiously he moved along, peering around corners. He encountered no one. It was past midnight; the guards were probably dozing. Most Templar prisoners had long ago been moved to other locations; some released. Only a few old men were still confined here.

The cells were secured by heavy wooden doors. Each had a small grille through which a jailer might observe the prisoner. Guy went from door to door. At each opening he would softly call de Charny's and de Molay's names, and then identify himself. He paused at more than a dozen barred windows before he heard a response.

"Thanks to God!" came a hoarse whisper out of the blackness.

Guy could see nothing, but heard shuffling sounds. Then he made out in the dull light of the passage a face pressed against the aperture. The man's eyes were dark and sunken, his hair and beard matted, his face eroded with sores. Guy barely recognized Geoffroy de Charny.

"Water!" croaked de Charny.

A search of the passageways produced a water barrel and wooden ladle. Filling the ladle, Guy carried it back and carefully poured the liquid through the bars. Much of it missed Geoffroy's open mouth. Three more trips were necessary before the Templar's thirst was relieved. Only then could he speak.

"Bless you," he said fervently. "For years I have prayed you would find me, Guy." He slowly shook his head. "That it would come to this!"

"There are troubling rumors throughout the city," said Guy. "I felt I should not stay away longer even though I was not summoned."

"You were right. We are helpless here. God sent you. That is the truth." Quickly Geoffroy explained in careful detail where he had hidden the shroud. "I have been told the king will soon make his move against us. I thought I had nothing with which to influence my jailer. One day I prayed for his sick son. The boy recovered. Now the man pleads for my prayers. He keeps me informed. We are to be taken from here for a further proceeding. The outcome . . . ?" He left his statement incomplete.

"When you find the time to be right, take the shroud to my nephew, the knight Jean de Charny, Sire of Lirey. The jailer learned Jean had married a de Joinville. Alas, we had hoped he would revive the Order. But, little matter. What is gone is gone. His estate at Lirey is a few hours' walk south of Troyes."

"I shall find him," said Guy.

"It is God's will that you bring the relic to safety. Listen carefully."

Guy moved his face closer to the opening. He caught the prisoner's fetid breath.

"You must promise to require a solemn vow of Jean. Never may he allow the shroud to fall into the hands of a ruler of France. He must keep all knowledge of the shroud secret until he passes it on. So, likewise, must his sons."

Guy promised.

"Have you found the grand master?"

"I reached you first."

"If he still lives, pray deliver this message. Tell him, 'Let us undo the deed.'"

With considerable difficulty Guy was able to find de Molay's cell off a corridor some distance away. Though the grand master looked in poorer condition than de Charny, his stubborn will was still evident. Guy assured the Templar leader that he would carry the shroud to Lirey as soon as it was feasible to do so. Upon hearing Geoffroy's cryptic message, de Molay nodded his grizzled head.

"Ah, yes, I plan just that. We both have the same thought."

Then, although he knew he had no right to do so, Guy was unable to resist questioning de Molay, for he had been shocked by the horrible accusations to which the grand master had confessed. "During my weekly visits to the Temple I never saw nor could I ever imagine such conduct as was reported. I do not understand why you said what you did." Indeed, though he had not admitted it, Guy had felt shame and more than a little anger about his own connection with the Order.

"Guy, hear me. You cannot know what happens to helpless prisoners. After these torturers had practiced their skills on me, I would gladly have confessed to slaying God Himself." He hesitated. "But it no longer matters. We have our understanding, Geoffroy and I. Tell him I have been comforted remembering the good times, our early years together on Cyprus."

After he had returned safely to his home, Guy le Meunier waited for the next act in the Templar tragedy. Sometimes he thought to enter Notre Dame, where de Charny had secreted the shroud, to see whether the relic was still in its hiding place. But he felt he must be cautious. Or maybe he was just a bit afraid. Better to wait until he could be certain of the Templars' fate. Part of him hoped for a miracle.

It never came. On a gray March morning, two weeks after Guy's visit to the prisoners, de Molay and de Charny, along with two others of the Templar hierarchy, were taken, manacled, in a tumbril to a wooden platform erected in the square that fronted Notre Dame. A fine drizzle was falling. The Templars were commanded to reaffirm their confessions before the people of Paris, thus justifying their sentences of life imprisonment.

The king awaited the end of the matter a short distance away at his palace. He was smugly satisfied that he had saved his conscience any pangs which might derive from the deaths of men who had done him no harm.

A few old people in the huge crowd that had gathered could recall these wretched figures when, in a better time, they had set out to fight the Infidel. Bearing high their piebald standard, the departing warriors would request prayers from onlookers gathered to cheer them on their way. Now only murmurs of sympathy could be heard.

When all was ready and everyone quiet, the recorded confessions were read out. Then the judgment: life imprisonment. Next the Templars were exhorted to reaffirm their guilt and express penitence for such crimes.

First, Hugues de Payraud, Temple Treasurer, former friend of the king. Bowing his head, he acquiesced in a faint voice. Geoffroy de Gonaville, Master of Poitou and Aquitaine, did likewise.

Now Grand Master de Molay was helped to the platform. With a rattling of chains he glanced briefly in the direction of the royal palace. Then, looking fiercely at the faces before him, in a voice still strong, he recanted his confession, telling the stunned crowd his earthly life held no value now. But concern for his soul prompted him to reveal the truth: such crimes had never been committed. The offer of life had no meaning when bought at the price of a lie.

After de Molay had spoken, people began weeping and crying out against the king. Officials looked alarmed and tried to quiet them. Only when de Charny, Master of Normandy, began to speak would they be still.

"I have served a pure and godly Order," began Geoffroy, firmly. "The only crime to which I confess is that I lied. I affirmed these disgusting and horrible charges as though they were true. They are *not* true!" As he raised his manacled arms, his clothes fell open revealing a scarred body. Geoffroy shouted, "I cry to God Himself—we are innocent!"

Within the hour Philippe IV received Guillaume de Nogaret, now his chancellor, who had been present at Notre Dame. The king's son, de Molay's godchild, stood nearby, listening, as they talked.

"Ah, Guillaume, let me hear the good news. It has been long in coming."

The chancellor feared his king's reaction. He had considered sending someone else to give the report.

"The good news is somewhat limited, Sire. Two of them reaffirmed, the others . . ."

Philippe's eyes grew wide with disbelief. "You mean, the others chose death? Who, de Nogaret, who?"

"Sire, reaffirming were de Gonaville and de Payraud."

"Fils de put!" screamed the king. "De Molay?"

De Nogaret nodded. "Recanted. De Charny, too. Of course, now they are relapsed heretics. We have no choice. As you said, Sire, they must die."

"No, Father!" cried Charles, moving to the king's side. "Not Jacques. Not my godfather." He was remembering how, as a boy, he had admired the illustrious Templar in his white mantle and beard, looking like a vision of God.

With terrible force Philippe struck his son, knocking him to the floor. Charles lay where he had fallen, staring up at his father. In an agony of frustration Philippe turned his face upward and howled like an animal. De Nogaret had never heard anything like it. Yet he understood. In death de Molay would be free; Philippe condemned.

At vespers that same evening Guy le Meunier was present on the tiny Île des Javiaux, close by Île de la Cité, to witness the death of the two Templars. As the tumbril clattered over cobblestones leading to the royal quay, Guy clenched his fists. Such an ignoble conveyance for men of knightly rank. A large and sympathetic crowd had gathered. They called out words of comfort and support.

Now Guy could see de Molay and de Charny. From the tumbril they were dragged to a boat and rowed to the island. The pair sat close together, their chained arms around each other's neck. A pair of stakes, side by side, awaited them. Their shackles were opened and rechained with their arms and legs behind the posts. The condemned men called out to a nearby priest. Following a whispered conference, the prisoners' positions were shifted. They would die facing Notre Dame. Only Guy knew why.

The kindling beneath their feet was set ablaze. As the flames rose around them, each man was heard to shout the Crusader battle cry, "Holy Sepulchre." And de Molay, with his dying breath, called, "Philippe! Clément! I summon you to meet me again at Heaven's judgment."

Darkness fell as the two bodies were consumed by the fire. The flames reflected redly across the Seine waters and on ramparts of Philippe's castle. Many in the crowd remained all night, waiting for the ashes to cool. Relics of such men were thought to possess great healing power.

Sickened by the spectacle, Guy soon departed. Pacing the streets, he finally made a decision and turned toward Notre Dame.

The cathedral was crowded with simple folk praying for the souls of the two Templars. Some already saw them as martyrs. Saints, possibly.

Guy went stealthily to a dark chapel on the northern side of the cathedral, where de Charny had said the shroud would be found. He could see the Virgin's statue. Making certain he was alone in the chapel, Guy tilted the polychrome figure toward him and reached beneath it. There, in the hollowed base, was a soft, yielding roll, sheathed in leather.

"*De par Dieu,* the shroud!" Reverently he ran his hands across the leather cylinder's cool surface. He tried to thrust it beneath his tunic, but it was too large. Tucking it under his arm and hoping he looked inconspicuous, he left the cathedral.

Outside, he had to resist breaking into a run. Walking briskly, he turned toward the Pont Saint Michel. Back home, Guy placed his treasure in the bedroom chest and expelled a great sigh of relief. Clotilde must ask no questions. Further decisions would have to be made soon enough. Until then the shroud of his ancestors was secure.

As he contemplated his trip to Lirey, Guy became increasingly concerned for the shroud's safety. Suppose he was stopped by the king's agents? Or robbers?

A solution presented itself one afternoon in mid-April, when a longtime customer, Barnabé de la Tour, entered the pastry shop. Barnabé, a knowledgeable, middle-aged man, and Guy were accustomed to engage in long conversations.

"Tell me, Barnabé," asked Guy, "suppose you were traveling to—ah—Troyes with something of high value. How could you protect yourself from the perils of the journey? Such as brigands, for instance?"

"Of course, you're speaking of money?"

Guy nodded.

"My friend, you're asking the right man at the right time. Have you forgotten I am a Fair Inspector for the Crown? I always travel south with the gold merchants from Saxony. They are jolly fellows, and one need not worry; their caravan is armed to repel any imaginable threat. My Saxons are in Paris now. We leave for the fair at Provins in three days. Get yourself a mule and join us. I shall enjoy your company, and Troyes is but two days from Provins. The road is well patrolled."

The journey south with Barnabé was a pleasant one, in spite of the responsibility Guy felt for the shroud's safekeeping. The Saxon gold merchants were, as reported, indeed good humored. They cooked their sausages with a strong-scented, salted cabbage which he came to relish.

Barnabé said his farewell to Guy at Provins, a week before the fair.

"We shall not travel to Troyes until the Hot Fair in July," he explained. "So it would please me if you would care to pay a visit to my dear, ancient cousin Noé le Jaillard, who operates a mill on the Meldançon Canal. Please extend my respects to him and tell him my brothers are all well. You will like Noé."

Guy's trip to Troyes was without incident, for there was much traffic going north to Provins. Entering the city by the Paris Gate, he made his way to the southeast corner, where le Jaillard had his mill. Guy's senses soared to see and hear the fresh rush of the current under the mill wheel. But the wheel was not turning.

He found Noé and a young assistant trying to replace a worn-out wooden gear. Introducing himself, Guy lent his efforts to the problem. Within minutes he had the new gear adjusted.

"You did that like a miller," Noé told him.

"I was once," said Guy, suddenly despondent as he thought back to his earlier days in Paris. He joined Noé for dinner, leaving his bundle under the trestle table, and was later persuaded to stay the night.

By noon the next day Noé had agreed to sell Guy the mill. Noé would live with Guy's family and be given a small annual stipend.

It was with a guilty start that Guy le Meunier's eyes finally fixed on his precious package. By the saints, he had forgotten it! The next morning, in exuberant spirits, he continued on his way to Lirey.

Chapter 16

Lirey—Poitiers, 1314–1356

Sundays for Jean de Charny, nephew of the martyred Geoffroy, had become a time of exhausting emotion. As he climbed the donjon steps, spiraling upward to Lirey Castle's highest tower chamber, it began again. Releasing his helpless left arm, which he invariably held with the right hand, Jean reached for his keys. Again he was seized by that grinding sense of humiliation he had known for several months since the notorious fall of his uncle. Where once the de Charny name had spelled great honor, it was now reduced to a justification for sneers. He turned the key and the ironbound door swung open.

When Guy le Meunier had arrived one day in April, he had brought with him not only the holy shroud but the true story of Geoffroy's suffering and end.

For a while Jean stood in the open doorway, burning with shame for his own private condemnation of the Templar. This noble man had sustained the most unspeakable tortures to induce his false confession. Jean slammed his fist against his thigh. By St. Loup, he should have realized! How could he possibly have accepted those damned stories? But people believe what they hear; he had been no exception. There were all those years of shameful reports and scabrous gossip. And now, even though his uncle was without guilt, the de Charny name had been dragged in the dust.

Following his usual sequence of thoughts, Jean clenched his teeth. It was that greedy, damned Capetian bastard, Philippe the Fair! Jean thrust the door closed behind him and bolted it. Then he bellowed with rage. That royal pig was always short of funds. Had he not debased the coinage, expropriated the Jews' wealth before he expelled them, and plundered the Lombard bankers? Then it was the Templars' vast riches he had sought. Along with the inestimably valuable shroud of Jesus.

His uncle had chosen death at the stake rather than affirm the vile acts with which he was charged. Jean recalled Guy's words, as he described de Charny's sublime courage while facing the flames. And despite everything Geoffroy had guarded the secret of the shroud.

Jean's eyes turned to the strongbox by the wall of the circular room. The morning sun shone through the greenish glass window he had installed in the east side of the conical roof. Breathing heavily, he moved to the chest. Kneeling in front, he carefully unlocked it with a second key and peered into its shadowed depths.

Jean thought of the sole condition Guy le Meunier had imposed upon him: the honoring of the Templars' demand of future shroud holders. Addressing the box, Jean passionately intoned, "I swear never to allow this sacred relic to fall into the hands of the Crown. Its existence shall be revealed to none but those who are wholly to be trusted." Then he added an additional pledge, his own: "Furthermore, I vow to renew this oath every seven days."

Then he carefully drew out the shroud and unfolded it on the cloth-covered floor. Sun illuminated the face of the Savior. Jean fell prostrate before the relic, sobbing. Jesus had suffered, Geoffroy had suffered, and now it was he who must bear the agony of his shame.

Thinking of his uncle, he cried, "Lord, forgive me. I saw evil where there was goodness."

He lay there, gazing at the features of Jesus in silence. Then, gradually, his spirit rose and he was filled with exaltation. The sunlight had shifted from the face to the spear wound in the Savior's side. Still on his knees, Jean returned the shroud to its hiding place. Leaving the room, he felt renewed, exhausted. Next Sunday he would come here again.

On a lower landing he encountered his wife. She knew nothing. He had explained, some time before, that he preferred to pray and meditate alone up there. In a way it was true.

"Would you like me to massage your arm?" she asked.

He nodded, smiling. It was his arm that had brought them together. Six years before, when he was eighteen, Jean had attempted to support himself by participating in tournaments throughout the land. The principle of primogeniture, the eldest son's exclusive right of inheritance, was a matter which presented substantial difficulties to younger sons such as Jean. These hapless knights, trained only for war, lacking a fief to bring them an income, were usually compelled to seek employment as mercenaries. Their major gains came from battle plunder and ransom monies. Tournaments, a sort of mock warfare, could bring riches to winners through their claims to the loser's horse, armor, and baggage.

In 1311 young Jean had participated in a great tournament held by King Philippe on a field near Paris. Jean had triumphed in his first joust, and was now facing a new challenger. With smashing force Jean's lance struck his opponent's helmet, reversing it on the man's head. The stunned and blinded knight held in his saddle as the horse charged at a wild angle directly toward the royal pavilion. The knight's lance was pointed at a young female spectator. Spurring viciously, Jean raced toward his opponent's mount. A moment before the impact of Jean's horse against the flank of the other animal deflected it into a harmless course, the tip of his opponent's lance drove under a pauldron protecting Jean's shoulder, ripping into his armpit, tearing nerves. It was later discovered that the lance's metal tip had been improperly flattened.

While his wound was being bound, Jean was visited by the young woman whom he had saved. She was Marguerite de Joinville, youngest granddaughter of Jean, Sire de Joinville. The remarkable old Crusader and companion of St. Louis had begun his important career as historian at the age of seventy-five.

Marguerite, accompanied by her father, Anselm, and the lively old man, now in his eighty-seventh year, were profuse in their words of gratitude and admiration of Jean's bravery. Marguerite was worried; Jean's arm hung limply at his side. He was unable to raise it. While the young knight was recovering, the Sire de Joinville insisted that he be their guest at the de Joinville castle on the Marne.

The wound became infected and for several weeks de Charny lay ill with fever. It was Marguerite who cared for him, and it seemed not extraordinary that Jean should fall in love with this sympathetic, dark-haired girl. For Marguerite, her love of Jean had been at first sight.

The old nobleman liked de Charny, and upon his father's warm urging, Anselm agreed to give his daughter in marriage to the young man. The minor castle in Lirey, with its modest revenues, became Marguerite's dowry.

That Sunday Jean and Marguerite were finishing dinner as a servant rushed in to report that some men-at-arms were approaching the castle. Jean studied the distant, mounted figures, then he made out their banner.

"Marguerite, they are the king's knights!"

Marguerite took a deep breath and said, steadily, "We must change its location. The top of the keep is the first place they will look."

"You *know!* How?"

Marguerite replied, "Why do you think man invented keyholes? But there's little time. You must greet them by the entrance portal. Give me the keys, quickly."

Accompanied by squires, serjeants, and dagger-armed soldiers bearing axes, Guillaume de Marcilly and Hugues de la Celle presented themselves to Jean. Bowing with a smirk, the short, icy, blue-eyed de Marcilly said, "By your leave, Messire de Charny, we are here at the command of King Philippe to search your properties."

The giant-statured de la Celle contracted his heavy brows and pushed a warrant of royal order under Jean's nose. "Read this," he growled. "It may keep you entertained while we look for something the king seeks."

De Marcilly giggled. "Don't disturb yourself, messire, we can find our own way about."

Turning to a serjeant, he said, "Station your men by all the outer doorways. We shall start at the top of the tower and work our way down."

"What have I done? What are you looking for?" asked Jean.

Brushing past him, de Marcilly said, "We didn't get it out of the Templar Geoffroy when we were—ah—examining him."

"And we tried much," scowled de la Celle, who was mounting the stairs.

Said de Marcilly, "Before he flew to heaven, one of the Templars confessed to Hugues that the late Master of Normandy had been visited by a nephew. Then a court herald came across your shield and name in a roll of arms from a royal tournament. The rest was simple." Without further words he began to climb the steps.

Back in the hall Marguerite was calmly sitting at the table, eating an apple. "Sit down, my dear," she said, pleasantly, "and finish your dinner."

"They'll break down that door."

"Not at all, it's unlocked."

"Where is *it*?" whispered Jean.

"I have to arrange something in the kitchen before they come back." And, the half-eaten apple in her hand, Marguerite hurried away.

After a long while the king's two knights returned empty handed to the hall where Jean was still sitting, staring at a partially dismembered game bird. Marguerite appeared an instant later.

"You gentlemen must be hungry," she said. "Will you partake of some nice rabbit?"

"By St. Denis, I can't find it," growled de la Celle. "Maybe we should personally examine de Charny here."

De Marcilly said, "Come on, let's stop for now and eat, Hugues."

The two moved to the table and made themselves comfortable. A boy entered from the kitchen and placed trenchers, large slabs of stale bread that served as plates, before the knights. Another serving-boy arranged pieces of stewed rabbit on the trenchers.

"More," ordered de la Celle. And the youth piled the large knight's trencher high with meaty rabbit bones.

De Marcilly turned genially to Jean and said, "De Charny was a hard nut to crack, or should I say, to roast. For my part, I prefer a bit of fire in my work."

"I'm a bone man," muttered de la Celle. He picked up a rabbit thigh and, holding it above his head, broke it with one hand. The crack of the bone giving way resounded off the stone walls.

De la Celle reached down to wipe his hands on the tablecloth. As he lifted it, he exclaimed, "These de Charnys really live well, Guillaume. Look, two tablecloths!"

Beneath de la Celle's huge, greasy hand, Jean saw the familiar herringbone weave of the shroud.

Marguerite, who had returned, said, "Gentlemen, I wish to offer you our very finest wine." She clapped her hands and ordered the bread server to bring in the special vintage. A moment later, two scullery boys entered from the kitchen, along with the cook, who was carrying the legs of an inert serving-boy. Each scullion held an arm of the body, whose head lolled and jounced as they moved. The veins of the body's neck were jet black.

"May the Lord save us," murmured Marguerite. "Another one, on the same day."

"Another what?" cried de Marcilly.

"What can I say?" sighed a distressed Marguerite. "It's the *peste foudroyante,* the fulminant plague. It strikes like lightning, but it only seems to affect the kitchen people . . . so far."

"Jesus," roared de la Celle. "That was the fellow who served our meat."

"Forgive me," said Marguerite, "but I'm afraid your wine will be a little delayed."

De Marcilly rose. "Consider, Hugues, we have done what we were directed to. There's nothing here—absolutely nothing! Let us depart."

"I agree," said de la Celle, looking squeamishly at the rabbit meat, and he followed de Marcilly down the stairs.

Shouts and commands came from below, and in a minute the sound of departing troops could be heard.

Jean stood facing Marguerite, then he dropped to one knee. He took her right hand in his and, bending his head, kissed it reverently.

Marguerite smiled and said, "Arise, dear knight." Then she added, "Be careful of my fingers, Jean, or you'll get soot all over you."

By late November Jean felt further justified in his fierce antagonism toward the Crown. As if in answer to Jacques de Molay's call to God, as the flames rose, to bring justice upon those who had so cruelly destroyed the Templars, both Philippe the Fair and head of the church's Inquisition, Pope Clément, died painful deaths.

In the summer of 1323 the de Charny family's four daughters finally gained a brother. He was baptized Geoffroy.

At the age of eight Geoffroy was sent to the nearby castle of a family friend, Count Robert d'Ervy, to begin his training for knighthood.

Summoned before d'Ervy, the youngster stood at nervous attention as the count addressed him sternly, saying, "Geoffroy, I have decided after some reflection to accept you into my service as a squire, although, as you may know, your family name is not regarded with a special honor in Champagne. Your relative—a great-uncle, I believe—was burned at the stake for certain acts of unspeakable abomination."

The shock of these words burned through the boy's mind. He forced himself to hold back his tears.

"But my father . . . ?"

"A noble exception. He has proved himself, and he is my friend. But I shall expect from you twice the dedication and twice the merit of my other squires. Your future must be more than exemplary."

Geoffroy never forgot that hurtful moment nor his resolve to achieve the highest honor for himself and, from all the world, renewed respect for the de Charny name.

During the next eight years the young squire served the table, polished armor, cared for the horses, practiced the skills of weapon handling, and constantly attended d'Ervy. Additionally he learned to read and write.

It was in May of his sixteenth year that d'Ervy announced to the powerfully muscled Geoffroy that he could expect to be knighted the following month. Meanwhile he was permitted to visit his parents and sisters at Lirey.

Returning from Lirey, Geoffroy chose his favorite route, a short day's walk through the shadowy trails of Cogny Forest. He loved to observe the woodland animals: red and fallow deer, martens, foxes, hares, wildcats, and badgers. He could move through Cogny more swiftly than most could travel the outer road. This day the distant sounds told him much.

He heard the baying of lymers, the bloodhound-like dogs used to track deer. Later came the single-pitched, staccato notes of an olifant, signaling the release of *lévriers,* the fleet, oversized grey-hounds used to bring a stag to bay. But something was wrong. The *lévriers'* excited barks became intermixed with piercing yelps. Then, abruptly, there was silence. Geoffroy started on the run toward the origin of these sounds.

Farther in the forest the small hunting party had dined merrily on cold venison with mustard and bread, washed down with large draughts of white wine. Returning on foot with his two leashed lymers, d'Ervy's huntsman, a seasoned professional, extended his cupped hand, into which he poured deer droppings from his hunting horn. One could see they had come from a large, mature animal. The huntsman added that the tracks verified this opinion. D'Ervy looked deferentially toward one of his guests, a tall, robust, auburn-haired young man who sat nearest him. The man nodded. Then d'Ervy blew his own ivory olifant. Dog handlers released the *lévriers* and the chase was on. Quickly gulping down some wine, the huntsman mounted his horse and started after the hounds. A few moments later d'Ervy and his two guests followed.

As they rode up, they saw the crouching huntsman studying

the ground around the bloodied bodies of the dead greyhounds. No deer was in sight.

"Boar!" called the huntsman. As if summoned, the beast exploded out of the bushes and, with a scythelike sweep of its large tusks, opened the huntsman from knee to chest. He pitched forward, mortally wounded. The full-grown boar was young, the most dangerous sort. Unlike older ones, who were supremely cautious, its ferocity was matched by speed and a cunning sense of maneuver.

"Get the alaunts," called one of d'Ervy's guests, referring to the huge dogs used to bring down wild pig.

Longsword in hand, d'Ervy dismounted. Annoyed, he yelled, "They're back at the castle. Look, de la Cerda, we hunt boar in *winter*."

The boar now wheeled and flashed toward the second guest, a young man still on horseback. Alarmed, de la Cerda drew his bow and let fly an arrow. The missile ricocheted off the beast's tusk, striking deep into d'Ervy's breast. His death was instantaneous.

The tall young rider galloped forward, extending a short lance which according to custom, the honored member of the hunt used on foot to finish off a deer. The boar moved away. As the rider leaned over to stab ineffectually at the boar's hindquarters, it suddenly reversed course, racing under the horse. The deadly tusks slashed out, severing the tendons in the mount's forefoot. With a screaming sound the horse crashed forward, throwing the rider violently to the ground.

At that instant Geoffroy arrived on the scene. He could hear a distinct snap as one of the rider's bones broke.

Groaning, the injured man tried to drag himself away. The boar killed the horse. Then, foam spilling from its mouth, it stared at the man on the ground. Springing forward, Geoffroy seized d'Ervy's longsword and placed himself between the man and the boar. The animal trotted away. Suddenly it feinted toward the unnerved de la Cerda, changed direction, and charged at an angle toward the fallen rider. Raising the weapon above his head with both hands, Geoffroy waited. Then he swept the sword downward, like an axe, cleaving the boar's skull and killing it.

One of the squires, whom Geoffroy did not recognize, started to help the injured man to his feet.

"Don't touch him, his leg is broken," ordered Geoffroy, who had just felt the break in the man's left shinbone near the ankle. Appropriating both de la Cerda's and the dead huntsman's scabbards, he placed them in opposite directions on each side of the injured leg and spread out the long leather straps used to attach them to the wearer's waist. He had seen this done several times at tournaments, where fractures were commonplace.

Addressing d'Ervy's younger squire, Geoffroy said, "Bernard, when I tell you, bind those scabbards like a splint to his leg." Assuring de la Cerda that he knew what he was doing, Geoffroy asked Bernard to hold the injured man steady at the waist. Then Geoffroy took hold of the foot and, raising it slightly, pulled backward, rotating the ankle to a normal position. The injured man gritted his teeth and grunted.

"Bernard, now!" directed Geoffroy.

Afterward the man managed a grin as he studied the sweet-faced, blue-eyed youth.

"To whom do I owe so much pain?" The grin broadened. "And my life?"

Geoffroy gave his name, and the other said, "I am a very grateful Jean de Valois. I thank you with all my heart, Geoffroy."

Looking over his shoulder at d'Ervy's body, de la Cerda raised his voice. "It was an accident, my prince. I was trying to protect you."

My prince? Valois? With a start Geoffroy realized that the life he had saved was that of Prince Jean, oldest son of Philippe VI, king of France.

Geoffroy politely urged the prince to allow himself to be carried to Lirey, several hours closer than the d'Ervy castle. Prince Jean would be spared much discomfort. The prince agreed and a litter was prepared.

The Lady Marguerite was pleased and gracious, expressing her pleasure in the honor of the prince's presence and regrets for his unfortunate mishap. Jean de Charny was stiffly correct.

Later, he drew his son aside, saying, "Don't tell me you have never learned my sentiments about the Crown. Was all this truly unavoidable?"

Placing an arm around her son's waist, Marguerite broke in. "Jean, my dear, you are not thinking clearly. The prince is no descendant of Hugues Capet, like that dreadful Philippe IV. The Capetian line terminated with the death of his last son. Our guest is a Valois. There is scarcely a connection. Anyhow, don't you think that was a truly splendid deed performed by your son? Rather like your own acts of courage."

"Yes, of course, exceptional," said his father. "He will become an outstanding knight." Then, in a vaguely sulky tone, he added, "But Prince Jean is Philippe's grand nephew."

Marguerite's shoulders raised in the slightest of shrugs. "So?" she murmured.

The prince requested his close friend, Charles de la Cerda, to travel at once to the d'Ervy castle and express the prince's profound condolences to Héloïse, d'Ervy's widow. Jean's squires were also commanded to ride to Troyes and fetch the town's physician of highest repute. The accompanying servants were to return with all manner of excellent wines and fine foodstuffs. Jean enjoyed a luxurious table, and he had observed that the de Charnys served rather simple fare.

Resplendent in a scarlet robe with its fur-lined hood, the doctor from Troyes carefully attached wooden splints to the broken leg. He suggested that Geoffroy should seriously consider the study of medicine. Pocketing a handful of silver coins, the doctor jovially told the prince that there was nothing to worry about, and to take his medicine. Before leaving, he deposited a bottle of mandrake infusion by the prince's bedside, telling Marguerite to give no more than two fingers four times a day.

The narcotic medicine relieved Jean's pain but usually left him drowsy. His early days of healing were marked by long hours of sleep. Later, more alert, he would spend the day talking with Geoffroy, for whom he developed the warmest regard. Three years older than Geoffroy, Prince Jean shared with him an intense devotion to the ideals of knighthood. They regaled each other with tales of high chivalry, heard or witnessed.

Prince Jean had also directed de la Cerda to Paris to tell the Princess Bonne, his wife, of his accident and to reassure her of his continuing recovery. Jean had married at the age of thirteen, which for royals was somewhat late in life. While in Paris de la Cerda was also to make arrangements for Jean's favorite falcons to be brought back. The prince missed them and felt a desire to share their fleet, fierce abilities with Geoffroy.

The day that Prince Jean first hobbled across the room using a crutch, he turned to Geoffroy and announced that shortly he would be visited by an excellent armorer who would take the necessary measurements.

"It is my plan personally to knight you."

Geoffroy's spirit sang. Asked if there was any special detail he would like to have, he said, "If it be possible, I should like a motto engraved on each epaulet, Honor Conquers All."

De la Cerda returned bearing news that all was well with the prince's family. With him was the falconer, who had brought four birds and a handler with several brachets, the small hunting hounds trained to eat and work with the falcons.

Geoffroy, Charles, and Prince Jean, followed by the falconer, beaters, and dog handlers, set out at dawn with the prince's favorite falcon, a pretty little merlin which he kept in his bedchamber. The falcon, "waiting on," followed the riders from high in the air. Whenever a lark was sighted, the merlin dove to catch it. Before it was rehooded at the end of the hunt, the merlin was given two of the succulent quarry.

The prince next placed a goshawk, the short-winged accipiter he had owned for eight years, on his left wrist. One of the dog handlers released the hounds trained to flush out rabbits. When it was younger, the female goshawk—for all the finest falcons and hawks were females—had been used to hunt grouse. Now it was best for game. The hounds drove out a rabbit which the goshawk caught easily and brought, still alive, close by the prince. Short-winged hawks did not kill in midair, like the falcon. They seemed not always to know where the killing-point was, clutching the quarry tenaciously and rarely shifting their hold, even to defend themselves.

As the goshawk rose again to "pitch," an effective diving

height above its new quarry, a lone heron en route to a stream passed in front of it. Sighting the hawk and far from the safety of water, the heron began rapidly to "take the air," seeking to rise above the threat. Flying in tight circles with its large bowed wings, it rose almost vertically to what it thought was a safe altitude. But the goshawk, spotting the heron, began flying at a fast rate of speed in wide spirals until it finally reached pitch above the heron.

"Oh, no!" called Geoffroy. Prince Jean looked solemn.

Diving with great force, the hawk clutched the heron. In the air the heron had no inclination to fight the goshawk and they came down to earth together. The heron's formidable, daggerlike beak stabbed at the hawk, piercing its breast but the goshawk held its grip, seeking to squeeze out the heron's life. The heron's second frantic stab went through the hawk's eye, reaching the brain. As Prince Jean galloped forward, the goshawk fell dead and the heron escaped.

Later, as Jean was helped to dismount, Charles said, "It would seem wiser for the hawk to have released its prey and saved itself. Then it might have killed the heron some other day."

Prince Jean had been silent since the loss of the goshawk. Limping slightly, he now turned to de Charny and de la Cerda. "The goshawk is a noble bird," he said, "with courage and dignity. It is better that it held fast and did not retreat. Though the hawk did not defend its life, it defended its honor."

Guests began arriving the day before Geoffroy's knighting. Among them were Marguerite's parents, d'Ervy's widow Héloïse and her two children, and a number of Prince Jean's friends who were to escort him back to Paris. Also among the guests was Jeanne de Toucy and her father. Geoffroy had met Jeanne during her visit to d'Ervy castle. The Count de Toucy now regarded Geoffroy with considerably more interest than previously, having just learned that the son of the king of France would officiate at the ceremony. It promised much for Geoffroy's future. After the dinner Geoffroy, his father, and Henri de Poitiers, the young bishop of Troyes, retired to Lirey's small chapel. A sword was lying on the altar. Jean de Charny handed it to the bishop.

Geoffroy recognized the weapon as his father's. It had hung in the great hall beside his shield.

Smiling to the bishop, Jean said, "His mother, a de Joinville, has placed three hairs from the head of Saint Louis in the hilt."

Bishop Henri nodded approvingly and blessed the sword, which was replaced on the altar. Then he said, "I shall pray for you and your acts of merit, which will restore glory to the de Charnys." For an instant Geoffroy felt the familiar pain as he recalled the past.

Alone, the knight-to-be began his night of vigil and prayer before the altar's simple cross. At midnight he was surprised when his father returned with a bundle of cloth.

Jean de Charny sighed deeply, and then enjoined Geoffroy to listen with all his attention. Still on his knees, twin candles guttering in their iron stands by the sides of the altar, Geoffroy heard the true story of his namesake, the Templar Geoffroy.

His father's voice took on a husky quaver as he said, "In a few hours you will become a knight. I do not know how much longer the good Lord will sustain my life on earth. It is therefore right that I now hand over to your care the holy shroud of Jesus for which the noble Templar Geoffroy gave his life. But first you must take the oath which he required."

It was with a profound sense of awe that young Geoffroy repeated the vow and watched his father unfold the shroud and stretch it over the altar. Gently Jean placed his sword at the folded linen's edge and departed.

As the first cock crowed in the distance, Geoffroy rose from prayer, reverently lifted the shroud, and carried it up to the tower room. Pocketing the keys, he returned to the chapel.

When the sky became lighter, servants carried a wooden tub into a small courtyard tent. Laughing and joking, they filled it with buckets of warm water from the kitchen as Geoffroy watched. Then, as various male friends appeared, he disrobed and stepped into the water. He would cleanse his body, as the night's vigil had cleansed his soul. In a sense it was a second baptism. Then he was dressed in a white silk shirt, white underpants, hose, and padded doublet. Afterward everyone attended Mass, celebrated by the bishop.

Moving to the hall, Geoffroy was helped into his armor by his father, Prince Jean, and others. All smiles and excitement was d'Ervy's thirteen-year-old former squire, Bernard de Bercenay, who had joyously agreed to serve Geoffroy. Prince Jean came forward with a round leather sack. Lifting it from its bag, he handed Geoffroy his helmet. Cresting its gleaming surface was a small golden boar. Everyone knew the story of Geoffroy's saving the prince's life. Laughter and cheers drowned out young de Charny's words of thanks.

The minstrels outside began to play—Prince Jean particularly favored the bagpipes—and the guests assembled in front of a raised platform erected for the occasion.

Prince Jean stepped before the glowing Geoffroy and began to address him.

"It is good and right that this day you join the noble ranks of the knights of France. Your courage and resolve shall make you invincible, but you shall always hold sacred the knight's greatest possession, his honor."

In a clear voice Geoffroy declared, "I this day swear to maintain the honor and fulfill the duties of my knighthood; to love God and serve my liege lord."

Then the prince girded Geoffroy with the sword as his father extended a buckler displaying the de Charny heraldic bearings: three small silver shields on a red background. The prince hung it around Geoffroy's neck and, stepping back, declared: "May God grant you all strength and blessings on your knighthood."

"As God so wishes," responded Geoffroy.

Quiet fell over the onlookers, as they awaited the final ceremonial act, the *collé*. It was a powerful, open-handed blow intended to make the knight forever remember the moment and his oath. Often its recipient was knocked to the ground.

Prince Jean brought his left hand forward to hold Geoffroy firmly behind the neck. Drawing Geoffroy's head closer, the prince bent downward and kissed him on the forehead. With this affectionate *collé* Geoffroy de Charny became a knight.

Turning to the cheering crowd, Prince Jean said, "And now we introduce the knight Geoffroy to Bélisaire."

From behind a wall Bernard emerged leading a handsome

gray stallion of Spanish breed. No knight ever rode a mare or gelding. The big warhorse was in multicolored caparison. Geoffroy adjusted his helmet and leaped nimbly to Bélisaire's saddle. Ahead, in the castle bailey, stood three quintains, hinged dummies used for tilting practice. Neatly Geoffroy charged down the line, upsetting each quintain as he struck their wooden shields with his lance amid shouts of delight from the guests. Riding back, Geoffroy once more demonstrated his skill. As the elder de Charny turned from the crowd to conceal his emotion, Marguerite gripped his hand.

After Geoffroy's knighting it was evident that his father no longer visited the shroud, for Jean never requested the tower key from his son. Without the weekly ritual of twenty-four years his mood gradually turned to melancholy.

Geoffroy was married to Jeanne de Toucy on Christmas Eve of that year. His father sat silently at the festivities, with a rigid smile. He had to be coaxed to eat. As the weeks passed, Marguerite was compelled to feed him. Her husband would remain in the same position for hours until he was carried to bed. Ultimately he ceased to eat altogether. Jean de Charny died at the outset of 1339.

Geoffroy viewed the shroud whenever opportunity permitted, often with his mother, who suggested it might be prudent to introduce his wife to the secret of the holy linen. Should any ill befall him—his profession as an active knight was a perilous one —then, as Marguerite suggested, there would always be someone to care for the relic.

As his wife and mother knelt beside him in prayer, Geoffroy would sometimes think of the vast dishonor thrust upon the Knights Templars and his family name. He resolved someday to right this great wrong. His mother had told him of Guy le Meunier's family and their connection to the relic. When journeying through Troyes he would usually pay them a visit. Matthieu le Meunier, Guy's eldest son, was now running the business. He was pleased that Geoffroy always requested a loaf of bread baked from flour which Matthieu had milled, claiming this bread tasted better than any other. Though not a rich man, Geoffroy always left a silver coin on the le Meunier table.

That the fate of the shroud and its new owner should be affected by an event so remote as the Norman Conquest or so seemingly irrelevant as a lady's divorce and remarriage one hundred and seventy-one years before de Charny's birth may seem strange. However, the Hundred Years War, which grew out of these circumstances, determined Geoffroy's life as a knight and the future of the great relic.

The problem began when Guillaume of Normandy conquered the English king Harold in 1066 to create a state on both sides of the Channel. Then the marriage of Éléonore of Aquitaine to King Louis VII of France was terminated after she bore him two daughters and no sons. She soon married Henry II, Duke of Normandy, who became the first Plantagenet king of England, taking with him the enormously desirable duchy of Aquitaine. In time the struggle which followed between the French Valois and the English Plantagenets was principally over this very rich land. King Louis's decision to rid himself of Éléonore appeared something of a misjudgment. She produced five sons for the English monarch, among them two kings, Richard Lion-Heart and John.

It was the Plantagenet Edward III who finally took decisive action. Paradoxically, as holder of French territory, he was a vassal to the French king. Resenting payment of homage to a foreign ruler, Edward declared himself king of France and set about establishing his absolute sovereignty by force of arms.

The war, which lasted more than a decade beyond a century, was actually a discontinuous series of raids, sieges, counterattacks, three major battles, and a succession of lapsed treaties. The greatest losers were the noncombatant people of France, who suffered loss of life and ruined lands at the hands of the adversaries, both English and French.

The year after his father's death, when Geoffroy was not in Brittany under command of the Count d'Eu, he found himself idling away four months before the walls of Aiguillon, while Prince Jean attempted to besiege the English-held town. The action was a failure. Nevertheless Geoffroy's affection for Jean only grew surer as he defended his prince from the criticism of more experienced knights. In the privacy of their tents they complained that Jean was hardheaded and obstinate. He resisted good advice, and once he had made up his mind, that was the end of the matter. A straight-talking fellow, Geoffroy gained much esteem for his unaffected loyalty.

In fact his prowess, chivalry, and magnanimity led the Count d'Eu to declare before the court of Prince Jean's father, Philippe VI, that of all the warriors he knew, Geoffroy alone could be called a perfect knight. This brought small satisfaction in 1349, as the Black Death ravaged France.

Returning from an operation in the northeast, Geoffroy learned that the plague had scourged Lirey. His mother, wife, and his two small children had perished.

Geoffroy requested an immediate military assignment. Camped near Calais, he planned a late-night operation to take its very important citadel. The action had become possible through an understanding with the commander of the fortress, who had agreed, for a substantial bribe, to open the gate to the French. However, Edward III's spies informed on the venal captain, who nervously explained to the king that he had had every intention of telling him and, anyhow, he hadn't received the money yet.

Thus, on New Year's Eve, with his main force waiting some distance away, Geoffroy and his knights were welcomed into the castle. Doors closed behind them and doors opened in front of them to reveal an enormous contingent of armed English knights, headed by a fiercely grinning Edward III. Geoffroy fought valiantly, but was knocked unconscious from behind.

During his captivity in England, de Charny spent much time in prayer and review of his past. Often he thought about the shroud, lying in its tower strongbox. Requesting paper, he occupied himself in writing somber poems of chivalry and religious faith. The two were becoming inseparable in his mind. He recalled a tale of certain imprisoned Knights Templars who were awaiting a fearsome fate. They had composed a prayer imploring "Mary, star of the sea, to guide us to a safe harbor." Each day Geoffroy prayed to the Virgin to hasten his release from prison. The ransom demand was far beyond his means. Edward

III's sense of chivalry never interfered with his utterly ruining a knight in order to exact a fat ransom. Since the tenets of chivalry only applied to gentry, lower-class soldiers were customarily slaughtered with total indifference. Because impoverished nobles were rarely treated better, the situation looked bleak for Geoffroy. He vowed that, if freed, he would somehow build a church in Lirey dedicated to the Virgin.

During the first year of his captivity, Geoffroy learned that Jean had succeeded his father on the throne. It was then that Geoffroy came upon an exciting idea. Perhaps now the Templars could be revived in an aura of acceptance and respectability. The organization would require a new name: the Order of the Star. Possibly the shroud might again become a prime object of veneration, and the Templar Geoffroy's name would once more be honored.

Eighteen months after Geoffroy's incarceration King Jean paid his ransom. In actuality the king owed him for several unpaid years of service. He explained to de Charny that the royal treasury was seriously depleted. So, regretfully, he was compelled to cut the knight's annual grant from one thousand livres to five hundred. But Geoffroy's devotion to Jean never wavered. As for the Lirey church which Geoffroy had vowed to build, Jean suggested that the present moment was inopportune. Possibly in a year or so.

But the idea of an Order of the Star was attractive to the king for a reason concerned with neither chivalry nor religion, but rather with a quite practical military consideration. A rule of the Templars had been that no member might quit the field of battle without consent of his commander. But in Jean's France each individual *grand seigneur* zealously preserved his right of independent withdrawal. The effectiveness of a fighting force as a cohesive group was, therefore, constantly threatened.

King Jean relished the idea of incorporating such an oath into the rules of a new Order. From his first day as king Jean had notified his leading barons to hold themselves in readiness for a major thrust against the English. The Order of the Star, as proposed by Geoffroy, would substantially abet the king's intentions. Additionally there was the matter of personal prestige which accrued to the head of a noble order. Had not Edward III established his Order of the Garter? The Knights of the Blue Garter were reminded by their leg bands not to move their limbs in flight from the field of action. Though the Order of the Garter involved no more than twenty-odd barons, King Jean contemplated a less select group, possibly as many as five hundred.

The Templars had sworn to the principles of obedience, poverty, and chastity. The king pointed out that poverty was, after all, a relative thing. In fact he did not consider himself to be a rich monarch. The last of these rules raised a genuine problem. The solution appeared when Charles de la Cerda, now Constable of France and second in power to the king, proposed that instead of chastity, the members should simply vow to be faithful to their wives. De la Cerda was unmarried.

Despite the serious reductions in royal revenues, the installation and first banquet of the Order of the Star was an occasion for some excess. Seated on specially made gilded chairs and wearing their star insignia and handsome regalia furnished by the king, the boisterous participants exploded in drunken carouse. To the skirling of a dozen bagpipes, silver chalices were smashed, members drenched in wine, and, in the end, several of the king's valuable tapestries disappeared. While the feast rolled merrily on, the English seized the highly strategic castle at Guînes near Calais. Throughout the festivities Geoffroy alone remained both sober and thoughtful.

The vow not to flee combat was soon tested at Mauron. A company of members of the Order, led by a marshal of France, was trapped in ambush by a force of Anglo-Bretons. Readily possible was an escape to safety. But, true to their oath, the knights held their ground until all were either captured or killed. The loss to the Order of the Star was substantial.

Geoffroy de Charny, at Lirey while a minor wound was healing, spent much of his time supervising the construction of his small church. King Jean had finally paid some of the monies Geoffroy had requested. Not enough for a stone structure: Geoffroy had to settle for wood.

The late afternoons and long nights seemed sadly empty in

Geoffroy's castle. Few of the servants had survived the plague. Geoffroy visited the shroud more frequently.

Héloïse, d'Ervy's widow, who had remarried, invited Geoffroy to be her guest. Thinking it would be a cheerful change, he accepted. Her young, unwed sister-in-law, Jeanne de Vergy, granddaughter of a marshal of France, begged Geoffroy to recount every story of his adventures. It thrilled her, she said, to sit beside one known as the Perfect Knight. In turn Geoffroy claimed the greater privilege was to be in the presence of the perfect beauty. When she exclaimed with delight over his latest poem, describing a battle from the viewpoint of an angel—French, of course—the matter was settled.

The first ceremony after Bishop Henri dedicated the modest church was the marriage of Jeanne and Geoffroy. A month later Geoffroy was summoned to Paris.

Upon his arrival de Charny learned that the king's favorite, Charles de la Cerda, had been murdered by an enemy of the Crown. Moreover, the French treaty with the English was about to lapse. War seemed inevitable.

As he embraced Geoffroy, tears spilled down King Jean's cheeks. "With Charles gone, there's only you, my last true friend." Not long after, Jean publicly expressed his regard at a lavish banquet attended by all the court. The king awarded Geoffroy the country's most honored office: Porte-Oriflamme, bearer in battle of the mystical royal standard of St. Denis, a scarlet, swallow-tailed pennant, scattered with gold-embroidered flames. As a further act of affection Jean promised his friend the rich lands and castle of Montfort.

While the king issued and reissued the general summons for all men between eighteen and sixty, the treaty with the English expired. By November, Edward III had landed with knights and archers at Calais. Then he headed south. Unable to obtain wine or ale from a land laid bare by King Jean's scorched-earth strategy, the English were forced to the dreadful alternative of drinking water. Ten days of campaigning were enough for King Edward. He sailed back to Portsmouth.

In the south the Plantagenet activity was led by Edward III's son Edward, Prince of Wales, known, because of his dark armor, as the Black Prince, and for his valor as the "Flower of Chivalry." His objective was twofold: to impress inhabitants of the surrounding territories that the English were a fearsome force to resist, and to gain as much plunder as possible. For neighboring Gascons the promise of potential loot further reinforced their alliance with the English.

The Black Prince, young, powerful, sporting a heavy mustache, did his work with enthusiasm and an untroubled mind. Avoiding strongly defended areas, such as Toulouse, his men burned food supplies and towns, cut down fruit trees and vines, as well as villagers and their livestock. To Geoffroy's misfortune the Black Prince ravaged and put to flames the town of Carcassonne, avoiding attack on its fortress. Carcassonne had been one of the towns furnishing revenues for Geoffroy's annual grant. Resistance from the French lords was not evident. When a town offered a sum to buy its immunity, the Black Prince might order all the inhabitants slaughtered, to demonstrate his right to absolute power.

With his baggage wagons loaded with looted tapestries, rugs, jewels, precious church objects, hams, grain, and butts of wine, he returned with fellow members of the Order of the Garter to his winter quarters in Bordeaux.

The following summer, 1356, Edward rode up from Bordeaux in high spirits. His mission was an enjoyable one and his fighting men were the best. In planning the overseas expedition, he profited from the practical necessity of transporting a relatively small but highly professional body of men. They had gained experience in two previous campaigns. The prince had thirty-five hundred gentlemen-at-arms, twenty-five hundred longbowmen on horseback, and one thousand mounted infantrymen. It was a highly mobile force, and for good reason. When danger threatened, he planned to race southward.

For King Jean the systematic depredations by the Black Prince as he rode north were a matter of surprisingly good cheer. Alarmed by this invasion of central France, the *grands seigneurs* from everywhere—Auvergne to Hainault—finally overcame their disaffection for the Crown and, with their knightly levies, rallied to the royal summons at Chartres. No one stayed home. The

French forces, more than double that of the Anglo-Gascons, were something to marvel at. King Jean was all confidence. He would drive the English back to Bordeaux. Maybe right out into the Atlantic.

So poor was the Black Prince's military intelligence that it was three days before he learned the French were closing in. According to plan he turned his troops around and headed back toward his Bordeaux base. The French pursued him along a parallel course separated by a broad forest. Edward never knew exactly where the Valois forces were. Calmly he rested his mounts for an astonishing two days while the French overtook and passed him on the other side of the forest. When the Black Prince started up again toward Poitiers and the coast road to Bordeaux, he made a shocking discovery. His scouts spotted the rear guard of the French, moving through the Poitiers gates. They were cutting across the English line of march. Edward had miscalculated; the plain before him was covered with men-at-arms.

At dawn next morning the Black Prince found a nearby location that appeared to be a fair defensive position. Edward still had his mind directed to the south and escape. But if an engagement was unavoidable, a stand here was his only hope.

Chapter 17

Poitiers, 1356

The Plantagenet forces were positioned on top of a slope facing westward toward Poitiers and the two-mile-distant French bivouac. Directly in front of the three English lines of battle was a hedge and long expanse of vineyard. This cultivated area was densely studded with four-foot stakes which supported the ripening grapes. Below, to the left of the hollow at the slope's bottom, was marshland and a steep descent to the Miosson River. At the right was high ground, covered with scrub and scattered groves of trees. Beyond the trees was an old Roman road.

The Valois army straddled the main country road which twisted eastward finally to bisect the vineyard where the English waited. Here the roadbed sank below the level of the grapes and stretched onward behind the Plantagenet lines. It continued through a wood to the village of Nouaillé and its stone bridge. The Miosson could also be crossed by a ford at a descending cart path behind the Plantagenet left flank.

It was Sunday morning.

The pope, Innocent VI, through his emissary, was desperately trying to forestall the battle. Turks had crossed the Hellespont at Gallipoli and now were threatening all of Christian Europe. This was no time for the two greatest Christian powers to be at each other's throats.

Innocent's prime delegate was the haughty Cardinal Talleyrand de Périgord, reputed son of Pope Clément V and his beautiful mistress, the Countess of Périgord. Clément had been the pontiff who abolished the Order of the Templars pursuant to Philippe IV's wishes.

Surrounded by a cloud of clerics the cardinal rode his mule back and forth between the two camps in a feat of tireless shuttle diplomacy. But so confident of eluding the enemy was the Black Prince that, at first, he rejected the idea of any truce. Equally sure of his superior numbers, Jean II refused to consider the cardinal's proposal to postpone military action until after Christmas.

Then the Plantagenet prince, reconsidering his situation more carefully, decided to play for time. In return for being allowed a safe retreat with honor and booty intact, he offered the release without ransom of all prisoners taken in his two campaigns, a seven-year pledge of nonbelligerency, and, unbelievably, the abandonment of Calais and Guînes. Meanwhile he strengthened his archers' positions among the vines with a formidable addition of sharpened stakes. At the same time he began shunting the most valuable loot-wagons out of the massed baggage train which barricaded his right flank.

Jean turned down the offer: its profusion of material advantages seemed to obscure the honor of the situation. He counterproposed through Talleyrand that, in exchange for a lifting of the Valois threat, he would accept the surrender of the Black Prince and one hundred knights. These terms Edward flatly refused.

The cardinal finally convinced the king to accept at least a Truce of God until the following morning. This despite the bitter remonstrances of Marshal d'Audrehem, who argued that any delay favored the English. The time to begin was now.

Marshal Clermont submitted that the most sensible tactic was simply to surround the Plantagenet force and wait. A blockade would predictably starve them out. It was precisely this possibility which gave the thoughtful Edward a distinct sense of anxiety. But the concept was unacceptable to the knightly instincts of the French.

D'Audrehem jeered, "My dear Clermont, you sound like you fear a little combat."

Smiling, Clermont replied, "When I run from battle, I expect to find your horse's nose in my horse's ass."

It was late afternoon.

Then Geoffroy proposed that one hundred knights from each camp should formally join in combat. He was recalling the Combat of Thirty which had taken place in Brittany some years before. Though only nine of the sixty knights were killed, and all had been wounded to some degree, the French champions triumphed to live in undying fame. Although the idea held a certain appeal for the king, it was shouted down. By such a course too many noble men-at-arms would be denied the glory of combat and the chance to gain rich ransoms.

King Jean's chief tactical advisor, Douglas, an elderly Scot who had participated forty-two years before in the defeat of the Plantagenets at Bannockburn, was now ordered to address the assembled warriors and set forth the order of battle.

"There will be a vanguard led by Marshals Clermont and d'Audrehem. They will be mounted."

Puzzled looks passed among the nobles. Why say that?

"There will be the usual three lines of battle," the Scot continued. "They shall, however, dismount and attack on foot."

Now there came the sound of many breaths being drawn in. Without warhorses there could not be the customary cavalry charge. In effect the knights would all now be infantry. Not having their strong *destriers* to bear them forward was like being without legs.

Geoffroy de Charny, carrying a flat leather case under his arm, passed the six knights-guardsmen as he approached the red silk pavilion of King Jean. The present Constable of France, Gauthier de Brienne, Duke of Athens, nodded affirmatively to Geoffroy, who glanced for a moment at the oriflamme staked by the entrance and moved within.

Jean was talking to Douglas, the tactician.

"Geoffroy, come in, come in!" he cried jovially. "Tell us what you think of Douglas's plan."

Bowing to the king, Geoffroy turned to the Scot. "As I have understood it, Messire Douglas, the knights on foot at Bannockburn were holding a *defensive* position. They were waiting for Edward II's 'battles' to ride through the marshes toward them—toward you Scots. Here our situation is exactly the opposite."

The old fellow stroked his beard and replied in his shrill French, "Messire le Porte-Oriflamme, your horses can easily be taken down by the English longbowmen. I know. That was the case in other battles. Is it not better to stride the ground safely than to drop with a falling horse and crash to earth in your armor?"

Geoffroy turned to the king. "But the vanguard of Clermont and d'Audrehem will be mounted."

"Someone must chance it to open the way. And the marshals will have our strongest lances, our fastest horses, and more than half of our crossbowmen," said Jean.

"As you wish, Sire," said Geoffroy. "By your leave, my king, I must speak alone with you."

Jean dismissed Douglas with a wave of the hand. Geoffroy placed the leather case on the long, map-covered table. Then he began.

"My father, Jean—you may remember, Sire—had much pain in his spirit. He felt less a man for the loss of his arm and less a knight for the cruel dishonor brought upon the name de Charny. That was the work of that damned Capetian, Philippe IV. Then, one day, my father came into possession of something of unspeakable importance. It changed much for him, and when he charged me with its care, I repeated his vow never to reveal its existence to the Crown of France.

"I think he would have agreed the time, now, is especially right, and you—a Valois—are worthy, Sire, to share this blessed knowledge."

Outside Jean's tent a horse neighed. There was the sound of laughter and the smell of campfires. In the distance some soldiers were singing a rondeau of Auvergne.

"Tomorrow the Valois knights face a battle which, with God's love, we shall surely win." Lowering his tone, Geoffroy continued. "We two have hunted together, hawked together, and faced the enemy together. With a full heart and trust, I ask, my king, may we now pray together?"

Opening the case and laying out the shroud along the camp table, Geoffroy said, "The shroud of Our Savior, the sacred relic of the Templars. May it speed our victory and someday find its place in the hall of our Order of the Star."

Tingling chills coursed through Jean's body. His skin seemed to tighten; he did not realize tears were pouring down his cheeks. The king sank to his knees beside Geoffroy.

"His shroud," Jean whispered.

Later he asked faintly, "May I touch it?"

Geoffroy smiled. The king reached out, then quickly withdrew his hand, gazing at his fingers. He took a deep breath and rose, pulling Geoffroy with him. He clasped his friend and, holding him tightly, looked into his eyes.

"Your trust gives me something I value beyond words, something I have never known before in my life. And you ask nothing in return. But you must not keep this here, dear friend. It is too precious."

Geoffroy nodded. "I have arranged for my squire, Guiscard de Bercenay—you knew my first squire, his father—and three mounted pikemen to bear the holy shroud, at once, to safety in Lirey. Later, when the Order desires, it will be presented to them."

King Jean said, "Young de Bercenay has the Right of Combat."

"True, but when I reminded him that a knight must also honor those things which are God's, Guiscard understood and agreed. He knows he carries a blessed relic. And there will always be other battles."

"But, of course," the king said. "And I shall direct two of my squires and six crossbows to depart immediately with your squire."

As Geoffroy carefully folded the sacred linen into its case, the setting sun beyond Poitiers cast a deep crimson light across the shroud. A fresh breeze from the far-off sea rippled the red silk pavilion, and Geoffroy was filled with a sweet sadness.

"Tell me," said Jean, with new firmness in his voice, "what do you think when you look on the shroud?"

Geoffroy's face lightened.

"Some have foolishly called me a knight who is perfect. When I look at the image of Our Lord, I think, here is one who lived by the highest code of honor. One who had for all the greatest mercy and magnanimity. One who faced peril with the truest valor. I think, here is the Perfect Knight."

Outside the tent pink clouds were toppled on the horizon. The sky above seemed strangely empty, and Geoffroy thought of a line for a new poem, "Gone are the great, swift hawks of memory. . . ."

Dawn, September 19, 1356—a Monday. Edward, the Black Prince, stood on the high ground behind the wagon park staring toward the French camp. There was no visible movement. The Earl of Warwick rode up.

"The wagons are moving toward the ford now, my prince."

"Good," said Edward.

A servant helped him to mount. Splendid luck, he thought as he rode south behind his lines, which were dismounted and waiting. Absolutely no French scouts had been observed since his Sunday arrival. No enemy activity in the next hour or so, and the retreat would begin by the Nouaillé road. It joined the little cart trail in the wood beyond the ford. In passing, the prince nodded to the Earls of Salisbury and Suffolk, whose battle lines backed the hedge. The archers stood restless in sawtooth formation on the ridge in front of the two earls. Edward's own battle line of Anglo-Gascons was behind and parallel to them.

The prince joined Warwick and Oxford at the edge of the steep slope to the river. Men were straining at ropes, trying to hold back the forward rush of the heavy loot-wagons. Curses, neighing, orders shouted. A sweating serjeant roared to another, "It would be damned easier if our loot were ladies. At least they could get off their backs and walk!"

"It should take another hour or so to get them all to the other side," said Oxford.

Warwick was across the river. Oxford rode down to join him.

Seven A.M. The prince, merely overseeing the work, was actually sweating in his armor. The sun hadn't even risen over the

Nouaillé wood. No, here it came. In a cloudless sky. By Saint George, the day was going to be a hot one. No movement from the Valois camp yet. Maybe they wouldn't attack. But if they did, thought Edward, let it not be by the Roman road beyond the trees. If they ride behind us and cut off our retreat, my goose will be cooked—by a Parisian chef this Christmas. But then, he reassured himself, they won't maneuver. Honor always demands a frontal attack. Edward watched another wagon roll out of the river to disappear into the far wood.

Seven fifteen A.M. A knight skidded down the ravine and, splashing across the river, yelled at the disappearing troops.

"The French are on the move!"

Edward immediately canceled all orders to retire the troops, assigned a detachment with Oxford to guard the wagons on the far side of the Miosson, and returned to high ground to direct his forces.

Heading the three parallel battle lines, the French vanguard moved slowly across the fields. Three hundred fully armored and mounted men, under Marshals d'Audrehem and Clermont, one hundred mounted German mercenaries, twenty-five hundred spearmen on foot, and the entire twenty-five hundred crossbowmen. It was one third of King Jean's whole force, and fully half of the trained men.

Eight A.M. The French forces, riding with the marshals, came over a rise and could see about seven hundred yards ahead past the hollow, the vineyard and hedge, and beyond the massed first English line. In the distance the Black Prince's banner was disappearing over the shoulder of a cart track. Warwick and Oxford's forces were out of sight. It looked as though the Plantagenet retreat had begun.

By eight twenty the vanguard had descended the far slope and crossed the hollow. As the mounted nobles started their charge up the English slope toward the bowmen, Clermont called to d'Audrehem, "Watch your horse's nose!"

D'Audrehem yelled back, "Guard your ass!"

Roaring with laughter, the two marshals spurred their mounts, followed by three hundred knights who were funneled by the stakes into the stricture of the sunken roadway. They came under a double cloud of arrows from both sides of their path. The arrows darkened the sky above them as they met their end.

The knights' sacrifice gained time for the experienced German mercenaries and the first of the infantry to make their way up the slope and engage the first battle line in fierce hand-to-hand fighting.

The Plantagenet longbowmen demonstrated their superiority in rate of fire: three longbow arrows to one bolt from a crossbowman's arbalest. Unlike the French, the English archers had no complicated loading procedure, no ratchet to draw, no trigger that might jam, variable control of their missiles—and their ranks were greater.

Just before the mass of the vanguard engaged the English, Warwick and his invisible men came storming up from the Miosson. Instead of reinforcing the frontal forces, they moved the shorter distance to the left below the hedge and enfiladed the shaken French attackers with flank fire from their archers.

Into the melee of fleeing infantry and wounded horses marched the first line of Valois battle led by the nineteen-year-old dauphin, Charles, heir to France's throne. By itself the eight-hundred-yard march in armor was exhausting. The shirts of linked mail alone weighed fifty pounds. All the Valois knights carried iron plates at their elbows, shoulders, and knees. Many wore frontal armor. The men had broken their long lances to a length suitable for use on foot. They took surprising toll of the English. Young Charles's attack was the most glorious feat of arms in the Hundred Years War.

Yet there were no miracles to save them. The dauphin and his fellow survivors staggered back along with stampeding horses into the advancing second line of battle, led by King Jean's brother, the Duke of Orléans. The panicked, riderless horses and men falling back mixed with the advancing troops to confuse and terrify the second line. Disobedient to the king's command, many were still mounted or had their chargers close by.

Orléans's force fled the battle without engaging the enemy. Whether because of cowardice, ineptitude of command, or political calculation, Orléans effectively decided the course of battle by his failure to rally his troops. The time was ten fifteen A.M.

By his vast sin of omission the king's brother gave the exhausted forces of Edward time to recover. Time to gather up fallen missiles. Time for the Black Prince to reorganize.

He ordered all men capable of combat to mount up, knights and archers, those mobile warriors who had sped through Aquitaine. Four hundred being held in reserve joined the battle lines. All the horses were still fresh.

Eleven twenty A.M. Edward, in a dazzling tactic, now called on the young cavalry captain, Jean de Grailly, the Captal de Buch. This exceptional and dashing Gascon hated the Valois. With the prince's standard-bearer, Woodland, and two hundred men—half knights, half archers—the *captal* received his instructions. He was to ride, unobserved, to the northwest, behind the groves of trees, along the ancient Roman road until he arrived at the rear of the third Valois line of battle. Then he was to attack.

The third "battle" was led by King Jean. He had no archers.

Lances leveled, the Black Prince's men slowly started forward down the slope. King Jean's knights-in-armor had traveled on foot twice the distance which had sapped the energies of the dauphin's line. The hour was approaching noon; the day was warming up.

Had Jean now retreated, his honor might have been dented but the political disaster could have been avoided. He had about five thousand men remaining. Most were inexperienced. With exhausted energies and unexhausted courage, the men trudged forward. They met the charging Plantagenets at the base of the hollow. The mounted lances had the best of it.

Suddenly, galloping toward the rear of Jean's tattered line, came Woodland with the banner of St. George, followed by the small contingent of the Captal de Buch. The effect was devastating. Surrounded, frightened French infantrymen searched frantically for a direction in which to flee. The king was part of a central group of nineteen knights, all wearing identical dark armor and white surcoats with embroidered fleurs de lys. But one stood out from the rest. In his left hand he gripped the gilded staff of the scarlet-tongued oriflamme. In his right, the sword whose hilt held three hairs from the head of St. Louis. As the Plantagenets closed in, the nineteen were falling. Beside the unhelmeted, bleeding King Jean stood his fourteen-year-old son, Philippe.

Philippe cried, "Guard to the right, Father! To the left, quick, guard!"

The main thrust of the attack was on the man with the oriflamme. Then, in a fierce rush, a knight with his lance aimed at Jean's heart charged forward. Oriflamme firm in his left hand, sword slashing ahead, Geoffroy de Charny threw his body between the lance and his king. As Geoffroy fell forward, he plunged the upright staff of the banner of St. Denis solidly into the earth.

A rider called down to the king. "Sire! I am a knight of Artois whose lands have been confiscated. My allegiance is now to the Plantagenets. Surrender to me, and I shall lead you to our prince."

Jean looked at Philippe, standing alone, and at Geoffroy's fallen body. He handed his sword to the Artésien knight. The battle of Poitiers was ended.

However humiliating the shame of surrender, its bitterness was somewhat sweetened that evening for King Jean. At the banquet given by the Black Prince to honor the king and the surviving French knights, Edward declared the privilege of standing before the valorous Jean was so exceptional that he would remain on his feet and personally serve his esteemed prisoner.

Though the ransom of three million gold écus was exorbitantly high—unpayable, actually—Jean's four-year stay in England was not unpleasant. He enjoyed high respect and honors, an elegant suite at the Duke of Lancaster's newly built Savoy Palace in London, front-row seats at the royal tournaments, and special luxuries imported from Paris.

Jean raised only a fraction of the ransom, but he was permitted to return to France following the Treaty of Bretigny, which gave half of what was then France to England.

Back in Paris there was the usual rash of problems: falling revenues, higher prices, unstable currency, immigration of peasants to the city, intransigence of the French barons, ex-soldiers throughout the land spreading terrorism, and universal resistance to the treaty.

Among other things the treaty designated the king's son, Louis of Anjou, as captive in his stead. Louis promptly escaped from his Calais castle prison, adding further embarrassment to Jean's bruised sense of honor. The king was now known as Jean le Bon, meaning "brave" rather than good.

Still unable to raise the money for his own ransom, Jean insisted on returning to England and resuming his former status as prisoner. Upon his departure he uttered the notable statement, "If integrity and good faith were banished from the earth, they would be rediscovered in the hearts and mouths of kings." Because of French raids on English coastal towns, the king was transferred to the Tower of London.

Throughout this imprisonment, which hastened his end, the balance of the ransom still remained unpaid. But King Jean never took the step which would buy him freedom. Resolutely he chose to honor Geoffroy's secret. The secret of the shroud. At any time Jean could have ordered the relic to be seized; its price would easily have paid for his release. The cloth was worth a king's ransom.

The Order of the Star died with the death of most of its members on the fields of combat against the English. Never did word come to Lirey to deliver the shroud to the Order's great hall.

Geoffroy de Charny's widow, Jeanne de Vergy, was hard pressed for funds. Only a month after Poitiers she begged the regents of France to make Geoffroy's grant over to his infant son, Geoffroy II. The financial pinch eased a bit for Jeanne in 1358 when Geoffroy II was granted the estates long promised to his father for valor at the siege of Breteuil.

Geoffroy II de Charny married the niece of the late Bishop Henri. The de Charnys moved to the castle at Montfort which had been awarded Geoffroy I. Geoffroy II, now attached to the court, carried out confidential diplomatic work for Charles the Wise, who, as dauphin, had led the Valois first battle line at Poitiers and later succeeded Jean le Bon to the French throne. Geoffroy II was rewarded with important and lucrative posts.

But, moved by his mother's tales of the past, his thoughts were often on the shroud and on his desire to reveal it to the people of France.

Finally Geoffroy consulted the papal legate and the shroud at last came before the public. Marguerite de Charny, Geoffroy II's young daughter, was awestruck upon first seeing it.

Before her death, Jeanne de Vergy, joined by her family, witnessed the dedication of her husband's new tomb in the Paris Church of the Célestins. Laid to final rest beside the remains of Maréchal d'Audrehem, Geoffroy's monument bore the inscription "Here lies Geoffroy de Charny, Knight. His valor and integrity were greater than that of all the others."

The de Charny name had at last achieved the highest regard. Jeanne remembered her husband's armor, the words on his epaulets which read HONOR CONQUERS ALL.

Chapter 18

Turin, 1978

At last word had come through. The shroud commission announced that the Shroud of Turin Research Project was authorized to start its tests beginning midnight Sunday, and continuing for five days, through the following Friday night. The STURP scientists were jubilant, the press was relieved, Nico was pleased, but Vittorio Monti was not.

On October eighth, Sunday, a few minutes before midnight, Vittorio walked to the old royal palace next to the Duomo. As he crossed the square in front of the darkened cathedral, he realized how desolate it was. All activity was now concentrated in the brightly lighted palace to which the scientists and their assistants were hurrying.

The guard on duty greeted the monsignore, as a representative of the shroud commission handed Vittorio the requisite badge. It was a plastic-encased white rectangle signed by the archbishop and bearing the printed words R. CAPPELLA SANTA SINDONE. The guard said, "Father, a great moment, yes? We will finally get the real story." Monti repressed a scowl.

He continued along the hallway through many sumptuous, high-ceilinged rooms to the former prince's reception hall, where the temporary laboratory had been installed. It was incongruous, all that equipment—tons of it—lying about in a setting of classical murals, gold-trimmed doorways, crystal chandeliers, and parquetry floors. Floodlights had been turned on, and fifteen of the scientists moved about, preparing for the moment to come.

Finally the shroud arrived, solemnly borne by a procession of scientists and representatives of the archbishop. As shroud keeper, Monti had been entitled to supervise the cloth's removal from the Duomo to this laboratory. He had not done so. The relic was, for the moment, in other hands.

Six nuns of the Order of Poor Clares, in white-piped, dark bonnets, walked beside the long tray on which the relic lay wrapped in red silk. They hovered anxiously as several scientists wearing white laboratory gloves carefully transferred the shroud from the tray to a Mylar-covered metal tilt-table.

One of the Americans, recognizing Vittorio, came over and explained, "Monsignore, this device was specially constructed. It can be adjusted from horizontal to vertical, depending on the angle required for any particular test. And you need not worry. The fabric is secured by these Teflon-coated magnets. They are really quite safe."

Vittorio felt outraged. This great symbol of Christian devotion, affixed to a board like some pathetic specimen on a dissection table. He reached out and touched the linen. It had always surprised him to realize how durable it was. Maybe durable enough to survive all this.

Preliminaries over, the Poor Clares began removing a portion of the backing cloth that had been sewn onto the fabric by nuns of their Order after the fire at Chambéry, four centuries before.

This is all I can bear, thought Monti, as he watched the sisters ripping stitches. He left, feeling it might be the worst evening of his life.

Richard arrived at the test site shortly after midnight. Unauthorized persons were not being allowed near the laboratory, but, through Molly, he had been able to obtain credentials which gave him access to a press room set up next to the palace entrance. He hoped to question the scientists on their way to or from the laboratory; maybe volunteer his personal expertise.

Already he had made contact with two persons from the research team. There was the fabric expert and archaeologist, Sforzini, and a biophysicist from Cal Tech, Harrison Berg. Berg was attentive when Richard briefly outlined his Coolidge Theory. The scientist requested the loan of Richard's photo of the de Gaulle image, proposing to examine it in a VP-8 Image Analyzer. The VP-8 analysis of shroud photographs showed the central portion of the image with undistorted, realistic three-dimensional quality, distortion occurring only at the image's edges, where the cloth had fallen away from the figure. By whatever means the image of the man on the shroud had been created, the process acted uniformly on the front and back of the body and was in operation even where the cloth could not have contacted the body. If Coolidge's de Gaulle demonstrated the same properties, the scientists might be onto something.

Richard waited uneasily until he saw Berg's tall, slightly stooped figure appear in the hallway. The scientist, a kind man with a thoughtful drawl, shook Richard's hand. Then he said, "Sorry to report this, Coolidge, but we got somewhat different results from your photo. There was some distortion in the central area of your de Gaulle face. The features appeared coarser and broader, however, the facial edges showed no distortion because the cloth lay on the plaque's essentially flat surface. This is the opposite of what we see in the VP-8 shroud analysis. You haven't hit it yet, I'm afraid. That is, insofar as the three-dimensionality is concerned. The only way we're going to get an explanation here is to keep sending up ideas and trying to shoot them down. When one stays up there, regardless of our scientific ammunition, we'll figure that possibly we've got our answer."

Disheartened, Richard was not ready yet to go down in flames. His theory was still right. He had probably overlooked some small detail. Besides, he had not been shown the photos. He decided, at this point, that a little more publicity was in order. Something to keep his name and theory alive. He thought of Molly. She cared for him. In fact, they might be moving toward a romance that could have greater value than that brief, long-ago affair had been. At the right moment he planned to ask her to help. She would not turn him down.

They met next day for a walk in the Parco del Valentino. The afternoon was cool and sunny. The huge park, stretched along the Po's left bank, had acres of paths and trees, beds of fall flowers, and many fountains. Though its buildings were principally used for national and international exhibitions, the Valentino's chief attraction was a medieval village. A fanciful assemblage of structures, this recreation had been built in the nineteenth century by a group of Torinese architects, to recreate a Piedmontese hamlet of the Middle Ages.

After having an espresso in a flower-bedecked trattoria along the riverbank, Richard and Molly walked down to a small dock beneath the shadow of a red brick, turreted castle of the replicated village. Sitting dockside, they dangled their legs above the river's dark surface. Richard took Molly's hand.

"You mustn't be angry with me for deserting you at the monsignore's reception," he said.

"I'm not. But I wondered why you haven't called."

"I telephoned you all weekend. There was no answer."

Molly explained she had been in Venice, checking some information for the article. She chose not to elaborate.

"Darling," he looked at her earnestly, "there are so many issues at stake here for me. But the most important is you. I think about you a lot." His arm went around her. She liked his touch.

"You've been on my mind, Richard. Maybe the old thing could still be there."

"For me it seems more than before. You've grown up, little M." He tilted her chin upward, close to his face, then kissed her lips tenderly. She looked into his gray eyes. Her arms went around his neck.

"Come back with me," she whispered.

Arms enlaced, they moved through the park toward a place where taxis waited.

During the drive to the Regno, Richard remembered what he had wanted to ask Molly. Distracted by desire, he had momentarily forgotten the matter. He leaned back in the seat and stretched his legs. An anxious tension gripped him.

"Darling," he said urgently, "I'm in a bind. Things aren't going well for me at the moment. I need something to keep the

Coolidge Theory alive. Do you think you could give me a little journalistic boost?"

She felt a sudden chill, as though cold water had been poured onto a warm place in the middle of her. "What do you want, Richard?"

"Oh, possibly a small paragraph in *View*. Just mentioning my news conference, the ideas I proposed." He speeded his words. "I realize you can't say anything too strongly in my favor so prematurely, but you did tell me at the time you thought what I had to say was interesting. And that you would check on the possibility of a story. How about it?"

The cab had pulled up in front of the Regno. Molly looked at him. "I have no intention of writing about you, Richard. Certainly not at this time. And you had better save your amorous energies for more responsive journalists."

"I didn't mean to offend you, Molly. Damn it! Just ignore what I said. You're getting the wrong idea."

"Oh? I don't have the wrong idea. You forget, I'm not your gullible little student anymore." She stepped out and, when he moved to follow her, closed the door quickly. She felt tears coming and did not want him to see.

Nicolò Sforzini called that evening. After the painful scene with Coolidge, Molly was especially happy to hear from Nico, and she let him know it. They agreed to meet next afternoon at three o'clock for ice cream at a little *gelateria* near the Duomo. It was the only time Nico could get away from the laboratory. His knowledge of ancient weaving, as well as his overall historical and archaeological background, was proving valuable.

The ice cream parlor was delightful, with its round pink marble tables and hanging greenery. A large glass window looked onto a small piazza. Nico was exhilarated. The scientists, he reported, had just discovered a tiny smudge of dirt on a heelprint. It had become visible during one of the wide-spectrum photographic tests. The figure's foot might have been dusty from the walk to his crucifixion, or perhaps his body had been dragged afterward. It seemed a supportive bit of evidence. Molly took notes, as Nico continued to discuss other early surprises. The bloodstains had remained surprisingly red, not grown dark brown as would be expected of old blood. The lash marks were vivid. More significantly, the blood had soaked through to the cloth's reverse side, whereas the body image had not. Some different process was operating here.

"The photographers find at times it is difficult to focus the image. It is elusive," remarked Nico. "But I have examined those threads, Molly. They were woven by an ancient method, like a first-century technique. I believe it could well be a burial cloth from Judaea."

His excitement was contagious. She could feel her own enthusiasm growing. What if the relic were genuine and they could prove it? This would be the supreme discovery of the age. Greater, perhaps, than a walk on the moon. Spontaneously she reached out and took Nico's hand. She told about her research of the Gospels. How closely they conformed to the pathologist's report. Wistfully she added, "I confess I'm a bit jealous of Doubting Thomas. He could finally believe and be happy." Nico smiled and squeezed her hand. He looked into her eyes.

"Molly, there is another reason I wanted to see you today. A very important reason." From his pocket he took a ring. She recognized it as the Roman ring he had found near Masada. Holding it out to her, he said, "I am not sure what you feel for me, *carina*. But I know I love you. I am asking you to accept this gift from me. If you will have it."

She remembered his words in Venice. The ring would be for the person he wished to marry. She stared at the gold circlet with its intaglio of three trees. Not wanting to face the immediate issue, she thought about the unknown woman to whom this had once belonged.

"Molly?" Nico's voice brought her back.

"Oh, Nico, please understand. I can't take your ring. Not now." The hurt from Richard, the way he had tried to use her, was still too fresh. Nico was not even to be compared. She had long ago perceived that. Yet they had known each other so briefly. She had spent a lot of years avoiding entanglements. Then there was her career.

She saw the pain in his eyes. "Forgive me, Nico. You are very special to me. The kind of man I could love. But the differences between us are so great."

He spoke softly, gentle pleading in his voice. "Differences? Superficial ones. I believe that in the important matters we would agree."

She spoke of her hesitation to open up to religious faith. This could prove a substantial barrier.

"I understand what you feel about religion, Molly. And about a commitment to another. You are afraid of both, I think. Having once been hurt, you are unwilling to try love again. You know, faith and commitment are not so very different. When you find one, you will know the other." He rose and touched her hand lightly. "I shall wait, *cara*. I sense you may be very close to a discovery about yourself."

Walking back to the laboratory, Nico experienced a heaviness of spirit he had not known since his breakup with Livia. The joy of the morning's efforts had vanished. But leaden as he now felt, he could not bring himself to believe his relationship with Molly was finished.

In the hallway of the Royal Palace he encountered Richard Coolidge. At this moment Coolidge was the last man Nico wanted to meet. Richard walked up to him. "May I have a word with you, Count Sforzini?"

"I must get back to the laboratory. Might we speak later?"

Ignoring the request, Coolidge explained he was interested in knowing just what tests were scheduled to take place, and when. Would Nico fill him in? Normally Nico would have been curious about this sort of query from an outsider. But Coolidge, because of his theory, was known to the team. He seemed a serious scholar. No reason to question his motives. Besides, Nico was in a dark frame of mind; anything to get rid of the man and return to the comforting impersonality of the laboratory.

He unfolded a white sheet which he handed to Richard. It was the schedule of tests, listing the estimated time and date of each. While Nico fidgeted, Richard scribbled a copy. "This infrared analysis, midnight Thursday. Doesn't infrared have to be done in the dark?"

"Correct," replied Nico. "I must be going."

Richard stared at the schedule. "This is incomplete. It doesn't say how many will be present for the—"

"Not many," snapped Nico, pulling back the paper. "Goodbye."

Upon his return to the Ambasciatori, Richard received word that Acciaro had called and would call again. As he entered his room, the phone rang. Richard reported that he had been able to obtain the requested information. Camillo said he was on the way to an important business meeting. Would Richard understand if they had to pass up dinner that evening? But he would stop by the hotel at nine. He could spare a few minutes. Of course, this conversation would be counted at the agreed price. He asked Coolidge to be waiting outside the Ambasciatori. No, the corner across the street would be more convenient. It was in the direction of his meeting.

As Richard waited opposite his hotel, an aging American auto pulled up beside him. It was a Buick Roadmaster. My God, he thought, were such cars still in use? The driver, a tough-looking fellow with a purple scar across his cheek, stepped out and, touching his chauffeur's cap, opened the rear door. Acciaro was seated inside.

"I must apologize for this rather inadequate vehicle," said Camillo. "My Bentley is in the shop for servicing, and this is the only car they could lend me. Let us drive a bit."

The auto pulled away and he turned on the interior lights. "Now, Riccardo, you said you have the scientists' schedule." Richard handed over the schedule and some notes he had made. Acciaro studied them. "What does this word 'darkness' mean, after 'infrared'?"

Coolidge explained that all laboratory lights must be extinguished during this test.

"How many people will be present?"

"Very few, I understand."

"No lighting, few people," repeated Acciaro. "Very interesting."

"Jesus Christ!" exclaimed the chauffeur.

"*Zitto*, Raffaele!" ordered Camillo sharply. In a confiding tone, he commented, "We allow our servants far too much familiarity these days. They are spoiled—all of them."

The driver made a covert, obscene gesture and muttered something indistinct.

"Why should the infrared analysis be of such particular interest to you?" asked Richard. "It is a standard procedure."

"The key to a thorough book is exactitude."

"I don't get it. Are you planning a blow-by-blow account? I should imagine a general review of these tests would be sufficient."

"Every writer has his own methods. I am something of a perfectionist. So tell me, how much time will that test require?"

"How should I know?"

"But I am paying you for accurate details."

"Okay, let's call it fifteen minutes," said an annoyed Coolidge, thinking, the hell with him—maybe it takes four hours.

"Very good," said his employer. Acciaro glanced at his wristwatch and announced in a friendly manner, "Please understand, I am most appreciative of your efforts. And since I am not pressed, we have time to stop for a sip of wine. Raffaele, park at the next respectable-looking café. Dr. Coolidge and I shall pause for a drink. No more than ten minutes."

They settled on tall stools at the bar. "You are more than justifying your modest honorarium," said Acciaro. "I find you altogether simpatico."

"Camillo, this drink is on me. After all, I ought to reciprocate now and then."

Acciaro reviewed the row of bottles on the back bar. "You are very gracious. I should prefer the Chivas Regal. I find your American drinks quite agreeable."

Irritated that Acciaro had ordered one of the most expensive liquors, Richard said, "Chivas Regal is not American. If you will allow the truism, Scotch comes from Scotland."

Half an hour had passed and Acciaro was starting his fourth Chivas. The chauffeur entered and grimaced. "*Padrone*, that ten minutes has long passed. You should be leaving."

Acciaro waved a hand airily. "Later, Raffaele, later."

The driver shrugged, walked to the far end of the bar, and ordered a Martini and Rossi.

Coolidge and Acciaro continued to talk about the shroud. Expansively Acciaro said, "It is a shameful crime to perpetrate so great a fraud upon the innocent. The thing should be removed; it is worth nothing."

"It is my experience," replied Richard, "that even a good fake has no commercial value. Possibly it could serve as an amusement for some collector with a sense of humor."

"So if it were to be carried off, there would actually be no loss at all," continued the Italian.

"No loss at all," responded Coolidge.

"I am now considering the validity of doing exactly that. It should amuse you."

"Are you thinking clearly?" demanded Richard, astonished. "And, anyway, you could never succeed. I think we should call it a night."

"I would succeed," declared Acciaro, loudly. "The key to success is clear thinking!"

The chauffeur moved over to Camillo and, seizing an arm, said, "*Padrone*, we are leaving now." He determinedly pulled Camillo toward the door.

As they stepped into the street, Acciaro called back, "*Grazie, grazie, caro* Riccardo!"

Chapter 19

Montfort, 1429–1431

Marguerite de Charny, granddaughter of Geoffroy, renowned knight of Poitiers, knelt on the stone floor of her chapel. Stretched above its small altar was the shroud of Jesus, hers since the death of her father. A forthright and attractive woman, now thirty-nine, Marguerite was childless. Each day for many years she had gotten to her knees and prayed the Lord for a child. A child to warm her loveless life and to inherit this relic, supreme possession of the de Charny family.

The afternoon was especially fine for Marguerite's daily ride. One of her grooms, Guillaume le Meunier, waited with her palfrey, as she emerged from the chapel. She had directed that Guillaume accompany her this day. A husky young man of sixteen, he was descended from Guy le Meunier, who had carried the shroud to her great-grandfather, Jean.

Nine years before, Guillaume had been brought to Montfort castle by an aunt. His parents, who lived in the city of Troyes, had been slaughtered by a band of marauding men-at-arms while bringing a wagonload of wheat back from the countryside. Far from their native Flanders, these mercenaries had been hired by a *châtelain* of the region in his private war with another noble. A problem common to the times was to get these soldiers-turned-brigands to return home once the conflict was over. Until so inclined they would cut a brutal swath through the country-side.

In view of his family's connection with the shroud, Marguerite had always taken a special interest in Guillaume. Lately, however, her interest had deepened. Guillaume was to figure in a plan of hers, one she hoped to initiate that very day. It was a desperate measure, but she could no longer delay. Appraising the good-looking youth, she knew he would admirably suit her purpose.

Guillaume looked forward to his occasional rides with Marguerite. They nourished his secret fantasy: the dream that he served as her worshipful knight, and she, the courtly mistress of his heart. Since his arrival at Montfort he had delighted in listening to the songs of the visiting minstrels. Hiding behind the portals to the great hall or lurking in the shadows when his duties as food-bearer allowed, Guillaume would hungrily absorb their tales of romance and chivalry. As he understood it, the object of chivalrous devotion should be quite unobtainable, a virgin or another man's wife. And the nobly beautiful Marguerite belonged to another.

One day Marguerite had asked if he were happy and if he had any particular needs. Without considering his words, Guillaume burst out that he only wished for a horse and armor. This was followed by an intense blush.

Laughing gently, his lady said, "I'm not certain about the armor, Guillaume, but the matter of a horse is simple. I shall have you assigned to the stables, and you will become a groom."

Today Marguerite was dressed in jade-green silk. He noticed how attractively the color complemented her rich brown hair and gray-green eyes. They took a familiar river path between the Armonçon and the edge of the woodlands. For a while they talked little; Marguerite was thinking of her first husband, the dashing Jean de Baufremont. What passion she had felt for him during the early days of their marriage! But Jean had a fickle and mercurial nature. He seemed to lose interest in her almost immediately. His eyes invariably followed the young noble-women who visited the castle. He was often absent without explanation. Unhappily she realized that de Baufremont was constantly involved in liaisons with other females. The marriage which had begun with such high expectations for Marguerite soon became one of emptiness. Throughout their years together, she reasoned, he had been too little in her bed to produce an heir.

De Baufremont died in the disastrous battle of Agincourt. As time passed, Marguerite became deeply concerned with proving her womanhood. It was, therefore, with little hesitation, three years later, that she had married Humbert de Villersexel, Count de la Roche. The wealthy Humbert, though long past his prime, radiated an attractive quality of intense masculinity. All too quickly it reflected itself in hunting parties and long, boisterous drinking sessions with his male companions. He would divide his time between a sporting life with friends at one of his estates and occasional visits to Marguerite. As Humbert reached his fifty-second year, the drinking, the gaming, the falconry, and the hunting became even more obsessive. He rarely showed up at Montfort, and his attentions to his wife grew even fewer. Maybe he was too old, she thought. But by then she no longer cared.

Marguerite turned to glance at Guillaume, who rode a few paces behind. A romantic youth, he had fair skin and sensual lips. A good mind, too, she thought approvingly. But was he still innocent?

"Guillaume, I shall dismount now."

They had reached a large chestnut tree. She decided here it would happen.

The young groom took her arm and helped her to the ground. Then Guillaume stood by the horses, a short distance away.

"Come, sit beside me."

Guillaume thought he must have misunderstood her words. Never had his lady offered such a privilege! Uncertainly he moved a bit nearer.

"Guillaume, I'd like you to sit down. Here." She patted the grass at her side.

Looking as if he wanted to flee, Guillaume gingerly sat where she had indicated.

Marguerite wasted no words. "Have you ever made a girl pregnant?"

His face turned crimson. Speechless, he tried to adjust his mind to the question. It was altogether unlike what one would expect from such a noble lady. "I have not."

Looking into his eyes, Marguerite asked, "Guillaume, do you find me attractive?"

He gulped twice and managed a faint yes. What could she mean? The ideal lady of his fantasies would never speak in this manner. He started to rise and move to a safer distance.

"Stay here." Marguerite smiled. Then, matter-of-factly, "Guillaume, have you ever made love to a woman?"

Disturbed by strange feelings, he stared at his feet. Marguerite brought her face close to his and whispered the question again. He feared she could hear his breathing. It had become a series of short gasps. "No, madame, I have never . . ."

"But certainly you have the feelings of a man?"

What was she up to? He simply did not understand.

"Answer me, Guillaume."

He supposed he had such feelings. She asked whether he had ever felt them for her.

"My lady," he responded fervently, "you have always been the purest object of my devotion."

"Good," said she. "Then kiss me."

"But the rules of courtly love forbid such license!"

"Courtly love?" She thought it tactful to suppress her laughter. Guillaume was certainly no knight to be bound by the code of chivalry. Where had he picked up such ideas?

She demanded, "Can you possibly imagine we are suited to a relationship of courtly love?"

"You are rich, I am poor. You are noble, I am obscure. And above all, I wish to serve you." Then he spoke of the minstrels he had heard in the castle—how they celebrated the lover who could never possess the object of his affection. His must always be a chaste love.

Marguerite sighed. "Surely you have heard of the *Roman de la Rose*? It is the most esteemed literary work of the times."

"I do not read, my lady." He hung his head.

She chuckled. "It is a pity you're not familiar with it. The poem condemns virginity as abhorrent to nature. Man's duty is to procreate. One must observe the commandments of natural love." She looked at him knowingly. "Otherwise one is bound for hell."

Guillaume protested, "It would be a profane thing even to touch you. I want only to serve your commands, regardless of the hazards. I only wish to bleed before you."

Marguerite held a leaf before her lips. "Very well," she said. "I command you to kiss this leaf."

As he did, she pulled it away, and Guillaume felt her bare lips on his. In horror he leaped up and backed away, bumping against a dangling branch. It scraped his arm slightly.

Marguerite laughed. "Look, you are bleeding before me."

Getting to her feet, she took his arm and, placing her wet, open mouth upon it, began to suck a tiny drop of blood. Guillaume's pulse was surging fiercely. This was all wrong! He carefully withdrew his arm.

Their debate continued, as each defended a point of view, until it grew late and a cool breeze began to blow. Marguerite recognized that she was not going to win over her young virgin with words alone. Perhaps she should take more direct action. The shamelessness of this idea excited her.

"Help me onto my horse, Guillaume," she ordered briskly. "We are riding back." She thought what a fine, healthy baby Guillaume would give her.

A sealed letter in hand, Marguerite's steward was awaiting her return by the main gate of Montfort castle. Bowing, he explained that her courier had just returned from Paris. Marguerite dismounted and tore open the seal. The message was from Christine de Pisan, her beloved friend since childhood.

Christine, historian, moralist, and advocate of women, was one of the most eminent and influential poets of the era. Her husband, Étienne du Castel, and Marguerite's father had been close friends while serving in the court of Charles VI. Christine had presented Marguerite with a ballade on her tenth birthday. Across the years the two women had maintained contact by the exchange of long, chatty letters. Always Marguerite's message would close with a plea to Christine to be her guest at Montfort, and always Christine would graciously decline.

Christine's letter opened on a more cheerful note than Marguerite could recall since, personally threatened by civil strife, Christine had retired to the royal convent at Poissy. She had just returned, she wrote, with Marie de Berry, granddaughter of the late king, Jean le Bon, from the coronation of Charles VII at Reims. This was a happy event for the Orléanists, whom Christine had supported at great risk.

She was paying a visit to Marie at Hôtel de Nesle, the great Paris residence of her father, the late Duke de Berry. And, surprise of surprises, Christine had accepted Marguerite's perennial offer and planned to visit Montfort two weeks hence, in mid-August. She would be accompanied by Marie.

May the good Lord save me, thought a disconcerted Marguerite. Only fourteen days to prepare for the visit—and a thousand things to do! Alas, her plans for Guillaume would clearly have to be postponed.

The day of her guests' arrival, Marguerite had posted Guillaume on the Montbard road. Now he galloped back, calling out, "They are coming." The entire castle staff, joined by field hands, assembled in the courtyard. Two young knights, one bearing Marie de Berry's banner, cantered through the arch of the castle gate. Then a murmur of excitement rose from the onlookers as Marie's carriage rumbled over the drawbridge. It was unique in France, a long-wagon which her father had ordered built from an English design. The arch-roofed, unsprung vehicle, pulled by five horses in tandem, was controlled by two riders. A cheer went up from the people of Montfort and nearby Montbard, when Marie and Christine waved from the large square windows.

As the two ladies alighted, followed by their serving women, Marguerite rushed forward to embrace Christine. Remarkably, at sixty-five, the slender, white-haired woman still possessed that lovely porcelain complexion which Marguerite remembered.

"My dear little Marguerite," murmured Christine.

Marguerite laughed. "Not so little anymore. Oh, Christine, it's been so long!" And looking into each other's eyes, they beamed with joy. Then Marguerite was introduced to Marie de Berry, a handsome woman her own age. Marie had the same pointy, retroussé nose of her cousin, the late Charles VI.

Marie said, "Marguerite, Christine talked so much of you on our way here that I, too, wish to embrace you." And the two younger women kissed.

Even before the visitors were escorted to their guest chambers, Christine told Marguerite that, above all else, she desired to see the Savior's holy shroud. Kneeling together in the chapel, the three women raised their eyes to the relic, suspended above the tiny altar. It was lighted by the morning sun, which streamed like gold through a window of yellow glass. Tears poured down the cheeks of the aging poetess, and Marguerite squeezed her hand.

"I feel that I am in His presence," said Christine. "The reality of His suffering cuts through my heart. And I think of the pain and death of so very many of our young men on that frightful, tragic field that was Agincourt."

Later, together in Marguerite's private antechamber, they were served hot spiced wine sweetened with honey.

"Here we are," said Marguerite, smiling faintly, "the three widows."

"Oh, no," cried Christine. "You never told me."

Marguerite shrugged slightly. "Humbert is still alive—wherever he is and whatever he's doing. But I might as well be a widow. I almost never see him. My loneliness is without end. And my most constant prayer, for a child to love, has seemed hopeless."

Trying to console her, Christine said, "I am no stranger to loneliness. But often a child can bring even more heartache. At least you have never known the agony of a child dying. Marie and I have both lost sons."

Marie broke in. "I can understand and sympathize, Marguerite. Your life must seem very bleak at times."

Lowering her voice, Marguerite continued. "Perhaps not for long. If I cannot have the love I want, then at least I shall have a child to comfort me. May I trust you with a secret? It is, of course, most confidential. My barren years will soon end. There is a young man who serves me here. He cares for me. . . ."

"No, no, no, Marguerite," cried Christine. "What you contemplate is wrong and unworthy of you. Not only is it adultery, but above all, it dishonors your husband. Regardless of Humbert's faults, you must be faithful. Not because he is or is not good and decent, but because you are."

And then Christine discoursed on the importance of morality and virtue in women. But her words began to come more slowly. Finally she closed her eyes for a moment and fell asleep.

"She must be exhausted," said Marguerite. Gently awakening Christine, the two younger women solicitously led her to her bedchamber.

They returned to their wine. There was a thoughtful silence between them.

Then Marie said, "Christine doesn't understand. She forgets."

"Forgets?"

"Yes, Christine has known great love. The memory of her Étienne will last a lifetime. She has her daughter with whom she has shared years at the convent. And Jean, her surviving son, whom she adores. Even I, who have deeply loved and lost two husbands and a son, have sweet recollections to cherish. And then there are my other children. All this fulfills me. So forgive me, dear Marguerite, but I see that your life has been barren in many ways. I can feel your great need to love. Surely that is not an evil thing. You must do what you can to redeem your life."

Marguerite reached over and gripped Marie's hand. "Thank you," she said.

Before noon the following day guests began arriving for the banquet to honor Christine. First to appear was Marguerite's half-brother, Charles de Noyers, a widower with whom she shared a pleasant relationship. Next came her friends from a nearby castle, Donatien de Ligny and his wife, Odette. Then her cousin, Antoine-Guerry des Essars, with his wife, Ursule. And finally there appeared—the invitation was a gesture to her absent husband—Humbert's nephew, François de la Palud. François was notable in several ways. He never walked, but rather strutted. His shrill voice was that of a distressed child, and his nose, memento of an unfortunate incident while fleeing the battlefield at Anthon, was crafted of silver and neatly strapped to his face.

Having had time to refresh themselves in their quarters and quench their thirst with wine, the guests assembled at the entrance to the great hall. Escorted by the two knights, Marie and Christine were the first to approach Marguerite, who stood beside a solemn little serving-boy. The lad held a tray with pieces of bread and a small dish of salt. Marguerite welcomed each guest as she offered them the bread and salt of hospitality.

At noon a horn sounded from within the great hall. With a crunching sound everyone moved across the floor, treading on fresh rushes which had been laid down throughout the castle. As Christine paused like the others to wash her hands at the built-in laver, she complimented Marguerite on the attractive fragrance of the floor covering.

"I remember your love of flowers," said the smiling Marguerite, "so I have intermixed our garden flowers with the rushes —lavender, roses, dittany, rue, and sage. And to honor you," she added, "there will be flowers served in many of the dishes."

Christine thanked Marguerite, saying, "Nowadays my appetite is no greater than a butterfly's. But I shall linger with delight over each floral delicacy."

Guests were seated along one side of the high table, with Marguerite at the center, Christine on her left, and Marie de Berry to the right. Marguerite nodded to her chaplain, who loudly offered up a prayer to Jesus Christ and all the saints. Then Marguerite looked up to the musicians stationed on a small balcony at the far end of the room. Playing vielle, psaltery, and crumhorn, they struck up a lively picaresque tune and afterward their leader, who bowed the vielle, silenced the others and accompanied himself as he sang verses of the song. The guests applauded by pounding the table with knives and spoons in their fists.

The loudest pounding came from the lower table, where a generally younger group was seated. Among them were the squires to the two knights, Marie de Berry's servingwomen, and members of Marguerite's household, which, at her direction, included Guillaume.

François de la Palud, seated next to Christine, turned and

piped, "Is it not splendid the way Marguerite, who is, after all, only a woman, has arranged this feast?"

Christine, who had been sipping hyssop-flavored broth, put down her silver-edged bowl, delicately wiped her mouth on the edge of the tablecloth, and sighed. "Sir," she said in a firm voice, "is it not also splendid that women oversee the dispensing of accounts, wages, and alms? They can run estates, bring lawsuits, make financial decisions, have their own business, and—"

Marie de Berry broke in. "And write beautiful poetry!"

"But," protested François, "what of the really important things, matters of state?"

"Countess Mathilda of Tuscany headed the most important state in Italy. Blanche of Castile ruled France for a quarter of a century. Éléonore of Aquitaine was decisive in placing a second son on the throne of England."

Those at the high table were all listening to Christine.

"But forgive me, sir. It is wrong to speak of the English here. Thoughts of them will only sour this excellent food."

Everybody cheered and pounded the table.

"But—but—" de la Palud protested.

Sensing a quarrel, Marguerite looked up at the musicians and clapped her hands. The vielle player announced, "By your leave, ladies and gentlemen, a ballade by Dame Christine."

> " 'Dear friend, let no more tears begin.
> They make me feel for you
> Such care, my heart gives in
> To the love you bring, sweetly true.
> So let your spirits rise; displace,
> For the good Lord's sake, your mournful view.
> Please show me now a happy face
> And I'll bestow what you wish me to.' "

Both tables were pounded with enthusiasm.

"Oh, dear," murmured Christine to Marguerite, "I thank you. But I wrote that so long ago—so very long ago." And she turned somewhat sadly to her salad of violets minced with onions and lettuce.

De la Palud said, "Madame, were you trying to tell me that women are equal to men?"

"No, they're kinder. And sometimes they're as brave. When Jesus was dying, it was the women who stayed with him. Sir, I believe women should play a supporting role to their husbands. But husbands should be loyal to their wives." She smiled. "I trust Our Lord would agree."

"What has the Lord to do with all this?"

"It's a matter you will have to figure out for yourself. God made Adam from the dust and the soil. Eve, we understand, was fashioned by Him from the earth's most noble creature, man."

"Well said," cried de Ligny's little wife, Odette. The table resounded with laughter.

But de la Palud would not drop his contest with Christine. "Madame, you're supposed to be a good writer. How can you possibly find fault with the greatest work of all times, *Le Roman de la Rose*?"

Christine sighed again, recalling her part in the most important literary debate of the era. "That was more than half a lifetime ago. The trouble with *Le Roman de la Rose* is simply its contempt for women, and its corrupt plea for immorality, for bastards."

Marguerite looked desperately toward Guillaume, and then to Marie de Berry, who glanced at the lower table and whispered to Marguerite, "That's he?"

Marguerite nodded and then silently mouthed, "Stop her."

Marie's voice rose, as she interrupted Christine. "Dearest Christine, I know you have been writing a new poem since we returned from Reims. Would it be importunate of me to ask you if you would share it with us?"

The table was silent for a moment. Then Christine spoke out. "Not at all, Marie. I have it with me. Perhaps this is the right time and place." And she withdrew a small journal from the purse that hung at her belt. In a voice that, but for the faintest quaver, was young and true, Christine began by explaining, "On the seventeenth of July I beheld a wonderful and blessed thing. Together with my dear friend Marie de Berry I attended the coronation at Reims of the Dauphin Charles. The siege of Orléans had been lifted and the English, with their evil accomplice the Duke of Burgundy, had been pushed out of the north. The way to the redemption of our land was begun. And all this, accomplished through the extraordinary pluck and leadership of a girl. A virgin. The council of matrons verified that. You all know I speak of Jeanne d'Arc, our Jeanneton.

"I can see her now, standing beside Charles in the cathedral. She bears her white banner, embroidered with the lilies of France, and showing the Lord sitting in the clouds, holding the world in His hands. This shall be my final poem. It is a hymn for Jeanne."

Then Christine read of the good times that had returned to France because of this young virgin. "Oh! What honor for the female sex," which God must love. To a girl of sixteen, "who does not even notice the weight of the arms she bears," He has given the power to drive out France's enemies. "Never did anyone see greater strength, even in hundreds or thousands of men." She has led the king with her own hand to his coronation. So, loyal Frenchmen, "submit your hearts and yourselves to him . . . that you may live your lives in peace . . . and that he may be a good overlord to you. Amen."

When Christine had finished, no one spoke. Then François de la Palud raised his goblet of wine, saying, "A cup of health for the Maid of Orléans!" And everyone repeated the toast with fervor.

"A cup of health to the king," cried Marie. And all joined in.

Then, from the far end of the table, the young knight, Gilles de Meaux, touched with a profound sense of nation, called out, "*Vive la France!*" And the hall exploded with pounding and cheers. It was a happy day.

Shortly after Christine's departure, Marguerite requested Guillaume to prepare the horses for another outing. This time they followed a path that led into the woods. Marguerite reined her horse to a halt beside a small stream. Again she invited Guillaume to sit beside her. This time he did not hesitate, though he still sought the right words to defend his knightly concepts.

But conversation was not on Marguerite's mind. Quickly she

reached for his face, and he felt her tongue glide between his lips. The effect was astonishing. What remained of Guillaume's courtly ideal gave way to an urgency between his legs. Soon Marguerite's roving hand confirmed the fact.

They made love. And when it was over, Marguerite straightened her clothes, becoming once more the proper countess.

Returning to the castle, she ordered the groom to ride again with her the following day. Somewhat giddily Guillaume realized he was entirely willing, untroubled even, to compromise his knightly code.

Marguerite de Charny encouraged her young lover to couple with her many times during the next year. He found her passionate and tender during lovemaking, but remote and pensive afterward. He, on the other hand, began opening his soul to her. It was a long time before Guillaume knew he had, at last, touched his lady's heart. One warm day they lay naked together, hidden by a thick grove of trees. He stroked her cheek, but now she did not hurry to rise and dress.

Deeply happy, he told her, "Though we have had each other's bodies, I still feel as I did before. You shall forever be the pure object of my love. I wish to serve you always."

A look of pain shadowed her face. "Then give me a child, Guillaume."

"Mistress, I shall. You will bear our child, I promise."

Seeing the fervor in Guillaume's eyes, Marguerite felt it was finally right to let her inner feelings pour out.

"All my life I have felt alone. It aches in me, Guillaume, like an illness. I have yearned for a child to let me feel needed. And a companion to ease my loneliness. But Humbert is cold. And so much older. He will never give me the love or the child I live for."

"The count leaves you too much alone."

"Perhaps it is my fault. After we married, he knew I looked forward to an heir. When none arrived, I blamed him. He took it as an attack on his manliness, and resentment grew between us. Then came his long absences from Montfort."

"How could he possibly stay far from you? You are so good and beautiful."

With a tender smile she put her arms about him. Guillaume felt a wave of joy. Never before had his lady allowed herself to open up to him, to show affection that reached beyond the act of love.

The months passed, bringing a time of inexpressible happiness to Guillaume, but growing despair for Marguerite. A year after her affair began, Humbert died and Marguerite reached her menopause. Now all chance to conceive had passed. She had grown old.

With widowhood came many suitors, all hoping to gain Marguerite's substantial estates and possession of the shroud. The most persistent of these was François de la Palud. His silver nose gleaming in the summer sunlight, François paid ardent court to Marguerite. His exaggerated declarations of love and vainglorious tales of heroism only amused her. When he bent to kiss her cheek, however, she flinched. His metallic nose seemed as cold and contrived as his motives.

Finally she had had enough of François. Yet ridding herself of him required a certain amount of tact. She argued the issue of consanguinity; his close connection to her late husband made marriage inappropriate. Such a union would forever upset her sensibilities. She must oppose it, and reminded François that, in his great wisdom, he could only come to the identical conclusion.

Observing de la Palud and the countess from a distance, Guillaume discovered jealousy. After the nobleman departed for the last time, Guillaume went to Marguerite.

"Your husband is in heaven, my lady. Let me be with you always. I shall share your bed, and give you the child you have wanted. I wish only to live for you."

Knowing her hopes were now futile, and suffering the discomforts of a change of life, Marguerite cried, angrily, "You, too, Guillaume? You, too, want my estates?"

"No, no! You misunderstand me. I want only you."

She felt old and despairing. "Leave me, please. Go love some high-breasted girl in the village. Someone your own age. Have sons and leave me alone."

Tears misting his vision, the young man ran from the room.

For more than half a year Marguerite avoided Guillaume, always choosing another groom to ride with her. But she found her thoughts persistently returning to him. He had offered the only love in her wasted life. And she had driven him off.

Finally she devised a plan by which they could be openly together. She would purchase Guillaume a title and then they could marry. Even without children there would be the reassurance of companionship, and someone to care for her in her old age. Guillaume could inherit the shroud. At once her depression lifted. She thought how good it would be to return the relic to Guillaume, whose forebears had carried it to the de Charnys.

She found an impoverished nobleman in the district around Sens. Owner of a run-down château, he was agreeable to selling, for the right amount, his title and coat-of-arms. Yes, it would work! Marguerite dreamed of the happy life ahead.

She summoned Guillaume. They had not spoken in eight months. He stood, staring at the floor.

"I treated you badly, dear Guillaume. Can you forgive me?" She smiled tenderly at him, waiting to see again the love in his eyes. He did not look up. "We should remain together for the rest of our lives. God sent you to me; I know that now. No one has ever given me so much."

Pausing, she relished the moment to come. "I know a knight of noble family who will sell his title. I shall buy it for you. Then you will be of proper station for us to marry. You will inherit my estates, the shroud."

Perceiving his lack of response, she spilled her words out faster and faster. Finally there was no more she could say. She fell silent.

Guillaume slowly shook his head. "You are kind and generous, my lady. The Lord once blessed me, a groom, with your love. I could wish for nothing greater."

Unsatisfied with this answer, Marguerite insisted her scheme would make everything possible. She revealed her vision for them: marriage, a life together, contentment. "And the shroud, Guillaume. It is rightfully yours. When I am gone, you must marry again and have children. Then the relic can continue to be where it belongs, with your heirs."

Embarrassed, Guillaume looked at her. "There is a girl in the village. . . . We plan to marry. I made her pregnant. You will remember you told me to go and have sons."

So Guillaume's woman was pregnant! Marguerite turned away, knowing, at last, the bitter truth. She could never have had a child. It was she, all along, who had been barren.

Chapter 20

Montfort—Liège—Chambéry, 1452–1453

After the marriage of Guillaume le Meunier, Marguerite wearied of relationships without purpose and put a stop to visits from eligible nobles. Having no illusions about her fading beauty, she realized that an offer of marriage, now, meant nothing more than an obvious ploy by some suitor to gain a rich estate.

She began devoting herself to prayer and the shroud. The relic became so important to her sense of well-being that she would not travel without it. The image of the Man of the Cross focused Marguerite's thoughts upon her own mortality. In a private way it became her talisman against death.

Guillaume and his girl from the village, Julienne, had two sons and a daughter. The family lived at Montfort. Thus Guillaume could continue to adore and serve his countess. Although his marriage was, of course, an ironically bitter matter for Marguerite, she still cared for him. As the years advanced, she cherished Guillaume as a friend and grew to depend on his presence.

Now Marguerite was compelled to face another reality; the fate of the shroud after her death. She had no likely heir, except for the foolish François de la Palud. In actuality the silver-nosed one had already inherited her late husband's properties. There were also her half-brother and a couple of irreligious cousins, whom she refused to consider. A proper and valid solution must be found.

She resolved to undertake a series of visits to European courts, in the hope of locating a suitable home for the de Charnys' most valuable possession. Traveling by horse-litter, a wheelless carriage with twin shafts supported by horses fore and aft, Marguerite was accompanied by Guillaume, whom she had elevated to the position of steward.

They went first to Liège. For centuries a center of learning, the great Flemish city was now the seat of powerful bishop-princes, who brought great hardship upon a miserable citizenry by the imposition of excessive taxes.

Arriving early one morning at the imposing palace of the current bishop, Marguerite requested an audience. The bishop's secretary rudely kept her waiting until noon. When finally she was admitted to the prelate's reception room, she sensed at once that she had made a mistake in coming to Liège.

Seated on a fanciful throne was a potbellied and pretentious prig. Clutching a pomander whose sweet odors he sniffed constantly, while wrinkling his brow as if he smelled something bad, the bishop contrived a chilly smile as Marguerite approached.

"So, madame, we are informed you come bearing a gift for us."

"Your Grace, I am here simply to discuss the possibility of a gift. As you are aware, my ancestors have long been possessors of the blessed shroud of Our Lord Jesus. Since I have no heirs, I am embarked upon a search for a suitable home for the relic." Lowering her eyes, she said, "It is, of course, painful for me to think of disposing of it."

The bishop took another sniff of his pomander and wrinkled his brow fiercely. "We have heard of this so-called shroud. Have you brought it with you?"

"Yes. It travels with me always. Allow me, Your Grace, to show it to you." Returning to the door, she motioned to Guillaume, who entered, bowing, and unrolled the shroud upon a long table at the room's center.

The prelate arose from his throne and strolled around the linen. His perpetual frown changed not at all.

When he returned to the throne, and Guillaume had rerolled the relic and left the chamber, the bishop fixed narrowed eyes upon his visitor. "A very nice representation, I would say. Yes, quite good. It is painted, of course."

Marguerite fought to hold back her anger. "There is an ancient legend that the blessed Lord's image was miraculously imprinted on the cloth. Certainly not painted on, as you suggest."

"And what official papers have you to that effect?"

Marguerite sputtered. "Why—none. None at all. It has belonged to my family for two centuries. We have never doubted its authenticity."

"However, madame, such documentation would be absolutely required before we could possibly accept such a gift as authentic. A papal bull, perhaps. Surely, you possess something of the sort."

Marguerite kept quiet. It was hard not to turn and walk out. How dare he!

"Tell me, good lady, how did your family acquire the—ah—shroud?"

"It came from the Knights Templars. It was their most cherished possession. But how they obtained it—"

He did not let her finish. Leaping up, the bishop pointed an accusing finger. "The Templars! Do you not know their history, madame? Damned by all, burned at the stake for their obscene and idolatrous practices. Say no more to me about this heretical object. I strongly recommend you quit my presence now, or you shall face a tribunal."

Angry and fearful, Marguerite fled the room.

It was with a deep sense of humiliation that she climbed back into her horse-litter. For many miles she was too upset to discuss the fiasco with Guillaume. It had been extremely difficult for the aging woman even to consider parting with this precious possession, her talisman against the years. And to have her generous offer acknowledged by an indignity!

Several years passed before Marguerite could bring herself, once more, to ponder the disposition of the shroud. During the spring of 1453 she received a message from an important court, that of Duke Louis of Savoy. The duke invited her to be the guest of him and his wife, Anne de Lusignan, at their castle in Chambéry. Remembering with revulsion her reception at Liège, Marguerite was tempted to decline. But she knew she could not; the shroud must eventually be provided with a reverent and royal home.

The countess had never been to Chambéry. Savoy's capital was situated in a green valley below snowcapped alpine peaks. It was enclosed by ramparts and high stone walls pierced by nine gates, each with a drawbridge spanning the moat.

The many-towered castle of Duke Louis stood on a low hill overlooking the town. Entrance was achieved by means of a ramp that curved under two huge gateways and emerged into a spacious courtyard, with a fountain at its center.

Upon her arrival Marguerite was escorted up a broad staircase that led from the courtyard into a large hall graced by a great rose window. She was graciously received by the duke and his duchess. Anne was a delicately radiant young woman, with rose-petal cheeks and cornflower eyes. She was in a late state of pregnancy. It was obvious to Marguerite that, while the duke remained kindly and restrained in his remarks, Anne could barely contain her eagerness to obtain the shroud.

"May we see it now?" she asked, shortly after they had greeted each other. Guillaume had already been dispatched to the duke's private chapel to place the relic on the altar.

"How truly wonderful!" cried Anne upon first viewing the shroud. "As a child I heard tales of it. On my native Cyprus the relic is still revered." She stared at it raptly. "At last I can see for myself. This is indeed the true image of Our Lord." Heavily she got to her knees and kissed the cloth.

Marguerite felt distressed. The duchess was too anxious. Why would she think she, rather than some other royal personage, should be the chosen one? Inside the older woman's heart lay something of which she was only dimly aware. It was jealousy, for Anne possessed everything Marguerite had so desired in her unfulfilled and lonely life. Now was this handsome, pregnant young woman to have the shroud, too? The countess found herself reconsidering her resolve.

The days at Chambéry passed pleasantly enough. Though the

girl tried to win her friendship, Marguerite maintained a subtle distance from Anne. They spoke at length about religion. Anne de Lusignan was much concerned with matters of the spirit. Marguerite, having come to a deep faith after much misery, wondered why the young duchess seemed so serious. Why did she not laugh and gossip like the other women of her court?

One night, after prayers in the chapel, Anne turned to Marguerite. "Dear Countess, it is the greatest comfort for me that you are here. I have prayed for someone like you with whom to share my deeper thoughts."

Marguerite nodded stiffly.

Continuing, Anne said, "There is something I should like you to know. The shroud—you see, it means more to me than it might to others."

So that is the tactic, thought the suspicious old lady. I was right all along. She countered acidly, "It has meant much to me, also. And I'm sure it might be the same for other royal personages."

"But there is a reason, now especially. I pray to it night and day." The duchess's face was troubled.

"I, too," responded Marguerite, not wanting to let her have the advantage. "It prevents me from fearing my own death." She paused, then added, "I may well keep the relic for myself. Then, when I am gone . . ." She shrugged her shoulders.

Anne's expression grew even more distressed. "So, we are not to be the chosen? You know, we would be willing to make many concessions in order to have it."

Marguerite felt a growing agitation. "It is not something I wish to discuss now. I should leave soon. When I return to Montfort, then perhaps—we must see." Her voice had grown taut.

"Oh, please, dear Marguerite," the duchess urged, "please do not leave before my child is born. I implore you!"

Marguerite knew perfectly well that the duchess wanted not her but the shroud, which she obviously coveted. It made her angry because, surprisingly, she had begun to value the younger woman's companionship.

Rising quickly, she said, "Whether I remain or not, the shroud is mine to dispose of. And I may choose not to do so." With that she left the chapel.

Next morning Marguerite felt the same agitation that had come upon her in the chapel. Since the day was sunny, she decided upon a walk in the castle bailey, outside the kitchens. The garden there was planted with fruit trees and vines to the north, with herbs and flowers to the south. Many of the flowers—lilies, violets, and anemones—were blooming. At the garden's center was a large pond, stocked with trout and pike for the duke's table.

As her anxiety increased, Marguerite began pacing the grounds. She resolved to leave as soon as possible. And something else: she would no longer think of giving up the shroud. It was hers; it sustained her as she faced old age. She would keep it until her last breath.

She was about to return to her rooms, summon Guillaume, and announce her decision, when the Duchess Anne appeared.

"Marguerite," she said gently, "I am afraid I angered you yesterday. Forgive me."

Now that she had made a firm decision, Marguerite was able to be more indulgent than before. "My dear Anne, do forgive me. I am so sorry to have led you to believe the shroud would be yours. But now I know I must hold it for myself. And I believe it is time to depart. I have enjoyed your gracious hospitality far too long."

Anne was upset. Her eyes were clouded with tears. "Though you have made your decision about the shroud, Marguerite, stay with me, at least until the child comes. Please!"

Anne was obviously desperate. Thinking this to be the natural fear of a woman expecting her first child, Marguerite smiled reassuringly and patted her hand. "My dear, there is nothing to fear. You and your baby will be fine."

Anne shook her head despairingly. "This is not my first pregnancy. I have suffered through labor twice before. And both babies"—she gave Marguerite a look of infinite sadness—"died." Shocked, the countess put an arm about the younger woman's shoulders.

"I fear—no, I believe—this child, too, will never live. The idea tortures me night and day. The last two times I nearly died. Each labor was long and terrible. Because my life was endangered, the midwives used those horrible extractors and crushers. . . ." She hid her head in her hands. "I am certain, this time, I am going to die. And, as before, they will tear my baby to pieces to bring it out of me. I pray constantly for God's protection. Oh, Marguerite!" The duchess began to sob.

Letting go of the hardness in her heart, Marguerite took Anne into her arms and rocked her like a child.

At last the tears stopped. Marguerite continued holding Anne close to her. Out of a wisdom that loneliness and despair had bred in her spirit, she spoke of life and death and the lessons they held. "God's goodness, dearest Anne, is very real. You must not forget that Our Lord protects those with faith. Your faith, my dear child, is very touching and must please Our Lord greatly."

Anne stopped sobbing and looked up at Marguerite. "Perhaps my fear is greater," she explained, "because my own mother died while bearing me. All my life I have been terrified that the same fate would be mine. And then those excruciating labors—oh, my dear friend."

Marguerite looked at the troubled duchess. "You do not realize your good fortune, child. You have a devoted husband, and fate has not denied you the chance to conceive. I was given neither. Can I tell you what bitterness it is not to know the relief of loving arms, the feeling of a child growing within you?" Never before had Marguerite voiced, to anyone but Guillaume, the lonely despair with which she had lived for so long.

Now aware of the older woman's pain, Anne forgot herself. She took Marguerite's face in her hands and kissed it with tender emotion.

That evening, alone in her bedchamber, the countess thought back upon her conversation with Anne. Though the young woman had much in life that was good, like Marguerite, she, too, now feared the approach of death. And neither a man's love nor a relic would prevent what was inevitable. Yet God existed apart from all else. And at the end only He would be there.

Marguerite knew now she could live out her life without the

shroud. Yet she was still faintly reluctant. It had been the de Charnys' greatest possession. Giving it up only accentuated her failure to carry on the line. That was the sad truth from which she could never escape.

Several days later, as Marguerite and Guillaume entered the great hall for dinner, Duke Louis's steward hurried over. "My lady, the duke asked me to summon you. Duchess Anne is in labor and calls out your name."

Marguerite went at once to the lying-in chamber, which had been prepared for many weeks. Already in attendance was the midwife, dressed in black, along with several other women.

Anne's enormous bed had been hung in blue silk and velvet. A large cradle alongside was covered in snowy holland cloth. Since the chamber was quite small, there was scarcely room for Marguerite. As contractions racked the duchess, she grasped two silk ropes which hung from the bed's canopy frame.

Marguerite bent and wiped sweat from the suffering face. "Please don't leave me," Anne whispered. Marguerite tried to reassure her, feeling a slow fear creep across her own heart. The pretty duchess had become very dear to her.

Hours went by, and as Anne began to tire, the midwife conferred with her assistants. Anne heard them mention the crusher that had mangled her other infants. Gathering strength, she screamed for Marguerite. "Don't let them. I may die, but not my baby!"

Fearful, Marguerite hurried to the chapel. She had an inspired thought. With Guillaume assisting, she carried the shroud back to Anne's lying-in chamber. Placing it over the duchess's swollen stomach, she said, in reassuring tones, "There, your baby and you will be safe."

From that moment Anne's panic departed and she bore her contractions with more ease.

Marguerite remained beside the young duchess, holding her hand and speaking constant words of comfort. As she watched, the old woman felt strange sensations happening in her own body; pains and something resembling contractions. In a marvelous way she felt that Anne's struggle to give birth was also her own. Now she knew the shroud must stay here with the duchess and her child, soon to enter this world.

Finally, with a last scream from its mother, a girl was born. Everyone relaxed. Soon, however, pandemonium broke out. Another girl appeared! The healthy twin babies began crying lustily for their first dinner. A wet nurse stood ready. Anne, exhausted but triumphant, took Marguerite's hand.

"Please stay awhile longer. We need you," she said faintly. Marguerite, weeping with relief that all was well, took the two babies in her arms. At last she knew the happiness that had been so long denied her.

Each day she came to visit Anne and her infants. As the duchess grew stronger, they spoke again about the shroud. Marguerite had decided to bestow it upon the House of Savoy. Anne promised that many important gifts would be heaped upon Marguerite. But the old lady had only one concern. Provision must be made for her steward, Guillaume le Meunier. Upon her death there would be nowhere for him to go. After Marguerite explained that Guillaume's ancestor had saved the shroud from destruction and originally brought it to the de Charnys, the duchess had an idea. Guillaume must stay on at Chambéry; her husband would appoint him Keeper of the Shroud. It would be a position of honor, and hereditary. When Guillaume died, his son and his son's son could assume the position. Marguerite smiled gratefully. Her work was complete.

And now she must leave. She did not want to presume any longer upon the Savoyards' hospitality. More than anything she dreaded the parting from Guillaume. They had been together so very long. Shortly before she was to depart, the countess summoned her steward.

"Please, sit down, Guillaume." She pointed to the chair next to her own. "There is something you must know."

They both smiled, remembering the first time she had commanded him to sit beside her.

"Guillaume, I have come to a decision. The shroud will remain here at Chambéry."

He nodded. "It is a wise decision, my lady. The duke and

duchess are pious. They will offer it the proper reverence. And, of course, the House of Savoy is one of the most noble."

"You know that I have always depended upon you to watch over the shroud."

"I have tried to serve you well in all things, mistress."

Marguerite looked at his face, now grown wrinkled. But she did not see the lines of age, only the innocent sweetness that had been there at the beginning. Anguish gripped her, and she spoke firmly; otherwise she could not have spoken at all.

"I wish you to stay with the shroud. Duke Louis will appoint you its keeper. You may bring your family and live here at the castle. It is all arranged."

He protested, saying his place was with her. He wanted only to be at her side. "You need me. You are not young. I cannot leave you."

"You must leave me. I order it!"

Deeply hurt, he looked as though he might cry. "Madame, if that is what you want."

No longer able to hide her feelings, she exclaimed, "It is not what I want. But I have no choice. There is little time left for me. And when I am gone, what will become of you? My needs are not important."

Guillaume fell before her, grasping her hands in his. "My lady, my lady, I have always loved you. I married and raised three children. Still, it is you who own my heart. Permit me, please, to stay with you forever."

She placed her head against his, feeling for a moment as she had long ago. "Oh, my dearest . . ."

Yet no persuasion could change Marguerite's mind. Guillaume must remain. She would dispatch his wife and family upon her return to Montfort.

Three days later all was in readiness for Marguerite's departure. Farewells had been said, and Guillaume had seen to her horse-litter and escort. They stood ready at the castle gate.

As she crossed the lovely courtyard, Marguerite felt a deep depression. Here, at Chambéry, she was leaving everything that had mattered in an otherwise empty life. The shroud, Guillaume, the little twins, Duchess Anne . . .

"Marguerite, Marguerite!" It was Anne, calling from a distance. Marguerite had believed her still confined to bed. But here she was, hurrying across the courtyard, blond hair streaming behind her.

Breathlessly she said, "I saw that you were leaving. I simply had to hug you again." She rushed into Marguerite's arms.

Unable to endure more, Marguerite gently thrust Anne from her and quickly climbed the little steps into her litter. As Guillaume stood by, she drew its curtains. No one would witness her tears.

She was about to call the order to set forth when she heard the duke's voice. "Marguerite de Charny!" She could not ignore him. Thrusting back the curtains, she looked out.

"The Lady Anne and I have talked together about you. You are very dear to her. She grew up without a mother, you know. And—"

"What he is trying to explain, dearest Marguerite," broke in the duchess, "what I wanted myself to ask before but could not, for fear of your refusal . . ." She hesitated. "Please stay with us here at Chambéry. We sincerely pray you will say yes."

"No, I could not. I have been your guest too long. It is time for leavetaking." She began to draw the curtains.

"Marguerite, what I mean is, I know that you have estates of your own; a household to run. But could you not find a way to return and—and—live here with us?"

Marguerite could not be sure she had heard correctly. Live at Chambéry? That would be impossible. She could never do such a thing. What would become of Montfort? She had responsibilities.

"If you do not return," said Anne, "my daughters will not have a *grand'mère*. Come back. Help them grow up."

The countess reflected a moment. Yes, it was true. Youngsters should be given the benefit of much older and wiser heads. Actually, they might need her.

Marguerite had some years remaining. Leaving Montfort in the custody of her cousin, she returned to Chambéry to spend them with Anne's enchanting twins. They played together in the castle gardens, the babies and the aged lady. And when they were old enough, the little girls delighted in picking violets each spring for their adored, adopted grandmother, Marguerite de Charny.

Chapter 21

Turin, 1978

Molly had been dreaming she was lying beside Nico in a broad meadow. Small groups of trees, three to a cluster, were scattered across the field. Nico took her in his arms and they made love. Afterward she laughed with happiness.

When she woke up, Molly lay with her eyes closed, trying to revive the dream. It was eight o'clock in the morning. On impulse she telephoned Nico. Had she awakened him? she asked. No, he was just about to go to bed to get a few hours sleep. He had been working all night in the palace laboratory.

"I just had the loveliest dream about you," Molly said with a little giggle.

He laughed then and said he would be right over. There was plenty of time for sleep when he was an old man. He would take her to breakfast.

Sitting over their empty dishes, they talked for a while about an archaeologist's work. Later, forgetting Nico's reticence on the subject, Molly said, "You have never told me why you quit racing."

"It gives me black memories."

"Wouldn't it help if you talked about it with me? You sound so sad, Nico."

He looked at his plate, then searched Molly's face for long minutes.

"I have killed a man."

Nico returned his gaze to the table.

"He was a member of my team. Livia's twin brother. It happened in the United States, on a dark, very fast corner at Sebring, Florida. Sebring is a punishing twelve-hour race on airport runways and rough taxiways. At night not Spa, Le Mans, or any other track is more dangerous or darker. The American aviation authorities foolishly imagine an airplane may land there during the race, so it takes place with all the runway lights turned off.

"I was in the lead and Gianni was ten meters behind me. We had been running for two hours in the darkness. Gianni was holding a steady speed.

"When I braked and shifted down at each bend, Gianni would follow an instant later. He could see my brake lights flash on, and it would cue him to do the same. Perhaps, after those nighttime hours, his reflexes had become automatic and he was relying on my brake lights.

"My radio was attached to the instrument panel next to all my switches. It was time to come in for a pit stop and refueling. When I went to turn on my transmitter to acknowledge the team manager's orders, I was looking straight ahead. Somehow—I still ask myself why—my fingers reached slightly beyond the radio toggle switch and turned off my entire lighting system. But I had seen enough to slide through the curve safely.

"Gianni was probably waiting for my usual brake lights. He slowed down a second too late. His car overshot the curve and rolled. He died on the way to the hospital."

"God, how awful!" Molly said. "But surely it wasn't your fault."

"It was. I turned off my lights. It was my error. I killed Gianni."

"Who could ever think that?"

"My fiancée did. Livia said some very terrible things to me, and she was right. She threw her engagement ring at my face and called me 'murderer.' That was the end for us. I have never driven a race car since."

"Nico, can't you see, it was just an accident. You must try to understand and forgive yourself. You've suffered so many years." She reached across the table for his hand. Nico withdrew it.

He continued, "That was the beginning of my 'dark night of the soul.' I learned to place my faith in Our Lord. He has become my greatest comfort."

"And you are still as deeply pained?"

"It is more than that. I resolved never again to be involved with high risk, with danger. Others could be harmed once more. Who could I hurt at a dig? Post holes . . . corroded bronze tools . . . a Roman mosaic . . . some ancient bones?

"Molly, I must tell you this. As an American, you would say I have lost my nerve." He bit his lip, then said in an anguished voice, "It is still not right inside of me. I am afraid."

She reached out again and took his hand. Tensely he held on to her fingers.

"Nico, I care for you and I am so sorry."

At the bar of the Hotel Sitea, the STURP team's hotel, Richard sat alone, staring into his drink. The scientists came here during their off-duty hours. Coolidge was waiting for Harrison Berg, who usually showed up midafternoon.

Richard was troubled. Certain things about Acciaro did not add up. Those phony keys on his watch chain, his excessive talk of wealth when he said his father had left him nothing. Writers, generally, were not all that rich. He soon expected to come into a large sum of money. Why? Acciaro always wore the same suit. And that beat-up Buick from a garage which serviced Bentleys. The way that weird chauffeur had dragged him from the bar. And his talk about carrying away the shroud. But most of all, his questions. Acciaro's insistence upon exact times of the tests and the number of people to be present.

These details could in no sense be considered vital or even significant to a treatise on fake church relics. Coolidge pondered the matter, and his half-formed suspicions made him uneasy. He tried not to think of his logical conclusion. Best to put it out of mind.

The scientist arrived with a group of colleagues. Spotting

Richard, he walked over and greeted him. Berg was in a very good mood.

"It's simply amazing, Richard," he said. "Under high magnification the image becomes, not continuous strokes of color, but millions of tiny dots on the top surface of the fibrils. It reminds me of the Ben Day process of mechanical reproduction used for ordinary newspaper illustrations. You know, a newspaper picture of a face becomes just an assemblage of black dots— all the same color." He went on to explain that in the shadow of a nose there would be many dots—densely bunched. On a lighter cheek there would be scarcely any. This was how the shroud image was constructed. "That a counterfeiter could accurately apply all these countless dots is out of the question."

"Does that eliminate things like powders? Myrrh and aloes?"

"Absolutely."

"You're positive?"

"Completely positive."

Richard felt ill for a moment. Recovering, he queried, "You're Jewish, right? Why should you be so involved with this Christian matter?"

"First of all, I am a scientist. The shroud presents a fascinating challenge. I have been on the STURP team since its inception. Does it surprise you that we Jews give a damn about the rest of the world? You might be amused to learn that my fellow workers refer to me as their 'conscience.'

"If you wondered, I can report that our tests have been carried out very, very scrupulously." He chuckled. "I might even term the procedures as strictly kosher. In any event my presence seems not so foreign in a place where we might be viewing the image of someone with the same roots as my own. Actually that image is beginning to strike me as rather miraculous."

Berg started to turn back to his friends at a nearby table. Richard was puzzled. "Tell me, Dr. Berg, do Jews believe in miracles?"

Smiling, Harrison Berg replied, "If a Jew didn't believe in miracles, he wouldn't be realistic."

Downing his drink, Coolidge put some lire on the bar and headed out of the Sitea, bound for his hotel.

At the Ambasciatori the room clerk handed him his key and a cablegram. Richard took the elevator to his floor. When he entered his room, he placed the cablegram on the telephone table beside an armchair. Settling into it, he lit a cigarette and slowly smoked, while staring at the envelope. Coolidge had an impulse to order dinner and read it later. But what was he afraid of? He lit another cigarette, reached for the cablegram, and tore it open. It was from the United States. With an effort of will Richard directed his eyes to the text:

TEST RESULTS SUGGEST FIRST CENTURY ORIGIN. RANGE 50 BC TO 110 AD. GOOD LUCK. SCOTT.

Richard saw the Coolidge Theory going down in flames. He sat with his head in his hands. Twice, he reread the cable. Finally he ripped it into bits and flushed it down the toilet.

Drawing a deep breath, he went to his suitcase and extracted a small address book. Returning to the chair, he picked up the telephone and requested the operator to get him Mexico City. Enrique D. Morán, D for Dagoberto.

When the call finally came through, the line between Mexico and Italy grew alive with words of ebullient greeting. Richard explained that he was about to leave Turin and was thinking of the project his friend had proposed in New York some months before. Was he still interested in studying the image of the Virgin of Guadalupe?

It had been discovered in the early sixteenth century by an Indian boy. Following a series of miraculous visions, the youth saw an unlikely hillside of roses growing in the barren, December soil. Wrapping the flowers in his serape, he carried them to his church's bishop. As he opened his serape, the roses tumbled to the ground, and an image of a dark-skinned Virgin was seen to be imprinted on the coarse fabric. The Virgin, now patroness of Mexico, was the focal point of the most celebrated religious pilgrimage in the hemisphere.

The Mexican told Coolidge he was ready to begin their investigation of the image whenever Richard could join him. He said some now claimed to see the tiny figure of the Indian boy in each of the Virgin's eyes.

"Marvelous! This is for me," said Coolidge. "I'm flying to Rome in a few hours. Then off on KLM to the Distrito Federal. Chill some Margaritas, my friend. *Ciao* and *hasta la vista*."

Coolidge made his next call to the airport ticket office. Whistling his off-key tune, he began to pack.

When Richard called Molly from Turin's Aeroporto Caselle, he begged her to get there quickly. It was urgent. She found him standing by the Rome departure gate. His attaché case lay by his feet.

"Molly, you must listen carefully to what I say. I owe you this one. In a way what has happened is partially my fault. I am convinced that by late tomorrow, the shroud will very probably be stolen."

Then he told her the story of his strange relationship with Camillo Acciaro—the suspicious questions and circumstances, Acciaro's declaration that he was thinking of carrying off the shroud. "I believe he means it."

"But how could you ever get yourself involved in this mess?"

"It was the money, I suppose. You know the shaky position my Institute is in."

"When exactly will all this happen?"

"I can't be sure. But the most likely time seems to be midnight tomorrow. The infrared tests. They will be conducted with all lights out. I told Acciaro it would take fifteen minutes. For all I know, it could take fifteen hours, but that's what I told him."

"How do you know this test will be carried out in darkness?"

"Count Sforzini confirmed it."

"Nico!"

"Well, I sort of pried it out of him. He had no idea of my reason for questioning him."

"I thought you didn't give a damn about the shroud."

"True. But that was yesterday. I will not explain my reason, but the shroud is genuine. The real McCoy. I know."

This unexpected turnabout was hard to believe. There could

be no real basis for it. Molly thought of all of Richard's bad calls. She dismissed this example of his off-the-wall opinion.

"Somebody should stop Acciaro," said Richard. "That guy is thoroughly unprincipled." Molly composed a wry smile. "Look, Molly, I'm not a crook. I'm essentially honest."

"Okay," she said, taking a notebook from her purse. "Let's get this story straight. First, what does Acciaro look like, and describe any people you associate with him."

Richard did his best, including Raffaele the chauffeur. He did not know where Acciaro lived, and he suspected the telephone number he had been given was a public phone booth. It either never answered his calls or was busy.

When Richard could tell her no more, she glanced at his attaché case. Where was he going? He explained his flight to Mexico City and his new project, the Virgin of Guadalupe.

An announcement came over the public address system. The Rome flight was now boarding.

"Molly, believe me when I tell you I sincerely regret that we never got off to a decent start again. It's my biggest regret. I think I loved you once."

Passengers began to brush past them. Molly stood motionless, feeling the sadness in her throat, knowing that a part of her life had finally ended. She gave Richard an honest kiss.

"Good luck, you bastard." Turning away, she ran for the taxi stand.

Whistling his tune as he moved along the passageway, Richard found himself correcting the melody, and suddenly the lyrics repeated themselves in his mind. It was a popular song of years past, "Street of Dreams." The words told of a magic place in dreamland where one's frustrated hopes came true, and all the riches one could wish for were right there for the taking.

He was annoyed this idiotic melody had fixed itself so reassuringly in his subconscious. Certainly he had not been dreaming all these years. And in any case such nonsense was over now. One way or the other he would wake up the world.

Quickening his stride, filled with renewed hope, Richard Coolidge disappeared down the departure ramp.

Camillo Acciaro and his two associates were holding their final planning session.

"What did you find out?" demanded Acciaro.

Rozza replied, "The door from the Duomo chapel to the palace is unlocked. I tried it."

"Very good. Ugo, it is most important that you obtain a heavy padlock and a length of chain to attach the transceiver to something secure in the helicopter. The pilot could get the bright idea to toss our radio out the window."

"Done," said Rozza.

"Now you will hear the ransom note I wrote. By the way, Bruno, does your boy understand all about delivering it?"

Strà said, "He is a smart kid. If you think he is stupid, deliver it yourself."

Looking pained, Acciaro said, "The arrangement will be satisfactory. This letter is directed to the Turin headquarters of the Italian Radio-Television Network." He began:

"Distinguished Gentlemen of RAI: By this time your facilities will have been active with news bulletins about the incredible disappearance of the Shroud of Turin. Please forgive my taking a moment of your time, but I alone can cast light on the truth of the situation. And I alone can tell you how to procure the shroud's safe return.

"You will observe I have enclosed a corner of your miraculous relic, which I have severed, to verify my relationship to this matter.

"Payment for the shroud's return to the Duomo will come from all those faithful believers who think the shroud is worth rescuing. You will broadcast to all Europe, if not the world, my demand for cash contributions to this end. All monies shall be forwarded to you. And they must be substantial.

"Then you shall place the money, of course unmarked, in solid bundles, appropriately wrapped to withstand a short drop. You shall also direct a pilot, with his assistant, to proceed with the money to a helicopter which I shall designate in a later message.

"The pilot is to take off with all the cash bundles sixty minutes before the last daylight hour on the thirtieth day after your receipt of this letter. And without any concealed transmitter devices within the bundles or on the helicopter. Thereafter the pilot will receive all orders directly from me. I have electronic devices to ascertain if you are cheating.

"Be warned: I can, at any time, blow up the helicopter and its passengers. This will be followed by total destruction of the shroud. So forget about tracking planes or devices. In such a case I shall know. The result will be disastrous for your relic.

"Be so good as to promulgate this message to all the press services. And don't forget, your time limit for collecting the money is thirty days.

"The Church, which is a corrupt organization, will be taught a lesson. With all good wishes, Giasone II."

"Who is this Giasone?" asked Strà.

"The man who stole the Golden Fleece."

"The golden what?"

"Oh, forget it," said Acciaro. "Now listen, gentlemen—you especially, Bruno. Our weapons are merely for intimidation. I want no rough stuff. Do you understand?"

Strà grunted. Acciaro continued, "You are all to be here at ten P.M. tomorrow evening. Don't forget any of your equipment, and wear overcoats or raincoats to conceal your weapons. Is everything clear? Very good, gentlemen, we are ready for our magnificent adventure."

Monsignore Monti decided to pay the shroud scientists another call. It was only correct. He had not visited the Royal Palace laboratory since that Sunday night the shroud had been carried over from the Duomo. It was now Wednesday. Only two days of testing remained. He had tried to keep aloof from what was happening, refusing to listen to any of the gossip that filtered from the palace. But he could no longer postpone an appearance. His position demanded it.

Entering the laboratory, he noticed that black plastic sheets had been hung over the room's high windows. A bright overhead lamp glared from the ceiling onto the shroud. Six scientists were on duty. The table to which the relic was affixed by parallel lines of magnets was now in vertical position, and a photomicroscope, looking like binoculars, but actually part of a large camera, was being moved horizontally along tracks, some two inches from the relic's surface.

Monti stepped into the circle of light and Nico, one of the group, greeted him. "Vittorio, we are about to begin our color photomicroscopy studies. We expect to turn up some surprises."

Sternly the monsignore regarded his friend. "You are not wearing your gloves. I thought all the scientists had agreed to wear laboratory gloves."

Patiently Nico replied, "We cannot use them when it is necessary to feel the fabric. There is no need to be concerned, Vittorio. You must know the linen is remarkably sturdy."

As Nico rejoined the scientists, the monsignore moved anxiously to the tilt-table. He lingered there, asking no questions, watching these men he so mistrusted, now intent upon their work. They spoke very little and when they did, it was in hushed tones. Monti was surprised by the quality of respect in their manner.

Selected details of the shroud were to be photographed through the microscope. But this test had presented problems. Because footsteps on the palace's fifteenth-century floors set up strong vibrations, the team could effectively work with only twenty-power magnification. Otherwise unavoidable blurriness would ruin their results. Even so it was necessary before each exposure, to call out in Italian and English, "*Alto*—stop," halting all movement in the vicinity.

Vittorio realized from the smoothness and precision with which the tests were carried out that the scientists had spent much advance effort on details of proper lighting and exposure time. He questioned one of the Americans.

"Father," the man replied, "we worked out our specifications and parameters long before we left the States. No one wanted to risk mistakes, or expose the relic to this bright light any longer than was absolutely necessary."

Now the team trained their lens upon the shroud figure's right side, where the apparent lance wound was located. There was silence as one of the researchers peered through the microscope.

"Fascinating," he reported. "Very interesting contrast here. A heavily colored stain, quite red. It has not spread very far. Must have been viscous. But I also see evidence of some colorless fluid which has diffused further out than the dark stain." He turned to the others, and Monti caught the surprise in his face. "The color-less matter seems to be something entirely different—clearly thin-ner than the blood-colored substance."

Someone quoted the Gospel of John: ". . . one of the soldiers pierced his side with a lance; and immediately there came out blood and water." The scientists stared at the linen in awed si-lence.

Watching and listening, Monti became convinced he had pre-judged the scientists unfairly. These men, indeed, grasped the deeper significance of what they were doing. Here were no cold, indifferent individuals. The priest realized the tests were being carried out by persons with heart and conscience.

"Lord," whispered the monsignore, "You are here."

Later Monti drove directly to the archbishop's residence.

"Vittorio, to what do I owe this pleasant and unexpected visit?" asked Archbishop Severini, who, with the pope, Italy's former king, and Vittorio, held the only keys to the shroud's reliquary.

Monti got right to the point, revealing in detail the informa-tion he had been withholding. After he had finished, the arch-bishop leaned back in his gilded chair. "Vittorio, you can relax now. All is well. You must talk to the scientists about this. They are responsible men. They tell me they can already confirm the fact that there is no pigment on that linen. So, even if there was a mixup long ago in Venezia, our shroud is not the copy. Of that you can be sure. Take things easier, my friend."

Vittorio felt the heaviness lift, all eight hundred years of it. His fears had been groundless. In fact the information Nico had uncovered in the Marciana archive could be viewed in a new way, since it added another century and a half to the shroud's lengthening provenance. Whatever turned up in that laboratory, Turin's shroud was the original. Now, Vittorio concluded, was the appropriate time to unburden himself of another concern.

"Your Excellency, I believe there should be radiocarbon testing as soon as the commission approves the method. We must leave no doubt in the minds of others."

"I cannot fault your logic. As you know, one proposal for the carbon-14 testing has already been presented to us. It comes from a laboratory in the United States with newer, more modern equipment. I understand it can be effective with a sample the size of your fingertip. But first we shall want a test made on cloth known to be two thousand years old. Let us study the result. Then we shall learn the relative accuracy of this process."

Vittorio felt better than he had in months. The archbishop said, "You look so happy, Vittorio. I did not realize you were eager for the carbon-14 test. After all, you might have something to lose should the device give us an unfavorable response."

"Not so much as I had once thought, Your Excellency. The love and devotion my family has brought to Christ's cloth all these centuries gives me profound joy and satisfaction. Alone, that is a sincere gift to God."

"Do you know how I view this testing?" said the archbishop. "These scientists will eventually tell us the truth about our shroud. And if that truth proves it is not the Lord's burial cloth, we still possess a work of great faith. The image, if made by man, remains a beautiful expression of devotion."

Suddenly Vittorio recalled Jesus' words to Thomas: "You believe because you can see me. Happy are those who have not seen and yet believe." He blushed to have understood so little.

Vittorio returned to his residence, delighted with the day's events. But his relief was short lived. Awaiting him was an unsmiling visitor, Molly Madrigal.

Chapter 22

Chambéry—Grenoble—Turin, 1532–1578

The wind was rising that December night. Snow had been falling all day. By dusk it began gusting into deep drifts. Chambéry's inhabitants stayed close to their hearths.

Young Jacques Meunier had arrived home before twilight, bearing three pages from a book that Gilbert Fichet, the printer, had allowed him to set by himself. Three years ago, at the age of nine, Jacques had been apprenticed to Gilbert, who had established the first printing press in Chambéry. Jacques could hardly wait to begin work each day. Some time before, he had learned reading, writing, and Latin from the Franciscans in the nearby friary. The previous spring he had asked Gilbert whether he might be given odd jobs at the shop. Gilbert had agreed. Jacques's quick intelligence and interest had impressed the printer, who decided the boy should learn the trade.

After supper, as François, Jacques's father, who was Keeper of the Shroud, sat by the fireside in a drunken stupor, Jacques spread out the three pages. They were from a Latin psalter, the hundred and fifty psalms of David. Gilbert had chosen the italic Aldine type, said to be copied from the handwriting of Plutarch. Firelight dappled the pages as Jacques reviewed with pride the work he had done.

Suddenly he noticed a strange brightness illuminating the

pages before him. Glancing at the small front window, which was partially covered by snow, he saw a terrifying red glow. Then he became aware of muffled shouts from the street. Fire, he realized, feeling the panic of it.

He unlatched the door, which blew open in a blast of cold wind. A few townspeople were hurrying up the hill. He saw the flames. They were rising from the roof of Sainte Chapelle.

"Father!" he screamed. "Father, it's on fire, it's on fire!" He shook the snoring François, whose heavy body slid to the floor.

"Mother!" shouted Jacques. She ran down the stairs. "Sainte Chapelle, it's burning! Father must save the shroud."

His mother tried to rouse her husband. Quickly she turned to Jacques. "It's no use. Jacques, you must go. Hurry."

He raced into the street and headed up the hill toward the church. The fire had started at the back of the wooden building. The shroud's reliquary was there.

Jacques recognized two Franciscans, young Brother Domini and Brother Fidèle.

"Where is your father?" yelled Fidèle.

Ignoring the question, Jacques asked whether anyone had gone inside to rescue the shroud.

"No," cried Domini. "The roof beams are burning. The whole roof could collapse any minute."

"I'll try," called Jacques.

As he ran toward the church portal, Jacques was full of fear. But it was his duty to confront the danger. Not for the shroud alone; for his family's pride. He was the great-great-grandson of Guillaume, Marguerite de Charny's steward and first Keeper of the Shroud. Since Guillaume's death, nearly a century before, members of the family—now known simply as Meunier—had been charged with the duty of tending the shroud. They were the only lay persons, besides the Dukes of Savoy, allowed access to the holy relic.

Inside the church Jacques and two townsmen who had joined him fell back at the rush of heat and smoke. Flames from a fallen candlestand had reached the altar and were racing toward the sacristy beyond. Burning ceiling beams crashed downward at random and flames rose steadily through the gaping roof. The church's three stained-glass windows, scenes of the Passion, appeared to be lighted by a scarlet sun.

Dropping to their knees on the less smoky floor, the three rescuers crept toward the flaming altar. Jacques pointed to a grilled recess where the silver reliquary rested. Flames were licking the iron bars.

"It's locked," Jacques said, coughing. "My father has the key."

"Wait," shouted one of the men. Standing, he grabbed a tall iron candlestand.

"We'll pry the grill open. You reach in, Jacques," he ordered.

The two men placed the candlestand between the bars and heaved. The grill burst open.

Jacques took hold of the silver reliquary, but screamed with pain. "It's too hot." The metal had started melting.

One of them grabbed a ewer of holy water. When he threw it over the reliquary, the silver box gave off a cloud of steam.

Jacques reached in and seized the reliquary. It was still searingly hot but he fixed his attention on one thing only: holding on to the box long enough to get it to safety. Ignoring the falling timbers, he made for the door. As he escaped the flaming building, there was a terrible sound. The belfry had fallen in. The bronze bells clattered to earth clanging crazily, and then grew silent.

Jacques dropped the reliquary into a snowbank. The snow sizzled and steamed upon contact with the hot metal.

Gritting his teeth with pain, Jacques plunged his hands into the deep snow. The two priests and the other folk had forgotten him, concerned only for the shroud. They crowded about the partially melted silver box while Brother Fidèle pulled out the holy cloth and carefully examined it.

Jacques drew his hands out of the snow. His mother, who had followed him to the church, screamed. Both palms and wrists were covered with huge blisters. The sight of the burns, the pain in his lungs, and the shock of what he had just been through, were too much for Jacques. He fainted.

François Meunier did not learn until next day of his son's heroism. Bored with his duties as shroud keeper, François believed he deserved more out of life than the monotonous task of bringing out the silver casket, unwrapping the cloth for public exhibitions, then putting it back again. After his other child, a daughter, had been born, he had started to drink. Now he had become an ugly sot, abusive toward his wife and children.

Jacques, a quiet boy with a long, serious face and dark hair, continually irritated his illiterate father, who found every excuse to deride him. Jacques lived for the day he could leave his father and go off to Grenoble. Gilbert talked about a printer he knew there. Jacques hoped, someday, the man might offer him a position.

But now the youngster lay on his cot, breathing in agony. The smoke he had inhaled had hurt his lungs. Fever consumed his weakened body. His mother called the midwife but the old woman, who knew only about delivering babies, stood helplessly staring at Jacques's blistered palms. His mother, more wise than the midwife, eased Jacques briefly with snow packs applied to his burned palms and feverish forehead. Each morning Brother Fidèle stopped by to pray and offer a soothing elixir of opium and wine.

At last Jacques's lungs felt better; he could breathe more easily and his fever abated. The blisters on his palms and wrists dried up; his burns started to heal. Now he could come down from his garret room to join the family for meals. However, he preferred that his mother feed him, since trying to hold cup or spoon was still painful.

Jacques was anxious for his hands to heal so he could return to the printing press. He hated being around his father. Brooding over his failure to rescue the shroud himself, the man was drinking more heavily than usual. And he had become even more abusive toward Jacques.

One evening, at the table, François stared across at his son, now trying to feed himself. "So, you think you'll be a printer of books?" He laughed. "Not with those paws you won't. You couldn't set type for the devil."

Jacques's head throbbed with hatred. He yearned to smash his father's bloated face. But it would be a sin to strike one's father. Then he glanced at his hands. Something terrible had happened. His fingers coiled inward. He could not force them to straighten.

Weeks came and went. Though the burns healed completely, Jacques's fingers remained unusable, curved like the talons of a falcon. His mother told him not to worry; he was a hero. A grateful Duke Charles summoned Jacques and his father to the château and gave them a generous reward, which the elder Meunier pocketed.

In time Jacques was able to move his thumbs, enabling him to do simple tasks. This heartened him and he returned to Gilbert's establishment. But he could do little more there than hold a broom to sweep the floor. One day he saw a finished copy of the psalter, with the three pages of type he had set. He wanted to fling them away. Three pages to last a lifetime! A bitterness rose within him—toward his father, toward the shroud, and even toward Chambéry, which he could no longer bear.

As he reached manhood, Jacques longed for a woman he could love. But girls of the town were repelled by his hands. Once, in desperation, he approached a whore in the marketplace. She turned away, screaming that he was possessed of the devil.

By the time he was sixteen, Jacques had had enough. He determined to leave Chambéry forever. He would go to Grenoble. It had been his dream. He did not believe much could await him there; large cities required abilities he no longer possessed. Still, the hope had sustained him all those bad years. Whatever happened, he must go.

One warm morning in May he packed his few things and kissed his mother and sister good-bye. Following him into the street, his mother placed a few coins in his pocket.

She whispered, "I took these while your father was asleep." She looked tenderly at him. "You are very dear to me, Jacques. This will always be your home."

Following the right bank of the Isère, Jacques arrived in Grenoble at noon the following day. Distracted from his almost constant sense of defeat, he was suddenly filled with delight by the lovely city which rose before him. By the quayside was the imposing Palais de Justice. Opposite stood the ancient brick church of St. André, and not far off, the Cathedral of Notre Dame. Beyond lay the tortuous, narrow streets of the walled city, which stretched toward the edge of Mont Rachais. Its slope was covered with a succession of fortresses. In the distance he could make out the snowcapped grandeur of Mont Blanc.

Jacques had an impulse to enter St. André and give thanks for the hope of a new life. But, as quickly, the familiar bitterness returned and he made off toward the streets of the town, his hands concealed in his cloak. Munching the last of the bread and cheese he had brought with him, he wandered around within the city walls. Frequently he paused to marvel at the shops and fine houses. A seller of spices directed him to Grenoble's printing establishment.

"So you worked for my friend Gilbert Fichet," said Roger le Grand, wiping his hands on a leather apron. Behind him the apprentice, a snaggle-toothed youth, grinned at Jacques, but his eyes were hostile.

Le Grand pointed to a box of pied type. "Suppose you show me what you can do. Straighten out that mess alphabetically. Then, if you're up to it, let's see you set up a row of type—say, the first line of the Lord's Prayer."

Forgetting his disability, Jacques rushed forward and thrust his hands into the jumbled letters. But the metal type spilled through his grasp like grain in the fingers of a palsied man. Biting his lip in humiliation, Jacques drew back his hands into the folds of his clothing.

"What have we here?" cried le Grand, pulling Jacques's wrists out for inspection. "Jésus, what happened to them?"

"They were burned," muttered Jacques.

"That's too bad," said the printer. "What could Fichet have had in mind, sending you here?"

"Coming here was my idea," said Jacques.

"If your idea was to work for me, you're mad."

The apprentice let out a yip of amusement. Murmuring apologies, Jacques backed out of the shop into the street.

The next few hours were an embarrassment and a misery for Jacques. Most of the other tradesmen on the street were equally unkind. The familiar quips assailed him. But finally he found a few menial jobs, plying a broom and emptying ordure into buckets which he carried to a distant ditch. If anything Jacques's

lot had fallen even lower than in Chambéry. The new life looked
hopelessly dismal, but at least it promised a few weekly sous. He
could survive.

Returning with much diffidence to the printer's shop, he
begged le Grand to allow him to sleep there at nights—the floor
would be fine. He would gladly sweep out the place daily and
clean as best he could. Le Grand, not averse to something for
nothing, acquiesced and life in Grenoble began for Jacques.

One fine morning in June, his chores finished, Jacques idled in
the printer's doorway. The distant peaks seemed as remote as a
chance for happiness. Finding Jacques a trustworthy fellow, the
printer had left him in charge of the shop, while he and his apprentice, Gautier, carted some loose sheets of Dauphiné law over
to the bookbinder. At that moment Jacques saw such an odd procession approaching the shop that Mont Blanc was instantly
robbed of any interest. Leading the group was a remarkably
powerful man in elaborate livery who was pulling the shafts of a
strange, four-wheeled carriage. On a huge silk-cushioned chair
fixed to its platform sat the largest, fattest man Jacques had ever
seen. Lavender plumes were bouncing from his cap and he was
wearing long lavender kid gloves. Walking to one side of the vehicle was a beautiful young woman with wide blue eyes and
flowing blond hair. On the opposite side strode an elegantly
gowned woman of about forty. Her strong features bore the imprint of chronic disapproval. Behind, dressed in matching cos-
tumes, were two young men in their twenties, of similar appearance, including vaguely bored expressions. The fat man's florid
face was glowing with pleasure. He was carefully eating a pear.

"*Holà*, Baptiste," he shouted, "we stop here!"

The muscled servant gently lowered the shafts to the ground
and set the wheel brake.

Smiling down at Jacques, the passenger called out, "Be so
good as to invite le Grand out here. We have business to discuss."

"He's visiting the bookbinder, sir," said Jacques. "Forgive me,
sir, I am alone."

"Fine, fine," said the fat man. "Then you will serve me, young
man. I wish to purchase some books for our voyage."

"Books?" repeated Jacques, distracted by the scene.

"But of course." The fat man smiled. "To pass the time more graciously."

There were about three-dozen volumes in a cabinet at the front of the shop. Some demonstrated the quality of le Grand's work, others came from the presses of distant printers.

Jacques asked if there were some particular volumes he sought. The fat man replied that he had no special books in mind, but since the young fellow worked for the printer, perhaps he could recommend a few. Jacques returned from the shop with an armful, some on paper bound in leather, others with parchment covers. Clumsily extending one toward the fat man, Jacques said, "It is always good to carry a breviary when one travels."

Letting the cover fall open, Jacques leafed through its contents. "Here you have the prayers for the canonical hours, the Psalms, and much else."

"I'll buy it," said the fat man. "But we do not plan to spend all our time in prayer. Happily there are other things worth thinking about in this world."

"We have books on hunting, falconry, history, cooking . . ."

"Cooking!" cried the fat man in a burst of interest. "I think I should like that better."

Jacques went back to the shop, returning with other books. "Here is *Le Viandier* by Taillevent. He was master chef to Philippe VI de Valois, to the Dauphin, and to Charles VI."

Jacques handed the volume to the fat man, who withdrew from his purse a strange object with two round glass lenses in a leather frame which he held before his eyes. He riffled through the book, pausing at a woodcut of four nobles dining.

"Very interesting," said the fat man, moving his nose closer to the woodcut. "My eyes aren't what they used to be. Of course, I can do accounts and computations, but these letters that crawl like insects across a page . . . very hard to read." He was still looking at the illustration.

He can't read, mused Jacques. "Would you care to hear some of the recipes?"

"You can read!" exclaimed the fat man. "How totally splendid. You should be going with us. You are exactly the sort of person we need on our pilgrimage. But please commence."

Jacques let the book fall open to a random page and began. "'Wild peacocks, which are born in the mountains, should have their feathers plucked like those of the swan. But save the heads and tails. Then they should be boiled in wine with a little vinegar. . . .'" The fat man's eyes were half closed, his lips formed a beatific smile.

The elder woman muttered, "Hah, peacock is too stringy, and swan too oily."

"'Then they should be well larded and roasted on a spit,'" Jacques continued. "'It is better to eat them cold than hot, for they last a long time. Some parts of the flesh resemble beef, others hare or quail. . . .'"

"I have had peacock in Gascony," murmured the fat man, "served along with the incomparable ham of Bayonne. But, ah, the ladies of Bayonne, with their eyes dark as ripe olives and their soft skin the color of pale caramel cream." He sighed deeply. "Yes," he declared, "I shall gladly buy that book. But what is the slender volume you have there?"

"The Canticles, Solomon's Song of Songs."

"Good. I like songs."

And Jacques read, "'Your lips, my promised one, distill a honeycomb. Milk and honey are under your tongue. . . .'"

Again the fat man sighed, "Such delicious phrases, and so quite true. Yes, I want that book also."

It was just then that le Grand and his apprentice turned the corner and came upon the cluster of people. As Jacques offered the slim volume to the fat man, le Grand stared angrily.

"This is not your proper work. Have you emptied all the chamberpots yet?"

"Oh, you poor, poor boy," cried the fat man, noticing Jacques's hands for the first time. "How did it happen?"

"They were burned," said Jacques laconically.

"What a tragedy," said the fat man. "But how?"

Bowing first to the fat man, le Grand turned to Jacques. "Move your stupid self into the shop and start sweeping the floor."

Jacques regarded him with pure hatred for a moment, then turned to the fat man and explained, "There was a terrible fire at the Sainte Chapelle in Chambéry. My hands were injured when I carried the holy shroud out to safety."

After a moment of silence the printer said, faintly, "I didn't know." And then, accusingly, "You never told me."

The fat man cried, "The sacred shroud of Chambéry! And you were the person who saved it. Now I shall insist that you come with us. It is meaningful and right that you, with your noble connection to the blessed shroud, should join us on our pilgrimage to the Cathedral of St. Jacques de Compostelle in Spain."

"He works for me," said the printer, contemplating some practical exploitation of Jacques's heroics.

"I think otherwise," said the fat man, pleasantly. "What is your name, son?"

"Jacques Meunier."

"You must agree to join us, Jacques. It will be a glorious adventure. You shall receive three times what the printer pays you."

"He pays me nothing," said Jacques.

"In that case, if you agree, you will earn an annual stipend of twenty-four livres."

Jacques looked toward the jovial fat man and the lovely blonde beside him; then at the scowling le Grand and his gaping apprentice. He nodded affirmatively.

"Splendid, splendid," cried the fat man. "Then you are one of us. At this moment we are all on our way to the draper's. It is right that we be clothed properly, as simple pilgrims." To the printer he added softly, "Le Grand, you will deliver to my house all the books this young man, Jacques, selects." Then turning to Jacques and waving a lavender glove, he said, "Make haste, Jacques, and collect all your belongings."

"I'm wearing them," said Jacques.

"Then we're off to the draper's." And with some astonishment Jacques realized he was now part of the strange procession.

Looking down at Jacques and grinning, his new benefactor asked, "How do you like my chariot? I designed it myself to fit on the boat, and when we reach Spain we can hitch horses to it—

take no offense, Baptiste. But forgive me, I am Gaston Bouboule, the glover. May I introduce my strong right hand, Baptiste." The husky one smiled and bowed. Turning to the lovely girl, he said, "And Isabeau, she sleeps with me."

Jacques blinked. The fair young woman smiled and curtsied. The middle-aged woman grimaced. "She is a virgin."

Gaston continued, "And Agnès, Isabeau's aunt. And my brother's sons, Hervé and Hercule—they are my companions."

The two young men looked toward Jacques and faintly nodded.

The draper studied each person and measured off appropriate lengths of gray woolen cloth, the *de rigueur* suiting of pilgrims. Then the tailor worked carefully with his tape, the hatter calculated the crown size for their traditional wide-brimmed pilgrims' hats, the cobbler determined the dimensions of their feet for sturdy traveling shoes, and the woodwright took the order for pilgrims' staffs.

Gaston Bouboule was happy. Everything was as it should be. And with Jacques, savior of the shroud, in attendance, special merit would be lent to their pilgrimage to the bones of St. James.

When the entourage reached the rich doorway of Gaston's residence, Jacques gasped. This was a house of great beauty. Clearly Gaston Bouboule was no mere glover. Jacques stared with fascination at the six identical stone-carved maidens with exuberant breasts who apparently supported the curved arches of the second-story windows.

Gaston, looking down from his carriage, said to Jacques, "Indeed they are worth gazing upon. How well I knew the lovely creature who posed for them. I furnished a dowry for her. Alas, I understand she is now settled in Vizille with ten children. She could bake a pigeon pasty that was also unforgettable." And he rolled his eyes skyward, seeing in the clouds the lady's bounteous contours or perhaps the steaming pasty.

The process of Gaston's forward ambulation, which Jacques had observed at the tailor's, was repeated as the large man descended and proceeded to his doorway. A nephew gripped each arm and Baptiste supported him from behind. His smiles were severely strained as, grunting and puffing, face reddened with effort, Gaston Bouboule slowly made his way into the house. His ankles and legs were swollen; the shoe on one foot was slashed open.

The ground story, used for storage, had been divided by curtains of red velvet into a dining area and bedchamber.

"My condition makes ascending the steps to the great hall a trifle incommodious," Gaston said. "So I have arranged my quarters here. But you, Jacques, will be installed in an upper story."

In midafternoon, when everyone was assembling by the linen-covered refectory table, Jacques met Gaston's younger brother, Martin. The bones stood out on his thin, pale face. His cadaverous body suggested that he might just have been released from long imprisonment.

"My dear brother is in charge of affairs at my little shop," said Gaston. "Have the black pearls from Venice arrived yet?"

"The emeralds are fine," Martin replied. "The pearls, though, were not perfectly matched; but with a slight change in design the archbishop will find them satisfactory. The ivory clyster syringe I ordered for myself has finally arrived. It is a thing of great beauty."

As the group were taking their places around Gaston at the head of the table, Martin on his right and Hervé and Hercule to his left, Bouboule raised a hand, halting the two young men. "Take no offense, my dear nephews, but I wish to speak to Jacques, here. Be so kind as to move one chair's distance from me. You well know that *fraternité* and *égalité* are the rule in this house. When you travel to all the fairs of the land, as I have, and mingle with the merchants of many lands, you must believe in the brotherhood of men."

Jacques saw the flashes of rage in the nephews' eyes as they were displaced. Had he already made enemies?

Course after course was served. Jacques, accustomed to meager table scraps from le Grand, was overwhelmed by the abundance of food. He had just finished the pâté of carp when a roast pig was brought in and carved at the sideboard by Baptiste.

While the others tore at the pig with their hands, Bouboule produced what seemed to be a little two-pronged pitchfork. He thrust the tines into a piece of pork and delicately inserted it into his open mouth.

"This is called a *fourchette*," he explained. "They are beginning to have great popularity in the courts of Italy. My Italian agent brought it as a gift. It avoids smearing grease from the fingers to one's clothes."

Martin's voice rose above the others, as he called across the table to Agnès. "The herbalist from Lyons sent me a new purgative yesterday—the oily seeds of a rare plant. The results were magnificent. I shall have some delivered to your chamber."

Gaston leaned toward Jacques. "My powers of digestion sometimes abandon me these days. There is my gout; my chest often pains me; I'm losing my vision; but"—he beamed a warm glance at Isabeau, who sweetly returned the smile—"as is well known, the heat from the body of a very young woman renews the vitality of an old body, cures many infirmities, and halts the ravages of age. The unkindest gift from life is not death, but age. However, it is my belief that if everything fails at the end, one has used oneself well and completely. A horse that is not winded at the end of a race has not raced well."

Gaston put an arm around Jacques and winked. "One day you will understand that there is a time when we must face the future. Accordingly I have taken a vow to make a pilgrimage to visit the bones of St. Jacques at Compostelle. It is time to acquire merits, to balance a life of sins. Not mortal ones, of course, but those heartening cardinal ones of gluttony and lust which, in whatever amount, are the source of man's joy." And he summoned a servant boy to refill his goblet.

That night, lying under warm coverlets in a real bed, Jacques listened to the bells of Notre Dame and St. André. Dare he think that a better life lay ahead? As he fell asleep he saw the blue eyes of Isabeau smiling through the mist of his first dreams.

The next morning he was summoned to the chamber of Gaston Bouboule, who lay in bed with a misery of dyspepsia and gout. Isabeau, beside him, was applying a poultice to his aching foot.

"You must visit my shop today, Jacques. Martin will show you around." And Gaston fell back on his pillows with a groan.

"Our father was a glover, and his father before him," Martin explained, as he led Jacques through the boutiques and workshops of Gaston's domain.

They passed through a room where men were carrying piles of varicolored leathers to their worktables, tracing the outline of wooden hand forms, and carefully following these contours with shears.

"We import goatskins from Spain, calfskins from Normandy, and chamois, as you know, from our own Alps. Our famed specialty is kid. Bouboule gloves are sold in the shops of Paris, London, and Ghent. Some of them go to the papal residence."

Moving to a cabinet, he produced some templates of hands, cut in thin silver. "That was Clément VIII, and this, Paul III. Care to see some kings and princes?"

From the far part of the long room emanated an unbelievable effusion of scents. Here two men were carefully rubbing fragrant substances into the glove halves.

"This," said Martin, "is what Gaston created, and the heart of our success. Dressed leather, at best, is hardly fragrant stuff. Gaston realized that, if perfumed, gloves would become a thing of elegant delight. We use cyclamen from the Alps on white gloves, lavender from Nîmes on lavender, and attar of roses from Bulgaria on pink leather, of course. It was Gaston's thought to match color and scent. An enormous success among the rich and noble."

They had arrived at a small room where a jeweler and his assistants were drilling holes in pearls and mounting jewels on silver medallions for the back of silk gloves. The gloves had been fashioned in appropriate liturgical colors.

Martin continued, "Many buyers were demanding new and varied scents for their persons. It was a simple matter for us to import additional essences from abroad. Also, civet from Africa, myrrh from Arabia. Our glass perfume vials are made in Venice."

He reached into his purse and withdrew a small, embossed leather box. "Try one of these pastilles," he said, offering it to Jacques. It had a sweet, earthy taste which was quite pleasant.

"Ambergris flavor," said Martin. "Restores depressed spirits, and returns sexual vigor—a splendid confection. Very costly. Merchant-traders are purchasing more and more. Gaston, who is a devotee of ambergris, devised these bonbons. He is truly a genius."

When Gaston felt better, and daily thereafter, it became a practice for Jacques to read and converse with him. Wide eyed and silent, Isabeau would look on, absorbing every word. This new relationship quickly became one of mutual affection, which had scarcely been the case between Jacques and his father. Jacques had found a friend.

One day, Gaston believed he had discerned an interesting point in the Twenty-third Psalm, which Jacques had been reading. "The line about 'my cup brimming over.' Doesn't that suggest that the Lord, Who has provided it, approves a little excess? I tell you, my dear Jacques, that psalm is most reassuring."

The pilgrimage to Santiago de Compostela was a frequent subject of discussion. In view of his difficulty in traveling, Gaston had acquired a boat for the first leg of the journey. The *Ste. Vierge*, as he had christened it, would sail down the Isère from Grenoble to the Rhône and southwest to the mouth of the Petit Rhône at Les-Saintes-Maries. A seagoing vessel would be awaiting them there that would proceed around the Atlantic coast of Spain to the port of Vigo. The remainder of the trip would be a brief overland journey.

The inventive Bouboule was proud of the alterations he had devised for the riverboat. A large sheltered sleeping compartment had been constructed for all the pilgrims except himself. He had separate quarters. And the boat even housed a large brazier, for cooking and roasting.

Shortly before the group's departure Hervé and Hercule cornered Jacques in a dark hallway. They each seized an arm. Hervé leaned close to Jacques and said, in an ominous tone, "We think it would be most wise of you to abandon the pilgrimage. Why do you need always to hover around our Uncle Gaston? We are his nephews and we don't like it."

Jacques angrily broke loose. "You are not my masters. I am here because your uncle wishes it and I want to please him."

Hercule said, "Be intelligent, Meunier. We shall give you now what you would have earned in a year. It's in your best interest."

Jacques uttered a sharp laugh and walked away.

On the morning of embarcation Gaston and his entourage attended Mass at the cathedral. The archbishop himself blessed their journey.

Aboard the *Ste. Vierge* Gaston was ebullient. "Think," he cried, "in a few weeks we shall all be privileged to wear the symbol of a pilgrimage to St. Jacques de Compostelle, the scallop shell. I promise you I shall have made for each of you a shell of solid gold."

As the *Ste. Vierge* cruised with the current along the Isère, Jacques sat at Bouboule's feet and spoke of his deep sense of loneliness.

"Jacques," said Gaston, "you are ignorant of the nature of woman. Happily there is a woman for every man—be he one legged or even a dwarf. Time will answer your need. So take heart. Being young, you have a great advantage. For the difference between age and youth is hope."

At Romans the boat was tied to a tree and a gangplank was put over the side. Gaston said, "There is no need for haste on the river. You must all visit the great fair at Beaucaire which opens the first day of July. It would be foolish to sail past before the fair commences. It is a splendid sight and many delicacies may be obtained there. I remember the first time I tasted whale's tongue cooked in *court-bouillon*. I showed no embonpoint then."

Jacques tried to imagine a slender Gaston and all he could visualize were the Bouboule eyes and smile.

"That was the year I met a jewel merchant from Persia, with two beautiful, dark-eyed daughters. Oh, those splendid girls . . . so fiery, so sympathetic! I bought several gems."

Across the deck Agnès muttered to the nephews, "If they were that merchant's daughters, I am the queen of France."

Bouboule remained on board but the rest of the party went ashore. Following Gaston's wishes, they purchased a large *salmis* of thrush, sweet buns, and a sack of walnuts. Baptiste drew the coins from a stout purse he always carried.

In the morning they reached the Rhône above Valence. Jacques elected this time to stay on board with Gaston, as the others wanted to visit the Cathedral of St. Apollinaire. Since his experience with the shroud he wanted nothing to do with churches or praying. They had also been directed to return with peaches, apricots, and wild strawberries.

During the reading session Gaston drew out the strange pair of eyeglasses from the purse on his belt to look at an illustration. He let Jacques examine them closely.

"They help me to see," he said.

Jacques was astonished. The neat, printed letters seemed crude and gigantic; the back of his forearm was covered with a forest of mammoth hairs.

Jacques said, "It is a sad thing that sight should grow less with the years."

Gaston smiled. "No, dear Jacques, it is a good thing. As a woman's beauty fades, so does a man's vision. Therefore women will always look beautiful to me."

That night they dined on young quail Baptiste had persuaded a trapper to part with, roasted on the spit above the brazier and washed down with draughts of good Côtes du Rhône wine.

Later Jacques was awakened by tugging at his arm. Hervé was leaning over him.

"Quiet," he cautioned. "Get up and follow me; we have something for you."

They joined Hercule on deck. He was holding a lantern.

Said Hervé, "We are about to present you with a gift far greater than those few coins you hope to earn. Look!"

Hercule drew out a glove which sparkled with rubies and pearls.

"This is yours, Meunier. We have our interests and you have yours. Take it and leave us here at Valence. The jewels can be sold easily. They will bring you a small fortune."

Jacques, inclined to look at the dark side of things, was alarmed. Was this a ruse? Would he later be accused of theft? Indeed, was the glove truly the property of the nephews? And how could he abandon Gaston for any price?

"If you offered me both gloves, I should say no."

At that moment in every sense Jacques had thrown down the gauntlet. He knew he would have to be ever alert from now on as the brothers obviously thought him a rival for their uncle's affection.

The river grew wider as they cruised south. Sometimes, alone at the bow, Isabeau would softly sing ballads of love.

> *"Cueur sans lequel les yeulx sont insensibles;*
> *Cueur sans lequel les baisers sont penibles;*
> *Cueur enchanteur, par lequel est heureuse*
> *La main tremblant de frisson amoureuse. . . ."*

"Heart, without which eyes are unperceiving; heart, without which kisses are a bother; heart, the enchanter, by which the amorous hand is made happy, trembling with a thrill. . . ."

For Jacques, Isabeau's small, sweet voice was the loveliest sound he had ever heard.

At Montélimar, after the river toll was paid, Gaston requested the pilgrims to seek out a woman of the town who made a candy he craved called nougat. She had beautiful red hair, he remembered. They found several villagers who were boiling down the fragrant honey-and-egg-white mixture. But none were redheads. An aging woman with white hair thought she remembered the name Bouboule. She wasn't certain. Baptiste bought all of her sweets. And that night, among other things, the pilgrims dined on truffle-filled omelets and nougat.

The *Ste. Vierge* passed under the first bridge at Pont St. Esprit. Along with the span at Avignon, the structure had been built by an Order of religious engineers, Les Frères Pontifs. Bouboule decided to moor at Orange, just below the city. The craft was tied by a long rope to a tree at a bend which curved northwest.

It was the dark night of a new moon. Jacques lay aft on the river side of the boat. He had taken to sleeping on deck, feeling uncomfortable too near the brothers. At midnight the mistral, a strong, dry wind from the north, began to blow. The boat, whose stern had been pointed downstream, began to swing in the opposite direction.

Jacques was asleep and did not hear the brothers stealthily approach. Quickly Hervé slammed his pilgrim's staff down on Jacques's skull, then together they shoved him off the deck.

"*Adieu, Maincrochet*," intoned Hervé. However, "Hook-hand"

had landed, not in the Rhône, but on the soft mud of the river-bank.

A few hours later the mistral abated, and the stern of the *Ste. Vierge* swung downstream with the current.

At dawn Baptiste, leaning over the rail, sighted Jacques on his back in the mud. He carried him on board and, rousing him, declared, "It is not wise to sleep near the rail, after so much wine."

Jacques rubbed his sore head. "Yes, it is easy to roll off."

When the nephews saw Jacques, on deck and unharmed, they were terrified. This deformed fellow obviously possessed some impressive magic power. It would be prudent to avoid him.

One morning Gaston called them all together. "Tomorrow is a day to which I look forward," he said. "We will reach the great fair at Beaucaire. It is the sweet memory of times past. There are beautiful women from many lands. You will see. And we shall be able to buy the fat livers of geese. The goose," he rhapsodized, "is a sort of living garden in which grows that most delectable of fruits, *foie gras*."

Thousands were camped from the shores of Beaucaire to the base of the Castle Rock. Ranged before them were rows of barrel-shaped tents of the merchants, laid out between a rainbow of pennants and gonfalons.

With a cry of delight Gaston rose by himself and hastened to the boat's railing. Suddenly he gasped and clutched his left arm. Baptiste and Jacques hurried to his side and helped him back into his chair. Sweat ran down Bouboule's face; his breathing was labored. In a voice of pain and fright, he cried to Jacques, "In God's name, fetch the pardoner—there is always a pardoner at the fair. Quickly, Jacques—my vow—it must be forgiven. I need an indulgence."

Into the crowds, past the stands of vendors, Jacques ran, crying, "Where is the pardoner? Please, can you direct me to the pardoner?"

Finally an old man who was selling sausages pointed to a small tent in the distance.

"I need you," cried Jacques in desperation to a rat-faced fellow in monk's robes.

"All men need me. I have precious relics to sell for the church.

A vial of the Virgin's milk, a thorn from Our Savior's crown . . ."

"No, no," cried Jacques. "My master is a pilgrim. He's ill. He needs an indulgence. Be quick."

The pardoner smiled, "Oh, one of those." He pulled loose from Jacques's grasp and moved into his tent, returning with a parchment from which dangled an array of seals and ribbons.

Jacques implored the man to follow him quickly to the *Ste. Vierge.*

Gaston's face was pale; he seemed in great pain. "The indulgence . . . to release my vow!"

The pardoner said in an unctuous voice, "It is customary to pay the entire estimated cost of the pilgrimage for such an exceptional indulgence. Let us carefully calculate all the expenses."

"I am dying," said Gaston weakly.

Baptiste took a gold *écu d'or* from his purse and, seizing the pardoner by the throat, growled, "You have your choice—gold, or my closed hand."

The pardoner grabbed the coin and stuffed it in his robe. He placed the parchment in Bouboule's lap.

"Now," said Baptiste hoarsely, "perform the last rites."

After the pardoner had left, it became difficult to hear what Gaston was saying. Both Jacques and Baptiste were close by. Isabeau, with tearful eyes, stood behind them.

"Pay Jacques all," whispered Bouboule, and Baptiste counted out twenty-four livres.

"It is well," said Bouboule.

Gaston closed his eyes. He murmured faintly, "Soon the fat liver of the goose will be for others . . . the sweet wood strawberries for other mouths . . . the kisses . . ." His head fell back.

With a sob Baptiste dropped to his knees, his arms clasping his master's legs.

Hervé stepped forward, facing Jacques. "My dear Monsieur Jacques, your services are no longer required. You shall leave the boat immediately."

Weighted with sadness, Jacques wandered aimlessly along the aisles of the fair, past rope dancers, jugglers, musicians, hawkers, a crowd of laughing persons watching four battered blind men trying to fell a pig with their cudgels. Then he spotted the pardoner's tent. The flap was closed, but mindlessly Jacques lurched inside. His back to the entrance, the pardoner was dipping thorns into the blood of a dead chicken. Beside him was a long blackthorn branch and his knife.

Jacques felt nauseated by such vile fakery. A terrible thought struck him: the holy shroud! Might that, too, be false? Had he ruined his hands for nothing? Had it merely been an absurd sacrifice? He backed out of the tent.

Wearied and heartsick, he paused by the old sausage vendor, who remembered him and nodded. Jacques bought a steaming *andouillette*.

Sitting on the ground, he stared at the dark sausage and began to weep.

A soft voice by his side said, "Surely, Jacques, the sausage has sufficient salt without your tears." It was Isabeau.

She sat beside him, and suddenly threw her arms around him and sobbed, her head on his shoulder. "He was so good, so kind." And together they vented their grief. Then, with a tiny laugh, Isabeau asked, "Would you share your sausage with me?" She touched his hand with hers. No one had ever touched his hands. Jacques realized that Isabeau had never before addressed him directly. He found himself laughing unexpectedly, and together they shared the *andouillette*.

"I, too, was ordered to leave the boat," she explained.

"But your aunt?"

"The nephews like her, and she likes the money they will possess. When my parents died, Agnès constantly chided me because of the expense I caused her. Now that dear Gaston is gone, I can no longer be of value to her."

"Where will he be buried?" asked Jacques.

"They intend to continue the pilgrimage; Gaston will be buried at the church in Les-Saintes-Maries. Baptiste is returning to Grenoble with half of Gaston's money. He says it properly belongs to Gaston's brother, Martin." She was silent for a while and then, looking at Jacques she asked, "If you would permit, I should like to return with you."

A strange feeling crept into Jacques's heart. Other men could have identified it easily. It was hope.

They traveled on foot with merchants returning from the fair, bearing silks and linens. One night they lodged together at an inn. And out of their mutual innocence, they found happiness. Jacques and Isabeau were married in Avignon.

Despite her new husband's reluctance to return to Chambéry, Isabeau insisted. She wanted to meet his parents.

Jacques's mother greeted her daughter-in-law with pleasure. She told them with small regret that her husband had recently died. The hereditary position of shroud keeper, provided by the dukes of Savoy, now awaited Jacques.

The responsibility of marriage compelled Jacques to face a new reality. Where else could he earn a decent living and have an ample house? He believed his present happiness over-balanced his disaffection for the shroud. So Jacques assumed the post.

Gaston Meunier was born as the fruit trees of Chambéry flowered in April.

Jacques's happiness with the beautiful Isabeau was short lived. Following the birth of their second child, Paul, Isabeau died of childbed fever. Their love had lasted only two years. Jacques never remarried. He raised his two sons with the help of his mother. Gaston, now a printer, lived in Lyons, while Paul, a Franciscan, awaited his time as shroud keeper.

Jacques had continued to serve in the post. Years before, upon agreeing to take on the hereditary responsibilities, he had thought only of providing for the woman he loved and their future family. He had accepted the return to Chambéry, a place of bad memories. After Isabeau's death, however, the old bitterness returned. So much had been taken from him; his hands, his profession, his friend Bouboule, and finally his beloved wife. Never to know happiness is one thing; to taste it briefly, then lose it, is quite another.

During the spring of 1578 a great rumor flew about Chambéry. The court of Duke Emmanuel Philibert was to move permanently to Turin. The duke's neighbors, the French, with whom Savoy had often been at war, would have liked the Savoyard capital to remain at Chambéry, a more vulnerable location. But the wily ruler regarded Turin as safer and more defensible, protected from France on the north by a high crescent of mountains. Such a move would necessitate traversing those peaks with all the belongings of the royal house. Jacques was to make the journey with the shroud. Though he knew the eight-day trip would be arduous at his age of fifty-eight, he was elated. Turin, a great city and an escape from Chambéry!

The move was to be accomplished in stages. Throughout the summer various householders and retainers would cross with mule trains loaded with the duke's belongings. Then the ducal family and retinue, Jacques among them, would follow in early autumn.

Assisted by his son, Jacques started the journey on the sixth day of September. The shroud, its silver reliquary enclosed in a protective case, was strapped to the back of a pack mule. Behind and before it ranged the duke's personal entourage. It was customary for travelers through these passes to move in large groups, especially during the warmer months when brigands were likely to attack.

The first few days brought only light breezes. Along the route peasants were bringing in the last of their harvest. Haystacks gleamed under a bright sun. The caravan planned to cross the Isère River at Montmélian; go from there to Aiguebelle, and then across the Mont Cenis pass. There would be the steep descent to Susa, then on to Avigliana and finally Turin.

Once into the mountains the narrow path threaded the heights in complex convolutions. There were frequent halts as horses stumbled, throwing their riders. Now and then, as the road climbed, there would be a patch of tiny alpine flowers.

The royal caravan, with its armed escort, spent each night at an inn, hospice, or monastery along the way. Late one afternoon a sudden fog enveloped the party. It was a fearful time as each person groped his perilous way along the line of posts which had been placed every few paces to mark the route. It grew dark, and in the distance there sounded the mournful blasts of alphorns, as mountainfolk were summoned to evening devotions.

Then came the faint tolling of a bell, a joyous sound, for such bells were mounted atop alpine inns to guide travelers in bad weather. Arriving for their night's stay, the duke and his retinue thankfully dismounted. Grooms led horses to the stable. The travelers crowded into a large common room.

Some minstrels and a jongleur, who had arrived earlier in expectation of the duke's visit, were performing before the blazing fireplace. One man cranked a hurdy-gurdy, another blew a *tournebout,* while the jongleur sang bawdy tunes. They broke off as the duke's party entered. The jongleur danced over to Emmanuel Philibert and bowed, while tossing colored balls in the air with a graceful gesture. The duke indicated that the entertainment should continue, as he and his party were seated at long tables in the overheated room.

After dinner had been served, the innkeeper placed a wooden trencher before the duke. It was marked with chalk circles, corresponding to the number of diners. Emmanuel Philibert motioned his purser to come forward. When all the circles on the board were covered with coins, the innkeeper bowed and carried it off.

Next morning the innkeeper suspected bad weather was coming, so Duke Emmanuel requested the assistance of *marones,* the experienced mountain guides. As the party prepared for the steep descent from Mont Cenis, the predicted snowstorm struck. Jacques and Paul covered their faces with hoods cut like masks. They protected their chests from the chilling winds with the sheets of parchment all had been advised to bring. Still, clothes froze to their bodies. The mule carrying the shroud's reliquary was blinded when his eyelids iced shut.

The *marones,* who wore spiked boots and carried long, spiked poles to probe for the path when snow buried it, advised the Savoyards to follow them closely. Deep crevasses could be hidden by the heavy snows.

As daylight temperatures slightly warmed, the falling snow became wet and froze when it struck the ground. The caravan halted. Jacques decided it would be necessary, since his mule's footing had become unsteady, to lower the shroud in another manner. One of the *marones* suggested that the relic be slid down the slippery mountainside on a *ramasse,* a rough mattress fashioned of rope-tied boughs. The shroud's lead case was lashed to the makeshift sledge. Paul stood behind, holding one of the ropes, and Jacques in front. In that way, by sliding or restraining the *ramasse,* the precious cargo was eased down the mountain.

Behind them Duke Emmanuel and his duchess and other ladies of their party, strapped into ox-hides, were carefully being slid down the mountainside. One moment the women would shriek with fear, the next, scream with nervous laughter.

Jacques's mule, unable to traverse the icy slopes, was blindfolded. With its legs tied together, it was lowered in much the same way as the palace entourage.

At last the Savoyard party reached more level terrain. The snow abated. The *marones,* richly rewarded by a grateful duke, turned back into the mountains.

Next morning the party first saw Turin, lying at the confluence of two large rivers. Very high, thick Roman walls belted the city. Jacques was fascinated by the neatly laid-out streets, intersecting each other to form rectangular blocks. The city plan, unlike any other he had seen, reflected a special sense of order and dignity. Even at a distance he could observe the newly built citadel, the royal palace, the cathedral, and numerous great houses fronting on wide piazze.

The duke and his company entered Turin from the north, through a great double gate flanked by impressive brick towers. The exhausted Jacques, dreaming of a comfortable bed, had first to tend the shroud. He and Paul went immediately to the ducal chapel, where they examined the relic, saw that it was unharmed by travel, and then deposited it in a locked grill behind the altar.

A week after Jacques's arrival in Turin he was summoned by the duke.

"Jacques," announced the ruler in his sonorous voice, "the great Carlo Borromeo has vowed to walk on pilgrimage from Milan to venerate the image." Rather gratuitously he added, "We could not, in good conscience, have allowed the saintly cardinal to travel across the high mountains to Chambéry."

Jacques smiled inwardly at the disingenuousness of the duke, who had used the relic and Borromeo's pending visit as the ostensible motive for permanently relocating his court.

"Now, Jacques," continued Emmanuel Philibert, "I wish you to go to Milan, meet the cardinal, and accompany him on his pilgrimage."

Hardly recovered from his exhausting journey across the Alps, Jacques groaned.

The duke laughed. "Don't look so unhappy. Though the cardinal has vowed to walk the entire distance barefoot, you are permitted shoes and a donkey."

Chapter 23

Turin, 1978

The assembled persons at Monsignore Monti's residence had been talking for more than an hour about the threat to the shroud. They were now awaiting the arrival of the Archbishop of Turin. Present with Monti were Molly and Nico; Mike Whitridge, who represented the American scientists; and, from the *Commissariato di Pubblica Sicurezza*, the commissario himself, Massimo Drioli. Alongside Drioli sat his top detective, Ispettore Brocca.

The idea Molly presented to the group had been very well received. All were in accord. It made sense.

"Speaking for the research team," drawled Whitridge thoughtfully, "you have our okay, if, as I understand, we might lose no more than a quarter of an hour from the test schedule."

Drioli listened to Nico's plea that he should be allowed to face the Acciaro gang alone.

"It will mean more to me than I can ever tell you. The expected raid on the shroud is, in a large measure, my fault. And, therefore, my responsibility. No one else should be at risk."

"Acciaro and the others with him will be armed, of course," said Drioli, a serious-looking middle-aged man in an elegant suit.

"I shall avoid anything rash or foolish. And I fully recognize the danger. But you must please permit me to do this thing by myself. It will redeem my mistakes now and in the past. I beg you to say yes."

Brocca, a large, powerful fellow, winked at the commissario and said, "It seems a fair request. After all, the count looks and talks like the scientist he is. That will be good. And we can always plant a few of our people nearby."

Drioli agreed, and the matter was closed. Molly glanced apprehensively at Nico, who was sitting beside her. She forced a smile, saying softly, "It will be all right. I understand, Nico."

The group had covered all the essential details. For the moment there was not much more to say. Drioli looked at Nico. "Tell me, Sforzini, what have you people turned up over at the palace?"

"I suppose it will be a disappointment to many, but the data we have collected will require several years to analyze fully. Then reports will have to be written. The press services, no doubt, would like us to announce the discovery of Jesus' monogram on the shroud." Molly laughed.

"Nico," said Monti, recalling his recent visit to the laboratory, "tell them about the blood."

Nico explained that the separation of various components of the stains indicated that the exudate actually came from real wounds in contact with the cloth, penetrating it; not from blood applied by a forger. He added that he had been thinking about its unexpectedly bright color—as if it were still fresh. It had occurred to him that first-century linen was usually washed and bleached with soapweed. "I suspect the chemical reaction of soapweed with the blood may have fixed its bright color in many areas."

"Nico's the expert on that," commented Whitridge.

Nico continued, "But we have not done too badly so far. We have certainly ascertained that the relic is the original and no forgery. And we have learned much else. The most exciting thing to come up, in my opinion, is not a test result but a conjecture now held by many of us: the flash photolysis theory. We had been unable to explain the process by which the image was transferred to the shroud until one of our scientists, a thermochemist, proposed this theory. To put it simply, the image appears to have been lightly scorched on the topmost fibrils. It looks like a dehydrated oxidation process. Flash photolysis may be the causative mechanism. It would be a short, very intense burst of radiation coming from within the body itself."

Then Nico told Monti's guests that a STURP chemist had explained to him that soapweed might also figure in another aspect of their theory. Exposed to bursts of radiant energy, the soapweed residual in the cloth releases a sugar which caramelizes, producing exactly the color of the shroud's body image.

"This all seems very difficult to believe," said Drioli.

"Not so very difficult," responded Nico. "You may remember that Jesus was aware of a special power within his body. You can read about it in—"

"Mark 5:25–34 and Luke 8:43–48," interjected Monti.

"It was described as being drawn out of him when a hemorrhaging woman touched his cloak and was cured."

Monti broke in again. "Luke records Jesus telling his disciples, 'Somebody touched me. I felt that power had gone out from me.'"

Silence followed. Then Whitridge said, "I go along with that theory. It's one we haven't been able to shoot down yet."

Brocca, in the voice of an interrogating detective, asked, "Can you tell us about the radiocarbon dating business?"

"Oh, that," said Nico. "I shall not resist a full confession. I am utterly convinced of the shroud's great antiquity. There are many indications to justify this inference. And my past studies have led to a fairly extensive experience with these early textiles. One could begin by noting that the shroud had been woven on a four-pedal loom, but I shall not bore you with other details. When the C-14 test is authorized—and it will be—it can only confirm the very obvious age of the relic. And no more. Radiocarbon analysis cannot prove this to be Jesus' burial cloth."

The archbishop had entered and was listening to Nico. He interposed a thought. "For that is an answer which only the vast numbers of our faithful can know."

"Exactly, Your Excellency," said Nico, rising like the others. "And no matter how advanced our technologies will ever become, science can merely take the matter so far and no farther.

There will always be a gap between our understanding and the ultimate reality. How can we bridge that distance? For me the answer is faith."

After the archbishop had listened to Drioli's recital of the menace to the relic, he declared, "I understand you are all agreed upon this plan proposed by Signora Madrigal. So am I, but with one proviso, and I speak for absent members of the shroud commission. It is a matter of fixed policy that a member of our clergy, my representative, should always be near when the shroud is exposed. There seems no good reason for an exception in this case. Vittorio, you are Keeper of the Shroud. It will be your duty to be present in the laboratory during the time after midnight tonight."

Monti bowed his head.

"Pardon me," said Molly, starting toward the monsignore's study. "I must make a telephone call at once. We'd better not delay this another minute."

Chapter 24

Milan—Turin, 1569–1578

"Then it is agreed, the cardinal must die." One of three leaders of the Humiliati Brotherhood, the provost of Vercelli, reached out and shook hands with two other conspirators, the provosts of Caravaggio and Verona.

Near them sat Gerolamo Donati, a priest of the Society, whom they called Farina. The three turned to him and he nodded. "Very well, it shall be done. But I'll require a generous reward for such work. Say . . . forty gold crowns?"

Verona looked at Vercelli. "Not from my pocket."

Agreed Vercelli, "Of course, that is understood. We can sell plate from one of the churches."

Caravaggio slapped his knee. "Ah hah! The jeweled altarpieces from Brera. They will clearly bring the required sum."

Farina smiled with easy confidence. No one could handle an arquebus like he. The Humiliati need worry no longer.

The previous day Cardinal Carlo Borromeo had faced leaders of the Humiliati, whom he had ordered to gather in their Milan chapterhouse. Originally founded in the eleventh century as a lay religious fraternity, the Humiliati was so named because of its members' plain, colorless clothing. Two centuries later the organization established a monastic Order. Though as monks the

Humiliati were expected to lead simple and ascetic lives, they continued to mingle freely with the world.

As archbishop of the diocese of Milan, Borromeo began an intensive campaign to cleanse this and other religious Orders of nearly a century of self-indulgent and licentious living. He viewed such conduct as a flagrant disregard of the vow to serve God.

Borromeo was an arresting figure: tall, with close-cropped, dark chestnut hair, a prominent beaked nose, and great blue eyes. The eyes, in fact, dominated his face even more than his emphatic nose. They could light with tender compassion for the innocents in his care, or grow dark with anger toward miscreants.

That day his glance burned with fury. These leaders of the Humiliati had grown rich and powerful, while enjoying the pleasures and luxury of worldly lives. They gambled, fornicated, and traveled grandly. The impulse for debauchery had filtered down even to the monks in their monasteries.

"For t-t-too long," the cardinal told the assembled provosts with his slight stammer, "you have disregarded the wishes not only of your superiors in this diocese, but of the Holy Father himself. You shall now learn the true meaning of that name by which you call yourselves!" He proceeded to read a new order, drawn up by himself, which levied stiff fines on their ninety monasteries, and provided stricter rules of discipline and comportment.

"If," he continued, "I learn that these reforms have not been carried out by you, I shall have no other choice than to write the Holy Father, recommending that your Order be disbanded."

Quitting the chamber, he was accosted by the provost from Vercelli, who demanded a repeal of the punitive taxes. The man's voice was heavy with animosity and threat. Yet the cardinal was indifferent. Two months before he had been shot at while entering the church of Santa Maria de la Scala, to which he had come on similar business. A lead ball struck his crozier and harmlessly bounced off. Believing himself designated by God to undertake this mission of reform, Borromeo redoubled his efforts, restoring the Inquisition to Milan, and traveling throughout the diocese, handling all relevant matters himself.

Wednesday evening, October twenty-fifth, a week after his visit to the Humiliati, Cardinal Borromeo and members of his household gathered, as usual, for vespers in the chapel of the Archiepiscopal Palace. The cardinal knelt at the altar, intoning words from the Gospel of St. John, "Do not let your heart be troubled or afraid." Suddenly there was a loud report. Borromeo felt something thud against his back. The cardinal wheeled and, losing his balance, fell to the marble floor. Behind him a hooded figure retreated up the aisle. A door flashed open and he was gone.

Shouts erupted. Some of the householders rushed to the prelate's side, crying for aid from the Blessed Virgin. Others, realizing there had been an attempt on Borromeo's life, ran from the room to pursue the assassin.

Only one ball from the arquebus had struck the cardinal. It had merely grazed his cope. But scattered shot was found to have lodged throughout the chapel. Having used an arquebus himself in hunting, Borromeo surmised that the gun must have blown up in the assassin's hands. Later some drops of blood were found where the man had been standing.

Unhurt, he rose, then dropped back onto his knees, thanking God for this miraculous deliverance.

In the weeks that followed, Carlo Borromeo's escape from certain death was hailed as a miracle by the Milanese faithful. There was talk that one day he would be canonized. For God was surely very close to him. When finally the would-be assassin was found and the plot uncovered, Borromeo's plea for leniency was disregarded by the authorities. All the accomplices were executed, and Pius V acted quickly to disband the Order.

As a result of the two attempts on his life Borromeo's resolve was reinforced. The rules of God's church, he preached, were beyond challenge. He filled the prisons below his residence with malfeasants who refused to obey his orders. And his soft voice grew sharp with anger at any questioning of his authority.

Because of the deplorable state into which Milan's clergy had fallen, the cardinal feared God's punishment for the city. He was not surprised when, in 1576, bubonic plague struck Milan.

Most called it the Black Death because of the dark spots it brought to a victim's body. This time it was said to have come by way of Constantinople. First an ominous sign: rats crawling by the hundreds into streets and houses, dying suddenly with blood-flecked mouths. Then the first citizens falling ill, revealing unmistakable symptoms: swelling buboes, large as oranges, afflicting groins and armpits; terrible fevers and bloody, foul-smelling issues. Very few survived. If the infection attacked the lungs, death was sure and swift.

As deaths increased, the city was gripped in panic. Physicians, in their red velvet gowns, hurried from house to house, offering little in the way of real help, except the vain belief that they knew more than others about the scourge. They could bleed the patient, purge him with enemas, lance the buboes, or apply hot plasters. But this did nothing to prevent the spread of the pestilence.

Commerce in the city virtually halted. People avoided going near their neighbors or into marketplaces and shops, for fear of contamination. Food supplies were no longer brought into the city. The possibility of starvation became as grave a problem as the Black Death.

Day and night, death carts traveled the deserted city, collecting bodies shoved out of desperate houses. The *campana a morto*, a bell which rang to announce deaths, now incessantly tolled a grim carillon, further terrifying citizens. It seemed to many that the devil himself stalked their city, fanning the flames of pestilence which now afflicted almost every family. Many believed they were witnessing the end of the world.

On this day Cardinal Carlo Borromeo hurried through the desolate streets, to a district he had not visited in more than a week. Following in his steps was a young Franciscan, Fra Voto, who served him as secretary and companion. Driven beyond their strength, both men were exhausted. During more than a year this plague had gripped Milan.

For the first time the cardinal and his secretary were relieved not to hear the tolling *campana a morto*. Borromeo had finally convinced the authorities to cease ringing it. He hoped this might offer the frightened residents some measure of calm. More than ever he was certain that the answer to their panic lay in absolute faith in God's protection. Only through the prayers of the entire population could this scourge be abated. Months before, he had instituted penitential processions, which, three times weekly, wound through the streets, stopping at one shrine or another. The cardinal had become a familiar and reassuring figure, as he carried his large crucifix beneath a black velvet canopy, calling out the rosary and the psalms to the long and somber processions.

Recently, however, they had had to be abandoned. The plague was now so widespread that persons were ordered by civil authorities not to leave their houses, except to seek food. Borromeo was forced to move from district to district, offering Mass at the doorways of sufferers. Frequently he went to the Lazzaretto, located to one side of the Porta Orientale. He had ordered that this hospital be reserved for plague victims. Eight hundred could be accommodated there.

At the height of the city's misery shopkeepers fled, and famine became a further horror. Borromeo had ordered that the city be divided into districts, each placed under the supervision of a group of charitable citizens, who visited every house and attempted to provide food and clothing where needed. The cardinal, one of Italy's wealthiest men, exhausted his personal fortune and incurred a huge debt by his attempts to assure that sixty or seventy thousand of the poor were fed daily.

Today Borromeo and his secretary walked in silence through Milan's empty streets. Occasionally they heard isolated screams coming from behind bolted doors, or the clatter of a death cart.

Borromeo spotted one of the carts, partially empty. It was driven by a shriveled old man. Hailing him, the prelate gave him a soldo to turn onto the Via del Pesce, where a great stinking pile of bodies had accumulated.

"Father Borromeo, Father Borromeo . . ." A door flew open and a man, nearly naked, fell to his knees upon the threshold. Borromeo could see the ghastly, suppurating buboes that infected his groin. They had burst and were emitting a foul-smelling pus. The man's face was flushed with fever. He spasmodically jerked his head from side to side while repeating, "Father, help me," in a weak voice. Finally he pitched forward, partially into the street, where he lay twitching and writhing with pain. A woman cowering behind him would not come nearer.

Human values have disappeared, thought Borromeo. Mothers, afraid of contracting the illness, would not care for their infected young. Lovers refused to comfort each other. Having expired without prayers, the dead were tossed into the streets like garbage.

Borromeo regarded many members of Milan's religious orders with disgust. He had demanded that they visit the sick in their homes or the places of refuge he had established, to provide spiritual comfort and last rites. Refusing, most clerics had run for the countryside where they thought they would be safe.

Stopping near the dying victim's threshold, Borromeo gestured to Fra Voto, who produced a crucifix and articles of the Mass. Then he called out. Slowly some doors opened. The afflicted and the still untouched knelt to hear the comforting words and receive the cardinal's blessing. Robed in his chasuble, and assisted by Fra Voto, Borromeo intoned the familiar words, "*In nomine Patris . . .*" He spoke haltingly, due to the stammer which had afflicted him since birth. If he were to stumble over a word, he stopped, crossed himself, then was able to continue with no hesitation.

"*Credo in unum Deum . . .*" The ancient ritual continued. Borromeo's transcendent expression as he offered the words to God caused sobbing to break out among many of the victims and their families. When finally he stretched up his hands, intoning "*Dominus vobiscum,*" he could feel his own tears.

So much pain, so much anguish. Borromeo did not spare himself. Fearless, he roved the city, daily exposing himself to the dying, in order to comfort them and their families. Yet it seemed that all he did was never enough.

Fra Voto, whose courage and faith were as great as the cardinal's, followed Borromeo on his rounds each day until his legs felt leaden.

Returning now to the Archiepiscopal Palace, Voto was unable

to hold back his frustration. "When will it end, Your Eminence?" he cried. "I learned this morning that twenty-five thousand souls have departed. And still it rages. I pray constantly for God's intercession. But where—where is He?" A moment later, he looked at Borromeo, embarrassed. "Forgive me, Your Eminence. I am tired. . . . I do not know what I am saying. . . ."

As always, after a day among the sick, the cardinal took certain precautions he urged upon all who had contact with the victims. He washed his hands in vinegar, ran his fingers through a candle flame, removed his vestments and ordered that they be cleansed. Then, freshly clothed, he retired to his private chapel, to prostrate himself before the Cross and pray for the city's deliverance.

This day he had a vision of a length of white cloth, bearing the image of Jesus' suffering. The shroud of Chambéry. Surely this was a sign! Fervently Borromeo prayed that should Milan be delivered from the Black Death, he would make a pilgrimage, on foot, across the Alps, to behold the cloth and venerate it.

From that moment Carlo Borromeo believed that prayers to the miraculous relic would save Milan. And, in truth, the pestilence began to weaken. But not before it had taken Fra Voto. During his secretary's illness the cardinal himself nursed the young man. "Father, Father," Voto cried in his last fevered moments, clinging to Borromeo's hands. It was many months before the cardinal could recover from his grief.

There came a day when no deaths were reported. It was during Christmas week of 1577. The plague had finally burned itself out. People with nervous eyes crept from their shuttered houses to wander about the streets. Shops opened again, and the life of the city briefly assumed a hysterical gaiety.

Remembering his vow, the cardinal sent word to Duke Emmanuel Philibert at Chambéry. But the work of restoring spirit and life to Milan's ravaged population occupied him for nearly a year. When at last Carlo Borromeo was ready to make his pilgrimage, he learned he would not have to cross the Alps; the shroud had been brought to Turin.

Jacques Meunier had never been to Milan, although he was

aware of its reputation as a center of commerce and home of the great bankers and moneylenders of Lombardy. As he entered the city, he was taken by another aspect of Milan's grandeur, its immense white marble cathedral. He had never seen anything to compare with the cathedral's many and graceful spires, which reached prayerfully into the sky like pale fingers. Evidence of great wealth abounded in the elegant city: the impressive red brick Castello di Porta Giovia, the Palazzo della Ragione, with its fine piazza, and the numerous lesser but sumptuous houses belonging to rich noblemen.

After arriving at the Archiepiscopal Palace, Jacques concluded that the cardinal's residence was far grander than all the others. Its vast rooms and salons, crammed with costly tapestries, paintings, and furnishings, were even more opulent than the duke's palace at Turin. Such excess is just about what one would expect of a prince of the Church, thought Jacques sourly.

His opinion quickly changed after being directed up several long stairways to the cardinal's private quarters. Climbing the steep steps until he panted, Jacques at last reached the palace garret.

"C-c-come in," called a halting voice from behind a closed door. Startled, Jacques realized it must belong to the cardinal. Entering by the low-beamed portal, he was astonished to see where the great man lived. One small chamber, with a passageway to a tiny adjoining chapel. The living quarters were furnished with a simple bed and straw mattress, a prie-dieu, two wooden stools, a sideboard and table. The sole item of value was a mechanical clock. Hastily Jacques knelt and kissed the episcopal ring.

"You are out of breath, my brother," said Borromeo. "Rest a moment. Then I shall be ready to leave with you."

The cardinal indicated that Jacques should be seated on one of his stools, while he sat on the other. The aging shroud keeper could hardly believe what he was seeing. This great personage, scion of a powerful and ancient family, lived like an impoverished burgher. It did not make sense.

Borromeo wore a tattered brown monk's robe, belted with a knotted rope. His feet were unshod, and he carried his few belongings in a sack tied to a staff. Jacques thought the cardinal's homely face fascinating. Though the man was clearly no longer young, his features radiated both a youthful vitality and a melancholy sweetness. Jacques noted the occasional stammer which sometimes affected the prelate's speech. At such times Borromeo crossed himself and placed his hands together in a moment of prayer before continuing with a clear flow of words.

As the cardinal addressed him, Jacques realized something even more striking. The shroud keeper, as always, watched for that instant of recoil at the sight of his deformity. But there was none; Borromeo seemingly ignored Jacques's hands.

"Shall we be on our way?" suggested the cardinal.

No party to pious self-denial, the shroud keeper chose not to join his companion on foot. Borromeo set out, his eyes fixed steadily ahead, lips moving in prayer. The plain of the Po River, along which they traveled, was rocky and often harsh underfoot. Eventually the prelate's naked feet began to swell and bleed. He was uncomplaining. Jacques felt embarrassed to be mounted so comfortably on a donkey. He found himself unexpectedly touched by the extraordinary cardinal. Though the bitterness which lay within him like a stone—the belief that an indifferent God had dealt unfairly with him—prevented Jacques from understanding a nature like Borromeo's, he sensed that his companion was a man above most men.

As twilight neared, Borromeo proposed a halt and Jacques set out to prepare their supper, the one meal of the day. Having built a fire, he began roasting a large sausage which he expected to share. But Borromeo smiled and shook his head.

"I shall not eat very much," he said. "Have you some bread?"

Jacques brought out a fresh loaf which he had obtained in Milan. The cardinal broke off a modest piece. "This will be sufficient," he said.

Taken aback, Jacques offered his flask of cider.

"No, no. I prefer to drink only water. That is all."

They ate in silence. Finally the cardinal looked up. Eagerly he inquired, "What is it like—the blessed shroud? I long to see it. Perhaps you may have actually touched it."

Jacques laughed ironically. "Yes, I have touched it, and it is like any other old piece of cloth. Except for the figure on it. And that is very faint. To me the relic is not extraordinary."

As he regarded Jacques, Borromeo momentarily frowned. There was an uncomfortable silence between them. Then the prelate moved off to his prayers.

The next morning they spoke little. Borromeo seemed deeply absorbed in his meditations. He had begun limping and it was obvious that the abrasions to his feet were painful. When the two rested in the final daylight hours, Jacques soaked the edge of his shirt in the river and asked to bathe the cuts.

"You are very kind, my brother," said His Eminence.

A short time later Jacques spotted a rabbit. Clumsily grasping a rock, he threw it and luckily downed the animal.

"Tonight we'll feast!" he shouted gleefully.

Holding a knife awkwardly between his stiff fingers and flexible thumb, Jacques tried to skin the animal. But it kept slipping out of his grasp. Noticing the difficulty, Borromeo offered to do the job. Surprised, Jacques watched the cardinal deftly skin and gut the rabbit.

"Eminence, for a man who takes only bread and water, you handled my catch with great skill," he commented, as he began roasting the rabbit on a stick.

Borromeo smiled in reminiscence. "In my youth I used to enjoy hunting."

This was a new side to the cardinal. "So, Eminence, you were skilled with a bow?"

Borromeo took the stick and rotated it over the flames. "And with my favorite firearm, the *demihague*. I loved all sport." Then he looked away. "But that was very long ago—before Milano." He sighed. "Milano . . . a dark city."

Jacques protested. "But, Eminence, it is truly a most beautiful city."

"Ah, but not within its monasteries. I am speaking of spiritual beauty, Jacques. So many of those who serve the Lord in Milano are c-c-corrupt." Stammering over the last word, he stopped, laid down the roasting rabbit, and made the strange, prayerful gesture.

Jacques, who cared little about this subject, was silent.

"Twice my life has been threatened by them. The Humiliati . . . I earnestly tried to correct them for their grievous and multiple sins. Once I even directed all leaders of the Order to be whipped. But to no avail. Finally I threatened to urge His Holiness to disband the group." His words poured out, as he relived the memory. "I was praying with my household one evening at vespers. One of their monks had been paid forty gold pieces to kill me. He discharged his arquebus at my back, but I was unharmed. It was a miracle, my brother, God's miracle!"

Jacques, irritated by such an interpretation for what, no doubt, had some logical explanation, raised his voice slightly. "Forgive me, Eminence. You survived a terrible experience. But it seems no miracle—rather a lucky escape."

Distress crept into Borromeo's pale eyes. "You do not believe that miracles can happen?"

A certain tension had set in between them.

"There are no miracles, Eminence. I am a sorry witness to that."

Borromeo seemed about to erupt in anger, but kept silent. Instead he said, "As you know, I require only a piece of bread for my supper. Take all of the meat for yourself." Abruptly he rose and moved away.

Jacques watched his companion kneeling at the top of a nearby rise. The shroud keeper had thought perhaps Borromeo might join his little feast. He regretted that his statement appeared to have offended the cardinal. But it was what he believed.

At their halt the third afternoon Borromeo drew a book from his sack and began reading. Jacques had never forgotten his first and deepest interest. He tried to glance over the cardinal's shoulder.

Borromeo looked up. "You can read, Jacques?"

Jacques nodded.

"This book from my library contains the Psalms of David. I frequently carry it with me. It brings fresh vigor and inspiration."

"Your Eminence, may I?" Jacques took the book and examined it. He remembered. It had been published by Gilbert Fichet, the Chambéry printer.

"Eminence," he exclaimed, "this is, this is . . ." He didn't know how to continue.

"Is there something about this book, Jacques?"

Jacques said, "Once, years ago, I was learning to be a printer. I worked at the press in Chambéry. Your psalter, Eminence—it contains the only pages of type I ever set. When my hands were burned, I had to abandon any hope of being a printer." His voice was choked. "Eminence, you who believe so firmly that God dispenses miracles, would never understand a poor life like mine. It has been blessed by no miracles; nor can I believe in them. Everything I had of value has been taken from me." He held up his hands. "And this ugliness. When I was a boy, people avoided me because of it. I wanted to hide; I was ashamed. Prayers meant nothing."

Then the cardinal said, "I can understand why your disability" —he nodded toward Jacques's hands—"has made you bitter. But to question the goodness of God or that He cannot ordain great miracles—no! Indeed, it was God's lifting the plague from Milano that has brought me on this pilgrimage."

"You haven't burned your hands, Eminence," said Jacques. "You may pursue your vocation."

"True," said the cardinal. "But it has not always been so. As a young man I, too, suffered an affliction. It threatened my ability to carry out my priestly duties. Have you, by chance, noticed my slight stammer? It was once so bad I could scarcely celebrate the Mass. The words locked in my mouth. I felt shamed; all those people listening. You see, for me, my vocation in the priesthood has meant as much as your profession of printer."

Jacques was surprised and flattered that this great man would compare himself with a lowly shroud keeper.

The cardinal went on. "Only through prayer and faith could I continue."

"But faith—my faith is slight, Eminence," murmured Jacques.

Continued Borromeo, "Then I discovered a brief prayer would release the barrier to my speech." Here the cardinal made the sign of the Cross and brought his hands together in his familiar gesture. "At such times I call upon God to aid me. And always He does. He is very near to us, my brother, if only we open our hearts to Him."

Jacques felt uncomfortable, but said nothing. Borromeo watched him, his eyes inviting more conversation. But the shroud keeper went no further.

As they set out the following morning, Jacques observed that the cardinal was hobbling badly. He offered his linen undergarment as a bandage.

"Thank you, but I may not ease my way," responded Borromeo.

At supper that evening Borromeo said to Jacques, "These are our last hours together. We are almost at Torino. Let us talk awhile."

Later a gibbous moon climbed the star-filled sky as the two sat before their small fire. The shroud keeper ate a meal of cheese and dried fruit, the cardinal his usual bread and water.

"Jacques Meunier, why do you never say your prayers?" asked the prelate.

Startled, Jacques did not respond.

"You, a man charged with caring for the blessed shroud. Your indifference has greatly vexed me."

Jacques shrugged. "I am no priest, Your Eminence. The position is hereditary; bestowed upon my family by the dukes of Savoy."

"Still, I should think you might be stirred by the wonderful image of Our Lord. How can you avoid being moved when you view His suffering?"

Jacques's bitterness erupted. "I have my own suffering to think about."

The cardinal's eyes flashed with quick anger. "Be that as it may, I seriously doubt your qualifications to care for the blessed shroud. I wonder if it would not be best that I bring this matter to the duke's attention?"

And suddenly Jacques was surprised to hear himself defend his right to serve the relic.

"Your Eminence, I have cared for the holy cloth long and well. My misery is my own, but my duty to my obligation has never suffered. Long ago there was a great fire in the Sainte Chapelle. The relic, in its silver case, was threatened; the metal was melting. I carried the shroud to a place of safety." Raising his hands, he said, "This is the result of my devotion."

"The fire at Chambéry!" cried Borromeo. "It happened before I was born. So it was you who saved the shroud from destruction." The cardinal briefly covered his face with his hands, and then said softly, "What may I say but forgive me—I didn't know. You are truly qualified to guard the blessed cloth."

Borromeo sighed deeply. "Always my vile temper, my haste to judge others." He sighed again. "Jacques, this day you have taught me much. I wish that I could help you."

He pondered a moment, then spoke carefully. "You see, it is really very simple, not just a matter for saints or theologians—or even cardinals. An act of faith is uncomplicated—a request from the heart, made in the deep certainty there will be an answer." Abruptly he asked, "If God were to grant you one desire, my brother, what would it be?"

Jacques replied, "The use of my hands. Then I could believe my life had meaning."

The cardinal nodded. "Yes, I well understand how much all of us yearn to prove our worth. Jacques, you must try to ask simply, with innocence. And believe that He has been waiting for you to come to Him."

At noon the following day they arrived in Turin. The cardinal was received with great ceremony, being much loved for his spirituality and his sacrifices during the plague. As Borromeo entered the city gates, the guns of Duke Emmanuel's guard fired a volley of salutes. Crowds of cheering townsfolk jammed every street, and the duke, overcome with emotion, knelt and kissed the prelate's bleeding feet.

Jacques watched as Borromeo was swept away by dignitaries. He felt unexpectedly sad; their brief time together had ended.

Borromeo immediately requested a visit to the duke's chapel, where the shroud had been suspended by cords above the altar. It was his wish to spend forty hours in private worship.

As the relic's keeper, Jacques was present, but he kept out of sight. Borromeo's lips moved constantly, as he prostrated himself in prayer, then rose to face the relic. Often tears coursed down his face.

On the second night of his vigil he noticed Jacques, who drew close to place a vessel of water beside him.

"I have been thinking of you, Jacques. Come, pray with me. Together we shall ask the Lord for the gift of your hands."

After years of resentful resistance Jacques found it almost impossible to pray. Moreover, he was afraid that should he open himself to request a favor of God, his prayer would not be heard or answered. Then he would feel even more rejected. In such a life as his there could be no miracles.

Borromeo saw the hesitation. "We are all frightened the first time," he whispered gently, "offering our trust to a Presence we cannot see or touch. But you will never know whether there is a Father until you call for Him. Every child must learn that."

Uncertainly Jacques knelt beside the cardinal. Though he would not permit himself to believe God was there, he trusted Borromeo. Closing his eyes, he tried to pray. Finally, from deep within, a few tentative words took form. "Father, if You are with me, I would like to know it. It would make life so much sweeter. I pray to use my hands again. I do not know whether You will listen to this poor sinner. I'm afraid You aren't interested. But if You are, I will believe. I promise I will believe."

Opening his eyes, Jacques realized he had been in a kind of trance. Borromeo was beside him, and he imagined he could see a glow of light about the cardinal's head.

Then Jacques looked down at his hands. The fingers! They were slowly uncoiling. He could move them stiffly, a little at first, then more and more.

Jacques uttered a moan. Turning to him, the cardinal saw what had happened. Borromeo's face filled with joy. He could not speak. Jacques looked up again and the chapel seemed to glow like a thousand golden candles. An emotion of love gripped him so strongly that he could do nothing but give himself up to its power.

These two, the eminent cardinal and the Keeper of the

Shroud, having learned a profound lesson from each other, knelt together, sharing the wonder of God's presence.

And above them the mysterious cloth hung like a ghostly sail, moving on in time.

Chapter 25

Turin, 1978

It was Thursday night, October twelfth. The time, eleven P.M. Except for lights in the second-floor laboratory windows and the hall beyond, the palace and its courtyard were devoid of activity. The stillness of the streets offered no hint of the recent hordes of pilgrims who had given so much life to the now desolate scene.

Within the adjacent cathedral a few worshipers were still at prayer. Separated by an aisle, two men with bowed heads knelt in silence. At the Duomo's rear a lone nun was saying her Rosary.

The first-floor press room at the palace was darkened and apparently deserted. But behind its masked windows waited nine restive persons. There were Ispettore Brocca, six of his plainclothesmen, armed with machine pistols, the guard from the palace entrance and, by Commissario Drioli's special dispensation, Molly.

Brocca continually glanced at his wristwatch. He turned, once again, to the room's closed door, as if he could see through it. "I was reviewing our files a couple of hours ago," he said, "and I believe I have identified Raffaele, the chauffeur. The name is Bruno Strà and he has quite a record." Brocca extended both arms to their full length. "A very bad type. Among other things, suspected murder, plus two convictions for terrorist activities.

Only recently he was released from Regina Coeli." The six detectives remained silent, soberly nodding with professional interest.

"But the really important thing for the *commendatore*," continued Brocca, referring to his chief's honorary title, "is Camillo Acciaro. The commissioner is certain that Acciaro is a fellow we call 'the Bishop.' No police record, we do not even know his real name, but he has mulcted a fortune from gullible people for nonexistent Church missions in central Africa." The detectives nodded. "He is a man Drioli has decided not to stop at the front door, so to speak. The *commendatore* is not interested in an insignificant arrest, in charges of illegal entry or trespassing, but the entire range of the crime. He wants to bring Acciaro to trial, not in the Praetor or Tribunal Courts, but right up at the Assize Court, where he will get the longest sentence. That is, if this is ever going to happen." He looked at his watch again. "Acciaro may change his mind and not show up. And we have no idea how many others are going to be with him. We do not expect this to be a one-man job. And keep in mind, the whole business is purely a deductive matter."

Finally Brocca looked at his watch and announced, "It is now the first minute of Friday the thirteenth. If this business is a false alarm, we shall know in fourteen minutes. I am afraid it may not happen."

"I'm afraid it will happen," Molly said. She was thinking of Nico and Monti, up there alone in the laboratory. She found herself silently praying, please, protect Vittorio and my Nico. The minutes were passing.

A priest entered the Duomo and, walking down the nave, tapped the shoulder of one of the kneeling men. He arose, as did the other worshiper. They both followed the priest up a marble staircase into the Royal Chapel.

"Jesus, Camillo," muttered Strà, glaring at Acciaro, who was wearing a clerical collar and cassock, "it's about time. My knees are killing me."

"Be quiet," whispered Acciaro. "I was waiting for the lights to go out."

The "nun" at the Duomo's rear withdrew a small walkie-talkie from under his habit. He spoke into the microphone in a soft, husky voice.

In the press room Brocca's transceiver crackled. He put it to his ear. "They just entered the chapel," he said. "There seem to be only three of them."

The detective, hoisting his nun's skirts, tiptoed to the top of the chapel entrance and peered around the corner. The three had already disappeared through the passage door which led to the second floor corridor of the palace. The "nun" swiftly moved across the chapel floor to the passage entrance. He carefully locked its heavy door, cutting off their retreat. Then he drew out his automatic, and waited.

The Acciaro trio had their weapons at the ready. Walking slowly down the long corridor of connecting chambers, with lighted flashlights, they passed a sleeping scientist who was stretched out on a bench. Strà wheeled around, directing his Thompson submachine gun at the man.

"No," ordered Camillo, "let him sleep."

The Acciaro gang entered the darkened laboratory at the end of the hall. They could see two figures. One was standing by the shroud, which whitely reflected their lights. The other was sitting in a corner chair. Acciaro turned his flashlight on Monti, while Strà pointed his light in Nico's face. Rozza quickly swept his across the length of the relic.

Monti cried, "Not a brother priest! Are you out of your mind?"

"I am not your brother, you religious bloodsucker," called Acciaro, his voice rising. "You rotten priests should be squashed like worms!"

"Let me do it," said Strà, advancing with his submachine gun aimed at Monti.

"No shooting," ordered Acciaro loudly. Shrugging, Strà raised the butt of his weapon, ready to smash Monti's head. Nico rushed between them, pushing away Rozza's Kalashnikov and raising his arms protectively in front of Vittorio. Strà's blow descended, striking Nico across the forehead. He fell to the floor.

"Get the shroud," yelled Acciaro.

Rozza spun around and made for the tilt-table. The Teflon-coated magnets tore away easily. He bundled the relic into one arm.

"That's it," said Acciaro. "Now we're getting out of here. Ugo, turn on your blowtorch."

Rozza handed the shroud over to Strà and removed the blowtorch from his belt. He pushed a button and the torch burst into blue flame. As they backed out of the room, Monti ran over to the unconscious Nico.

When the three passed beyond the sleeping man, he rolled off his machine pistol and spoke some words into a radio. Then he raced toward the laboratory.

Brocca, who seemed desperately to be trying to see through the press-room door, ordered lights out. He crouched, peering through the keyhole. His detectives were standing behind him.

Descending the wide marble stairway to the ground floor, Rozza whispered, "The guard has gone." Strà lowered his weapon.

The three moved out of the palace entrance into the dark courtyard. The local streetlights had gone off.

"All ready? Let's go," said Brocca, and the seven moved out of the press room toward the palace portals.

Outside, for a moment, all was darkness. The three shroud-nappers felt an enormous sense of relief in the shelter of the quiet night.

"Now!" came the powerful voice of Drioli through a bullhorn. Suddenly the courtyard and the palace entrance were illumined by giant floodlights. In an encircling arc stood five police cars from which armed officers were descending. Some *carabiniere* stationed on a military vehicle were manning an efficient-looking machine gun. Beside the police cars were two panel trucks marked RAI. TV news cameramen on their roofs were running film equipment; soundmen aiming microphones.

"Acciaro, Strà, and you there—lay down your guns. Easy, now. Stay alive."

Acciaro shielded his eyes against the glaring lights. He could make out vehicles and people beyond. There were many. "Strà, hold up the shroud. Rozza, turn your torch full-flame." Acciaro yelled toward the lights, "Look at it, gentlemen, the holy shroud of Jesus Christ. Let us go safely through your lines to our auto. Do not follow, or the relic will burn. Do not force me to destroy it."

Unmoved, a semicircle of police began their forward advance. Acciaro turned back. Behind him were the six muzzles of the detectives' 9-mm. submachine guns. Brocca's automatic was pointed toward his head.

"Throw down your guns. Quick!" called Drioli. "You have no chance. We will shoot."

"Go ahead, drop them," ordered Acciaro. His small Beretta and Rozza's Kalashnikov clattered to the paving. Strà hesitated for a moment, scowling under his pearl-gray Borsalino. With the ancient Thompson submachine gun at his hip, he brought back memories of the twenties in Chicago.

Called Drioli, cajolingly, "Come on, Al Capone, we are waiting."

Strà gave a grunt of disgust, and his gun bounced against the other fallen weapons. He clutched the bundled shroud in one hand, above his head.

"Gentlemen," screamed Acciaro, "spare the relic. Let us go through your lines or we destroy the holy shroud, the shroud of Jesus Christ."

The semicircle of armed police moved slowly toward them.

"Stop!" screeched Acciaro. "Save the shroud. Ugo, get ready. Stop, gentlemen, before it is too late."

The police continued their forward advance.

"No, no, Ugo, that blowtorch—not so close!"

In a whuff of flame the shroud ignited. A moment later Strà had to drop it. It fell at their feet, a ball of orange fire. The police lines halted as everyone watched the shroud glow with a shower of sparks and collapse into blackened ash. A policeman walked over and carried off the weapons. Drioli moved in front of the trio, his hands on his hips. He stared at the ashes and then at Acciaro.

"Well, Signore Acciaro, how good to meet you—or should I address you as Father Camillo?" Acciaro shrugged glumly.

Above, on the second floor of the palace, the door from the

chapel reopened. All lights were back on in the hall and laboratory.

Vittorio, broadly smiling, was steadying Nico with one arm.
The count was pressing a handkerchief to his forehead. On
Monti's other side stood the plainclothesman. They composed a
motionless tableau. Then a sound was heard of many footsteps in
the distance.

Through the passage door from the Royal Chapel came a procession of Poor Clares, clergy, and STURP scientists. They carried a long tray which supported the Shroud of Turin. It was an
exact reenactment of the ceremony observed five days before.
The shroud was borne along the corridor toward the laboratory.

When the relic was fixed again to the tilt-table, Vittorio bent
forward and kissed its surface. Molly pushed past the crowd to
embrace Nico.

"Oh, they've hurt you!"

"Not really. It is nothing."

Monti gently patted Sforzini on the back, saying, "I think our
Nico just saved my life."

"Darling, how do you feel?" continued Molly in a worried
tone.

"Better than I have in years." He grinned. "That gunman
knocked something out of me. No more fears."

Molly kissed him and gently lifted away the bloodstained
handkerchief. "That looks nasty. We'd better get you to a
doctor."

"I do not want a doctor. I would rather light some candles."

"Please, Nico, let's go."

The detective who had posed as a sleeping scientist led the
way down the packed hall. As Nico and Molly passed, the research group broke into applause. In a moment everyone joined
in.

On the ground floor Drioli was talking to Brocca. Both turned
to Nico.

"Thank you," said the count.

Next morning Molly met Nico by the clinic door. The doctor

had detained him for observation during the night. The injury to his head turned out to be slight, a glancing blow.

Sforzini proudly announced he had five stitches in his forehead. Kissing her, he said happily, "Your plan was brilliant."

"Nico, you should have seen it on the early news. The coverage was marvelous."

"Is that RAI program chief angry that their shroud copy was destroyed?"

"Angry? Sciavone was ecstatic. When I called to apologize, he stopped me after the first sentence. Said he would gladly have sacrificed one hundred copies for that splendid footage. Actually, he thanked me for getting RAI in on it.

"And listen to this. An unbelievable ransom note was delivered to RAI early today. Obviously from Acciaro. They read part of it over the air and then sent it to Drioli."

Nico and Molly sat at the back of the Duomo. Monsignore Monti had just celebrated a Mass marking the shroud's return to its reliquary in the Royal Chapel. It might not be on public exhibition again for decades.

As the cathedral cleared, Nico said he wished to visit the chapel and pray awhile. There were many reasons to be thankful: his inner healing after so many years of fear, the shroud's escape from destruction, the end of Vittorio's worries. Gazing affectionately at Molly, he said he also wished to pray for her, for what she meant to his life. He asked her to join him in the chapel. Feeling that she did not belong, she shook her head.

He mounted a steep, black marble staircase beside the altar, which led from the cathedral to the Royal Chapel above. Molly watched him. How much he had become for her. Despite resistance her loving feeling for Nico had steadily intensified.

Directing her eyes upward to the golden nimbus which crowned the shroud's chapel resting-place, Molly speculated on her role in the relic's history. Maybe, she thought, just maybe, there really is a Someone up there, watching over us. Acceptance of the idea seemed easier after the events of the past month.

Molly began to feel anxious. I may have to switch from my comfortable agnosticism to something more doctrinaire. She thought of the plan which had occurred to her yesterday. All because of her sudden recollection of a television program five years before. It had saved the shroud. Yes, she told herself, I must find a new theology. Then she smiled. Considering what has been going on, it has already found me.

Thinking of Nico, she felt an overpowering wave of tenderness. It was difficult to resist the impulse to mount those marble stairs and join him.

So much had happened recently: the chance opportunity to cover this incredible story, the last of Richard for her. Nico. This urge to join him by the altar that held the shroud—was it absurd? Her desire persisted, growing even stronger.

Since the beginning, so many persons must have confronted the relic. One could imagine soldiers and saints, kings, fools, and lovers. And central to their encounter had been the image of a man. These generations of people, she reflected, were linked to each other—as she was to them.

Intently she stared at the marble staircase. Something was pulling her toward it, almost against her will. Standing up, she whispered, "No doubt You knew all along how it would turn out."

She hesitated at the top of the steps. The Royal Chapel was a circular chamber of white and black marble. At its center stood the high altar on which rested the shroud reliquary. Sunlight radiating through the skylights of a lofty dome lit the altar and its sunburst, spilling down on Nico's kneeling figure.

Quietly Molly joined him on the altar steps. At first he was unaware of her presence. Then he saw her kneeling beside him. Filled with joy, he thanked God for this miracle. Though they might never be together, Molly was now joined to him in a spiritual bond stronger than any other.

Molly felt strange, tingly. Turning, she faced Nico. And then they both knew. It was right. Their love was right. Once again he drew from his pocket the Roman ring. And this time she held out her hand. He slipped it on her finger.

No longer hesitant, Molly let her spirit be drawn upward, close to the sunburst, close to the shroud. It had not been enough. Her whole life until this moment had not been half enough.

Late that night Vittorio Monti reviewed the dynamic events just past. But he wanted to contemplate more than mere happenings. With all that had gone on, he had not permitted himself time to ponder the critical question. What did the authentication of this burial cloth, bearing Our Lord's image, mean, beyond the fact that the man Jesus had lived and died? Perhaps, he reasoned, Our Lord had chosen this moment in a violent and negative time to remind us of something.

The tired priest pulled himself to his feet and poured a glass of his favorite wine. He savored the Freisa as it caressed his throat.

Jesus is reaching out to us, once more, to affirm the truth of his teaching. Monti grappled with that a moment, reflecting how correctly the shroud's image mirrored Gospel accounts.

Faith is so difficult for most of us. So much beastliness in the world. Sometimes it seems everywhere.

He thought of Camillo Acciaro, his desire to commit violence upon this innocent cloth. No doubt the poor man had acted out of his own misery. As a priest Monti had seen such things before. Yet in the end, when there was no more escaping it, Acciaro, too, would cry out for God.

Yes, concluded Vittorio, the real miracle is quite clear. Not the image and how it got there. But the shroud itself, surviving two thousand years of man against man, not as an object but as an inspiration. Now and for times yet unrealized.

Setting down the empty wineglass, he switched off the lights. Love is still with us, he reminded himself, hanging on and maybe even winning.

With a serene smile the old monsignore went up his stairs, prepared for a peaceful night.

V. G. Bortin is the pen name of Virginia and George Bortin, a husband and wife writing team from Los Angeles whose background in journalism and interest in historical research, and in particular, the Shroud of Turin, led to the writing of this novel.